THE
SOUND *of*
ONE HAND
CLAPPING

Richard Flanagan

Atlantic Monthly Press
New York

'Goodbye Mr Pippin' by George Park, from A.C. Frost, *Green Gold,* 1976 (A. C. Frost and the Donnybrook and Balingup Shire Council, WA).

First published in 1997 by Pan Macmillan Australia Pty Limited, St Martins Tower, 31 Market Street, Sydney

Published simultaneously in Canada
Printed in the United States of America

FIRST ATLANTIC MONTHLY PRESS EDITION

Library of Congress Cataloging-in-Publication Data

Flanagan, Richard, 1961–
    The sound of one hand clapping / Richard Flanagan.
      p.   cm.
    ISBN 0-87113-802-6
    1. Fathers and daughters—Australia—Tasmania—Fiction. 2. Alcoholics—Australia—Tasmania—Fiction. I. Title.

PR9619.3.F525 S68   2000
823 21—dc21   99-045458

Designed by Mary Callahan

Atlantic Monthly Press
841 Broadway
New York, NY 10003

00 01 02 03 10 9 8 7 6 5 4 3 2 1

for

Archie Flanagan

Helen Flanagan

Anton Smolej

Forgive me its failings, but I tell it with love.

Sarajevo, 1946

Here, as in Belgrade, I see in the streets a considerable number of young women whose hair is greying, or completely grey. Their faces are tormented, but still young, while the form of their bodies betrays their youth even more clearly. It seems to me that I see how the hand of this last war has passed over the heads of these frail beings . . .

This sight cannot be preserved for the future; these heads will soon become even greyer and disappear. That is a pity. Nothing could speak more clearly to future generations about our times than these youthful grey heads, from which the nonchalance of youth has been stolen.

Let them at least have a memorial in this little note.

Ivo Andric

Chapter 1

1954

ALL THIS YOU WILL come to understand but can never know, and all of it took place long, long ago in a world that has since perished into peat, in a forgotten winter on an island of which few have ever heard. It began in that time before snow, completely and irrevocably, covers footprints. As black clouds shroud the star and moonlit heavens, as an unshadowable darkness comes upon the whispering land.

At that precise moment around which time was to cusp, Maria Buloh's burgundy-coloured shoes reached the third and lowest snow-powdered step outside their wooden hut. It was then, as she turned her face away from the hut, that Maria Buloh knew she had already gone too far and that she could no longer return.

Some people say she was simply blown out of the town that night with the furious blizzard winds; that the tempestuous, billowing breath of the storm picked her up and that she rose with it like an angel into the forest beyond, flew like a spectre into the wild lands that lay at every compass point beyond that place that burnt like a fresh bullet hole in flesh.

But that was not the way it was, of course.

Some people even say that she turned into the wind itself, became the gale that was to curse them all. But such terrible winds are not something one can ride as if in a dream. They can only be braced against and it was this which Maria Buloh did, for she was a sensible woman after all, despite what people say, and not a flighty woman whatsoever, and she braced against the wind as though it was a wall that might at any moment fall upon her and she pulled the scarlet coat, that tatty scarlet coat, pulled it tight around her small body. But even that gesture is getting ahead of this story, for the winds were not to blow hard until she had almost walked out of the settlement. And she had some walking to do to get that far.

'Mama,' Maria Buloh heard a small girl's voice coming from inside the hut. Then once again, this time more a whimper—'*Mama* . . .'

Maria Buloh stood there on the step, looking anywhere but at the hut behind her as she tried to soothe the child she had left within. Maria Buloh looked down at her burgundy-coloured shoes, looked at the beautiful impression such battered shoes made in new snow, saw, on the two wooden steps above where she stood, her footprints beginning to disappear in a fresh flurry of snow, and wondered at the nature of beauty, wondered at the small time allowed anything good before it was obliterated. 'Aja, aja,' said Maria Buloh, attempting to soothe

the child with the words mothers of her country always used to put their children to sleep. 'Aja, aja.'

As she then walked away she did not look back at the hut, but let her gaze drift upwards, let it wander beyond the rag-tag disorder of the settlement into the dark forest. Looked at the night-time blackness above. Looked at the snow falling into the cones of yellow electric light. Watched the snow circling its way earthwards. The way the white flakes eddied and whirled in the air as if they were time passing not constantly but erratically. Maria Buloh watched the way the falling snow showed that the air was never still, but held endless circling complexities, held infinite possibilities for graceful inexplicable movements.

Maria Buloh felt herself at that moment to be watching everything including herself, as if she were in a movie and this were a movie set. By thinking this way she did not hear the distant sounds of her daughter crying out to her from the hut she had just left. Strange sounds. Sounds she would not hear.

'Mama,' the child cried, but her mother would not hear it.

'Aja, aja,' Maria Buloh said soothingly, though whether the words were for her or for her child or for no reason whatsoever, nobody can know, for she was already far from their hut and the snow, in any case, deadened all sound. 'Aja, aja.'

She continued looking: seeing it all anew, as if it had no connection with her. She saw how the whole black-and-white scene was lit up by the stark electric lights that ran up and down what passed for a street, how on either side of the street were crude vertical-board huts with corrugated-iron roofs and corrugated-iron chimneys, and how to some who lived there it brought back all too painful memories of forced labour camps in the Urals or Siberia. But she knew it wasn't Stalin's USSR. Knew it wasn't Kolyma or Goli Otok or Birkenau. Knew it wasn't even Europe. Knew it to be a snow-covered Hydro-Electric Commission construction camp called Butlers Gorge that sat like a sore in a wilderness of rainforest.

In this land of infinite space, the huts were all built cheek by jowl, as if the buildings too cowered in shivering huddles before the force and weight and silence of the unknowable, that might possibly be benign, might possibly even not care about people, but which their terrible histories—chronicles of centuries of recurring inhumanities and horrors which they carried along with a few lace doilies and curling photographs and odd habits and peculiar ways of eating—could only allow them to fear.

Because not to fear was to imagine a world beyond experience.

And that was too much for anybody.

In those cowering corrals of huts had to live the workers, for in this remote highland country of the remote island of Tasmania that lay far off the remote land of Australia, there was no other human settlement for many miles. There were just wild rivers and wilder mountain ranges and everywhere rainforest that only ceded its reign over the land to intermittent buttongrass plains, or in the higher altitudes, to alpine moorland.

That is what she saw.

What she heard was precisely nothing.

It was the time of the beginning of the great dam-building boom. The time the new Australians came to such wild places to do the wog work of dam-building because work in the cities, which the new Australians would have preferred, was Australians' work. But Maria Buloh, wife of Bojan Buloh, mother of Sonja Buloh, wasn't coming to Butlers Gorge.

She was leaving it.

Forever.

So Maria Buloh continued walking down the empty street, a young woman clad in an old coat carrying a small cardboard suitcase, the tracks left by her shoes momentarily bisecting that grim, sour, snow-swept camp, her image already losing its earthly outlines in the falling snow.

The sheet of silence the snow had thrown over the settlement was ripped apart by the approaching clatter of a small engine. The diffuse yellow streaks of a single small headlight made a moving piss-coloured puddle in the drifting snowflakes. Then a hunched rider on a motorbike with empty sidecar shaped out of white nothingness and bore down the street toward her. The rider sped past Maria Buloh, then fifty yards or so beyond slowed as he turned right and slewed to a halt outside the canteen. Maria Buloh stopped, turned, and stared.

In front of the canteen's main entrance, a double wooden slat door, she saw a dozen women huddled around a fiery brazier improvised from an oil drum, preferring society under such conditions to a warmer solitude. They were clad in a quixotic motley of summer dresses and heavy winter coats, their heads covered with hats of varying exotic types—some berets, one slouch hat, two straw hats, a rainbow of beanies. Some women stood and some sat on the empty wooden beer barrels around the entrance, chatting and drinking beer brought out to them by their blokes—husbands and boyfriends and flirters—from the men-only canteen. When the doorway opened for a man to pass in or out, gossipy steam and steamy stories and laughter and the splintering of falling glasses spilt out over the women and onto the main street.

A leather-jacketed and helmeted figure got off the motorbike, and, conscious of making a dramatic entrance, strode past the women into the canteen. The barrel women were momentarily taken with this colourful new arrival. They heard his voice boom through the crowded canteen. 'Name's Eric Preston,' he yelled. 'I'm the AWU organiser and I've come to sort out the problem with the reffos. Who's the rep here?'

But then his strident voice was lost in the babble of tongues that was the canteen drinking its past away and the interest of the women swung to the sight of the solitary woman with a suitcase walking out of the town on such a Godforsaken night to God knew where; the solitary woman who was staring at them and through them as if they were there but had never been there, as if she saw a future akin to the past when they would all once more be scattered with the wind and nothing of this horrible time and place would remain. Her face (so young, so young that it now looks shocking) seemed almost Oriental: the structure of the bones and large eyes different from those of Australians, and the lines—only a few, but deep nevertheless—seemed induced neither by the passing of the years nor by the sun, but as if they had been chiselled into her face by a sculptor to accentuate a strange, exotic beauty.

Some later said she was wrong, condemning what it was beyond them to understand. Perhaps because of this judgement, or perhaps arising from an opposite emotion, some small measure of sympathy for a tragedy that might befall any of them, or perhaps for reasons none of them would ever figure out, they nudged one another and they stopped talking when Maria Buloh looked at them so, and all that any of them or Maria Buloh could hear was the ongoing noise of the men inside.

Maria Buloh turned away. She recommenced walking out of the town. From the canteen she could hear the faint, ever fainter strains of a new American country-and-western song being played on the gramophone. The song seemed to simmer tears, like a goulash stewed out of sadness. As Maria Buloh walked toward the dark forest the babble from the canteen died away. The song became lost in the soft whip of sleet. Maria Buloh's face was without emotion. Yes, that face—beautiful, *yes*; young, *yes*; but something else. What was it? As if fixing her mystery forever, tears—though only a few—slid from her eyes and glazed her face.

Behind Maria Buloh ran the tracks that led back to the place from where she came, the tracks that were being lost even as she made them in the falling snow, that were disappearing in the whiteness that threatened to enshroud everybody and everything in that grim little village long, long ago.

And it was some time afterwards, after the canteen had closed and the fighting finished and even the card players had given up for the night and were snoring yeasty breaths into the backs of women who wore their beanies to bed, that the gale rose and the wind began to cry such that it chilled even that wild wet earth.

Aja, aja, it seemed to howl. *Aja, aja.*

And the old, huge trees could be heard to crack and groan, and the new wires that scratched the vast night sky to whistle eerily, and none of the women who lay awake in their sagging beds that night were soothed by such sounds.

Chapter 2

1967

HE WORKED WOOD; that much Sonja Buloh wished to recall.

How often?

Whenever he could, at work and at play.

What sort of wood?

Tas oak, blackwood off-cuts retrieved from work wastebins, Huon pine when it went cheap from the Finns' sawmill; chipboard when it didn't. The white wood of old packing cases, the six-layer plywood used for boxing on some construction jobs, craggy with concrete dags. Celery top and King Billy and black-hearted sassy, when wood-yards cleared out odd lengths of local exotic timbers. But he made something of it all and it was something good of which she was part.

What did he make?

Anything and everything: cupboards and tables to sell, chests to keep for linen they never had, a console for the FJ in the manner of those he had seen in an airliner advertisement, handles for the old Frigidaire, chairs, stools, bookshelves for neighbours, and pot stands and toolboxes for themselves.

He would show her the qualities and uses of different woods: how sassy burnished and Huon shavings kept dog fleas away, how Tas oak framed beautifully and bad pine didn't, how plywood could be steamed and blackwood made you sneeze when it was sanded, how myrtle was for furniture and celery for windowsills.

He worked wood and he tried to make something of it and in his making make something of them. He worked wood and for her he was wood and she loved him for it, o God, how she so loved him for it.

But when that pungent odour of sour sweated bread and all that it grimly foretold came yet again to Sonja Buloh's nostrils and she looked up, it was unmistakeable. He was yet again drunk. He was not, it has to be said, a big man, but when the rage was upon him, he could appear so huge that he would be fit to burst out of a room and collapse its walls and crush its frame with the size of his anger and crush you like a steamroller would an ant and anyone else in the process. And the rage came upon him when the drink was within him, which was often and which was more and more with the passing of the years.

He stood above Sonja Buloh swaying, his head turned slightly to one side, and she could see the flesh at the back of his neck puckering red. Wild and dishevelled, part of a blue-checked flannelette shirt hanging out, fly at half-mast, trousers marked with florettes of dried urine— a roaring giant, a maelstrom of a man with pieces flying off everywhere but never quite breaking away and she one more piece, one more item of disarray that was half-stuck and half-unstuck, all only held together in motion by some huge unknowable enigma at his centre from where his arm raised in anger above his head which was shouting, 'You bloody don't call me drunk,' the arm flailing, pushing away something that could not be seen or apprehended, 'Nobody call me drunk, I have a few beers in pub with my mates, a bit of a good time, and I get home and you bloody say I'm a drunk.'

He was not big nor was Sonja Buloh big nor had she his unusual quality of growing to gigantic proportions. Her quality was precisely the opposite. To elude his wrath she had learnt the art of smallness, of rendering one's being so tiny as to be invisible to all but the closest scrutiny. Her body, at sixteen years, if stretched out and released from its obligation of smallness was in fact tall for her age, perhaps almost a full five foot ten inches, which made her as tall as him, a point of equality neither seemed to want to dwell upon, and which she had developed a slight stoop to deny.

But this was not the only quality Sonja Buloh possessed. Upon smelling the scent of sour sweated bread her soul had the wondrous ability to take leave of her body. In this way Sonja would see his rage only from far away. His voice she would only hear as if from a great distance, as if she were listening to a spirit caught in a sea shell held to her ear on some distant sand dune. This day she transported herself back out fishing with Bojan in a dinghy in the middle of the Derwent River. Against the immense forested blueness of the mountain behind it, the pepper shaker sandstone spire of the old Cromwell Street church in Battery Point sat yellow and solitary. She could see, but only incidentally, only as blurs, the houses of the city beneath it. It could have been the 1840s or the 1940s. It could have even been Eastern Europe. But it was, as she had written across her schoolgirl's folder, Hobart, Tasmania, Australia, Southern Hemisphere, the World, the Solar System, the Universe. It was 1967.

It was not him. It was not.

But in the far distance she saw her home and her home was breaking into pieces and a giant was exploding out of it and the giant would not stop growing and the sun was eclipsing behind his back and the world was darkness and the giant's anger had become a frenzy.

'I bet you been out with the bloody boys, I know, I know, you bloody slut, you little tart, you are just like your whore of a mother carrying on with—'

And at this point his top lip drew up and shivered and his head quivered and his body shook and his rage momentarily faltered, as if a memory long pushed down was suddenly rising up, but he fought it back, with every particle of strength remaining to him, he forced it way, way back down and he momentarily staggered like a charging wild pig catching a bullet and cried out but one word in vehement denial '—*bullshit.*'

Sonja heard his rage from far away. His slap across her face she wished to feel as if from a great distance, like an unexpected cold wave deflected by the dinghy's railings. But the slap was not a wave. It was a demand, that she leave the dinghy, leave watching the mountain, leave looking at the town that nestled in its thighs. His slap across her face demanded she leave the river and come back, and his voice was suddenly loud and his hand brought fire to her face. She saw him, a monster unrecognisable. She wanted her father. She did not want him. She did not.

She screamed. She screamed to bring her father back from the dinghy. 'No, it's not true, you are only angry because you are drunk, you only say . . .'

But before she could finish the monster again slapped her across her face, this time twice, this time with more force, this time saying, with anger so cold, the words scaring Sonja more than his open palm, saying, 'I show you who's bloody drunk.'

As he continued hitting her, Sonja remained impassive and did not cry, although his blows hurt her greatly. She did not cry, though the welts rose on her flesh and the blood dripping from her nose sprayed the walls each time her head spun with another blow or slap. She did not cry, but he was breaking something and she could not put it back together no matter how she tried, and the hurt opened up like an abyss within her heart. Sometimes she even perversely thought that it was this feeling she carried within her that caused him to be so. Every day she prayed that this faultline of emotion would not move and yet every night it invariably did. Huge subterranean, cataclysmic forces beyond her ken which destroyed that home, and both as powerless to stop it as the tree to stop the earth from collapsing beneath its roots.

She pleaded with the earth in Slovenian.

Saying: '*Ni, Artie, ni, ni, ni, ni . . .*'

But his rage was absolute, impervious even to her shrill cries, impervious even to his memory that he succeeded in drinking away evening after evening, only for it to return the next morning to drive him to drink again that night.

She ought to have wept, she really ought to have, or at least let a single tear flow, but something within her had long before shattered and though his blows brought forth cries in the way a bellows pumped hard emits air in bursts, he could never find reflected in her face the things he felt himself and so he had no choice but to continue searching that mute, inscrutable land of this girl's body with his punches and slaps for what he carried within himself. It was an unspeakable act of description, those blows, a painfully eloquent attempt to find what they had in common by sculpting with violent intent all that he felt. But there are good ways of describing pain and bad; and his only increased their agony.

The following morning the house seemed light and airy. He sat at the table freshly washed and shaven, looking only a little seedy. Sonja made some coffee to which she then added milk. She broke bread into two bowls and poured the coffee over the bread. Then she sat down and they began to eat. Without looking at her directly, he began to talk.

'Funny thing,' he said, stirring his spoon around the coffee-soaked bread. 'I can't remember a thing that happen to me after I left the pub last night.' Sonja said nothing. His eyes remained averted. He lifted a spoon of coffee and bread to his lips and was about to swallow it when he stopped.

And spoke once more.

'You remember what happen when I get home?' And then he looked up at Sonja for confirmation of what he knew to be a lie. 'I must have go straight to bed.' Sonja raised her face from her bowl of bread and sweet coffee. He pretended not to see what was so apparent, pretended not to notice how badly swollen the face was, how grotesque the one he thought so beautiful now looked, pretended not to see the puffiness and the purple welts and scarlet bruising.

'Yeh, you went straight to bed,' she said. There was a long silence. He said nothing, his face betrayed nothing. 'And you snored something terrible,' Sonja added.

He laughed at the small joke. He was satisfied. Sonja laughed too, because now he was sober and guilty, things would be good.

Until his next binge.

That was all many years past now, and as much as possible Sonja had spent her life since then attempting to divest herself of all things that were not necessary for day-to-day living: any extra possessions that were not totally needed, any recollections that were surplus to what she needed to work, to exist, to know who she was. But some things remained, some memories. Sonja remembered the place as possessed of a certain violence of emotion. The wind cuffed the house with sudden wild blows, the rain fell upon their tin roof with the intensity of an avalanche, and afterwards the sun shone so bright she screwed her eyes up every time she went outside, where the steam rose from the hot blue-black bitumen yard in splendid vents between her toes.

She would visit that place now, of course she would—that little hut in a backyard of a northern-suburbs home in Hobart, in which they spent that whole lifetime before this lifetime—she would, were it not that it would be disenchanting. She was a stranger to her past. No-one would see in the professional woman that skinny frightened child with eyes always cast sidewards in expectation of the unexpected blow.

And in that shack, there would be no wood to work, nor sour sweated bread to smell and thus no magic to conjure her soul away from her troubles. These—her troubles—she had in any case long ago learnt to live with, to accept as part of herself.

Therefore: no giants, no magic, no happy endings.

Chapter 3

1989

SONJA BULOH TRIED to remember the first thing that had formed in her belly but she was cold and her hands burnt and her nipples ached so and the chill tore through her flesh into her bones.

Something had seized her like a cramp, had gathered her guts together and cast them downwards that fateful morning in Sydney only a week before, something she at first only understood as a longing, curious and big and strange as the sky above. A wanting to once more see the peculiar Tasmanian light and what it touched upon, what it was that stood between the sun and the earth, that strange light of negative images, whereby the sky could be dark as pitch and the earth could glow ruby gold, and only shadows holding the two together.

She commented upon the cold to the service-station man who had appeared to fill her car with petrol. He was tall and skinny with short black hair and a moustache that belied his middle age, the years and then decades he had watched dissolve and run off the garage tarmac with the dirty oil and and pure rainwater.

'Mainlander, eh?' he asked. This was a big question which was not so easily answered, even by answering simply she belonged nowhere.

'No,' Sonja said, though it wasn't quite true, but what was quite true wasn't that easy to know, let alone say.

Sonja handed him some money and followed him back into his small office to collect her change. Sonja looked at herself in a mirror behind the counter, realised she was staring, not listening. The mirror was old and chipped and contained a large picture of a spark plug in a corner and the logo 'Moving into tomorrow to keep you moving today!' She saw in the mirror a woman approaching middle age, in her late thirties, elegant in what was almost office attire, as if off to some formal engagement with a stranger, which was, she supposed, effectively what she was about to do. At whose heart was a mystery few even apprehended and none could divine. And having not been divined, the mystery had grown into a swan of sadness, and in the mirror she saw reflected the wings of that swan growing out from her padded shoulders like those of an angel. Sonja saw her face, still smooth, still olive, if somewhat lined. Her bobbed hair, tipped blonde, but beneath still not grey. A body still not dried up, in the way she could see many of the women of her age were drying up. Still ripe, and she was shocked and amused at such a notion. Ripeness was not something she associated with herself. But she could not deny what she felt: ripe. Nor her pleasure, her folly and her pride, in feeling so. Even the wings in the mirror quivered slightly.

'We have a lot of mainlanders stop here,' the service-station man said, handing her the change. 'They like our heritage and things.' Sonja looked out beyond the office at the concrete-block toilet, a puddle of urine spreading out from it and at the puddle's edge where the urine had mixed with old sump oil she saw swimming all the colours of the rainbow, and beyond the extraordinary swirls of metallic wonder a beaten-up country town. She glanced back up at the mirror and saw reflected not herself, nor an angel, but a small frightened child holding a teapot. She involuntarily trembled. But when she looked back the child was gone and only her own image remained.

'Cold, missus,' said the man. 'Lot of mainlanders find it cold down here in Tassie.'

She would find him even after all these years, finally track him down and and ask him what was it that had happened to them? What was it? she would ask. Was it only life? Him? Her? Or was it the woman dressed in lace who tormented Sonja in her dreams?

She would find him, she thought. She would.

The man gave the old wooden cash drawer a forceful shove and as it slammed shut a bell rang within, its brief toll jolting Sonja. Her head swung to look at him. He flashed a smile of reassurance.

'Even colder out west.'

Chapter 4

————

1989

THROUGH THE BLOODY dark of the eclipsed morning Sonja Buloh drove along the road to the west, a writhing tapeworm of crumbling bitumen, empty save for Sonja's red hire car. In that year of revolutions, she was driving through a time grown momentarily molten. In a growing gyre, she felt time circling her, at first slowly, as if waiting. And though it seemed dreams were being born within dreams, it was not so. It was only Tasmania in spring.

When at length light returned—strangely, as if curious—it was to a land at once alien and familiar. Bearing the bruised country into hamlets' hearts, slow rivers carried broken willow and bastard gorse—those new Australians of the bush—into old convict towns now unravelling like used newspapers in the wind. Sonja Buloh drove through them and into the sheep country, in which occasional ancient gum trees stood as if brooding survivors of some terrible massacre, sharing their melancholia only with the rainbow-coloured rosella parrots that briefly called in upon the trees before flitting off elsewhere, as though unable to bear the tales told them by those aching branches.

Once this weary pastoral land had been open forest through which blackfellas hunted and camped and of a night filled with their stories of which one had no end: that of their fierce war against the invading whitefellas. Then the surveyors came with their barefooted convict track cutters and they gave the land strange new names and by their naming and by their describing they announced the coming of a terrible revolution. Where their indian-inked maps cut the new country into neat counties with quaint reassuring English names such as Cumberland and Bothwell, the surveyors' successors, the hydro-electricity engineers, made their straight lines reality in the form of the wires along which the new energy, electricity—the new god—hummed its song of promise, its seductive false prophecies that Tasmania would one day be Australia's Ruhr Valley. The island busily, almost hysterically tried to bury its memory of a recent, often hideous past in a future of heavy industry, of gigantic furnaces and enormous machines that were to be powered by the huge resources of water energy that the place possessed in abundance, and for a time the island was falsely praised as a virgin land without history.

There was in this nothing new: it is said the Chinese Emperor Shih Huang Ti ordered both the construction of the Great Wall of China and the destruction of all books preceding his reign, so that history would henceforth begin with him and his wall. And if the history of the place the migrants had come to live in was so completely denied, then that was only the rightful corollary of their ambition: to leave their own individual pasts behind. So for a time the goals of the state and of the capitalists and of those unfortunate enough to labour at turning such visions into reality seemed to have fused into one.

By such alchemy the dull fear of the past was transformed into electric power, the coveted gold of the new age, and at the bottom of the alchemists' distilling flask all that remained were the pestilential by-products of that magical process for which nobody cared: the cracked natural world and the broken human lives, both dregs easily discounted when their insignificant cost was tallied against the growing treasure of the burgeoning hydroelectricity grid, and no-one counted the growing cost and no-one thought that tomorrow might be worse than today, least of all on that day so long ago when Sonja's parents had steamed into the port of Hobart with their sixteen-month-old daughter, at what they thought was the end of their long flight from Europe.

As Sonja drove past the electricity transmission towers, strutting across this forlorn land like giant, musclebound warriors, she drank it all in, immersed herself in that world beyond the windows. She always did this: immerse herself in surfaces. In the appearance of things. She had succeeded in turning what was once a simple desire into a forceful habit that had now obtained for the greater part of her adult life. For which people liked her.

She did not trespass upon their hearts or memories. Nor did she reveal hers.

How could she? How could she?

My friendships are gone and my memories broken, thought Sonja, gone and broken.

Beyond this dead land of towers and sheep Sonja drove, into the highlands, only recently cleared by the woodchippers, leaving the land as if after war: a shock as far as the eye could see of churned up mud and ash, punctuated here and there by a massive charred stump, still smouldering weeks after the burn-off of the waste rainforest that could not be made into tissue paper for Japan. Parts of me are dead, Sonja thought. Her stomach knotted. Ashes and tissue paper, Sonja thought, looking at the wastelands around her. She drove on.

You are not your past, Sonja counselled herself, can never be reduced or explained by the past. You are your dreams, which is why Sydney—that sly city of alluring promise—is the place for me. I am what I am now. I lived here once, true, but that was then, and this is now. That's all. That's all there is and ever will be. I am my dreams of tomorrow. The past is not your fate, and you make your chances like you drive a car, either slowly, risking nothing, gaining nothing, or fast, where all that matters is just what is in front of you at this moment, and everything that is behind you is totally irrelevant.

As she turned off the main road onto a rutted gravel road, Sonja pressed her foot down as if in affirmation of these thoughts, but the car, a four cylinder, was sluggish in response. She drove along the road through the broken bush that arises after logging and fire until she came over a crest beyond which she saw the top of a dam giving way to an expanse of water so vast that it appeared an ocean. She halted, looking out past the wave-torn waters, to where rainforest and moorland and snow capped mountains merged into a single wild land stretching away as far as the eye could see.

That land did not welcome her or care for her, any more than it had welcomed or cared for her parents who had come to live here so long before. And yet this land had shaped her, shaped them all.

And they it.

Sonja switched the car radio on, lighted a cigarette. A radio newsreader was talking of bewildered border guards who, only a few months before, had shot dead a man trying to escape to West Berlin, and who were now waving huge crowds of East Berliners into the west through holes made by cranes. 'The Berlin Wall,' said the newsreader in a flat voice, as if doing a promo for a pizza parlour, 'the great symbol of the Cold War, has fallen.'

It meant nothing to her, this news, that history, and she sat there enveloped in smoke, both part of and beyond history, forgotten by history, irrelevant to history, yet shaped entirely by it, unintelligible without comprehending its frontiers and those, like her and her parents, who had come to live beyond them. Because in the end history—like the Berlin Wall—shapes people, had shaped her, but would not in the end determine her, because in the end it cannot account for the great irrational—the great *human*—forces: the destructive power of evil, the redeeming power of love. But all this lay before Sonja like the waters held back by the dam: immense, mysterious, waiting.

Sonja switched the radio off, stubbed the cigarette out without having drawn upon it, turned the car and drove slowly down the hill to the bottom of the aged dam.

Chapter 5

1989

THE CORROSION OF the years made it difficult to tell where the dam's concrete ended and the rock of the gorge in which it was built began. But there was no denying its power, its scale: she knew her hire car would appear only as a miserable, minuscule scratch of red at the base of the huge black dam wall. The mossed and slimed dam seemed to her a relic from another age—an historical oddity as curious and as inexplicable as a Mayan temple in a Mexican jungle—part of a dream that sought to transform the end of the world into a place just like all others, and failed. She switched off the engine, and summoning a breath and with it her courage, stepped out of the car.

There gathered in the pungent damp air about her the sense of imprisoned souls that clusters in the shadowed bases of such vast wet edifices, and that pressing dankness heightened within her a feeling of premonition.

She fingered an aged bronze plaque she found bolted onto the slimy black concrete wall, felt each upraised bronze letter with her fingertips. It read—

FOR THE MEN OF ALL NATIONS
WHO BY BUILDING THIS DAM
HELPED HARNESS NATURE
FOR THE BETTERMENT OF MANKIND
1955

—and Sonja felt the emptiness of each word, the utter insignificance of each bold upright shape, and wondered if they were ever anything other than hieroglyphics which none divined.

A memory suddenly burst upon Sonja and she abruptly butted her forehead into the dam face to force it all back down. Then as the memory receded and her fear abated, Sonja slowly turned her face to one side of the wet concrete and looked to the west, her cheek pressing upon one of the numerous cream-coloured stalactites that formed from leaching calcium to roll like tears down the face of the dam. As if trying to comprehend the cold dam's unfathomable mystery, Sonja stretched her arms out to embrace the bottom of that vast curved concrete wall—an engineer's grotesque pot belly that hummed and vibrated with the power of the swollen mass of water imprisoned upon the other side. She felt the dramatic raking angle of the dam, its curvature at once strident and restrained, its ongoing desire to render everything around it as industrial—even nature itself. But she could see that the ageing dam was decaying back into the natural world, rather than, as its makers had intended, the other way around.

She felt the power that still remained within the huge structure, the power not simply to make electricity but to summon visions of another time, a distant time of triumphant belief and total confidence. She felt all this through the damp, chilled flesh of her cheek, all this and more.

She felt the power pushing upon her skull, wondered what would happen were the dam suddenly to burst and its waters, so many years trapped and waiting on the other side silent and black and falsely still, to surge forth in monstrous cascades and carry her away.

Children grow frightened at such places. Unlike adults who have a faith in the infallibility of engineers' calculations, children unerringly know that what is made by people can break. Children know that ships sink, planes crash and dams burst. Adults, by and large, do not. At that moment Sonja felt herself a child once more. A child on a cold, snowy night. Leaning against the dam, spreading her arms out along the dam wall, she felt as a child searching for reassurance, as if the huge construction were some long lost parent.

She did not mean to do such a ludicrous thing, to be there looking such a fool hugging the wet black dam, an aphid upon a boulder, but as she clutched the dam so, she once more felt the strange sensation gathering her guts together, and the memory burst upon her again, like a skyrocket breaking a black night into a million fragments of colour. And Sonja Buloh knew without having words for knowing why she had not before allowed the scraps of memory shape and form, those ashes and shadows of the past that it was becoming increasingly difficult to turn away from, that in the soft mist of that afternoon were turning themselves from broken bush into saplings and the saplings into trees and the trees into a forest.

And in the midst of that forest grew a small rude town of long ago, and in one of its rough shacks, behind a white tablecloth, sat a small child playing with her mother once upon a time.

Chapter 6

1954

CAUGHT BETWEEN PLAY and enchantment, it all returned to her mind now as something akin to a magician's set. There was a table made from an upturned wooden box, down the side of which ran a single word stencilled in fading red paint: GELIGNITE. Upon it sat the white lace tablecloth that ought to have been crisp as it was freshly washed, but the all-pervasive dampness had overpowered even the stiffness of the starch and left the lace beautifully soft. And on the tablecloth sat a toy china teapot, small and delicate and elegantly circled with a motif of scarlet brambles, and around it three similarly decorated tea cups on saucers.

Sometimes then, often, forever, it rained, hailed, sleeted, snowed. The smell of the damp eucalypt palings that clad the walls exhaling their aromatic resin into the house, mingling with the fragrance of the myrtle burning in the fireplace. Above the low cracking of the flames a child's voice. The three-year-old child Sonja's voice.

Saying: 'Turska kava for Artie—turska kava for Mama—turska kava for Sonja.' And punctuating each phrase she pretend-poured from teapot into cup.

An adult woman's hand came down and its index finger rested on the spout of the teapot. The hand was young, oh so young, but rough, bearing already the marks of long years of harsh toil. And the voice somehow much older than the hand. Somehow more than a young adult's voice.

Maria Buloh's voice.

Saying: 'Tea, Sonja.' Her ring finger tapping the spout. 'We drink tea now.'

Sonja's fingers, still pudgy with the beautiful glowing flesh of small children, moved over to Maria's ring finger and began playing with it.

Sonja saying: 'Why Mama? Why we drink tea?'

And Maria wiggling her ring finger this way and that, that thin finger with the wedding ring loose upon it, Maria saying: 'Because it is Tasmania and not Slovenia. Because our world is upside down.' And as if to accentuate her point Maria grasped Sonja's hand firmly and then slowly turned it over revealing Sonja's palm. Maria ran her ring finger around Sonja's small palm, raising white circles upon the child's soft puffy flesh.

Maria saying: 'Because to have a future you must forget the past, my little knedel.'

Then she took Sonja's four small fingers in her hand and folded them shut over Sonja's palm.

And with that gesture the smell of the palings and the fire began to dissolve into the past, the *hish* of the snow to fade, and the lace-covered magician's set and the hope it promised was washing away with the memory and Maria was stepping outside into a snow-swept blackness and the door was already closing and it was the same as Sonja always dreamt: the lace was disappearing forever.

Chapter 7

1989

AND THEN THOSE FINGERS, those same elegant fingers
with the chewed nails that had felt the smooth and sensual
coldness of the stalactite-tears falling down the dam face,
those fingers were scrabbling in the bush-covered peat in
the middle of the rainforest, at a place only a kilometre or
so from the dam site, where once stood a construction
camp called Butlers Gorge and where there was now
nothing called anything, only strange bird cries and wind
and cold and ten elegant fingers with chewed nails clawing
at the bleak earth at first slowly and almost respectfully of
its secrets then with an urgency mounting into a fury.

The fingers momentarily stopped when Sonja spied
something glinting white in the greasy loam. But only
momentarily. Then her fingers lunged at this whiteness,
ripped it from the loose ground, and rubbed the dirt away
to reveal a shard of porcelain upon which was etched a
scarlet bramble.

Though the clouds above had now stopped moving
and had begun to empty their water upon the weird

beautiful earth, the falling rain did nothing to impede Sonja. Tall manferns dripped rain upon the ageing stumps of huge eucalypts felled long ago to clear the site for the camp. Above the soft noise of the rain were the desolate, harsh noises of Tasmanian rainforest, the wind up high in the forest canopy, the cries of black cockatoos and crows. But Sonja paid no heed to any of it. Her frenzied fingers were ripping up large sods and flailing them to pieces, pulling the heavy soil apart and in the process finding other porcelain pieces, all similarly broken at odd, sharp angles.

Until the ten elegant fingers with chewed nails were digging beneath the peat and beyond the wild wet earth below and seemed so frantic and wild as though they were digging into a land within her own skull. As she dug so, Sonja did not scream nor say a thing other than grunts and brief pants.

As if trying to give birth to that land lost within her skull.

Chapter 8

1989

BOOKENDING EITHER END of the Tullah pub were two massive fireplaces in which huge logs were daily burnt in vain, for the pub was always cold and had the mildewy look of a building that, like many of its patrons, had never properly dried out. Sonja, still damp from being caught in the downpour at Butlers Gorge a few hours earlier, wisely bought a double vodka and found a table in a corner, where she sat and waited.

The pub's future was as uncertain as that of the remote mountain hamlet it serviced, and perhaps this explained a certain melancholia Sonja felt as she sat there. It had taken all changes and all types in its stride: both the boom that came when Tullah was made the base for dam-building projects in the mid-1970s, and the winding down that was now under way. Every day more men were leaving, heading out of town early to avoid being caught on the winding mountain passes behind the semi-trailers slowly hauling the mobile homes and single men's quarters away to be used as the new housing of the poor elsewhere.

A country band playing at the other end of the room competed, with little success, against the rain on the tin roof. Perhaps because of the noise of the rain the punters' talk was desultory, reduced to a shrug, an ironic smile, a murmured laugh, a soft shake of the head, and there was in it all a strange tranquillity that Sonja had not expected.

Halfway through a song Sonja saw him arrive, and she watched him looking for her. The sound of the rain thrashing at the tin roof outside was now deafening to those drinking inside, and for this reason she excused herself not calling to him. In any case he seemed so little changed from her memory of him that she was at first too shocked to know what to do. Sonja had prepared herself to see someone whom she would have difficulty recognising after so long. She had expected him to have grown fat with drink, or frail with emptiness. His life ought have left him shrivelled or bloated, ought have collapsed his face or made it coarse and jowly. She had supposed that she would find a man only roughly approximating him, a man pretending to the looks and figure of his youth with clothes that did not suit.

But there he was, just the same now as then, neat as a pin as always, hair amazingly still thick and falling in its carefully clipped lustrous waves, a little grey, but only a little. He still seemed the handsome man she had known then. For whatever else she remembered, she could not deny his looks, gentle, almost feminine, a heart shaped face atop a small body that even at a distance she could see retained a measured grace of action and gesture she had inherited. With a small joy that Sonja managed to quash as quickly as it arose in her, she noted how he had dressed up for the occasion—wearing dress pants, a striped cotton shirt and bone cardigan—in a dapper way she forever associated with the working-class Europeans of her childhood. He still has his pride, she thought, and it was that which perhaps surprised her more than anything.

At length Bojan Buloh spotted Sonja and hailed her with a smile and a nervous wave of his hand. He crossed over to her table, she stood up but they did not embrace. They had both come too far for such false intimacy. Not only his mouth, but his whole body reeked of tobacco and drink, the same as it always had, only now it recalled the past as well as suggesting, as it always had, a future with little hope. Up close Sonja saw that her first impression had not been entirely correct, and that the years had taken some toll. His olive complexion could not hide the broken veins that blotched his cheeks. She sensed his movements growing somehow blurred upon being with her as if his body were confused at sudden purpose. She wondered what to call him, whether to say Bojan with its suggestion of equality, or Artie, the affectionate Slovenian word for father. In the end she used neither but settled for a word foreign to her and him, which carried for them both a slight formality.

'Dad,' Sonja said finally, 'you look well.' She knew it wasn't quite true nor was it untrue. Something had changed but she didn't know what it was, and not knowing what it was she focused on what had seemingly not altered. 'Funny,' Sonja said, 'twenty-two years and you don't look a day different.'

In his face she saw her own, in his mannerisms her very gestures. Curious that she might have forgotten such things: her memory—or rather the tricks her memory played—was of a stranger with whom she had spent some years she would rather not have. Nothing more. But here he was, his hard hands making the same deft, elegant movements that her hands made, lifting, holding, moving, carrying.

Bojan smiled. That charming, disarming smile, that she had with so much else forgotten. That smile with which he nervously punctuated his sentences—easy and soft and reassuring—that smile was the same she used when unsure of herself, the same smile that made people like her, made her look open when she knew herself to be closed. In him she saw all of herself and was simultaneously comforted and frightened. In her he saw something that struck him as a curious mockery: that there was something good that had issued from his lousy life.

So both averted their gaze so that they would not see in the other those parts of themselves that they preferred to hide.

'Let's not lie to each other,' he said after a time, his words heavy with accent and something more, something else.

Sonja looked up.

'I look what I am,' said Sonja's father. 'An old wog drunk.'

And he laughed quietly, sadly.

In the Tullah pub the fires blazed and the rain fell with a passion and neither spoke for some time, both lost in their thoughts and in their embarrassment at knowing each other so well and having everything to tell and nothing to say.

Bojan sought to speak once more. 'I . . . ah, no. No . . .' He halted, gathered his thoughts in his head, and tried to rearrange them into a semblance of correct English. 'I would have write you, eh, letters, but, eh, my English, good for work, good for pub, not so good on paper.'

He shrugged his shoulders and held his hands outwards in embarrassment. Sonja gave a small smile, at his unease, at his beautiful movements, so familiar, so forgotten, so unlike anybody else she had ever known, and forgave him with a wave of her hand.

'There are things that matter more than words,' she said. Then paused. Her comment had however struck Bojan. He became almost garrulous, though not angry in his refutation of it.

'Perhaps you say this because you have plenty of words,' he said. 'You find a language. But I lose mine. And I never had enough words to tell people what I think, what I feel. Never enough words for a good job.'

He stopped. Abruptly. Sonja looked at him, felt something so huge rise up within her that she wondered how she had for so long not known it was there. Without meaning it, for she had never intended to touch him so, she reached out and with the back of her hand softly stroked his leathery cheek.

As they both became conscious of her offering of grace Bojan recoiled as if shot. His hand flew upwards and it slapped Sonja's hand away, so forcibly she bit her lip to stop from yelling out in pain.

Then his hand too fell, as abruptly as it had risen, and he stared hard at her. Bojan Buloh spoke quietly, as if to himself, so quietly that she had to lean forward to hear him say what was almost an apology for his life.

Hear in him a broken voice.

Whispering: 'Never enough words for you.'

Chapter 9

1954

ONCE IT HAD NOT been this way, thought Bojan Buloh. Once he had been able to find within even his broken self the thing, the mystery that he shared with all other men and women. But the thing that made him one with himself and with others, that thing was gone, the mystery had flown into the forest with the furious blizzard winds of the evening before, and all he had left was one terrifying certainty, that he was no longer a man, but fragments exploding ever outwards.

On that day after the night Maria Buloh walked out into a blizzard, Bojan Buloh stood silently with all the other prospective new Australians and their families and their friends in the large vertical-board hut that was the Butlers Gorge movie hall, waiting for a local politician to conclude his address from the dusty stage.

'You men and women have decided to join your fate with that of Australia's by today being naturalised,' the politician told them, his words as burnished from use as his greasy suit collar. 'In so doing you are making a better world for yourself and your children. This fifth day of May, 1954, is a momentous one for you. You and your children are part of a new vision of a new Australia.'

Behind the politician sat two officials at a table, and behind them the Australian red ensign and the union jack were crossed. In the forlorn hope of making the place appear festive, some tatty bunting was draped from the rafters and some portraits of the young girl-Queen and Ming Menzies hung off nails driven into the unlined studwork. For the Australian officials the naturalisation ceremony was a joyous, celebratory moment when the new Australians renounced their previous citizenship— their country, their past—to become Australians. For those being naturalised it was a sad but necessary step to take.

The politician looked up from the lectern at the crowd, chin uplifted in what he believed to be the correct pose of a visionary. The next part of the speech the politician delivered without the aid of his notes, because it came from his heart. 'The path to the new Australia is lit not only by the electricity that will come forth from your labours here at Butlers Gorge, but by your conviction that the new world can be better than the old.'

The room swirled in front of Bojan Buloh's eyes. The young girl-Queen and Ming Menzies circled around him like wolves, and all the crowd and all of that hall, all of it and all of them revolved around Bojan like some carnival merry-go-round. He felt dizzy, felt the floor beneath him rise and buck and roll at strange angles like the hall was at sea, like he was caught in some wild storm in the Adriatic and he was unable to do anything more than keep his balance and fight the terrible fear akin to vertigo that was shaking not only his body but his soul. He felt his head grow unbearably heavy, felt it grow huge with some unnameable pain, felt it loll grotesquely and felt some force of will that seemed alien yet was strangely, undeniably part of him force it back into a position that he hoped appeared normal. But he could not stop his bottom lip quivering, was unable to stop his head slightly shivering.

He felt the three-year-old hand of his daughter Sonja grasped around one of his fingers, felt it grip that finger with all its puny might, and it seemed as if his arm were in another country that he was leaving forever and to which he might never be allowed to return. So that his head would not drop off his shoulders and roll onto the floor, an orb out of whose empty eye sockets flames would dance, he very stiffly turned his head, to ensure it remained connected to his shoulders, to make sure that she, Sonja, was still there, standing next to him, a three-year-old girl pretty in a formal party frock, her hair done up in ribbons.

Bojan knew he had an arm because he could feel Sonja holding his finger. That must mean that it is connected to a hand and the hand to an arm, that must mean, thought Bojan Buloh. And he knew he must still have eyes even if he doubted that also, because he could see Sonja. That must mean eyes that I must have and they must be connected to my mind, that must mean, thought Bojan Buloh. But when he could no longer see Sonja, when he could no longer feel her presence, what would that mean? He had no answer to this, only a most terrible consuming fear that he could not deny.

'You bring your hope and determination,' continued the politician, 'and in return receive the great gift of English civilisation, the English language and our belief in justice and fair play.'

A Polish worker standing near Bojan spoke, though not to Bojan in particular but as an aside for all who stood near to hear. 'I'd rather the good meat and vegetables and fresh fruit that the Pommy engineers and their families get,' he said. There was a ripple of muted laughter.

There is only this, thought Bojan. Flesh and stretched bones and shit and wood that grows in trees that stretches flesh and flesh that flattens wood to make meaningless things such as this hut in which we are and this noise that means nothing. There was birth and there was love and there was death, and there were only these three stories in life and no others, but there was also this noise, this end-less noise that confused people, making them forget that there was only birth and love and that each and every-thing died. There is only that, thought Bojan, and he lifted Sonja to his chest. He began to sob, at first quietly, then uncontrollably, and it was then that Sonja put her small arms around her father's head, and cradled it as if it were the most fragile thing in the world, as if it were made of china and could as easily be broken.

The politician, after a sideways glance at Bojan, assumed that the weeping migrant was overcome with happiness on the occasion of this great day. To battle the embarrassment the politician shared with the officials at this untoward—though, he knew, for their race characteristic—display of emotion, the politician felt encouraged to extend his speech with some lengthy observations about the present world situation, formed on a fact-finding tour of the Empire he had recently made in the company of several other leading statesmen. Some friends of Bojan's came up to him. He felt their arms wrap around what he presumed was his body and he felt that body push them away, heard his mouth form and twist and say in a language he knew little of and found harsh '*Fuck off fuck off*,' and, shivering head erect, he stood alone and unsupported, looking through the politician, as if seeing beyond the enclosing walls into the forest and its terrible mystery, alone in the crowd with Sonja and sobbing.

When later in the afternoon two engineers' wives took Sonja away and he did not fight it—though she did, but to no avail—it was commented upon how blank was her face. She was still dressed in the same party frock. She appeared neither happy nor sad. For a long time she stood motionless upon the snow-covered ground as if part of a carefully composed painting: the tall eucalypts and wistful sky full of scudding clouds in the background, the harsh vertical-board shacks of the construction village in the mid-distance, their once sap-green swamp-gum timber now grey and twisted. In front of her the women had set up an upturned gelignite box, covered with a makeshift red chequered tablecloth, upon which was arrayed her toy china tea-set for her to play with.

Sonja picked up the teapot, moved it past the table-cloth, and let the teapot fall to the ground where it smashed.

There was no energy in what she did, rather an absence of energy, an absence of emotion, desire. There was no joy in the pot smashing nor anger in the dropping of it. And so she continued in a methodical, entirely impassive manner, smashing the tea-set. Though her face betrayed no such emotion she felt momentarily surprised that the sound of the smashing porcelain could not overwhelm the other sounds she carried within her. First the teapot, then the milk jug, then the saucers and the cups, all fell to the ground and broke into dozens of fragments. But no matter how many tea-set pieces fell to the ground the other noises always returned like a howling inside her head that would not leave: sounds of her father sobbing, of the blizzard wind that had beaten up their shack-home the night before, of her mother singing, of her mother singing. Teapot and milk jug, saucer and cup upon concrete. Porcelain, pearl-smooth on the outside, sharp as glass and dry as death upon breaking. Had they broken? Had they?

Teapot and milk jug smashing. Her mother singing. Her father sobbing. Saucer and cup breaking. A howling inside that would not leave. Her father and her mother.

Saucer and cup.

Singing.

Saucer and cup.

Breaking.

Chapter 10

1989

THE SMASHING AND singing and sobbing and howling eased and then was gone. The noise of the chill wind whinnying in the electric wires overhead, too, thankfully began washing into times long gone. Sonja took some deep breaths. To force it all away properly, hopefully forever, she focused on the sound of the rain that beat upon the motel room's aluminium window with a strange and insistent rhythm; sweeping, scratching, receding, as if hoping to gain entry, then despairing and leaving.

When finally she felt sure of her time and place, sure that time had not bent back around and taken her once more into a past she wanted nothing of, Sonja opened her eyes slowly. Switched on the bedside lamp. Assured herself that she felt better. Tried to forget her dream of then by immersing herself in that strange and peculiar detail of the motel room now. A low tide of dull light spreading out from a cheap bedside lamp to the built-in wardrobe with its peeling wood-grain laminex skin sticky-taped back into place. Assured herself. The sticky tape now curling.

Felt better. The sink set into the wardrobe. The mirror above it with corners browned.

The mattress's plastic cover crackled as she rolled off the bed and went over to the mirror, to stand before it gazing at her reflection. She raised her singlet and with her right hand described her belly as a circle, slowly rubbing the soft flesh round and round, as if trying to bring forth some new magical shape, a genie from the spirit lamp of her midriff. But there was in that place, on that evening, no magic to be had. Even in the dim yellow light she was able to observe, without either satisfaction or despair, that her stomach was flat.

Next to the bedroom sink lay a damp knotted scarf. Sonja let her singlet fall and picked the scarf up, untied the bow holding it together, and looked at the dirty porcelain pieces she had discovered earlier in the day. Piece by piece she carefully cleaned the dirt that stubbornly clung like long protective grease to the various jags of broken china, rinsing each one under the tap, knocking off the larger dags of dirt, then working each fragment more thoroughly by scrubbing them with her toothbrush. She watched the whiteness and scarlet bramble pattern gradually being brought out of the darkness, as if she were a painter for the first time discovering the mystery of her subject within the canvas. After, she dried the shards and fragments on a motel towel, placed them on her bed and there, in the direct light of the bed lamp, began to try and piece them together.

She worked carefully, patiently trying first one way, then another, until she succeeded in beginning to get some in an arrangement that suggested a small teapot of old design. In the end she managed to assemble perhaps a quarter of the teapot, before in frustration giving up. For the pieces would not fit, would not allow themselves to be made back into some order that might make sense, that might mean something, anything.

But within the mirror a small child clutching a teapot trembled.

Chapter 11

1989

SONJA STOOD UP and went to the open doorway of Bojan's room to look at the world outside. There it was late afternoon. For Sonja, the town of Tullah did not so much nestle in that high valley with wild mountains around all sides, as appear to be an industrial accident swept up into orderly piles, left sinking into swampy ground. Everybody, everything was temporary. Except the rainforest and the buttongrass that would come back when this brief intrusion was over. It was not a place in which people were born or would wish to die, but a place that they simply longed to leave.

The promise that had been made to the migrant workers, the offer of a better life in Australia than in war-ruined Europe, the elusive rainbow of prosperity and easier, more peaceable times, had grown thin and distant, till it was no longer something real but a half-remembered kaleidoscopic dream that it was better to try and forget. Till it was no more than an occasional aching shriek; sounding shrill and unexpected, that could, with sufficient effort, be crowded out with the low thrum of dull everyday certainties. Everybody brooded sullenly in the sour swamp that was Tullah, waiting for a moment of catharsis that might relieve the monotony: a death building the dam, a brawl at the canteen ending with an urn of boiling water being thrown, some prostitutes over from Melbourne for a hard-working weekend beginning with their being raffled at the pub.

In this manner the reffos grew old in the hydro construction camps before they knew their time had already gone. They gazed around at the young who laughed behind their backs but who were secretly frightened of the hardness of such men and what it prophesied of their own destiny; and the old men watched the new drugs, the dope and the speed and the acid, partly supplant the grog as the necessary corollary of such wretched lives. Nothing had changed except for the fact of variety, and whereas refuge and forgetting could once only be found with fluid, it could now also be found with innumerable tablets, powders, and herbs. The old had eyes like boiled saveloy water and the young had eyes like pin heads. The old drank beer a jug each a time, and the young smoked six paper joints and ingested stupendous quantities of amphetamines till their hearts raced as hard as their unhappy souls and they felt only tears of bitterness at such a union of body and spirit.

Sonja looked across from Bojan's room at the mirror-image of the single men's quarters in which she stood: another long skinny single-storey barracks clad in corrugated iron, doors running down its length, verandah above, washing hanging out the front upon pieces of nylon cord stretched from post to post, fraying singlets, khaki denim work trousers faded to the beautiful colour of eroded sandstone, coarse woollen jumpers in all colours, and t-shirts inscribed with the messages of a world that had no place for those who stretched into them, shift after shift after week after month after year. Men came and went from this battery-hen cage, and Sonja watched how at the far end of the single men's quarters opposite, a rolling fist of listless men folded and unfolded, tensed and untensed, as if forever unsure that their physical strength was not some cruel disability, talking in short sentences followed by long awkward laughs.

Behind each door was a miserable cell of a room, identical to the one in which she stood, the one which Bojan forever refused to call home, but in which he had lived for decades now, in various reincarnations at various hydro dam construction camps, each new cell sufficiently the same as the last for him to be confirmed in his belief that no single one could ever be special. It came with a steel bed and nothing else, because anything else the authorities rightly figured would be stolen. There was, in any case, scant space to contain much, but in spite of this some of the inhabitants would attempt to reform the cells as suburban lounge rooms, ludicrous and compressed dreams of stillborn domestic ambition. Others treated their room only as a bivouac, which they would soon be leaving forever as they headed out to meet their destiny somewhere else, anywhere else other than Tullah.

Bojan's room belonged, as did Bojan, nowhere. It was empty of aspirations, of delusions, of dreams. It was neat enough, sparkling in its austere emptiness on that day that Sonja visited, and she knew that her father would always keep it that way. He had always hated dirt, mess, evidence of what had been. In addition to his steel bed Bojan had a small TV. An old transistor in a leather case that she remembered from her childhood. A chest of drawers. A kitchen chair, steel tubed and orange vinyled. A small fridge. A small wooden wardrobe he had decorated himself, painting on each of its two doors a white flower with pointed petals. It was a quirk of his which she had forgotten, this painting of flowers on things, even on his construction helmet and her first hockey stick.

By day Bojan's room was lit, as each room was, by the dusty light that tumbled from the one small window set high up in the wall opposite the door. Sometimes he sat there, a silhouette of a man skewered into this world only by the shafts of light down which motes unrolled like illuminated letters in a mediaeval manuscript, and imagined himself a monk in some distant Balkan monastery. A man who had renounced everything and scourged his flesh daily in the hope, forever unrealised and unrealisable, of purging his soul of its terrible demons. He punished his innocent body terribly with drink and with labour, felt his flesh gnarl and wither, felt his guts bloat like a dead man's, felt his head throb with the dull agony of it all, but within him something sharp still cut, something undeniable, and as long as he felt that pain he knew there still remained within him a soul, and he would have done anything to be rid of it, would have renounced it, traded it, thrown it like rubbish on the road and walked on.

But it was not possible.

Chapter 12

1989

BOJAN BULOH'S SHADOW fell across the table, darkening the food, all that beautiful food of her childhood, the meats and salads he made with such gentleness and love that she knew that the man who hit her was not the same man who was her father whose fingers so gently stuffed the mince and herbs into the sausage skins, that the man who said such obscene things was not the same man who was her father who found such beauty in a tub of fermenting sauerkraut, who giggled when he saw the first shoots in his vegetable garden arise in early spring and who once wiped a tear away when he saw his tomatoes glistening in a sun shower.

She moved her seat slightly so that she would not be in his shadow and therefore could better see her father.

'What's wrong?' he asked. 'You don't like? Not Sydney tucker. Won't eat your wog tucker anymore?'

'No,' she said.

'I fucken love it,' he said, and smiled. 'Sorry.'

Sonja smiled too, in wonderment, in sadness, that he might boyishly apologise for a single bad word now when once he had used no others. Known few others.

Bojan was more confident now that he was on his own territory, but both he and Sonja still felt awkward with each other. So he talked upon a neutral subject, though an important one for him.

'In the canteen,' said Bojan, 'they serve Aussie food, you know these mountain camps, chops and stews and cakes and chops, it's orright you know, but it's not right for me, so—' and he halted, smiling, chortling a little to himself, waiting for Sonja to respond.

'So?'

'So,' he said with a hint of triumph, 'so I have to make my things for myself, or otherwise I bloody starve.'

And with a flourish he opened the fridge, which she saw was stacked full of smallgoods, the likes of which she had not seen since her childhood. From the fridge and from his wardrobe which he used to dry other foods in, Bojan prepared a sumptuous spread for their tea. Upon a card table he arranged salamis, cheeses, salads made of beans and potato and tomato, pickled mushrooms, grilled capsicums, smoked trout, and bread. Then they sat down to eat, he one side of the card table upon his bed, she on the other side sitting on the orange vinyled chair.

'What you think of that meat?' Bojan asked, pointing to a plate of sliced meat.

'It's lovely shinken,' Sonja said.

'Bloody shinken my arse,' Bojan said. 'You know what that is? That's a thousand times better than bloody shinken. That's kangaroo!'

Sonja looked up at him in surprise. Bojan laughed.

'Yeh, kangaroo. I shoot it, I pickle it, and then I smoke it. It's beautiful, bloody beautiful. No cholest-o-roll,' he said, labouring the word. 'And that's important for your health.'

Sonja smiled. A little.

'In Sydney,' Bojan continued, 'I bet you don't eat kangaroo.'

'No,' Sonja said.

'No,' Bojan said, pouring two serves of a clear liquid from a coke bottle into two small glasses. 'That's bloody right. No bloody way. And you are unhealthy, because you eat rubbish.' He passed one glass to Sonja. 'Now you drink this.'

Before drinking, Bojan gave the obligatory Slovenian toast—'Nostrarvia!'—and they both took a few sips.

'Is good, eh?' Bojan said. 'Apricot schnapps and leatherwood honey. Us and them.' He laughed at this unlikely union of central European drink and Tasmanian food. 'A Croatian down the road makes it.'

So they ate and drank, until little remained upon the card table apart from the honeyed schnapps bottle. So they drank, so they talked, until the talking became as easy as the food and drink. She asked him how he felt about all the rivers being dammed, whether he thought it good or bad, and he grew garrulous.

'Of course it's bad,' he said. 'It's fucken wrong. I tell you, I used to walk up the banks of that Murchison River and the Mackintosh River and the Pieman River, up that bloody rainforest and I love it up there. All fucken day and then sometimes even the night and the next day. I'd just make myself a nest like a fucken bird I would make this nest beautiful it was bloody beautiful branches of myrtle lined with soft dead-man fern fronds. I would catch trout and cook them for tea and for breakfast when I woke so beautiful I sleep you wouldn't believe the things I seen and then even more strange this one morning I am lying in my nest and I see him, a fucken Tassie tiger. Well I know they supposed to be extinct and I had been drinking all that night before in my nest, drinking peach schnapps and fruity lexia and I know I wasn't feeling that right but I know what I know I see, and I see this fucken Tassie tiger maybe this far away, maybe three metres at the most. And I laugh, because it's funny you know, me being in a nest and the tiger wandering about, and I start talking to him. I say: "Maybe it's me who should be dead." The tiger just looks at me. I say: "Maybe I am dead," and I thought maybe the fruity lexia had pushed me over the edge and I had died and this was heaven. Or maybe the other place. So I ask him: "Cobber—is this hell?" And I laugh again. The tiger still doesn't say anything but then he opens his mouth wide, so wide you wouldn't believe. Jeezuz Christ, I thought his jaw would fall apart, and in his mouth I saw all these terrible things from my childhood and well, I tell you, I never drink that bloody fruity lexia again.'

So they drank and they talked. Until the bottle was near empty, until Bojan looked at Sonja, sucked in his breath, and asked, 'You have a fella?'

Sonja tried to avoid having people become part of her life, because to allow them entry to her life was inevitably to invite their departure, and that was to make the pain of her loneliness as hard and visible and undeniable as first light. It was impossible, of course, to try and maintain such a position of isolation, to live only as a denial of life. She had known off and on the sweet warmth and heavy odours of a shared bed and a common life, had slept with many men, and, when younger, a few women, sometimes out of desire and more often simply for comfort. But then she found she could no longer satisfy desire nor find comfort.

So she said nothing, looked across at Bojan and smiling slightly, shook her head. Bojan sensed that perhaps he was on to something, though he guessed wrongly as to what that something was. He smiled as though he had just caught an animal.

'Ah. I know,' he said. 'You have a fella.'

How to please men, that she knew so well, that was so easy. With her body she was mostly generous. Her flesh she would feel moving in response to their thrusts and pulsations, and sometimes even moving in accordance with its own remote desires. But within her head nothing moved. Within her soul nothing trembled. She did all that men wanted of her, and did it with a cold vigour that they found erotic.

But if afterwards they rolled over in their sleep and spontaneously spooned into her, the sudden warmth would wake her instantly and she would wake them, would roll them back to the far side of the bed, would draw an imaginary line down the middle of the bed with her index finger and say, 'Don't touch me while I dream, I cannot bear it, to be touched so while I dream.'

And her dreams were strange, unknowable, unfathomable depths into which she descended searching for things lost long, long ago. The things that once moved, that once trembled with a force that was then irresistible.

'I've had too many fellas,' Sonja said flatly, finally.

But Bojan misread what Sonja was trying to tell him. 'No. I know,' he said, waggling a finger in the air. 'Now you have a special fella. No?'

Sometimes, though rarely, a man had got closer. She liked some of them: it was undeniable. Sometimes a vague longing came over her to touch, to cuddle. But the moment that feeling came upon her with a man, she began to grow cold, and she would allow them then to drift apart as a couple, quickly, quickly, before the feeling grew into something more. For they were worse than the men she disliked, for they shucked her open as if she were only an oyster and their love that only of the gourmand, opening her up where she wished to remain closed. Her coldness with them came upon her like a seasonal change; not turned on in anger as some shouted in frustrated rage; simply a chill that permeated her and which would not depart until the man who had brought the coldness on was also gone.

She had tended to end up with the easier, more straightforward company of the men who cheated on her, the men who came home late with bodies full of foreign scents and hands full of flowers, with the men who used her for sex or for company or for money or for any combination of the three. With them she at least felt comfortable, for they only posed bearable problems that existed in the present and never touched upon the unbearable nature of her past.

Sonja gave up any pretence of telling her father the truth and just shook her head in gentle reproach. Bojan Buloh continued with some conviction and determination.

'I know. It's none a my business, but this fella of yours, when do I get to meet him?'

He ran a hand through his neat wavy hair. His quarrelsome, foolish hair, she thought. It irritated her. The way he still thought he understood when he understood nothing, about them, least of all her. Least of all him. And, because it was despair that she felt, she smiled once more and lied.

'Not . . . not for a while. He didn't come. He's still in Sydney. Work.' She shrugged her shoulders. Her smile at that moment was enchanting. 'Busy.'

'He is honourable, yes?' Bojan asked. 'He will marry you proper, yeah?' Sonja said nothing and Bojan became strident. 'What did the bastard say? I tell you what he will say when Bojan Buloh finds him and puts a knife under his throat.'

As he talked Bojan Buloh made elaborate gestures indicating the fate of the fella should he be so unlucky as to fall into Bojan's hands. Sonja took his violently inclined hands and held them in hers, but it was a hollow gesture, for nothing had been bridged.

'It is alright. It will be alright,' she told her father.

Then she picked up the coke bottle of apricot schnapps and honey and emptied it, pouring generous nips into their two beer glasses. Bojan sensed that something was being hidden, and he thought it him from some new beau.

'I understand,' he said. 'You do not want him to meet me. I understand. Should you want him to meet me? No. I am nothing. Nothing to be proud of.' He shrugged his shoulders and spoke as he thought, without self pity, with no emotion. 'A nobody at the end of the world. If you love him, you would not want him to see what your father is.'

'No,' Sonja said. 'It's not like that.'

'But you love him, no?' Bojan said. 'And that is . . .'

But Sonja was passing a glass to her father, putting the other to her lips, and with another thin smile raising her glass, giving the toast, albeit in a melancholic way— 'Nostrarvia'—throwing her head back and draining the glass in the old world's fashion, with a single gulp. Then, also in the Mitteleuropean manner, placing the thumb of her right hand on her right cheek and with one swift movement of her index finger wiping her upper lip dry. Then the index finger fell. Again she smiled. But her face was curiously without expression, devoid of hope. The lacquer of liquor warmed Sonja's throat. The idea of love struck her once more as faintly comical, strongly treacherous, and forever elusive.

'Who,' she said in a flat, matter-of-fact way, 'who would hope for love?'

Bojan Buloh went to look down but his gaze caught Sonja's. His eyes like shards of shattered beer bottle. He pulled his bottom lip up, thought, went to repeat Sonja's necessary, sustaining lie but then halted. And looked away.

Who?

Chapter 13

1954

ALL THAT FOLLOWED should be told as quickly as possible, for that was the way it all seemed to happen, and now it seems as if it happened even faster still, within a matter of hours or even minutes, whereas of course it may have been longer, possibly days or even weeks. But it came upon Bojan Buloh and his small daughter as a cavalcade, a terrible disaster that seemed to spiral ever outwards, as though the worst thing were not the initial act of violence but its inevitable growing consequences.

No-one spoke much to Bojan Buloh. Some drank with him, but the drink had no effect upon his body for it was as though his soul had fled his body and followed his wife into the forest. He swallowed beer and home-distilled schnapps with the same indifference he swallowed the prayers of Father Flannery who came to see him. Once he would have thrown the priest out of his home, but now he simply poured drinks for himself and the priest in equally large measures until the man of the cloth was so drunk that he was later seen vomiting behind the truck depot.

While Bojan cared not whether he felt anything or nothing, cared not whether he could hold such prodigious amounts of drink, he simultaneously could not help but marvel at what he could hold within himself and not break, so much drink and so much more, as if he were transforming into the very dam he daily toiled upon. With this realisation he came close to weeping, because he recognised it as the shadow thrown by the huge shapeless things that had changed him. He felt as if he were in some huge dark tunnel down which he was travelling toward a pinprick of light a great distance away and with a sudden moment of clarity late one evening he was able to see that the pinprick of light was Sonja. But this feeling was succeeded by one of frustration and despair, for no matter how far and how long he travelled in blackness he could not reach the pinprick of light. All these confusing and contradictory things he felt and others beside. There was no clear line to follow in such thinking. Only a chaos and him existing only as its container.

It should all be told as slowly and carefully as possible, for such a thing demands explanation and understanding, but no way of telling does it any justice. Days and weeks fled by with the speed of a few seconds, and a few seconds stretched into an eternity of suffering. It was beyond any human tolerance and compressed beyond any human sense and none of it can be understood or explained.

The foreman spoke with the supervising engineer and the supervising engineer spoke with the project superintendent whose wife was full of the stories that were sweeping the camp as to why it had all happened and the strangeness of the reffo and of his wife and of their daughter who was not like a child at all, but whose face was a mask containing God knows what queer thoughts. And the project superintendent told the supervising engineer who told the foreman who told Bojan that he was being allowed a fortnight's compassionate leave which mystified Bojan who didn't understand what the English word 'compassion' meant. He ignored the foreman and continued turning up for work each day, because it offered him at least the sense of a life beyond the tunnel, even if he observed it only from a great, great distance as a land he might one day reach. Not that he went through the motions at his work. Far from it.

With a sledge hammer he broke stone as if it were his own mind. His hammer rose and fell as if it were a drumstick pounding out a crazed, cracked rhythm on the valley stone, and his extraordinary labour was watched by all around the dam site with wonder, as boulders crumbled to gravel beneath his blows. When a film unit turned up to shoot footage for the Commission recording the construction of the dam, the wild wog labouring was one of the more remarkable sights pointed out to the film crew as worthy of shooting.

Cameraman Earl Kane framed the peculiar scene in his fingers. Frankly he didn't have a damn clue how to capture it all with the pissant gear they had equipped him with for the job. Not like the old days with the newsreel mob back in Sydney. Good gear, good jobs, good operators. But work was work and there was bugger-all these days for a cameraman unless he wanted to go into one of the new television studios and be buggered if that had any appeal. Earl Kane sighed. He unscrewed the legs of the tripod only to discover one was broken. Jesus, thought Earl Kane, how the hell can I be expected . . . ? A voice from further up the rutted gravel road broke his thoughts.

'Eh, Earl! Get your arse up here. We can pan around the entire works from here.'

How the hell, thought Earl Kane. How the hell. But ultimately he knew it didn't matter. The Commission was just another big body that wanted it all recorded—on paper, on photographs, in film. No-one would ever watch it in a cinema. It was just archival material. By the time anyone got around to looking at it, he'd be long gone.

When they got the rushes back the week following the visit, Earl's boss, a one time Party man, was more than happy with the results.

'Look at it!' he said, American-style cigarette replete with a modern cork filter tip. 'You got the right feel this time, Earl. It's . . .' Earl's boss thought for the right word for a time, then said, '*heroic*, that's what it is, Earl, fucking heroic.'

He waved the cigarette at the editing screen where the black-and-white footage flickered back and forth.

'It could be some vast Soviet hydro scheme in Siberia or the Urals. Could be the Hoover dam.'

The footage, in its jerky sweeps and occasional over-exposure, suggested the inability to describe the enormity of what was taking place, of man finally, violently, and seemingly forever asserting himself over the natural world.

'But it's us, Earl. Fucking us. We're doing it, Earl,' he said, 'at long fucking last this country's finally doing it.'

The camera panned through the bottom of the dam works. Various men at work at various strange elevations, but whether they were excavating some exotic archaeo-logical site, some wonder of the ancient world, or creat-ing a wonder of the new world was not immediately clear. It looked monumental, half completed, half destroyed. The camera moved across the river to where steam shovels gnawed like rodents into the rock, then slowly up a new cliff hewn out of a rainforest-clad river valley. Above, roads, as if slash-marked by a mugger's knife, cut across at fierce angles. A slow tilt up the dam face, cul-minating in its half-finished top, upon which men scur-ried to and fro like ants on the face of a shovel. A large concrete bucket descended from an elaborate flying fox to the top of the dam face, its load released by men hanging in mid-air from its vast lever, like puppies hanging by their teeth from a trouser leg. Other men, ankle deep in cement, laboriously puddled the concrete into its rein-forcing, ensuring there were no gaps or holes. Cut to a single man wielding a pounding sledge hammer, framed by rocks all around. The man lifted and dropped the ham-mer with such ferocity that it impressed even the men in the dark editing room. At the end of each blow the sledge hammer bounced up as if it were rubber rather than rock being hit.

'Look at that bugger go, Earl,' said Earl's boss. 'You'd wonder what would drive a man to work like such a demon.'

And they watched Bojan's hammer swing.

Cut to a steel frame being lowered down the inside of the dam into its place as a debris snare at the entrance to the water tunnel. A man waiting at the bottom for the debris snare. Earl suddenly froze the frame, rewound and played it again.

'Look,' said Earl. 'It's that same crazy reffo.'

Earl let the film roll some more. The debris snare came to rest a foot or so above the concrete floor. They watched Bojan Buloh fitting the frame into position.

'Looks,' said Earl, 'as if he is being imprisoned behind them bars forever.'

Chapter 14

1989

LIKE AN ARMY of phantoms intent on malice, the bodiless coats and gowns swept through the air, hurtling down toward her. Without meaning to, Sonja braced, the reflex of one always ready for a blow, twisting sideways to offer only the smallest edge of her body for the swooping spectres to strike. And then her body uncoiled, though slowly, for her mind could not sufficiently reassure her body that there was nothing to fear where she stood. She felt embarrassed at being afraid in such a place, for behaving childishly. After a time that seemed long but was not, she realised that there was no cause for worry. As she gathered her wits and looked about, she could see that her foolish fear had passed unobserved. In the great noise and overwhelming activity of the vast sewing room of that Hobart textile factory, everyone was too intently focused on meeting their daily quotas, to notice, far less care about the behaviour of a passing stranger.

Sonja looked up at the cavernous ceiling, at the dust ascending in shafts of light that tapered away into small windows far above, as if containing all the escaping hopes and dreams of those who drudged for a living below. Through those millions of motes garments flew along motorised gantries from one worker to another, each intent on their separate tasks of cutting, sewing, embroidering, buttoning, and packaging.

As she resumed walking down the length of the enormous room, Sonja listened to the way the clatter of the overlockers and the rising and dipping hum of the sewing machines combined to place a strange powerful roar upon the room that was in some way comforting. She walked along row after row of women machinists, brushing past the occasional male supervisor, walking through garments as they swished past—the clothes draping over her to briefly describe a half-spectral, half-human form. She searched each lowered head for a face she was no longer sure she would even recognise. It was difficult enough to distinguish one woman from the next, far less remember one face from a muddied long ago past.

Near the end of the room Sonja noticed an operator's hands. She halted. All Sonja could see of the seated woman was a bowed, scarfed head and her hands. But there was about the movement of the hands something Sonja recalled, a flow in the way those hands were moving the material quickly and deftly under the needle that caught Sonja's attention. She stood there, watching. The hands finished a hem, and then the scarfed head rose slowly.

A small, strong face peered upwards at the stranger staring down at her.

Each searched the other's unchanging expression, without moving, letting their eyes roam quizzically around faces that had both long ago learnt to betray nothing.

And then the old woman's lips moved.

'My God. My God.'

It was not any of her particular features that Sonja initially recognised because time had changed her face, but a quirkiness at the edges, a mouth that seemed to be smiling even when it wasn't, an inviting generosity in the eyes that upon closer examination proved to be what at first no-one ever believed they were—one blue, one brown—those remarkable piebald eyes that Sonja had once found so entrancing.

Sonja found herself telling the old woman the truth in a tumble of words.

'I came back because I felt I had to see him, because . . .'

'I don't hear,' said the old woman, tapping her ear-lobe. 'My hearing here—' She lifted her head and cast her hands about at the rows of machinists, machinery, gantries, the whole industrial catastrophe that was her livelihood, in a gesture of helplessness '—my hearing cactus.'

Sonja got a grip back on herself. This was, in any case, hardly a confessional and the old woman certainly no priest.

'I came back for a holiday,' said Sonja, pretending to repeat herself, speaking in a much louder voice. 'It's good Tasmania. For a holiday. Lots of trees. And things. For a holiday.'

'I think so,' said the old woman. 'And I think, I don't blame that girl. Who would after all that?'

But then the old woman realised with a shock that she had misheard Sonja, that they were talking about entirely different matters, and that Sonja had no idea to what the old woman was referring.

The old woman's fingers rose to her eyes which were filling with tears. With her fingers, with movements no longer assured but rather shaky and awkward, with first one finger, and as that proved inadequate, a second and then a third, the old woman flicked the tears from her extraordinary eyes as if with this gesture her emotion might be similarly disposed of. Then she lowered her head so that all Sonja could see once more was her scarf softly shuddering and Sonja realised that the old woman was silently sobbing.

Sonja said the name she had not said for over twenty years.

'Helvi.'

And the old woman, though not hearing and without looking up, reached out and took hold of Sonja's hand.

Chapter 15

1989

PERHAPS IT WAS THEN that Sonja lost her resolve, though it didn't seem that way at the time. When Helvi's shift finished they had gone to a cafe down at Salamanca. They sat outside, at a small round table, a penny of a table really, beneath which they continued clasping their hands together like schoolgirls. But these hands will part, thought Sonja, this time forever—her hands soon to pass a boarding card to an airline steward, Helvi's hands to resume running a million more metres of fabric beneath the prancing point of her sewing machine.

At that late hour of the afternoon Salamanca was oddly empty of people and of movement. Where behind the venerable sandstone warehouses there ought to have been the architectural accumulation of centuries, there was only the cold wilderness of the mountain. Sonja was momentarily distracted by this thought, by the incongruity of this place that failed at being cosmopolitan but succeeded at being something altogether rarer: itself. It was a world at once skewed and strange and beautiful, and

Sonja suddenly saw that Helvi was actually a bird from a foreign land that had accidentally alighted here—heard Helvi's English speech with its Finnish warble as a finch-like twitter, saw Helvi's small, lithe movements as those of a sparrow darting from branch to twig to branch.

Sonja asked Helvi of names from their past, about Helvi's various children, all of whom had now left home, and some even Tasmania, leaving her and Jiri alone. Helvi talked of them and of others, and they laughed at the old stories they shared, and the new stories that Sonja did not know. Sonja was less animated when Helvi asked her of her life, for that was a subject that Sonja found of least interest. Other people—their histories, their stories, their evasions—always struck her as so much more interesting, somehow more real than what she had known. To wonder unduly about yourself seemed to her not only indulgent, but also—though of course she could hardly bring herself to think it, far less say it—dangerous. It was in any case—in the best of cases, and Sonja certainly wasn't one of those—it was in any case less than easy to explain her life, a life peculiar and mysterious, elusive even to her who lived within it.

Sonja looked at her life as a day-by-day proposition and on that basis it was, as she told Helvi, a good life and she was not lying when she said such a thing. Her job was not like those she had watched her father and his friends spend a lifetime ruining their bodies in. She had progressed from typist to secretary to a minor administrative position in an insurance company, then acquired a job as a production assistant in a television company that made game shows. It was not glamorous, and her pay was that of a clerk's. But it could not break backs or tear off fingers or ruin hearing, nor did it condemn you to life in the diaspora of desperate desires that were the construction camps and Hobart suburbs of her childhood. The unit Sonja rented was not in a fashionable area, but it had been the only place she had ever lived in longer than five years. Not *the* good life, but as good as, actually far better than she felt she had a right ever to expect. She could afford things she had never known as a child—good clothes, jewellery, occasionally eating out at a mid-priced restaurant.

'A good life, Helvi,' said Sonja. 'Not grand, but good.'

'And television too!' Helvi said, unable to imagine television as anything other than the most glamorous and wonderful of lives.

Sonja laughed. She reminded Helvi of the small-goods factory they had once worked in out at Derwent Park, Helvi full-time, Sonja after school and in the holidays, making salamis and sausages out of cheap meat.

'TV's no different, Helvi. Repackaging everything that is about to go off.'

Sonja knew although Helvi was wrong to think that any of what Sonja had done could be equated to success, there was in her story some small triumph that she had never before recognised about herself. But then Helvi had always made Sonja feel as if she were worth something.

'Not bad for a scrubber from Moonah, though,' said Sonja.

'You must go back soon?' Helvi asked.

Sonja nodded, then smiled, for she had to smile, because she had to believe every day turned out as well as one could ever hope, that every decision taken was the only and best decision to make. Sydney was the certainties of work and the person she had created as Sonja Buloh. Tasmania was the wind, and she could see it slowly sweeping along the pavement toward them tentatively jogging parking tickets and discarded food wrappers, could feel its first stirrings now beneath their table. And she spoke firmly into the wind, though she felt anything but resolved, felt a cud of fear deep within begin to slowly journey upwards, spoke slowly and definitely in the hope that then the wind might know her resolve and desist and leave her alone to return to her brittle certainties.

'Back to work, Helvi.' She paused. 'You know how it is.'

Sensing that this seemingly innocuous subject was somehow forbidden territory, Helvi alighted upon a new branch of conversation.

'Where you stay?'

'The Sundowner Motel,' Sonja said. 'Out Warrane.'

A waiter placed a short black and a cup of tea on the table.

'No, my child,' Helvi said, squeezing Sonja's hand. Sonja felt the calloused hardness, the way years of labour had worn the skin of Helvi's hand into a most exquisite leathery suppleness. 'No,' Helvi said, and her hold relaxed and her head shook. 'You stay with me and Jiri.'

Sonja protested, of course, said that it was impractical and unfair and unnecessary and anyway what would Jiri say?—went to withdraw her hand from Helvi's to gesticulate, to emphasise that she could not and how could she anyway?—but Helvi's grip tightened a second leathery time like a belt being pulled in on a belly girding itself for a fight and Helvi insisted and the wind was rustling cold, and Helvi said it was time to go, and Sonja, in spite of her misgivings, gave in.

So Sonja came to find herself where and as she had never intended to be, in the middle of the night screwing her eyes up in Helvi's bathroom, out of a weariness that was more than a lack of sleep, out of a feeling of helplessness at being unable to control her nausea, at being unable to adjust her vision to the glaring brightness of the harsh electric light bouncing off the white porcelain. Her hair she knew to be bedraggled, her face a sickly, waxy colour. Here, thought Sonja, to be here of all places, producing such strange, putrid odours, such violent sounds, to end up vomiting *here*.

Sonja raised her head up from the toilet bowl and turned around, realising as she did so that she had not closed the door behind her. At the far end of the darkened hallway she saw Helvi in her dressing gown, presumably having observed the whole sorry spectacle with her strange all-seeing eyes.

Helvi came into the bathroom, and without saying a word, placed her hand on Sonja's forearm, and looked up into Sonja's eyes.

She is so small, thought Sonja, and was struck at both how she had never before realised what a little woman Helvi really was, and how this was of all things the last thing she ought really to be thinking. So Sonja turned away and Helvi's grip loosened and Helvi left the bathroom to return with a bucket and mop. She spoke only to usher Sonja to bed. Then Helvi silently cleaned the bathroom and bowl.

Outside the weather had swung around. Lying in her bed Sonja could hear the westerly wind rattling hard the windows in their aluminium frames, like prisoners shaking their bars in rising anger.

Chapter 16

1959

FIVE YEARS PASSED.

Being five years, Sonja ought have remembered more things than she did. She was three when Bojan Buloh left her there and eight when he took her away for good. Being five years, she ought have remembered a great deal, but she didn't. Sonja remembered this—sitting on that crumbling concrete fence outside the house concentrating on cutting the blood off to her legs—just by concentrating, making them go all numb and tingly and trying to do the same to her heart but feeling nothing and wondering whether you could, wondering whether it had worked and whether her heart was as numb as her legs.

Foolish things, Sonja would later tell Helvi, dumb things—that's all she remembered. Not the important things you should remember.

She did remember her first communion dress, and herself standing flushing within it, feeling like the strawberries her father would later grow and serve covered with yoghurt—standing so upon an old wooden kitchen table recently refurbished with a linoleum top and red plastic edging; did remember slowly turning a circle, smiling, lifting the dress with her hands so proud in a flourish, and doing a little theatrical swirl, giggling, the three European women who stood around the table with pins and needles and cotton smiling back. The dress was beautiful, she remembered how beautiful it was and how much she loved it, pre-war in its design, length, and extravagance of lace. There in the middle of that small kitchen she twirled for a second time in her first communion dress, and despite a few pin tucks and unfinished edges, it was the most wonderful thing she had ever worn, a dress from another world that suggested life might be something other than what she knew it as, and for a brief glorious moment she thought she might begin to rise into the air like an angel and fly away.

Then it was evening. In a darkened bedroom lit only by the small light that fell from the kitchen through the partly opened door, she sat up in her bed, dressed in an old nightie. She looked intently at the back of her left hand. From the kitchen came the sound of the women talking.

Maybe they were sitting around the table she had danced upon, the linoleum-topped table upon which she had briefly known such grace. Maybe those women—their bodies, large and hard from labour and history, their faces bitter and narrow from being unable to escape or transcend either—maybe they were trying to reduce the wonder of that table to the smallness of their own lives, using it only as an insignificant platform for their tales of escape and retribution, of those who transgressed the agreed order and were invariably punished most terribly. Maybe they were drinking coffee.

But Sonja only remembered what she heard that night after she had realised it was possible to be an angel and to rise above sin, only remembered their voices.

The Italian woman saying, 'So now you've got her, Maritza.'

And Mrs Maritza Michnik replying, 'Someone has to. Her father can't. Working in those camps in the bush, that's no place for a child.'

'Not with the amount he drinks,' the Italian woman snorted.

Perhaps then Mrs Maritza Michnik and the Italian woman smiled knowingly. Perhaps then the third woman, who like Mrs Maritza Michnik was also a Pole, looked a little confused. Certainly it was her voice, gravelly like an old dog's, that the child Sonja then heard say, 'The mother? What sort of mother is she? What woman could treat her child so bad?'

Sonja remembered looking at her hands, at her left hand in particular, focusing upon nothing, hearing it all.

'You know the story,' Mrs Maritza Michnik said.

'It was a mortal sin,' the Italian woman said.

As she listened to them talk about her mother, she slowly turned the back of her left hand over, revealing her open palm. Then she ran the index finger of her right hand around her palm.

'Ach!—people talk about what they cannot know,' said Mrs Maritza Michnik. 'The mother is gone, the father is a drunk. But he pays us what we ask so the girl has a home. A good Cat-er-lic home. What does the past matter? The mother is long gone, and the girl wouldn't remember her. She was too small, and nobody talks about it. He pays well and she never speaks, that's all that matters.'

Then with her right hand Sonja took the four fingers of her open left hand and very slowly folded them shut over her palm.

So: a dress, an angel, and playing games with her fingers. That's all she remembered of five years. Stupid things, dumb things.

Not the things that matter.

Chapter 17

1959

IF SONJA COULD REMEMBER more she might have been able to call to mind how it all began. But really, she recalled only broken pieces, fragments of lucidity that emerged sharp and hard only to disappear back into meaninglessness, the moment she tried to focus upon them. As if she were once more chanting the decades of the rosary that bitter winter's night long ago, all kneeling in a circle in Mrs Maritza Michnik's lounge room holding rosary beads, her, the nine-year-old Sonja, dressed in a nightie, and the three sour women—the Polish woman, the Italian woman, and Mrs Maritza Michnik—in their work aprons. The women's rosary beads were elaborate stained wooden affairs, while Sonja's rosary was a small girl's cheap model, made of pink plastic beads. All their eyes looked at the ground, focused upon nothing in particular, as they chanted:

'HailMaryfullofgracetheLordiswiththee . . .'

From outside the sound of a car coming up a drive, switching off, and a car door opening and shutting. The particular dying rumble of the motor, the slight squeak in the door closing, Sonja knew as real, as belonging to her, as being the sounds of the Holden FJ her father had bought the year before and of which they were both so proud. There had been a few rare weekends when he had come to visit in the new car and they would spend all Saturday cleaning and washing and polishing the car until it shone like a precious jewel in the sun, and on the Sunday, much to Mrs Maritza Michnik's chagrin, they would drive down the Huon to pick mushrooms or to the beaches for a swim.

The FJ had been almost new when Bojan had purchased it, and the object of envy on the part of many who knew him. It was a lovely car at first, and at first Bojan possibly saw it as the future into which he could escape from an ever more unsatisfactory present. After all, it was what no-one he knew had had in Slovenia: a car like in the American movies. And it was proof to both those in Slovenia and Australia that he had become what he had set out to be: Australian.

'This,' he one day announced to Sonja, momentarily stopping rubbing cutting compound into the FJ, and holding his hand out toward the FJ as if it were a divine apparition, 'this why we come.' Later the FJ was to become the reduced circumstances of his present—his home and companion, lover and hearth and promise and solace all conveniently wrapped up in steel in one mobile bundle. And in the end, it was to become his past, of which he knew no way of dealing with, beyond a certain destructive contempt.

So when in Mrs Maritza Michnik's lounge room Sonja had heard the rumble of the FJ she momentarily forgot both her prayers and Mrs Maritza Michnik's fervent faith, and had dared to look up, only for Mrs Maritza Michnik to push Sonja's recalcitrant head firmly back toward the ground, hissing: *'Concentrate.'*

And they continued: '. . . *blessedisthefruitofthywomb* . . .'

Sonja's eyes rising back up slightly at the sound of the back door opening—

'. . . *JesusHolyMary* . . .'

—and closing—

'. . . *MotherofGodprayforussinnersnow* . . .'

—and then her heart was racing fit to blow up as she listened to the sound of the lounge-room door opening followed by two—three—four footsteps. Sonja summoned the courage once more to look up, and as she did so, she realised that the chanting had stopped, and that the others had also raised their heads. Standing in front of them was her father, Bojan Buloh.

He stood still, but his eyes roamed around the circle of those kneeling. There was beer on his breath and something akin to a great sadness in his gaze. This time Mrs Maritza Michnik did not push Sonja's head back down.

Finally Bojan walked up to his daughter and held out his hand which she took. 'Come,' he said to Sonja, 'you are leaving.'

They walked out of the lounge room to her bedroom where he quickly and uncharacteristically threw her few clothes and possessions in a messy tangle into her old cardboard suitcase. Neither spoke, not in the bedroom, not walking out of the house and through the women who tried to stand in front of them, not when Bojan threw the suitcase in the back of the FJ, not when Sonja, now in her dressing gown, climbed in the front seat. Mrs Maritza Michnik clasped her cardigan closed against the chill night air with one hand, and with the other began gesticulating wildly.

'How can you take her away?' she demanded.

Bojan was silently adamant, and, moreover, angry, burning with a rage that Mrs Maritza Michnik only dimly apprehended. For if she had, it is doubtful she would have had the courage to continue her harangue.

'You have nowhere to take her,' Mrs Maritza Michnik continued. 'And her first communion, it is this Sunday . . .'

Bojan, already hunkering down to get into the FJ, drew himself back fully erect, and leant across the car roof, fixing Mrs Maritza Michnik with such a chill look of fury that even she flinched.

'I don't want her near the bloody Church. I tell you that,' Bojan said in a voice, hard, clenched. 'At the beginning I bloody tell you. And then I come here and find you have her on her knees praying.' Mrs Maritza Michnik swallowed. 'I gave you good money.' Bojan rummaged in his trouser pocket for his keys, but finding there only a bundle of change left from his visit to the pub, pulled it out. 'Fucken money,' said Bojan Buloh and threw the pennies and shillings and sixpences down on the car roof with sufficient ferocity that they shot back up at Mrs Maritza Michnik as if they were shrapnel. 'Fucken church.'

He lowered himself into the driver's seat and slammed the car door. From the far side of the car Mrs Maritza Michnik, in an attempt to regain both dignity and strategic advantage, shouted back through Sonja's side window at what she saw as blasphemy—'What do you know of God?'

'I know what I see,' said Bojan, now visibly upset. As he continued fumbling in his pocket for his keys, Sonja wound down her window a third or so of the way. 'What I bloody see in Slovenia when the Germans march in,' Bojan was yelling, 'and the bloody Church back the bloody Fascists.'

Bojan finally found his key, and rammed it in the ignition. 'They were all there,' he continued haranguing Mrs Maritza Michnik, 'cheering the Domobran on, giving lists of our names to the SS.' He fired the FJ up, and shouted even louder to be heard over the engine. 'The SS! I know your God.'

With all the strength she had in her, Sonja threw her pink plastic rosary beads into Mrs Maritza Michnik's face, then quickly began winding the window back up. Bojan turned to see framed in the front passenger window the ludicrous sight of Mrs Maritza Michnik's face momentarily festooned with pink plastic rosary beads before gravity tumbled them earthwards, and burst out laughing.

Sonja though dared not smile, or even to look at the woman she had lived with for five years of what had not been her life, but sat up straight on the seat, staring without expression directly out of the windscreen. She focused only upon the darkness in front of her, ignoring the ferocious Mrs Maritza Michnik to her side, now waving about in a clenched fist the pink plastic rosary beads she had caught as they fell from her face. Above the roar of the revving 138 motor, she trained her anger on Sonja.

'You ungrateful little bitch. Just like your mother. Leaving the ones who love you. At least we never hit you.'

But Mrs Maritza Michnik's face, contorted with righteous rage, was already sliding into darkness as the car reversed into the black night, her abuse fading away.

'And don't think you can come back,' she was shouting at Sonja. 'You can never come back. You . . .'

But they were already fleeing out of that tired town, along the empty and lonely road heading toward Hobart, driving into the forest that the frost was already riming that clear, chill night. Sonja wiped the side window with her hand, and the moment before it misted back over she was reassured to see precisely nothing in the blackness to her side.

Inside the immensity of her father's bluey coat Sonja huddled upon the FJ's front seat, next to Bojan, his expressionless face illuminated in the dull nicotine glow of the speedo, hers cast in darkness. Sonja knew not where they were bound, only that it was away from the Michniks, that they were in flight, and that it was through the night and that was enough: any more might lead back to the reality of tomorrow, and in her eight years she had learned that tomorrow only ever brought worse things.

She looked up beyond the coat's coarse black wool flaps at the vast eucalypts that formed illuminated columns on all sides of the car, left, right, and to the front, rushing at her and Bojan. Through the gaps in those advancing trees she could make out the moon and stars. Where it led, this threatening and frightening corridor, to her past or to her future, she did not know. The trees, of course, gave no answer, did not call back to her, did not bring forth phantom voices that might somehow explain it all. They were only a question. But they would not go away.

After some time that seemed a very long time to Sonja, she looked away from the trees and up at her father. He lifted a hand from the steering wheel and knuckled his gritty eyes forcing them to focus better upon the dark empty road along which they travelled.

'I am not going back, am I, Artie?' she asked.

Bojan said nothing. Sonja continued to push.

'I can live with you now? In a home, our home?'

Bojan looked down at her, his eyes like discarded, rusty dog spikes, and looked troubled, for the truth was otherwise.

'I'm sorry, Sonja,' he said. He drew breath, and when he next spoke the tone of his voice had grown bleak. 'You know it is not possible. I must work at the hydro camp in the mountains and you . . . you must live elsewhere.'

Again Sonja looked up at the trees flying away from her, pierced and divided by the FJ's onward journey. She no longer knew if she and Bojan were in flight from the trees or the trees in flight from them. Then Sonja was struck by the thought that perhaps it was not the FJ moving at all, but rather the forest, pouring like a river around the boulder of the car.

At first this thought comforted her, then frightened her, for to stay with her father forever was her most heart-felt desire, but all that stood between their present serenity and the trees washing them away into oblivion was her father's will and she did not know if that was strong enough to withstand such a forest and still hold them together.

Bojan looked down again to see Sonja asleep, her damp head on his lap. He drove on further into the forest, until the car spluttered and coughed a few times, then cut out completely, and he realised that the FJ had run out of petrol. Cursing inwardly, he rolled the car to a stop on the side of the road. With the action of one who works with their body and hands and knows how to move with gentle yet deft and strong purpose, he very slowly slid his legs out from under Sonja. He took his jumper off, rolled it up, carefully lifted Sonja's head, put the jumper as a pillow under her, and then rearranged the bluey coat over Sonja's body as a blanket.

He closed the front door and stood in only his shirt and pants in the crackling cold of that night upon a forlorn roadside in a forest. He felt the brown gravel beneath his shoes, sensed with trembling flesh the cold rising up from the blasted earth of that roadside cutting, looked up at the vast southern night sky forever so slowly moving.

Then foetally curled he found strange sleep shivering on the FJ's back seat, curious and awestruck that such a fragile moment of serenity might exist at such a place at such a time.

Chapter 18

1959

WHERE THE MORNING that was seeping into the FJ was leading, neither Bojan nor Sonja could know.

Bojan knuckled his eyes and remembering the unfortunate fact of being out of petrol, swore in Italian rather than profane his native tongue. Sitting up, he saw that Sonja was still asleep on the front seat.

After she woke they hitched a lift with a passing log truck to the nearest town. The log-truck driver spoke plenty and Bojan nodded and smiled and swore often enough that the driver felt relaxed.

The log-truck driver's stories mostly came back to the day his son, who was working in a skidder on the same logging gang, was squashed beneath a big tree.

'It's not the windy days to be frightened of,' he said. 'It's the quiet days after the storm. When the tree's been weakening through the storm and the night after and then it dries. That's when them big bloody branches drop like rain, that's when stags fall, that's when no-one should go anywhere near those rotten big bastards. Such a beautiful day when Kenny went, such a day, such a grand day to die.

'Mum took it bad, real bad. I'm alright. Have to be. Got over it, I have, I say to myself, I have to.' He stopped, put a cigarette in his mouth, pushed the truck's lighter in.

'But Mum, no Mum never did.'

The driver never looked across at them, only down that road, as though perhaps beyond the road in the forest there might lurk ghosts that were too terrifying to acknowledge.

'No,' he said, 'Mum never could.'

Once they had the FJ back on the road they drove through to Hobart in heavier and heavier rain that was blowing in with a fresh westerly front. Sonja was silent, Bojan, for once, out of guilt and sadness, uncharacteristically talkative, his tone determinedly upbeat.

'Don't worry about nothing, Sonja,' he said. 'A few months and I find a job in Hobart, I leave the hydro camp, find a place for us, and we live together.'

Sonja said nothing.

'Until then you go live with Picottis, they look after you good.'

Sonja said nothing.

'I talk to Bertie, he good fella, he make sure nothing happen to you. No religion either. What you say, eh?'

'Will they take me to my first communion?'

Bojan looked at his daughter. He leered conspiratorially, hoping to evoke the same mocking contempt from Sonja. But she did not smile back.

'Eh!' he said, still smiling. 'Bloody communion—what good is that?' But she was serious. He stopped smiling. 'Eh—you get to go to better things.'

'Artie—my dress—my dress—I want to wear my communion dress.'

'I buy new dress, Sonja, a bloody beautiful bloody new dress.'

'But, Artie, can't we go together to my first communion? Like other families?'

Bojan nervously lighted a cigarette with a fuel lighter, puffed, took the cigarette out of his mouth and flicked what little ash there was out the window. He didn't know what to say in reply. Instead of looking at Sonja as he had done before, he ran his hand through his hair and kept his eyes resolutely fixed on the road ahead. She too looked ahead. Bojan slipped a furtive sideways glance at Sonja, and with a small gesture of great torment, put the cigarette back between his lips, then almost immediately took it out again.

'Sonja . . . I . . . Jesus Christ . . .'

'My communion,' Sonja said. 'You come and watch me.'

Bojan tried to speak, but finding no proper words put the cigarette back into his mouth. They both continued looking out past the swishing arcs cut into the windscreen by the wipers. A cat ran out in front of the car.

Bojan swerved to miss it, but failed. The car jolted slightly and there was a dull thud. Bojan's eyes flicked up to the rear-view mirror. He took the cigarette from his mouth, shook his head.

'Did we miss him?' Sonja asked.

'No,' Bojan said dully. 'Stupid bloody cat.'

Smoke fell out of his mouth in blue rolls. Sonja felt scared. She said, 'Mrs Michnik says that if I pray to God he will make things alright. If I pray the cat will be alright.' With a rising note of panic and fear in her voice, she said, 'That's right isn't it, Artie? If you pray, Artie, if you pray it's alright.'

'No,' Bojan said. 'It's dead, don't you see. Dead.'

In his anguish Bojan brought his right hand across his forehead and wiped it down his face, squeezing his hollow cheeks together as he did so. And he turned and looked at her, with a look of a suffering so great that the child instinctively recoiled from it and leant back into the door.

'And nothing can help the dead. See?'

Then realising that he had unintentionally frightened her, he patted her on the knee, forced a smile, then withdrew his hand to the gearstick to drop the engine into second gear so he could take a sharp corner. The car shuddered at the abrupt gear change, and shaking uncertainly father and child swerved down a new road.

Chapter 19

1989

WHEN SONJA CAME into the kitchen a little after seven, Helvi, for whom coffee seemed to be as necessary as air itself, was already on her fifth cup and grinding more beans to make a fresh jug. Jiri, dressed in khaki overalls, big chest pushing out a bigger belly like a bulldozer blade a boulder, fat fingers like salamis delicately holding a piece of toast, sat at the small hexagonal kitchen table he had made out of myrtle, leafing through a *Picture Post*.

While some mysteries can be readily seen as such, Sonja's mystery was one that she preferred to keep hidden. Sonja never tried to explain herself, nor did she believe there was much virtue in talking things out. She found words interesting, even powerful, but never reliable, far less trustworthy, particularly when it came to charting the unknown country of the heart. That morning there were things to explain to Helvi and Jiri that she did not wish to say, that she would avoid saying if she could, because in her heart she perversely cherished her mystery as the one thing that might one day redeem her.

So as early morning light fell through the kitchen window they all ate silently, and all were clearly uneasy. But something had to be said, and Helvi ended up saying it.

'A bad stomach?'

'*Helvi,*' said Jiri in exasperation, holding his hands wide open and apart as if trying to stop a wall falling down, and then took refuge in sipping his coffee behind the bunched-up *Picture Post* which he now brandished like a fly swat, ready to flatten any further untoward comments.

There was a long pause. Then Sonja replied, tersely.

'My stomach's fine.' Nothing was fine though, and they all knew it. Sonja tried to soften her words, by adding: 'Now.' Sonja took one of Jiri's cigarettes, put it in her mouth and went to light it.

'You're pregnant,' said Helvi.

Jiri looked up from the *Picture Post* in shock, and spluttered into his coffee.

Sonja's lighter froze in position at the tip of the unlit cigarette in her mouth. Her head was twisted to the left and raised in the falsely confident pose that some strike when first lighting a cigarette. Her eyes rolled right and she looked at Helvi. Although Sonja's face was empty of emotion, there was nevertheless a certain dignity. Still looking at Helvi, she snapped the lighter's striker back, igniting the flame. The low hiss of gas all that could be heard.

The cigarette tip flickered then glowed brightly as Sonja drew in a deep, defiant draught of smoke. Sonja's face, particularly around her cheeks and lips, twitched slightly as she inhaled, betraying a nervousness at odds with the angle of her head. She ran a slightly shaking index finger down the side of her cheek. She took the cigarette out of her lips and before exhaling spoke.

'Yes.'

Then she blew out a long cloud of smoke that obscured the others' vision of her.

'You won't be wanting coffee then, Sonja?' said Helvi. It was a joke, a small offering, and Sonja smiled.

'No.' Sonja laughed quietly. 'Not today. Not for a little while, I expect.'

They all smiled, though only politely and awkwardly. There was another long pause as each tried to think of what to say next.

'I am—' Sonja said, but almost simultaneously Helvi asked, 'When—' then halted to allow Sonja to finish —'I am . . . having it terminated. When I go back. To Sydney. Have to go back anyway. Must go back, Helvi.' With fingers extended, Sonja rubbed her forehead with the rump of her palm. Her cigarette had gone out. 'I have made a booking, you see. At a clinic. You know how it is.' She relighted the cigarette, but after a single light puff, she took it out and rested it in the ashtray where it smouldered, enveloping the three of them in its vaporous question marks.

Then Sonja shrugged her shoulders, picked the cigarette up, and took another long drag.

'What does it matter?' she said, though whether as a question or a statement, Helvi and Jiri were unsure. Jesus, thought Jiri. Everything, thought Helvi. But they did not reply.

Nothing, thought Sonja. Fucking nothing, just like me.

Chapter 20

1989

IN DREAMS SONJA hoped to find the innocence she felt evaded her in life. For she felt guilt in her waking life, felt that all things, most particularly her own self, were her fault, and the fault was one of character, of a person who was ultimately incapable of good. This was a foolish notion and she knew it to be so, but nevertheless it was more easily dismissed from her mind than purged from her soul. Possibly this was why she had endured so many bad men for so long and possibly also why, when finally she found a good man in the form of Koló Amado, she ended up treating him almost as badly as she had been treated by the previous men in her life. This was curious and she knew it to be so. But she felt no urge to hold him or caress him and in bed lay as still as the earth, marvelling only at the sweated labour he would waste in the useless task of trying to arouse her body. She would at such times imagine her body as earth covered by a highway over which innumerable cars roughly rode, and her body below souring into acrid, lifeless clay beneath layer after layer of blackness. And at the end of his ever more desperate, confused fumblings Koló Amado inevitably apologised as if it were his fault. She wanted to love him, sometimes even thought she might love him, but was unable to show any such love and was bemused that he could not understand this if he loved her.

'My poor suburban boy,' Sonja would sometimes whisper, though Koló Amado, the issue of a short affair between a Timorese shopkeeper and an Albanian nurse, was in age a year older than her and came from north Queensland. Nevertheless, there was about him a docility she both liked and resented.

In desperation Koló Amado turned to perversions to try and reach her, and while these afforded her mild amusement she grew quickly bored with this empty theatre of sexuality and felt guilty once more and advised him to do it simply and quickly and be done with it so that she might sleep, and dream. Yet much as she sought release in her dreams, they only returned her to what she was able to avoid in her waking hours. So she lived for many years, catapulting daily between the past of her dreams and the present of her waking hours, wanting neither, unable to reconcile one with the other.

So when she awoke lying on her side each morning to find Koló Amado still there, lying behind her, his arm thrown over her hip, his loins wrapped around her buttocks, she always felt a strange moment of anger. Which was perhaps why, upon realising she was pregnant, she had to ask him to leave.

Koló Amado protested that he would not leave. Being at heart a good man he would not have left her at all if he had known that within her was their growing child, and being at heart a good man he left her because that was her wish, however little he could understand it or make sense of it.

Unable to dream that night, stranded in a strange single bed covered with a handwoven Finnish quilt, resplendent in a worn pair of Jiri's flannelette pyjamas, Sonja sat up and looked down into the gully of the bedspread made by her legs, at the shards of broken china from Butlers Gorge that lay there. About her the silence that only exists within the womb of rain falling upon a tin roof. A child's ageing lamp cast its light, low and comforting, from the small, cheap chest of drawers upon which it sat. Her bed lay flush against a wall of dressed and estapoled pine logs that rose into darkness, and upon one shadowed wall was an old hunting rifle, and above it, a kangaroo skin as decoration. A Finnish interior with antipodean flourishes.

Once more she tried to piece the broken china fragments together. Roughly balanced, they were part of a three-dimensional jigsaw—something that once was a teapot, its base and part of its spout clearly identifiable— that kept falling apart.

After a time she gave up and let the shards drop from her cupped hands onto her quilted lap. Then she picked up the bottom of her shirt and pulled it up from her waist to her breasts, exposing her belly. With her right hand she took a porcelain jag, pushed its point into the softness of her lower stomach, and slowly pulled it straight up her stomach's centre toward her chest, pushing it hard into her flesh as though it were a knife. She felt that sharp edge threatening to tear her flesh, heard his voice once more.

Saying: *And nothing can help the dead.*

The jag left a hot, red streak in its wake. Upon reaching the well of Sonja's navel its journey altered. Without taking any tension off the porcelain, she dragged it across to the right of her stomach and then back down and around, until it was the full moon of her belly she was so describing. But then her grip grew looser and her movement slower and more rhythmical until she was caressing her belly with the porcelain shard. Then, as if by accident, the shard fell into her lap, and only her hand remained, gently rubbing her slowly swelling belly in curious marvel.

Chapter 21

1989

THE SAME NIGHT, but a different drumming of rain on a corrugated-iron roof. A different darkness. And within it, on the other side of the island, within a remote mountain camp, in his bed in his room in the Tullah single men's quarters Bojan Buloh suddenly sat up, switched on the light, rubbed his eyes and then his head with his hands.

He had the hunted look of a man beset with bad dreams.

Bojan looked at his arms, which were covered in sweat. And then ran a hand over his face for a second time and realised that his face was similarly affected.

Bojan got up and opened his door. Outside a gale raged. He did not shut his door, but left it open, pushing a jam under it to stop it slamming. Nor did he immediately go back and sit down on his bed but instead remained standing there, a dark figure framed in the doorway, the small room behind him brightly lit by the naked electric bulb, his breath forming a fog in the cold.

Sometimes there was a balance, very fine it was, and it could be struck and he could hold it. Hold it all down for weeks, months, even years. But then something would happen, a smell, a song, a white flower—and back everything would rush, a giant wave coming in to swamp him, and no matter how fast he ran it wasn't fast enough. He wished she had lived it too so that it would not divide them, this watery wall of memory which prickled his flesh nightly. Maybe that's why he liked drinking with Jo and Pavel and the others. Not because he liked them.

Because if anything he disliked them.

They were drunks. They were, at times, violent men. At times, bad men. That he could see. But it went beyond liking or disliking. If he had been asked what he thought of them, he would probably have had to say that he was even frightened by their hate and violence and desire for the dark things, was frightened most by how much like them he had become. But they too had seen some things, and they too rarely—if ever—talked about them.

Pavel had served first in the Polish Army, then the Red Army, then, when overrun by the Wehrmacht in 1941, had been pressed into serving in the Germans' Russian army. When in 1943 he had been captured once more by the Red Army he had, by fast talking and the production of a long hidden Komosol card, evaded a bullet and was instead sent for seven years to the labour camps of Kolyma. And of what did Pavel talk? How in the Arctic cold of Kolyma one got rid of lice by burying your jacket in the permafrost overnight, leaving only a tail of the jacket above ground. The Kolyma tail, Pavel would joke, for in it would gather all the lice living in the jacket to avoid being frozen to death. Then one would burn this gathering.

The Kolyma tail, Pavel would joke, that's us.

Those were the stories they told: funny stories, strange stories, that echoed into their present. Seven years in the Gulag. How on his job application form for the Hydro his English interviewer had written 'seven years forestry experience, Russia'. That was a funny thing about which they all laughed. That was something about which they could talk. But there was much more that they chose not to tell.

Of what did Pavel not talk?

That when he returned to Poland his wife and children had disappeared, executed, it was said by the Communist authorities, by the Germans who had in their time denied it and said it was the work of the Russians. Who did it, Pavel was beyond caring. His family was massacred with numberless others and thrown into a pit, the covering earth of which reportedly heaved for some hours afterwards.

Of what did Bojan Buloh tell? How when running messages as a child for the partisans in 1944 he had been sent to a house up a distant valley of which, when he came close to it, he felt suspicious. A few hundred metres from the house the boy Bojan suddenly turned and bolted, and then tumbling out of the house came a dozen German soldiers who pursued him, as Bojan told it, a little in the manner of the Keystone cops.

And of what did Bojan Buloh not tell?

That upon finally returning to his home at 4 a.m. the following day he had found his family already up, their preparations for flight complete, believing the boy Bojan must have been caught by the Germans, who would soon come for them after having made the child betray them. In a corner bound to a kitchen chair to prevent her harming herself further, he saw his mute Aunt Angelica who had grown so frightened that she had tried to kill herself earlier that evening, by slitting her throat. He had stared in horror at the thick blood-slubbed cloth wrapped around her neck, a dark red scarf of unspeakable fear.

He didn't tell of that, of any of the various wretched deaths he had seen, of the one he still had nightmares about—how, when shepherding cattle in the alps he had inadvertently witnessed a German column led by Slovenian fascists ambush a derelict border house, used occasionally by the partisans. Bojan had seen the German column marching toward the house and he had hidden in a pine tree a few hundred metres up the slope. He saw them shoot like rabbits the partisans as they ran out of the house, but nothing prepared the child for what next took place.

They killed all but one of the partisans, whom they made dig a hole in the ground. It was still early morning, and after half an hour or so of the partisan making very slow going of the rocky mountain soil, the German soldiers presumably grew sick of waiting, for the hole was nowhere deep enough for its purpose. They made the partisan squat in his shallow hole and they filled the hole back in, leaving only the partisan's head exposed.

Then they kicked that head back and forth like some weird fixed football until the partisan was dead. They left in a lighthearted mood, as if after a fine day's hunting. Bojan, fearful of being discovered, remained high up in the pine tree all the rest of the morning and all the afternoon, and only came down with the sun's descent. And all that long time he was in the pine tree Bojan sobbed silently, staring down at that head erupting from the earth at a broken angle, like a snapped flower stem.

Bojan's friendships now, such as they were, were with strangers who without being told, knew the horror of each other's story, who demanded no explanations, and gave no justification for their own bad behaviour. They never told these stories, perhaps because they knew there was nothing remarkable about any of them, because they knew they were shared by millions upon millions of people, because all that they had seen had taught them this one terrible truth that no-one should have to bear: that people are horrific and evil beyond imagining. There was worse. There were horrors Bojan kept within him without even a story to enclose them, that he kept shapeless in the hope of dissolving them.

But sometimes, if Bojan were out in the bush hunting early of a winter's morning, and the sky was clearing enough that the sun was chopping apart black clouds, he would feel the canker of dread growing out of his stomach into the bush around him, and though he wanted to look away he had to see it once more, yet again, looking up into the trees.

Into the trees, Christ, thought Bojan Buloh as he sat upon his bed, what sort of thought is that?

He took a towel off a hook on the back of the door and towelled the sweat from his arms and neck, then took off his wet singlet and towelled his torso. He put the towel neatly down on the rail at the end of his bed. He lighted a cigarette and sat on the side of his bed, clad only in his underpants, smoking, thinking.

Sonja went. Sonja come back.

Like a ghost I don't want to see. Like the ghosts that Maria screamed at when we went to bed, that she pleaded with to take her but not her father. Maria went. And her and her ghosts never came back. Till this. Till now.

Sonja come back.

What does she want, what does the fucken bitch want of me? I liked her better when she hated me. See, that you can understand, you follow. But this, there is no understanding, no following. Because it follows no sense, see. Like old things.

Outside a worker clad in a black bluey with a fluoro orange yoke scurried across the front of the quarters and into darkness. If he had momentarily turned and looked he would have seen the rain scratching diagonal dashes across an open doorway, within which a small hunched man sat semi-naked on a bed, the light from the room forming a yellow halo around his shrivelling body. But the fleeting figure never turned, of course. On such a night, simply to stare at an old wog-worker, why would he?

I hate them, bloody hell I hate them all the old things. Old houses that they like now, I think they just fucken rubbish and why do people bother. I like the laminex and the aluminium windows and the smell of drying mud between the bricks. That I like. The new things you see you can smell, and they only smell of a man's sweat that he put into making them. Oh yeh and glue, for sure, and all them smells.

Old things they smell of all the things of all the people who have lived there. Of all the things that have happened. They smell like shit. I hate that smell. I like the new smell of sweat and glue and mortar and gyprock dust. I like new, see, because it don't remember.

Fucken hell.

Why she come back?

After a time Bojan grew cold and began to shiver. He took his bluey coat down from a hook on the back of the door and pulled it over his shoulders. Encompassed in the coat's black stiffness, he sat back down, still shaking, smoking, thinking.

In contrast to those of his old friend Bojan Buloh's, Jiri's dreams were anything but troubled. He ate heavily, drank overmuch, and slept easily. In his dreams he had constant trouble remaining fixed to the earth, and had a tendency to begin to rise up into the air, sometimes only a matter of inches, at other times a matter of many metres. At which point and from which unique vantage he had this particular night the curious power of seeing into people's souls, which, he discovered, sat, somewhat peculiarly, like a luminous cockatoo's sulphur crest attached to the back of the crown of the head. He saw Bojan, an old bird in a cage, incessantly plucking out all his feathers and every day the feathers, to the bird's chagrin, growing back. He saw Sonja's crest and bizarrely it looked like a feathered egg. He smelt the sleeping form of Helvi who lay on her side next to him. A warm and heavy smell. Like compost, he thought. For all the many, many years he had been with her he had always loved the secret joy, the complicity, the extraordinary sensation of smelling Helvi as she slept. He gently pressed his nose a little closer to her windcheatered back, and, intoxicated with the strength of the heady smell of Helvi, a smell somewhere between fruit and bread, found himself soaring once more in his dreams, far, far above the ground, searching for cockatoo crests.

Then suddenly he was falling out of the sky and crashing into the earth, and he had awoken with a sudden start and a few wild groans and grunts to find that Helvi was no longer lying next to him but sitting up in the chair next to their bed, looking at some old photographs.

'I couldn't sleep,' Helvi said, seeing her husband awake.

Jiri merely murmured an acknowledgement, pulled the covers aside and went to the bathroom to relieve himself. A working man of some sixty-four and a half hard years, he shook his head in despair at the poor stream that slowly dribbled into the toilet bowl, and remembered with envy the high pressure days of his youth. Outside the rain poured with a taunting fury.

When he returned to their bedroom Helvi was still looking at the photographs.

'You know you interfering again,' said Jiri. 'It's hard enough for her, the poor girl—let her work it out herself.'

'I owe it to her mother,' said Helvi. She looked up at her husband, his face a battered bollard that appeared permanently startled.

'I do feel that, Jiri. For Maria,' said Helvi.

Jiri saw that she was even more troubled than he had first thought. He waved a big hand in a gesture of dismissal.

'Ah, Helvi—why you look at those old photographs, they just upset you. Put them away.'

Helvi's composure suddenly cracked and tears began to roll down her cheeks. Jiri sat next to her on the side of the bed. He put his hand around her back, but Helvi, preoccupied with her memories, would not be comforted and did not draw close. She continued sitting as she was and quietly wept. And as she wept she spoke once more, though her words seemed addressed not to Jiri, but to something both far away and omnipresent.

'After all these years,' said Helvi, 'I still grieve.'

WELL IT'S A FUNNY THING, thought Jiri as he lay back down in his bed, this life of mine. In Czechoslovakia he had drunk with the Gypsies. In Tasmania he drank with the Aborigines. He was never accepted by either, but then he, being half Sudeten German, half Czech, had never felt accepted anywhere.

After the great exodus of Sudeten Germans in the war's wake Jiri's family had remained in Moravia because they felt themselves to be what the Czechs believed his family were not: Czech. The Gypsies who arrived in Moravia in large numbers from Slovakia, where they had been persecuted during the war by the Slovak fascist Hlinka Guards, believed themselves to be only forever travelling *o lungo drom*, the long road, along which the abandoned German homes in Moravia that they occupied were but way-stations. Jiri was to them a *gadjo*, a non-gypsy, an outsider to that race of outsiders. Later, Jiri became to the Australians a reffo and then a wog. The Gypsies sang songs of forever travelling, not romantic ballads, but bleak laments and in them Jiri heard something of himself he had until then not known. They sang:

> The crack of doom
> Is coming soon
> Let it come
> It doesn't matter.

A short man, sturdy, fat head still full of fine blond hair even now, Jiri was given to smiling along with almost everything others said, partly because as a young man he had discovered that this eased his path through life, partly because it was a mask, and he delighted in the deception, in the way it kept people at bay, happy in presuming him to be the same. Like the Gypsies he used several masks: of speech, of behaviour, of personality. So that he might beneath remain true to himself. He still looked, in spite of his age and bulk, boyish, and often behaved accordingly, drinking excessively, behaving badly and flirting with women other than his wife, Helvi. He was fortunate that his vices, such as they were, found balance with his virtues, which were inclined to be equally large, sometimes outlandish. The truth was that he liked almost everybody, loved many and would do near anything to please anybody, whether it be foolish, constructive, or against his own interests. But he was this way because he was truly a *gadjo*, always outside, unable to enter. Jiri had made it a lifetime policy to make the best of it that he could, because like the Roma and the blackfellows he had never had any other choice.

On arriving in Australia as a young man Jiri was directed by the authorities to push trolleys of waste at the Hobart zinc works, a sprawling hideous establishment that looked as if it had been transported from another century. In its vast cavernous rusty wastelands he worked a year with Germans and Poles, with Ukrainians and Lithuanians and Byelorussians, with Bulgars and Magyars and fellow-Czechs and all that any of them wanted, even the most adventurous, was a world that was ordinary, a country that seemed a little smaller and less combustible and more comprehensible, more easily contained in the small ball of grey custard enclosed by a fragile human skull. Australia was ordinary, and even if it wasn't, they didn't want to know about that. They simply wanted a world that might be ordered with the hope that the order might last long enough to build a home and raise a family and have them in turn bring their children back, and then to die knowing one had as much as one could rightfully expect out of life without having to suffer cataclysmic wars, occupations, revolutions, destruction of homes, cities, nations, countries, languages, peoples.

Jiri lasted a year at the zinc, would have lasted longer still, but he teamed up with a Pole who had been a professor of history in Krakow until losing his post because of his supposed bourgeois sympathies. The professor of history took to his new role as little more than a beast of burden with some relish, for even if middle-aged, and a sparrow of a man, he seemed to find in his humiliation a form of private revenge. He discovered within himself an extraordinary capacity for physical labour, as if the spirit of a navvy had always existed within the mind of the scholar, and the harder the professor worked the more he laughed, for nothing struck him as funnier than the thought of a man once victimised for alleged bourgeois sympathies proving himself to be an excellent proletarian, the Stakhanovite of the Risdon zinc works. Correspondingly, the more the professor laughed the harder he worked, because he now clearly saw his destiny was to live a life that could only be understood as a joke and this was the punchline, the pay-off to the interminable gag that he had up until then been forced to suffer. Happy at last with how fate had allowed him this curious justice, one mid-morning he suffered a massive stroke. Like the dying fish that floated belly up around the zinc work's jetty, he rolled over onto the adjoining tramway. At that moment there was another tram being pushed along that tramway in the opposite direction by a Byelorussian called Wheelbarrow by the Australians because his name was deemed by them as unpronounce-able, and a Latvian whose name nobody knew. Before Jiri was able to get across to his stricken workmate, Wheelbarrow's tram ran straight over the top of the poor professor's head. So it was that the former professor of history from Krakow finished his life with his head split in two upon railway irons that led to a furnace at the Risdon zinc works, Tasmania, the tramway's blackened gravel glistening wet from where the small ball of grey custard formerly enclosed by his skull spilled outwards.

After that the zinc works lost what little interest they had held for Jiri and he made representations to the authorities to be transferred elsewhere—something which rarely led to any action, because it was expected that wogs would go wherever they were told to go for their first two years and be grateful. There was, after all, a price to being ordinary, as much as there was a price for being extraordinary.

But to his surprise Jiri was transferred, to his regret to a remote hydro construction camp in the Tasmanian highlands. Jiri had the letter explaining all this translated to him by a Rumanian linguist who worked in the cell room stripping metals. Jiri asked him to repeat the name of the camp to which he was going to live.

'Buttleroos Gorgeh,' said the Rumanian linguist, slowly enunciating each syllable. 'Buttle-roos Gorg-eh.' His specialty had been the Indian language group.

And at Butlers Gorge Jiri was to lie for the first time with the woman who would become his future wife, Helvi, while outside the wind howled worse than anything the two of them had ever heard. And it was there, that following morning, that Jiri was to take a fateful truck ride with a young Yugoslav labourer called Bojan Buloh.

Chapter 23

1959

IN THAT LONG AUTUMN of 1959, when elsewhere the world was sensing change so big and hard in its coming that it was like the trembling of the earth announcing the arrival of a yet to be seen locomotive, in that month of April in the city of Hobart, nothing much looked like it could ever change around a town that had grown used to never being anything but the arse end of everything: mean, hard and dirty, where civic ambition meant buying up old colonial buildings and bulldozing them quick and covering the dust promptly with asphalt for cars most people were yet to own, where town pride meant tossing any unlucky derro found lying in the park into the can, and where a sense of community equated with calling anybody with skin darker than fair a boong bastard unless he wore snappy clothes in which case he was a filthy wog bastard—in that month of April when the cold slowly began its winter's journey, spreading its way down over weeks from the mountain's steel-blue flanks, on an early Saturday morning, an FJ was wending its way through the scummy back streets of north Hobart to the home of Umberto Picotti.

If Sonja had been able to foresee what was coming to her, the feeling in the FJ that morning would have been different. She was fearful, true, but her fear was tempered by Bojan's promises that this time it was only temporary, that this time he would visit weekly, that they would spend every weekend together, and as soon as possible he would move to Hobart and get a house for them both to live, father and daughter, a family: '—what you say, Sonja?' and Sonja said, 'That is all I want, Artie, that is everything.'

Perhaps it was the shared intimacy of escape and flight from the Michniks, of waking in the huge, cold forest fearful of being lost and alone to suddenly see her father rising up from the back seat smiling, giggling, pulling a face and putting on a voice like a chook and mocking Mrs Maritza Michnik, saying, 'Don't think you can ever come back', and them both giggling and Bojan saying 'Bloody bitch, as if we ever would, as if ever.' And Sonja knew she was not alone, that they were bound amongst those huge trees that scratched the moon and the sun by something she had always known was extraordinarily powerful no matter how often she felt powerless, something unbetrayable no matter how many times her father betrayed it. And she felt it in the swoop and ocean-like roll of the FJ, smelt it in the upholstery and stale cigarette smoke, heard it in the road rumble and motor clatter.

But as she and Bojan drove up the pot-holed road to finally halt outside a run-down weatherboard cottage in

North Hobart that morning, the feeling was quickly evaporating, and replacing it a foreboding harrowing the pit of her belly.

Maja Picotti, full bodied and with a fulsome face like the flesh of a plum left too long in kirsch, was there greeting them before they were even out of the car. She hugged Sonja and lifted her into the air, told her she didn't have to blush because this was her home now. Sonja said she wasn't blushing. She did not say she was red because of the fever of fear. She did not ask how could it be her home if Bojan was not going to be there with her?

Umberto lingered at the front door. Short with a spiv's hawk-like face, his strong bristly black hair swept back with brilliantine—though some rebellious hairs still rose up—his eyes constantly searching those of his wife for any evidence of infidelity, and those of any other woman for the possibility of an affair. As they walked to the house, Umberto turned and withdrew inwards, like an echidna burrowing into the darkness of the ground. They found him inside, waiting for them, sitting at the kitchen table, both arms resting on the tabletop, smoking.

It was then that Sonja smelt him and understood him henceforth. His smell was that of uninvited proximity, of assumed and unwelcome intimacy. It was the smell of, among other things, cheap aftershave lotions and mouthwash and menthol cigarettes; of sweet things eaten for breakfast souring in an unwashed mouth, of homemade schnapps and strong instant coffee, of acrid industrial smoke impregnated in clothes mixed with naphthalene—

the smell, in short, of filth masquerading as cleanliness. Umberto Picotti looked at Sonja with a quick glance of indifference. Then on the tabletop he carefully counted out the money Bojan handed him for Sonja's board. And all the while Bojan laughed and joked with his daughter's new keeper, and she saw her father once more finding comfort in the cruel camaraderie of men.

If she had been older she might have cried out:

There is no honour!

But she could only watch in horrified fascination the way Picotti's gaudily ringed fingers felt each note, touched every coin with a slow sensuous pleasure, as if it were flesh and not cash he were fondling, and though they had not yet spoken so much as a word to each other she thought with the intensity and clarity that only children can think such things:

How much I hate him.

Chapter 24

1959

MUCH OF SONJA'S LIFE henceforth revolved around avoiding Picotti and helping Maja with the unending tedium of washing and drying and ironing and putting away clothes, cleaning dishes, bathroom, toilet, bedrooms, kitchen, cupboards, and tending the vegetable garden. Sonja discovered a certain pleasure in the tedium of work: a place where she avoided thinking. Bojan rang occasionally, normally from a pub and though she could not smell him over the telephone wires to make sure, she knew he was drunk. And after each such call she redoubled her efforts helping Maja split and stack firewood under the house, helping her make salamis and helping her slice cabbages and punch the crunchy shreds into plastic garbage barrels until her wrist was aching and her raw fist burning with pain. Each morning Sonja's job was to lift the stones off the board that compressed this fermenting sauerkraut and, as she mopped up the slow bubbling froth with a tea-towel, she wondered what it was that she was transforming into.

One morning in the school holidays after Picotti had gone to work, Maja opened all the windows he kept closed because the summer air gave him allergies and a breeze fluttered in like a welcome old friend finally come to visit, and she and Sonja spent the morning preserving apricots. Each apricot's old gold-red blotched flesh Sonja washed as if it were a rough aged face she loved, each apricot's plump flesh Sonja sliced in half, each apricot's gnarled stone she flicked into the sink, and with Maja she pushed apricot halves in their hundreds into the tall green glass bottles, those hundreds of apricots they had picked the afternoon before from the four gnarled old apricot trees that grew in the Picottis' backyard. There was a pleasure in filling the kitchen with that warm sweet smell of apricots and covering the table with bottles of preserved fruit. It was a good day, thought Sonja. 'The best of days,' said Maja.

Then when they were finished Maja went out shopping with the baby, leaving Sonja to wash up.

If Sonja could have chosen a colour for the clothing of Picotti, she thought as she filled the sink, she would have chosen black, not a raven's jet blue-black in which there is something at once alluring and magical, but simply a dull black like the bottom of the burnt pot she was about to scrub, as dark and scary and suffocating as a blanket pulled over your head. But Umberto Picotti did not dress in accordance with Sonja's vision of him, not any day and not on that day when he returned home from work early, having clearly been out somewhere else on his way home, for he wore not his grimy olive green work pants and old shirt and tatty brown jumper, but came in clad incongruously in a blue Hawaiian shirt covered in a yellow banana design, tucked into shiny grey rayon trousers. Finding Maja away, he at once suspected his wife of being with another man. He sat down at the kitchen table, lighted a cigarette, looked about. For all the new gaudy clothes, his gaunt face remained to Sonja a shadow. When he finally spoke, it was in a hushed, grieving voice, as if he had just suffered a terrible injury or loss.

'Where she?' he asked Sonja.

Sonja turned around from the sink to face him, but didn't reply immediately.

'Where she? Where Maja?'

'Getting meat for your tea,' said Sonja.

Picotti looked around, drew his bottom lip up and nodded his head, as he came to his own conclusion as to where Maja was. Within the shadowed country of his face she could see his eyes blinking in rapid spasms, a nervous condition which came on him whenever he and Sonja were alone together and which she detested. His mood seemed to change, though the tone of his speech remained low. He breathed out and then spoke.

'Yeh, she say that, sure she say that, but I know different. Most afternoons she not here.' He seemed weary, to be musing about something of great weight. Casually he flicked a bottle of the preserved fruit off the table. Sonja's body flinched involuntarily, but her face remained unchanged. She watched the bottle slowly roll through the air.

All that work.

All that love.

And when it bounced slightly upwards on hitting the floor she hoped it might not break. But the fractures in the glass merely took a split second to course the length of the bottle then open outwards, and the bottle collapsed back upon the floor into a mess of glass shards, syrup and fruit. And all the time she was watching the bottle fall and shatter he was watching her, staring at her, saying nothing, unmoving, an animal with semaphoring eyes sizing up its prey. The conversation had been transformed into an interrogation, though neither spoke for a few moments, until Picotti resumed.

'Where? Where she go?'

Picotti searched Sonja's face for confirmation of his suspicions, and he was infuriated to find none, to be reminded yet again of the complicity of wicked women as certain as it was obvious. He put his fingers under the table, felt its weight, lifted one end ever so slightly off the floor and held it there.

'Why? Why she go? Another man, that is what it is. You know?' murmured Picotti, his voice remaining ever so soft, his fingers so gently balancing the slanting table. 'She out in another man's bed. You know what they do?' He smiled, then the smile was gone and Sonja knew him to be displeased, as if it had been her who had smiled and had insulted him by doing so, as if it was her playing games with him. Still he talked quietly. 'You know?'

Then Picotti snapped. He suddenly threw the table up and over. Sonja leapt backwards. The table flew up into the air and then clattered down, bottle smashing against bottle, as both table and bottles fell to the linoleum floor with a horrifying crash.

'Of course you know!' roared Picotti, and his voice was a cyclone that Sonja thought might blow her away.

Terrified, gripping tightly the sink behind her, Sonja looked down at the linoleum, at its abstract pattern, bright colourful lines and squares repeated all over, which, despite constant effort upon the part of her and Maja, had seen better days. Parts of it were worn almost down to the hessian backing, and over this shabby lino landscape the smooth syrup and scores of apricots now rolled in a colourful glacial flow, leaving in their wake moraines of plump fruit and broken glass.

Then Sonja's head jerked up to see Picotti's blinking had ceased as strangely and inexplicably as it had begun, and that he was pointing an accusing finger at her.

Sonja did not know what to say or do, but feared what Picotti would do next if she said nothing. So she grabbed a mop, cried out, 'I'll clean it up, Mr Picotti,' her voice at first high, sounding as if it were her fault, then cracking, as she tried unsuccessfully to lower it to hide her fear from him.

'No,' said Picotti. 'No—*you* show me,' said Picotti swivelling his head up and sideways as if he had just won a knife-fight in a pub but was watching all angles in case of one final, unexpected feint, and Sonja could hear his shuddering breath, 'You show me where *she* is.'

He dropped his half-smoked cigarette into the mess of preserved apricots that lay upon the floor, as if there were something somehow offensive about the things women did and took pleasure in doing.

Picotti ordered Sonja to come with him for a drive in his bright burnt-orange Pontiac, to find his unfaithful wife and her phantom lover. In the back seat of the huge car Sonja felt trapped, the soft bone-coloured seats enveloping her like restraining arms. As she wriggled to the front of the seat, trying to find a place where the car had minimum purchase upon her body, she was belaboured by Picotti with details of his wife's supposed infidelity.

'That bitch,' he rued, 'she is sleeping with another man. I know this, I know Maja, I find them both now and make them pay for shaming me like this.' His lips, she noticed, were moist with saliva. He punctuated his points with an elaborate throw of his left hand sufficiently vigorous that his brilliantined fringe fell out of its neatly combed place.

'Me! Umberto Picotti! The bitch! The filthy whore! Women like her are no good, Sonja. They are bad to their husbands and bad to their children.' He put the fingers of his right hand under his drooping fringe that sat across his face like some outflow of sulphurous bitumen, and flicked the hair back into its correct position. 'Like your mother see.'

This was a throwaway line on Picotti's part, but in the rear-vision mirror he glimpsed Sonja looking up, and he sought to talk his way out of it, partly out of embarrassment, partly out of curiosity, to see what it was that interested Sonja in her mother whom he knew she had not seen for many years.

'I tell you now because you are a good girl,' he continued, studying her all the while in the rear-vision mirror, 'because you are like your father, I tell that your mother was not faithful to him and that is . . . that is why she is not here.' Sonja looked away from the front, from Picotti. She curled up against a side door and stared at the cars passing by, as though she was not listening. 'She did not love your father,' said Picotti, thinking, But you are listening. Listening to everything I say. 'She did not love you.'

He paused to light a cigarette.

'Your mother did not love you or she would be here now. Eh? She would. If she loved you, she would be here looking after you. You understand what I say—your mother did not love you. This is hard for you I know, but it is better you know it all.'

He paused again.

Inhaled.

Exhaled.

Carefully thinking what he would say next.

'She was whore, a filthy whore, and I tell you true you are better for her going.'

Without warning he pulled the Pontiac to a halt on the side of the road. The big car slewed and rolled like a rudderless boat buffeted by a wild sea.

'Eh! Sonja. Come over and sit in the front seat.'

Picotti smiled at the child's back as Sonja clambered over into the front seat without enthusiasm and without awareness. Sonja sat down and turned around to see Picotti had resumed his rapid blinking. He reached over and placed his hand on the inside of Sonja's leg and began to draw it up her thigh.

She felt a knotting in her stomach that would return to her often after, felt a terrible fear, felt herself falling into his power. But her stony face betrayed nothing. She knew to survive this movement, her face must be that way. His hand reached the hem of her dress and still it would not stop slithering upwards.

'What are you doing?' she asked, trying not to let her voice trill.

Picotti continued smiling and he spoke so softly, so gently, in such a pleasing way that Sonja wanted to believe what he said.

But she did not believe him.

'Do not be frightened, my child,' he said.

But she did not believe him, would never believe him. His hand was nearing the top of her thigh when he sneezed and at that moment of distraction Sonja drew away and reached for the door handle. With her gaze fixed upon his blinking eyes Sonja gingerly opened the door and eased herself out of the car. Picotti made no further movement toward her. Sonja walked away down the sidewalk. When she was ten yards or so distant Picotti leant across the front seat and shut the front door.

And, without looking back, drove off downhill, leaving Sonja to find her own way.

Chapter 25

1960

THE DAYS PASSED into weeks and then into months. Autumn gave way to winter and then winter passed into spring. Rains came with great force but Bojan did not come and the talk was of terrible floods up north and then spring too was gone and summer had arrived but Bojan still did not return, and Sonja had come to be part of the strange little household. Every night she prayed to the Madonna Mrs Michnik had taught her about and every night she begged the Madonna to bring her father back to her the next weekend, and every weekend she waited and her father did not return and she could only conclude that the Madonna, like so many other grownups, was inexplicably angry with her. Picotti was away a lot, working shifts at the cell room at the zinc works or drinking, which suited both Sonja and Maja Picotti, who, despite all her protestations to the contrary, seemed much happier without her husband.

Maja Picotti watched the child and wondered who she was. Sonja helped her around the house, but rarely spoke. Maja Picotti found her trustworthy, hardworking but strange. She did all tasks asked of her without complaint or comment. Until the day Maja Picotti had gone out shopping and had left her sleeping baby in Sonja's care.

Almost as soon as she had gone the baby had woken and begun to cry. Sonja watched and waited impassive. She did not move to help the baby, to pick it up and comfort it. She waited for Maja Picotti to return but Maja Picotti, who had been held up chatting to a friend, did not come and did not come and still the baby cried.

'She's like her papa,' Maja Picotti had said. 'She won't wake till it's time to eat and drink.'

But the baby had woken and still Maja Picotti did not come and the baby was crying and suddenly Sonja could not bear to hear its cries. She seized the cot, rattled it a little, and when that proved to no avail, shook it harder to stop the baby crying. The baby took to bellowing. With all her might Sonja heaved the cot back and forth. And it was at that moment that Maja Picotti walked in, saw what was happening, grabbed her baby, and admonished Sonja.

'Madonna!—what are you doing you stupid child! Can't you see the baby's upset?'

The baby's blubbering diminished as Maja Picotti rocked it back and forth on her shoulder. She turned and stared fiercely at Sonja. She searched the child's face for some explanation of her bizarre behaviour. Maja Picotti looked hard, but found nothing. Presumably the child was fearful of what might follow, but she did not flinch, nor did she try to apologise.

'Well?' said Maja Picotti. 'Well, what have you got to say?'

Sonja wished to say the baby had woken and the baby was crying and Sonja could not bear to hear its cries.

'You never cry,' said Sonja. 'No matter how bad you feel, you never cry.'

Sonja wished to say that she felt infinitely sorry for the baby, but the baby had to learn what she had or the baby would die. But Sonja wished to tell these things to the baby and not to the baby's mother; wished to say: Beware, beware, and learn from me—never feel, never feel like me.

The baby began to blubber again. Sonja didn't move toward the cot, but stood exactly where and as she was when admonished by Maja Picotti. Sonja stared past the baby and began to sing:

> *'Don't cry little fishy*
> *Don't cry don't cry*
> *Don't cry little fishy.'*

Maja Picotti stared at Sonja, not understanding, perplexed by the strangeness of the child. She shook her head, and momentarily wished she could pick Sonja up and hold her forever.

Sonja continued to sing:

> *'Don't cry don't cry*
> *U-fee little fishy*
> *Don't cry don't cry.'*

But later Maja Picotti felt troubled by all that had taken place and all that she had felt, and before she went to bed that night Maja Picotti said rosaries for the safe journey of Sonja's soul back from wherever it had so clearly fled.

'U-fee little fishy,'

Sonja sang in her bed that evening,

'Don't cry don't cry,'

Sonja sang.

But there were no proper words for the emptiness she wished to sing. In the end she gave up singing out loud songs she knew and instead took to slowly mouthing words that did not exist for feelings that had no name, her lips forming into a circle and then collapsing, circling and collapsing, like a fish panting for life-giving water as it dies in the foetid air of a fisherman's creel.

Not long after, Bojan returned.

He and Umberto and Maja Picotti and Sonja each sat at a side of the kitchen table. Sonja was filled with a sudden dreadful vision of Picotti sweeping them all aside like bottled apricots and them—Bojan, Maja, her—falling to the floor and breaking, and Picotti flicking ash upon them, smiling. Picotti blinked, once, twice, continuously.

Bojan smiled. Sonja shivered. Bojan was ignorant of what had passed, of why Umberto Picotti would have wanted to end the arrangement to look after Sonja. He had, after all, paid the Picottis handsomely. The atmosphere was brooding, the coffee that Maja had made undrunk, the cakes on the plate in the table's centre untouched. Umberto Picotti counted out some money and slid it across the table to Bojan, past a bowl of brodo he had not permitted Maja to take from the table when Bojan arrived.

'That your money back, minus when we look after her,' said Umberto Picotti.

Bojan didn't reply. He was confused. Umberto Picotti, without looking up at Bojan, addressed his soup.

'Take her now.'

He rubbed his blinking eyes, rolling his balled fingers hard like an auger, as if he were trying to bore them out.

Bojan felt perplexed. 'Oh, Bertie . . .' he began. But Picotti interrupted before he had finished.

'I won't miss her,' said Umberto Picotti, blinking to the noodles floating in his chicken soup. 'Disobedient little bitch.'

Chapter 26

TASMANIAN MADNESS—the bastard issue of a century
and a half of despair cleaving to ever more outrageous
fantasies—only intruded in the Hobart airport in a way
that wasn't immediately obvious: some years before, in the
vain delusion that such a facility must inevitably attract
sadly absent international custom, an international terminal had been built and the runway lengthened to take
jumbo jets. While local satraps, in the manner of previous
cargo cult chieftans, continued searching the sky for
fabled jumbos full of wealthy Asian tourists and made
speeches reassuring their followers that the island's
salvation as the Singapore of the south was nigh, the international terminal found use for a minuscule company flying locals in six-seater planes to the remoter edges of the
island.

Apart from such pleasing eccentricity, the Hobart
airport, though small, was of its type an undistinguished
example, and it was from this thought that Sonja derived
some solace as she waited with Helvi at her side in the

queue for the reservations counter, ready to return to Sydney. Airports always had a comforting effect upon her, of dissolving the familiar into the general, the important particular into a mass insignificance, acting as the chain-saws of life, clearing away the certainties of place into clearfelled wastelands that were the same the world over. People smoking, people weeping. Ashes and tissue paper, thought Sonja, handing her ticket over to the reservation clerk. Jiri, who had until then maintained a respectful dis-tance from the two women, stepped forward and, his best 1970s vinyl bum-hugger jacket squeaking, passed the suit-case to be checked in, and then stepped back.

'You could stay here,' said Helvi. The reservation clerk passed the ticket back to Sonja, complete with a boarding pass, as if to refute Helvi's words. 'You know that. It's not too late,' Helvi continued, but it was clear from the quiet way she spoke that she no longer believed this.

Sonja held the ticket and boarding pass in front of Helvi's face, as if it were a sentence she was condemned to accept. She shrugged her shoulders, then shook her head and smiled at such insistence. With a soft mock sternness, as though admonishing a child, she said, '*Helvi.*'

Helvi looked at Sonja and saw it all once more. Felt the grief, huge rocks pressing hard in her belly and on her forehead, felt it almost overwhelm her. Changing tack, Helvi said, 'You never tell your father you're pregnant?'

Sonja seemed detached. 'No,' she said. 'What could I say?'

'The truth.'

'Ah, that,' said Sonja unemotionally. She began walking at a brisk pace to the departure lounge. 'The truth.' She continued to stride, smiling a little, tried to swallow but found her mouth dry as sand, and then, without looking across at Helvi, said, 'He wants to believe I have some serious love in my life, that I at least am happy.' And though she was angry with Helvi, pushing her so, she laughed a small, wry laugh. 'The truth is rarely worth knowing, Helvi, you know that? It hurts. Lies are easier.' And all the time she was walking and all the time she was looking straight ahead and not at Helvi. 'What's the point of telling him there is no father who wants the child, no proper home, no time I can spare from working. Not enough money. No anything. That I could offer the child nothing.' Abruptly she stopped and fixed Helvi with a harsh stare. 'That I'm poor in everything and abortion is cheaper.'

Though the fight was lost, Helvi wasn't about to concede defeat.

'Sometimes an abortion is right,' Helvi said. 'Sometimes a baby destroys what little a woman has.' Sonja looked away, wondering how much more she had to endure before she could finally leave, though grateful that Helvi seemed to have finally swung around to her position. 'But sometimes,' continued Helvi, 'it is wrong. Sometimes a baby can help heal.'

This was too much for Sonja. She gave peremptory embraces and kisses to both Helvi and Jiri, then hurried away alone to the entrance of the departure lounge.

She walked through the security gate, watched her handbag slide out along the x-ray unit's conveyor belt, her mind empty, aware only of the most trivial details. So she saw the uniformed arm reach down and pull her handbag to one side but her mind did not weight this action with any significance. She saw only the pubic-like hairs of the fingers of the hand as it grabbed the handbag's strap, the chunky gold wedding ring, saw the blue pullover sleeve and wondered pointlessly whether it was pure wool or an acrylic wool mix. At first she did not even hear the security officer's words as being addressed to her.

'Excuse me, ma'am, do you mind opening your handbag for me?'

A middle-aged woman next to Sonja nudged her and she went around to the other side of the belt and opened her handbag on a melamine shelf. She unfolded the scarf that lay within to reveal some broken teapot pieces.

'Ah—that's what she was,' said the officer. 'Maybe you ought to take up coffee.' He smiled. 'Thank you, ma'am. That's all.'

But Sonja didn't touch the porcelain fragments, made no attempt to fold the scarf and close the handbag. She stared at the teapot pieces and her mind raced and her body felt hot and her head shaky.

'Thank you, ma'am,' said the security officer, conscious of the need to continue with other inspections. 'If you could take your bag now. Please. Ma'am? Are you okay, missus? It was a joke. About the coffee. A joke.'

Sonja stared into the teapot pieces, and she saw many things and felt her eyes go watery. Saw a door closing. A teapot smashing. Her father. Her mother. Herself. Had they broken? Had they?

Then suddenly she came to her senses, picked the handbag up, flashed an embarrassed, awkward smile at the security officer and muttered an apology.

'Yes,' she said. 'Coffee. Instead of tea. Such a good joke.'

But instead of heading into the departure lounge she turned and started walking away from it, at first with measured steps, then at a canter, finally breaking into a run. People turned away from her, slightly shocked by her untoward behaviour.

Sonja was in flight, not away from what she was, but back toward it. She scarcely paused when she bumped people, as she pushed past people, as she swam against the almighty undertow of movement seeking to sweep her away, so far away—and all of the people blurred to her and the airport dissolved into strange smudging dabs of colour and sound and she could only see one thing clearly: a piece of lace, and it was blowing away in the cyclonic swirl of people arriving and departing, arriving and departing, everybody now a reffo, fleeing the nameless, the unspeakable, and for a moment she actually thought she had been transported back to a postwar refugee camp, but still she chased the lace through all those businessmen and surfies and tourists and families who were now dressed in dun-coloured rags carrying not plastic suitcases and backpacks but brown paper parcels bound with string and they all, all looked lost, and still the lace eluded Sonja, then finally she gained upon it, and the lace transformed into a red nylon overcoat and a 1970s bum-hugger leather jacket and she was swimming toward it as hard as she could when suddenly she yelled—

'It's not too late?'

And in their bewilderment, a startled couple near an exit door began turning around, and, in so doing, without knowing it, Helvi and Jiri were answering Sonja's question.

Chapter 27

1960

THE LATE AFTERNOON SUN gilded the FJ in luminous wonder, so that in all its glorious metallic colours it glided like some huge Christmas beetle through the northern suburbs of Hobart, past the old brick and stone tenements and the new housing commission weatherboard and concrete-block houses, as if searching for a familiar gum branch that might prove to be home. Inside the FJ Sonja looked across at Bojan, hoping he might look at her.

But he did not. He kept on looking straight ahead. Neither spoke. She thought of Picotti. Saw him beckoning her to come over from the back seat. *Come!* Hated his spiv clothes. His oiled hair. Made the sight of him go away. Made herself breathe the sweet close smell of Bojan's cigarette smoke. Made herself observe the concrete-block and weatherboard box homes. Made herself memorise the gravel gutters in which children played. The lack of trees, ornamentation, difference. The bareness.

They shared their silence as a sustaining bread, and broke it accordingly.

Slowly. With some reverence of what breaking it might mean.

'Sonja,' said Bojan finally, 'you do not mind leaving the Picottis?'

'No,' said Sonja after a time. She did not look at him, only, as he had, straight ahead. She coughed. 'No,' said Sonja, her throat raspy.

Bojan looked away from her, looked back at the road unravelling.

'I don't know why they ask me to come and take you back,' he said, genuinely perplexed. 'You were a good girl for them?'

Sonja said nothing. Bojan had an intimation of what had passed.

'I never liked the bastard anyway.'

He felt an old, ceaseless terror within and kept driving as if he were racing away from it but it was within him and could not now or ever be so easily shaken off. The steering wheel trembling as if the wheels were being shaken out of alignment under his shuddering hands.

'Who do I live with now, Artie?'

'With me,' said Bojan. Quietly. Then he said it a second time, this time with a slight smile at the pleasurable strangeness of such an ordinary idea, and his hands' shuddering ceased. 'With me.'

At these words Sonja felt her spirits suddenly rise. A rush of exhilaration and curiosity.

'In the camp? You and I in the camp?'

'No,' said Bojan. 'Here. Here in Hobart. I throw my job with the hydro in and I find a place for us before I pick you up. When that prick ring and say I must collect you, well I, I—' He momentarily halted, flustered, then recommenced, the words now rushing out—'I think maybe it good now if we live together. I think it's not right you with these other people.'

Sonja was incredulous. 'You're going to look after me?'

Bojan threw a hand in the air in guilty exasperation. 'Jesus Christ—I'm your bloody artie—no?'

Sonja looked long and hard at Bojan.

He said, 'I know what you thinking.'

He felt her stare, terrible and searching, and knew she had the power of children to see beyond words.

And then he described what he felt, quietly, resolutely, as if it were his fate to which he now had to submit and from which there was no further running. He meant to say it as a flat statement but it ended up sounding somewhere between a query and a revelation.

He said, 'But I am your artie.'

The FJ came to a house with a long drive down its side, and Bojan turned into it, drove up past a newish weatherboard cottage, butterfly tin roofed and aqua-green painted. There in the back corner of the backyard, spitting distance from the Hills Hoist, sat a small shed, its undressed timber vertical boards black from coatings of sump oil.

They stepped out of the car. Bojan waved awkwardly to a woman—their landlord—washing dishes behind a nylon cafe-curtain in the main house. Sonja followed her father through the shed that had been converted into accommodation, albeit of a dirty and basic type. Then they walked around outside, Bojan showing where they would plant tomatoes and where they would build furniture. Then they went back inside and stood in the kitchen.

Bojan smiled wryly. Spread his arms out wide, as if what they embraced was vast beyond measure, rather than the three small, cramped rooms of the shed—the kitchen-cum-lounge, the bedroom, and the bathroom.

'Doma,' he said. 'You know what doma means, Sonja? It means home. In Slovenian doma means home. You know what Australians call these places, Sonja? Wog flats, that's what they call them. That means they are not for the Australian people. That means they are for the wogs. For us.' And then he smiled some more and laughed, a generous open happy laugh. Sonja looked up and, realising that he was happy, smiled and laughed too.

Over the next week they laboured at transforming the shed into a home. Bojan bought a second-hand bakelite wireless and sat it on the kitchen windowsill and they let it play nonstop. He bought a sofa, an armchair, and a Silent Knight refrigerator on hire-purchase, but paid cash for a Hoover vacuum cleaner and they were both utterly taken by its space rocket styling. He bought an old wardrobe, a new mattress, four saucepans, one frypan, and in an unconscious expectation of a future possibly better than the present, four sets of knives, forks, spoons, plates and bowls from Woolworths. As Elvis and Dean Martin poured in a slurry of staticky sound from the wireless, they carpeted the lino floors with old blankets, cut pictures out of the *Women's Weekly* and put them into frames which Bojan made from scrounged timber and Sonja painted in bright blues and purples.

At first they had only one bed and so they slept together. That was how he had grown up: that is, he would say, how it is, sharing a bed with older brothers and sisters, and though he would not admit it even to himself, he gained a certain comfort from sharing his bed, however much Sonja kicked and wriggled in her sleep. The Australian concept of a single bed for a single person struck him as odd and destructive. Sleeping alone was a punishment, a sadness, a lie that life was not shared in its most fundamental, mundane aspects. To be told that some might put a less than savoury gloss on such behaviour would have appalled him. He knew too well what some adults did with children, had suffered his own uncle one night when he was twelve. But if they knew Bojan Buloh, they would know that was not him, and, for Bojan, that was that. He knew himself: in his pigheaded way it never occurred to him that others might have an opinion of him also, somewhat at odds with who he was.

One evening Sonja was still sitting up when Bojan came to bed. She was looking through some old photographs that he kept in a cardboard shoebox. One photograph in particular intrigued her, a black-and-white snap of a thin middle-aged man laid out in a coffin full of flowers. Bojan got into bed and turned his back to Sonja, trying to get to sleep. Sonja pushed the photograph of the man in the coffin under Bojan's nose.

'And this one?'

'Your grandfather. Mama's artie,' mumbled Bojan into the blanket.

'Why have they put the flowers around him while he's sleeping?'

'Because he's dead. When you're dead they like covering you with flowers. That's how they do it over there. Now go to sleep.'

'It's beautiful.'

'Sure.'

'Mama? Where are the photos of Mama?'

'I don't know,' said Bojan untruthfully. 'Somewhere.'

'Can I look at them?'

'Sure.'

'Now?'

'No. Another time you look at them. Now we sleep.'

But he couldn't. Long after Sonja was asleep he was still awake. He prised the photograph of Maria's dead father out of Sonja's sweaty clasp and put it away, not looking at it any more than he had to, because that one picture was the best picture of Maria he had, but how could he ever explain that to his daughter, or any of what he could not even comprehend himself. A man can be as proud as he likes, thought Bojan Buloh, he can try and make a home out of a wog flat, he can try and make a good life out of a bad one but his past will always claim him back completely like a swamp does withering sedges. He can try and protect his daughter and he can fail, he can even be dressed up with flowers when he's dead, but all corpses are alike, even the one he had once seen that had eaten a flower at the moment of release.

But what did that mean? What did any of it mean? He could have wept, but he believed tears were to the living what flowers were to the dead: proof only of the futility of feeling.

Chapter 28

1960

EACH PLATE, each knife, each fork, Sonja washed with as much attention as if they were surgical instruments to be used in an operating theatre. Her father, she was discovering, was a meticulous man. Bojan could not bear what he termed 'filth'. 'Filth' served to cover anything that Bojan Buloh believed was not clinically clean, and that was just about everything. From dust on top of window frames to a beer glass in which the beer failed to sparkle because the detergent had not been rinsed properly—all was filth, all equally upset him, and all filth had to be exiled from his home. The rites of order and cleanliness were women's work, and such was Sonja's role from the age of nine, a relentless round of housework he expected her to do entirely in accordance with his own ways and standards.

Sonja was wiping up when Bojan came inside from working out on the porch on a set of cupboards he intended selling. He saw his daughter was crying quietly. He noticed her arms moving quickly but stiffly, how each movement seemed to cost her a certain measure of pain.

'Sonja?' he asked, and she turned and her watering eyes were wary. She stifled a sob. But when he spoke further, she knew that he was not angry with her for having washed or rinsed in transgression of his notions of cleanliness. 'Are you alright?' he asked softly, and came up to where she was standing on a stool.

She turned and buried her head in his chest. He noticed how her arms were covered in a hot red rash. Bojan ran his fingertips over her skin. He felt it dry and chapping in painful flakes, like dried-up pastry. Bojan had not felt such skin with his fingers since he had been with Maria, when she had suffered similarly. He slowly bent the arm at its joint, though carefully and only a little way back and forth, once, twice, then halted and cradling her arm, said, 'It hurts to bend, no?'

Sonja nodded.

'How long?'

'Since the Picottis,' said Sonja. She felt her thin fore-arm softly rest in his hand, marvelled at how he held her arm like it were some precious thing, delighted at how gentle his touch could be. She shrugged. 'It's alright,' she lied to impress him. 'It doesn't hurt really.'

'Eczema,' said Bojan. What he did not say: that this too, along with her temperament, her looks, she had inherited from her mother.

That night Bojan wrote a letter in his native language, the first time he had written such a letter in some years, and he had to write it out three times before it was right, for he never had been a scholar and after so many years away he found it very difficult to know what to say and to find a way even in his own tongue to say it all. He wrote slowly, painstakingly with a neat and old-fashioned hand that swirled and looped across the page, and he concentrated as much on making the script beautiful to look at, as the words meaningful to read. In his youth in Slovenia he had been in some demand as a painter of local beehives, which he adorned with scenes of alpine life, some conventional, some lewder, depending on his customer's fancy. In Tasmania beehives were, like so many other things, unadorned, so he had abandoned his rude art. All that remained was a certain reputation in the minds of others so very far away (and, he hoped, a few of the beehives also) that he was not about to jeopardise by penning a lousily scripted letter. When he was finally satisfied, he shook his writing hand a few times to relieve his aching wrist, sealed the letter in an envelope, and the address he wrote on its front finished with the word *Jugoslavia*.

Some weeks later Sonja found her father using a somewhat savage-looking knife he had fashioned out of a power hacksaw blade to cut the string of a brown paper parcel covered in Yugoslav stamps. Inside the first parcel, a letter and a second, smaller brown paper parcel. When Bojan carefully unfolded the second parcel Sonja was disappointed by what was revealed. It was not exotic, nor valuable, nor even interesting, but only a dusty pile of small dried flowers.

That night Bojan ran a deep bath in the old, stained bathtub. As Sonja undressed in the rising steam, Bojan scattered the flowers over the bath water, then stirred them in with his hands, till the bath resembled a swirling, watery compost-heap. Sonja giggled.

'What are you doing, Artie?'

Sonja put one foot then the other in the bath, stood for a minute as her body adjusted to the heat and then sat down in the flower-water. Bojan smiled and sprinkled a few flowers upon her hair.

'Is it not beautiful to swim in flowers?' he asked. He picked out one of the flowers and held it close to Sonja's face. 'Kamílica,' said Bojan. 'I write and tell your grand-mother in Slovenia about your skin and she pick and dry the kamílica for you, she send them across the oceans, she want to heal her Sonja.' He indicated the bath waters with a wet flowered hand. 'Now you must lie back.'

Bojan left the bathroom. And Sonja sank back into the chamomile flowers. With just her nose and eyes above water level, she picked out a single flower, turned it this way and that, gazing at it closely.

And to herself softly whispered.

'Kamílica . . . kamílica.'

That night Sonja had a strange and beautiful dream: of a magical land cobbled together from what she knew of Tasmania and what she imagined of Slovenia.

There was a strong smell, full and steaming and won-derful, and it was the smell of the grass and the earth below a wet mountain after the sun has come out. There was a green slope on a steep blue mountainside, and it was the country back of Mount Roland where Sonja had once been shooting roo with Bojan. Back bent, picking flowers on that green slope was an old woman, dressed like the Slovenian peasant women in Bojan's photographs—head scarfed and body long black dressed, floral smock tied at the back. A face, mottled and twisted like a spud grown in hard earth, betraying no emotion beyond a certain grim determination to endure. She stood up, flowers in the cup of an uplifted skirt, and started walking down the green mountainside to where there was—as though it were the most natural place in the world for such a thing to be—an open coffin, and in the coffin was laid out Sonja's dead grandfather, looking, Sonja could hear voices around her say, far better in death than he ever managed in life.

Yet when the old spud-woman got to the coffin and looked inside it she saw not the old man lying there but Sonja, and Sonja was looking up the coffin's walls and seeing a slow avalanche of flowers, the most beautiful flowers in the world falling on her. Sonja felt at peace lying in that coffin, felt no fear watching the flower petals raining down. Her gaze wandered up from the heavy boots and coarse stockings to the black dress and floral apron, until it finally arrived at that face, an extraordinary, scarfed face, angular, beautiful, and young, oh so young, no longer that of the old spud-woman, but the face of her own mother, Maria.

And through the shower of petals, she was smiling down at Sonja.

When Sonja woke the morning after her dream, she rose as she had done for many months, lifting herself up from her bed slowly, cautiously, fearing pain. But she found she was able to push herself up easily. She looked at her arms. They were clear. The red dryness of the eczema was almost entirely gone, her skin no longer dry pastry flaking.

It was a Sunday and Bojan was not working. She found him in the kitchen, placing onto a wooden chopping board on the table a large, old black cast-iron frying pan spitting and hissing sweet fatty sounds. Freshly fried eggs, yolks still wet, whites bubbling like living lava, studded with tomatoes and Polish sausage.

Before Bojan had even looked up to see her Sonja spoke: 'Artie! Artie! My arms are better!'

Bojan turned, picked Sonja up, examined her arms, smiled at her. He noticed a chamomile flower in her hair and picked it out, tickled her nose with it, and ran it down her arm to her elbow.

'Kamílica,' he laughed. Then in a mock serious voice repeated. '*Kamílica.*' And they both laughed.

Bojan put Sonja down.

'Now we eat,' said Bojan.

With pieces of thickly sliced continental bread they ate Slovenian fashion from the pan, bursting the yolks and scooping up bits of egg, sausage and tomato all together on a single piece of broken bread, laughing and smiling as they did so, for the food was good and the food they shared as one, pushing yellow and white and red into their mouths, feeling sweet and hot and sharp and fatty in their gobs.

Chapter 29

1960

THE HEANEYS were that sort of family who were everywhere, that sort whose kids spread unavoidably like spilt gravy over the street—dirty and brown and everywhere and difficult to avoid and difficult to be rid of, that sort who stood by neighbours' fences asking them questions as to why they did this or that in the garden, only to then belabour them with details on how *their* Dad—who, in the neighbours' view, by and large did nothing, except head back to work fishing when his family got too much for him, which was frequently—how their Dad did such things and how they really ought do it their Dad's way. That sort of family they were, whose kids terrorise the pavements on broken-down old bikes that seemed unsafe at any speed, let alone the subsonic speeds at which they hurtled into oncoming traffic, only to swerve out of its way with a gleeful laugh at the last moment, the sort whose mouths ran even more than their perpetually runny noses, but who would always help when neighbours needed help, and on several occasions when they didn't. How many Heaneys? Heaven knows, the street would declare with a sigh, for this was a matter of ongoing contention: sober estimates put their number at six, but the frequent influx of cousins who could stay any amount of time from a few hours to a few months made any sort of guesswork difficult.

For Sonja they were fascinating creatures from another world: freckly, snotty aliens; and she took to sitting at the head of the driveway leading down to the wog flat, watching with wonder the mob of Heaneys playing in and around the dilapidated, unpainted concrete-block house that was their home across the street, not so much in the hope of playing with them as simply observing them and their antics. For a long time she would not have been able to say what it was that attracted her to the Heaneys, until the day when she saw a Heaney boy bearing down the road, riding an old bike far too big for him no-hands, while at the same time trying to juggle three mandarins which, it transpired, were not his but those of the Greek shopkeeper Mr John Kerr—whose change of name by deed poll was to be later deemed by history as less than fortunate—who was loping behind at some distance, yelling angrily. It was a most magnificent sight: a stick-thin child on a ridiculous old bone-shaker, lost in his dreams of lightness and wonder, pursued by a rotund rocket of a man.

It was also folly. The boy failed at the juggling, dropping first one, then two mandarins, and with his harmony broken and dreams disappearing earthwards, he mistakenly leant a little too far out to his left trying to catch the third mandarin. The front wheel jack-knifed sideways, the bike lurched and came to an abrupt halt—unlike its rider who half-catapulted, half-fell what seemed to Sonja a considerable distance to the ground. Upon touching down, he was about to bellow when upon looking up he saw hovering over him the red-faced visage of Mr John Kerr glaring down.

'Well,' he then said, each word a gulp, 'I could hardly use watermelons.' As though his theft of the mandarins had been somehow appropriate and modest.

Sonja—unlike Mr John Kerr, who grabbed the boy by the ear and marched him off to see his mother—burst out laughing. The Heaneys, Sonja realised, made her feel happy.

The children's mother, a large, rapidly ageing, and perennially pregnant woman known to the street only as Mrs Heaney, was already coming out of the house having appraised herself of the situation from the lounge window. She hit the street in the manner of a beach landing by the marines in the movies, attempting to make up for a certain weakness in her position with an overwhelming display of force that was largely illusion. She hooled into Mr John Kerr to leave the poor child alone, asked the street what was the point having a tick if Mr John Kerr couldn't even put a few lousy bits of fruit on it, and why should any of them bother taking business to someone who didn't even understand how credit worked, blustering so much that in the end the shopkeeper did no more than give the boy's ear a final savage twist, turned on his heels and headed off, issuing under his breath several dreadful curses in the language of his forefathers.

Mrs Heaney then turned her fire onto the hapless juggler of mandarins. 'That'll be the last time you'll be allowed on that bloody thing if ya keep that nonsense up. And you're not to nick. You know that: no bloody nicking. When your father's back from sea—' She looked up and noticed Sonja sitting opposite. Halting her invective, Mrs Heaney called one of her girls to her side and as she spoke to her, pointed a finger in Sonja's direction.

The girl walked slowly over to Sonja, but even so her gait was a skipping one. She fronted up to Sonja and though both girls now faced each other, each looked anywhere but at the other.

'Gday,' the Heaney girl said after a time, twisting her mouth and looking downwards at the path where her right foot kicked at the brown gravel.

'Gday,' said Sonja, looking up at the hydro wires overhead.

'Mum says we should be playing with you,' said the girl, and she looked up, 'cos otherwise you might think we were just snubbin' you cos you're a wog like.'

The introduction had been well intentioned if appallingly delivered. Not knowing what to say, Sonja said nothing.

'Moira,' said the girl, after a long time waiting in vain for Sonja to speak. 'Moira Heaney.'

Unlike the rest of the Heaneys, who were inclined to be small and weedy, seeming to bear strongest resemblance in size and speed and proclivities to the ferrets which Mr Heaney kept in a cage in their backyard for his rabbiting, Moira, though also dark, was verging on chubby, and slightly clumsy in her movements. Her long hair, constantly messy, was today done in a rough top-knot that sat like an exhausted exclamation mark above her constantly grinning face. Her voice was loud, her laughter raucous, her games seemed inevitably to lead to some adventure or disaster or more normally both. Her voice was slow and sing-songy, the inflexion rising at the end of sentences, and it was this accent that Sonja was to take as her own for the rest of her life, for she unconsciously wished to be like this person who saw herself not as fat and awkward, but as having in life an invitation to an event that was to be enjoyed at all costs.

Over time this friendship grew, an attraction of opposites, Sonja as quiet and reserved as Moira was loud and ebullient. Sonja taught Moira Slovenian words. Moira taught her gammoning. To gammon was to imagine, and that was what Moira liked doing most of all, organising all the other Heaneys and anybody else she could find in the street, into all sorts of curious games.

Moira's method of introducing Sonja to the family was typical: Mr and Mrs Heaney's bedroom was organised by Moira into a riotous confusion, the double bed an elaborate theatre stage. The room was filled with Heaneys and assorted others. Moira stood up on the bed and announced—'And then from far away—' then waited, a dramatic pause, while Sonja, clad in an outrageous combination of old scarves and hats and clothes of Mrs Heaney's, all of which gave her an appearance at once slightly magnificent and somewhat ridiculous, slowly climbed up the chairs onto the bed. Moira dropped her head and theatrically swept her head right around as if taking them all into her confidence, and continued in a low hush '—came the Princess of the Orient.'

Like a queen Sonja walked into the centre of the bed and spread her arms out wide as Moira had instructed her. Moira looked at Sonja with affection and pride.

And then yelled: 'The Princess of the Orient! Best and fairest of them all!'

Everyone cheered Sonja.

At that moment a back leg gave way under the weight of a tribe of trampolining Heaneys. Before the bed had even finished collapsing, before Sonja had picked herself back off the floor onto which she had fallen, the room was empty of everybody, save Moira, who was tugging at Sonja's arm, telling her to scram before Mum found out.

But Mrs Heaney, who quickly arrived at the scene of the crime, was philosophical. 'That bed was buggered long before you kids got on it,' she said, helping Sonja to her feet. 'The main thing is—are you alright?'

Sonja smiled. She felt she was almost a real person. She felt her face stretch so much with smiling she worried that it might grow too tired to keep going. She felt she was somebody else. Different. And that it was possible to be somebody else and still be you. And she started to giggle at how funny it was, at how life could be so funny and so warm, and she laughed and brayed and cackled and giggled and no matter how hard she tried, she could not stop laughing.

Chapter 30

———

1989

THE SMELL OF FLESH, fallible and fecund, was slashed by the knife-sharp scent of the cleaners' methylated spirits. Shreds of odours came to Helvi's nose as lacerated suggestions of rancid sweat and clotting blood and mucus, and she found them difficult to match with birth, whose imminence is so often greeted with the expectation of a life better, more fulfilling, more meaningful than that which it is about to succeed.

She wiped her nose with a tissue, and turned to look down the long, caterpillaring row of cheap plastic chairs set against the public maternity hospital's waiting-room wall, minuscule segments of the chain punctuated by yet another woman's swollen belly. Some of the women were very young—fourteen and fifteen years old—and some of them looked already beaten and worn out by life. Their clothes, tracksuit pants and Esprit tops and the like, though suggestive of affluence, were rather the modern apparel of poverty. Here and there a mother's mother, old beyond their short age, hard-faced beyond sadness that their promise might have come to this despair. An occasional boy-father, lizard thin, all bum-fluff moustache and flannelette shirt and fingers searching for forbidden cigarettes, feigning a nonchalance that fooled nobody, least of all themselves. Upon the walls pasted and pinned posters telling of domestic violence and rape and child abuse and AIDS, the varied and bitter truths shrouded by the promise of hope whose name is birth.

One of the many bellies—though hers was yet little bloated—in the caterpillar chain belonged to Sonja, who sat next to Helvi. Sonja did not even wear looser clothes, though she felt her thickening as a tightness that pressed outwards, a heaviness that dragged her earthward with the power of sleep. She glanced at Helvi, still and observant as a bird on a branch, slightly bowed, but with the assured strength of those who have known only hard labour, and Sonja wondered if it was her own future she was seeing and if it was a future she wanted.

Some children were playing with a ball. Without warning the ball strayed and hit Helvi in the chest, dropping into her lap. The fixed, hard old face opened like land after a drought to welcoming rain, both brown and blue eyes sparkled, and the old woman chortled, then laughed, then chiacked the kids, and threw the ball elsewhere, laughing all the while with such gusto that a few mothers gave her a reproachful eye.

A nurse holding a clipboard looked down at her notes and then up in the vague direction of Sonja, eyes roaming back and forth.

'Ms Buloh?' she asked.

Without waiting for Helvi, Sonja headed through the door indicated. By the time Helvi had reached down, picked up her handbag, and looked up again, Sonja was disappearing into an examination room. Helvi felt slightly bewildered, but recognising she was not welcome to follow, sat back down to wait for Sonja's return.

A pair of translucent plastic gloves peeled off and fell into the alligator mouth of a bright yellow bin. The fleshy hands of an obstetrics registrar dropped to a wood-grained laminex desktop and picked up a pen.

In the windowless cell of the examination room his voice was young: sleek and full, of achievement, of expectations, of confidence. The accent was as smooth and deodorised as the skin of his ever so smooth, downturned face. The words purred forth with no rough edges, no betrayal of anything other than comfort.

'Congratulations,' he said, 'you're ten weeks pregnant.' Sonja rose from lying on her back to sitting in an upright position on the examination table. She looked blankly at him, saw a short, trim man with strong black hair already thinning, not good looking, but immaculately groomed as if he had been shot out of a hairdryer. Those oddly fleshy fingers began to fidget.

'Of course, we may have to run some blood tests. Being thirty-eight years of age and having had two previous abortions, the risks of complications in this pregnancy are, let us say, greater than for a younger woman without your medical history. But, in your case, everything for the time being seems fine.'

The obstetrics registrar felt obligated to continue until he gained some reaction.

'The risk of spontaneous abortion is of course increased.'

Noticing Sonja's face displaying some interest he continued.

'Spontaneous abortion—a miscarriage, as it is commonly termed.'

It was amazing, thought the obstetrics registrar, how shocked people were that miscarriages still occurred. He could have told her how they were in fact commonplace, of how foetuses and babies, for all the wonder and science of medicine, still died. And he could have told her how he had chosen obstetrics to specialise in because he hated the corporeality of flesh, its insistence in decay that medicine, for all its gaudy brilliance, was unable ultimately to deny. Yet even here, in a field that ought only to have been about aiding the gestation and delivery of life, life still revealed itself as inextricably linked with death. He had resolved to not accept this, to fight it with all his skill, and yet that morning he had to assist in the delivery of a still-born six-month foetus, whose parents, to his horror, had insisted on naming and even photographing—as if the dead foetus was something, when it was to him nothing, evidence only of the cruel anarchy of flesh. And now here was a woman who, presented with the possibility of a new life, seemed uninterested to the point of a mute hostility.

He found life was not only ignorant, but the more he learnt in his chosen profession, inexplicable. Of course, he said none of this, instead tried to focus upon the triathlon he was to compete in the following weekend.

'But I stress, at the moment all is well, and with careful management all will continue to be well.'

Sonja heard his words but not what was being said.

'All will be well?' she asked herself.

She stared at the obstetrics registrar, this young man striving hard to convey a sense of secure belief. She did not like the way his lower mouth protruded in a strangely belligerent way as he spoke.

'Yes.'

Sonja looked away, thinking.

The obstetrics registrar felt that she wished to say something.

'There is nothing else is there, Ms Buloh?'

Sonja looked up, her mind obviously elsewhere, and rose to her feet to leave.

'No,' said Sonja. 'Nothing.'

He could not remember her name when he bade her farewell, but he knew how to handle such lapses without causing embarrassment. Manner is half the battle, he thought. Out in the waiting room, patients and nurses looked up at the door opening.

He smiled.

Let them see, he thought, that I am a good and caring man.

Chapter 31

1990

SUCH WAS THE STRANGE, hesitant manner in which Sonja Buloh came slowly and with numerous second thoughts to accept that she was not to return to Sydney and not to have an abortion. Not through words, or by actions, but by a lack of actions, a resignation to letting things be. But it was to take her much longer to think of her life in terms of things that she was now to do, rather than in terms of things that she was no longer to do.

It was one thing to ring through her resignation from the job she suddenly realised with joy she had always hated and from which it was presumed, reasonably accurately, that she had simply fled; to make arrangements to have her Sydney flat packed up, vacated, and her few possessions shipped southwards to Tasmania, when it was simply costing her a great deal of money from a rapidly emptying account to keep the flat up. These affairs seemed to Sonja only acknowledging the obvious direction destiny had taken her. Like apologising for a hair appointment you missed the day before. They were but her agreement with life that it and not she determined what would be. But it was an entirely different matter to actually initiate new directions for her life, to find a new job, to find a new place to live, to say to others as she was unable to say even to herself for some months, 'I am having a baby come next year'.

Helvi disagreed with such foolish notions. In the time it would take Sonja to come around to her way of thinking, though, she had no choice but to do all she could for the poor child—though Sonja was almost middle-aged, she still could not help thinking of her so—and her yet-to-be-born baby.

Helvi wanted Sonja to stay with her and Jiri until the birth. 'You must,' said Helvi. 'It's not Buckingham Palace,' said Helvi—'But it is cheap.' So cheap that Sonja paid nothing, no matter how many times she tried to offer money, and had to resort to forestalling Helvi by buying groceries and presents. The days grew shorter and colder. And with the approach of winter Helvi's thoughts turned to the business of finding a place for Sonja to live once the baby arrived.

They sat in Helvi's old blue Corolla, looking across the narrow road from where they were parked next to a dog-torn garbage bag, at a squalid run-down weatherboard cottage, set tightly in a street of similarly withered houses. At one end of Barracouta Row was a closed video store, at the other an open pizza parlour, with nobody about either. As Helvi talked their eyes wandered over the dilapidated exterior: the broken letterbox overflowing with junk mail, the blistering paintwork faded to the colours of the earth, the rusty corro of the verandah roof, the partially rotted window frames more humus than homely.

'I run into Ahmet the Albanian's wife,' Helvi had said, 'and she say Ahmet has this place that might suit Sonja.'

They entered the house using the key Ahmet's wife had lent Helvi. The house was not derelict, but it had the terrible run-down feel of true poverty—the filth, the cracks in the wall, the peeling wallpaper, the broken windows, the stove with the door that didn't close properly, the cheap nylon carpet in which stains could not be discerned only because the whole carpet had taken on an undulating mustard tone, the cupboards in which Sonja noticed rat droppings. Sonja tried to flush the yellowed toilet. There was a noise like steel bolts being rattled in a rusty tin. Apart from which nothing happened.

For reasons that Sonja could not fully divine Helvi seemed hellbent on Sonja taking it.

'You could live here, eh?'

With not one jot of conviction or enthusiasm, Sonja agreed.

'I could.'

'It's cheap.' Not for a moment was Helvi going to let the reality of the house's condition alter her plans for Sonja, such as they were. 'I know it doesn't look much, but we could clean it up, Jiri fix what's broken, and Ahmet will let us have it for a quarter of what you will pay anywhere else.'

'He'd bloody need to,' said Sonja.

'So you decide to take it?'

'I've never decided anything, Helvi.'

'You decided to go. And to come back.'

'Maybe. Why, I don't know.'

'Because it's what you wanted. Because you choose what you want.'

'Do you?'

'Of course you do,' said Helvi. She pointed at a mantelpiece caked in numerous layers of bright chipped enamel paint, white, blue, with a final flaking overlay of red. A disintegrating union jack of a fireplace. 'Character, eh?'

Sonja smiled. Helvi pulled out the oven grill, which was caked in dirty, rancid fat.

'Oh God! Look at that. Bloody Ahmet.'

'Any oven as long as it is pre-greased,' said Sonja, and they both laughed.

Helvi slammed the filthy grill back into the stove with a triumphant clatter, her logic having unfolded without Sonja placing any serious obstacles in its way.

'You're wrong,' said Helvi. 'You can choose this place.'

Sonja gave a small laugh, more a polite exhalation of breath than anything else.

'I suppose I could.' Sonja slowly pulled the grill back out and gazed vacantly at the rancid fat. 'I suppose.' She was beyond caring. Helvi wanted her to take the place and she was indebted beyond measure to Helvi, and in any case she had so little money, that an absurdly low rental—even for such a hovel—was not something she could rashly disregard. She said, 'As long as the toilet flushes and the doors close I don't care.'

'Ahmet say he hold it till you are ready to move in summer. Maybe do a little work.'

She didn't feel sick or even tired that day as she and Helvi stood in the claustrophobic squalor of that near-derelict excuse for a house. She knew the worst thing was that she simply didn't care and that she should, but she didn't, and the more Helvi pushed, the more she felt nothing and that there was no excuse for this feeling nothing. Sonja knew Helvi was right. She had to get a home, had to get organised for when the—when *it* all happened—but before that there was something else. And because she didn't yet know what that something else was, she could only wait till it found her, unravelled her, awoke her.

And then she knew she would care.

'I'll take it,' said Sonja.

Chapter 32

1990

AFTER THEY LEFT Ahmet's house, it sleeted on the top of the large blue mountain that rumped and fingered the shivering town of Hobart, and then the sleet stopped and the clouds dissolved and the sun came strangely fierce as if angry at being denied, and then the wind was gone and the mountain was still.

From the vast wild lands of the south-west of the island, and beyond it an expanse of ocean that stretched unimpeded by land fully half of the planet to the west before its waves swept upon the beaches of South America and a quarter of the planet to the south before it began reforming as the icy shoals of the Antarctic, the weather most always came this way to Hobart: wild, mad, its reason lost somewhere out in the aching emptiness of the fish-fat sea, its rhythms those of the roaring forties and breaking waves, huge water-walls rising only to suddenly fall into frothy flatness, hot sun succeeding sleet succeeding harsh hail storms shrapnelling the sea succeeding snow succeeding sun, and all the world's weather experienced not with the steady waxing and waning of seasons, but known in a morning or afternoon, all time and all the world and all the seasons of life in the infinity of an hour.

In the short warmth of the late afternoon sun that followed, plants steamed, the earth gasped and amidst lichen-etched boulders and blasted heaths the mists rose in witches' wisps, and caught within each gasp in that damp-sweet gloaming was an immense aching.

Here upon the mountain's summit Sonja had once sometimes come with Bojan when returning from an early morning picking mushrooms down the Huon. Together they had then wandered dew heavy paddocks in long shadowed valleys, sharp-eyed, searching for the mushrooms that had only a few hours earlier arisen out of the damp dark fecundity into light. If they had umbrellaed out above their stalk, Bojan would tap their brim a few times before plucking them, so that their spores returned to the earth, ensuring that the next time there would be more mushrooms. Then, if there was snow on the mountain, they would return along the old Huon Road and play a while in the snow at the summit, before it became too cold and they headed home. Together, two spores blown by the wild wind, wandering the still, wet earth.

This afternoon Sonja was not still, nor her seasons or moods any more easily divined than those of the mountain. She was moving in thoughts of her mother, of how she had once written her mother a letter. There had been no address, of course, to put on the front of the envelope, so there could be no reply, she knew that, of course—that there would be no letter coming back beginning, 'My beloved Sonja . . .' but still she had imagined finding a reply from her mother in the letterbox in which Maria Buloh would tell her daughter what she ought do in her life, maybe a recipe or two, perhaps even just the smallest of sentences that might tell Sonja everything she ever needed to know, a sentence that would say 'I love you' but of course it was a stupid foolish idea in the first place, and though she knew there would be no reply, though she knew there could never be one, it broke her heart once more because it made her realise that in the end she could not even pretend to be other than alone.

Sonja believed herself to be neither a good person nor a strong person nor a kind person. She would wonder if, had she known her mother, and if her mother had been there when she was growing up, whether she would be otherwise: be better, kinder, stronger, and not forever punished. Because she did feel punished and she felt that her punishment must be entirely deserved because if it wasn't what reason was there for it? Because if there were no reason for such sorrow, then it was possible that there might be no reason for any of the suffering in the world, that it might just be the fate of men and women to beget suffering as they begot each other. And Sonja would suddenly switch the TV off and would scurry past the news-stand to avoid having to endure the unendurable and would rush home hoping against logic, hoping against reality, hoping, desperately hoping to find the letter from her mother that said it wasn't true that children were born to suffer, it wasn't, because she was her mother and she knew it wasn't. But every night Sonja came home and every night there were only department store catalogues boasting of family values, and insincere direct mail letters signed sincerely yours with the intent of soliciting money or votes, but from her mother there was no letter speaking of love.

Sonja turned to see Helvi coming toward her with a small bouquet of wild alpine flowers she had picked. She fixed Helvi with a stare.

'What happened to Mama, Helvi?' she asked. In the midst of banks of small bowed ti-trees, bent and crooked as if badly arthritic, forced to stoop by season after unrelenting season of cold cruel winds, Sonja's similarly bent figure abruptly stood upright, angle suddenly at odds with that of the plants around her. 'What?'

The gnarled fingers of Helvi's hand twitched around the small branches held in her other hand, twisting an unruly sprig off here and there, rearranging parts to make the whole more seemly. Helvi thought about all the things she could tell Sonja about her mother, and then all the reasons why she couldn't tell her any of it. She proffered the bouquet to Sonja as if it were some sort of answer, and Sonja accepted it with a smile, but it explained nothing.

'What happened, Helvi?' she asked again.

But Sonja didn't really want to know, any more than Helvi wanted to tell her. It was just something that came between them, and if there had been a way of picking it up like a stone and throwing it away into the boulder field around them, Sonja would have done that. Sonja wanted a new life, and it made her angry that somehow she felt the need to exorcise a part of her old life which in any case only had ever existed for her as an absence. She never had had a mother and it ought have been that simple, but it wasn't. She was thinking all that and also how beautiful the mountain was, and how it should be simple and beautiful like the mountain, but it wasn't and never would be. Sonja was thinking how she hated her mother at that moment because her mother would not let her be calm even on the mountain. She was also thinking how at that moment she hated the mountain.

Helvi had often wanted to tell Maria's story. But as much as it was Sonja's to hear, it was not hers to tell. She was no chronicler who might foolishly pretend it was possible to assemble all the details to begin at the beginning and end at the end, but only an old woman, a seamstress as foolish and inconsistent as her own eyes, who breathed in shallow gulps and understood only the unspeakable nature of it.

So avoiding Sonja's stare, Helvi continued gazing out over the channel.

'Tell me, Helvi. Please.'

Helvi spoke with what seemed disinterest, as if commenting upon the view.

'Maria was unhappy.'

'I know that,' said Sonja, 'but why, Helvi? Why? What happened?'

Helvi attempted to end the whole discussion with a statement that was as unsatisfactory as it was enigmatic.

'She saw bad things during the war,' said Helvi quietly. 'Very bad things.'

Sonja, coldly, said: 'She wasn't much of a mother.'

'She was a good mother,' said Helvi even more quietly, still not looking at Sonja. 'Maria was a good woman, a good mother. And she so love you. She used to call you her little knedel—dumpling, I think it means. But you know that. And everyone like your mama. She was funny, she could dance, she could put a man in his place with just a few quick words.'

Sonja had never heard that her mother called her anything. She should have known that story, for it was her story, as much as her arm belonged to her that story was hers, yet someone else had possessed it all those years and never even thought to give it back until now, and then so carelessly, so offhandedly thrown it in her face. She ought to know that and so much more about her mother, know more and feel more about her mother than she did. Because the worst was that she felt nothing, and Sonja hoped that if she knew something she might also feel something.

'Were they happy together? Mama and Artie?'

'They loved one another.'

Sonja's pleading became almost desperate: 'It's not the same thing, Helvi. Even if it were for only a day they must have been happy. Even if it were for only an hour, they must have been happy, mustn't they, Helvi?'

'Love is a bridge, Sonja,' said Helvi. 'And there are some weights bridges cannot bear without breaking.'

Sonja turned and began walking back across the vast mountain top to the distant point where they had parked their car. Helvi looked around, swallowed hard, and then followed.

Far below the sun spread over D'Entrecasteaux Channel. A huge expanse of gilded water, now still, expectant. Jiri watched from the considerable distance of the bleak summit car park as far, far away two small scratchings on an endless boulder field slowly, awkwardly found their way back. Behind them, an apricot sky, immense, open, wrapping around them as tenderly as a mother's palm.

Jiri wished he could do something to help Sonja, though he, even less than Helvi, had words, or knew what to do. But he would, he promised that sky, he would.

SOME OF THE strangeness of this tale may have been a consequence of character. But who of us ever determines the one thing we believe most fundamental, the thing that is the truest expression of their soul? Of course, it can be objected by those whose circumstances are sufficiently propitious, and who therefore are able to explore the end- less possibilities of character, reinventing themselves like some seventies rock star or nineties politician, that character is what makes and unmakes us, that character is destiny, and that we choose to live our life as a poem or as a tragedy, that we can be whoever we wish.

Bojan Buloh harboured no such fantasies.

Bojan Buloh held onto only what he could grasp in his hands, and when not working that tended to be an emptying bottle and a guttering smoke.

For years he lived however and wherever, in the indif- ferent company of men who were similarly afflicted. Maybe they chose such a life of their own free will or maybe they didn't. Maybe at the beginning they had intended to get out, to make something better of their lives from the poor warp and weft of their labour, to get ahead, to prosper, to know, if not happiness, then perhaps some serenity. But it tended not to be possible. A few got away, but only a handful. In the end what mattered was only that there seemed no escape, nothing really but death or grog. After a time everything else faded, and some were happy enough for it to be that way and some were not, but either way most ended up deciding that it was simply best not to dwell upon the yoke of fate that weighed them down so harshly. After a time they lost most things: family, money, hope. They did retain a certain camaraderie of the lost, for what it was worth, generally little, occasionally a great deal. A sense that they were as doomed as the trees that they felled for the geologists' tracks, as the rocks they blasted to gravel, as the rivers they were labouring to drown, and all this tended only to make them feel that the rivers and rocks and trees like them had had it coming for a long time and deserved to be destroyed. Cruelties, small and large, were dismissed as insignificant, as indeed they were. The men lived in limbo, and they allowed as little as possible to arouse them from their terrible waking sleep. If their souls they tried to preserve in a vacuum, their bodies they had long ago abandoned to the grog and the afflictions of a lifetime of physical labour. Their bodies bloated or took on the shrivelled appearance of long lifeless things bottled in alcohol, backs broke and hearing went with fingers and the occasional limb, brains atrophied and livers rotted, yet such raddled flesh managed to rise anew each morning to

undertake the labour that bound it to such curious punishment in a miraculous affirmation of the power of the
living over the dead. For their life may have been bitter to
them, but they preferred not to be reminded of it, to lose
themselves in the regular rhythms and coded language of
work, and dismissed as the foolishness of children the claim
that only the bold and stupid might make: that their situation was the consequence of character. Bojan Buloh held
onto only what he could grasp in his hands, and that night
it was a letter in one hand and a photograph in the other.

He sat on the edge of his bed in his single men's
quarters. He put the yellowing black-and-white photograph of a couple holding a baby down on his pillow. He
eyed the letter suspiciously, as if it were a bomb.

'It says that?' he asked for a second time.

'Sure,' said the Italian who sat opposite him on the
one chair Bojan possessed, a wooden kitchen chair. Bojan
suddenly thrust the letter back at the Italian.

Bojan did not like words, the insufferable swamp of
the English language, through which he had made his long,
awkward way in a rude raft constructed of a few straggly
branches of phrases he had torn from a scrubby tree here
and there. He did not believe in words like Nation. Like
History. Working Class. Management. Efficiency. National
Interest. Creeping Socialism. Or even words like Tech-
nology. Economics. Wilderness. Lifestyle. Or Future.

'What do they mean?' he would ask the Italian, who
they both pretended was cleverer. 'What the fucken hell do
any of that mean?' Bojan had the Italian even write them all

down, all these deceptive words, then made him define each one for Bojan. But for every definition the Italian threw up Bojan would demonstrate that the words actually really meant nothing at all, that they were simply ways of not understanding, not seeing, not hearing, as though they were some deliberate, conscious refusal to see the sad, mad, bad world as it is. Bojan sometimes wished he could believe in these words that clearly meant so much to others, wished for belief itself, but all he knew and comprehended was that bread was bread, some good, mostly bad, that paprika and tomato went well together particularly in a bowl with polenta, and that garlic and sauerkraut did not, that the Italian's explanations would give you a headache but that a strong turkish coffee with the juice of half a lemon would cure it, that laminex chipped, that wood could snap. He did not even believe in himself but only his hands' capacity to measure and cut and join wood. His words were few and rough, but he was rightly wary of using any others.

'You want me to finish reading it?' the Italian asked, tired of waiting for Bojan to say something.

'Sure,' said Bojan Buloh.

Bojan Buloh picked a half-empty long-necked bottle up off the floor, took a swig, folded his arms loosely across his lap, and looked down. The Italian scanned the letter until he found where he had got to before Bojan had snatched the letter out of his hands, coughed, looked up at Bojan, looked back down at the letter, asked Bojan once more, 'Sure?'

'Sure?' said Bojan. 'Sure I'm fucken sure.'

Chapter 34

——

1990

IN A HEAVY ACCENT, speaking in a stilted, slow voice, as though he were declaiming from a stage, the Italian resumed reading out aloud: '. . . *so I chose to stay in Tasmania to have the baby,*' adding as a narrator's aside, '— that's where I got to before.' Bojan's downward-cast head nodded. The Italian continued. '*It's due mid-year, the first of June in fact, or so the doctors reckon.*'

Bojan's eyes moved upwards from the floor to better see the Italian reading the letter. But his face remained fixed as if it were a mask.

Thinking that Bojan's shock was now over, his Italian workmate became genuinely excited.

'Eh, Bojan—so you are to be grandfather. Bloody Bojan poppa. Bloody hell. Congratulations.'

'Nothing to do with me. That's her business. Just fucken read the thing.'

The Italian stood up, letter in one hand, stubby in the other. Like Bojan he was middle-aged and had seen much hardship, though he was softer, more open, and more manipulative than Bojan. He was also embarrassed and a little mystified at Bojan's response. He rubbed the side of his head with the stubby. Then returned to his curious reading from the letter, at once stilted and dramatic, ludicrous yet poignant after his fashion.

'*Maybe when it's born we'll come over to see you, and you can come and visit us sometimes.*

'*At the moment I have a job in a pub and am staying with Helvi and Jiri who are lovely to me. We have a found a place for me to live in, which is not grand but is cheap. I move in next month. Helvi and Jiri send their love, as I do. I hope you are well. Your daughter, Sonja.*'

The Italian relaxed, sat back down, took a swig from his stubby, assumed a conversational tone, and said, 'There are some kisses at the bottom.' He took another good long guzzle of beer, burped, and said, 'I'll do you a good little reply to that. Only cost you a dozen stubbies.'

Bojan Buloh would have liked to believe that he and Sonja could find something together, he would have liked to believe that it was possible just to believe, but that, of course, he knew was not possible.

He remembered when he was a child, remembered how it was a time of war, how his mother—she of the third eye—how she had predicted that the rivers would run with blood, and how they had: on good days just the slightest tinge rapidly dissipating in the currents, on the bad days frothing pink. He remembered how people believed in lots of things then, in the national revolution that would throw the oppressors out, in the Domobran that would keep them in but on reasonable terms, how they believed in each other and how every belief was betrayed.

Bojan Buloh spoke often to his long-dead mother, not having anyone else much to talk to in Tullah, and particularly having no-one else to talk to of the food he ate as a child. He would ask her advice on recipes and most particularly tastes. He would hold a spoon wet with pot stirrings or salad dressing and say, 'But is that it, Mama? Is it right in here?' and point to his mouth, and then laugh, saying sheepishly, proudly, 'Well bloody hell Mama I think it's not too bloody bad I think.'

He would have liked to believe that he and Sonja might share such moments, but he had seen a world dissolve into blood and yet people still went about their daily lives, still were possessed of envy and avarice and saw others only as having somehow caused their misery, and yet as a child all he could see was blood. Blood spurting from the ten villagers they machine-gunned in front of the assembled schoolchildren in reprisal for a partisan killing of one of their soldiers, and no child allowed to close their eyes. Blood congealing in dark crusts over the partisan's body they shot outside the barn of his aunt's farm, that body they forbade anybody to move for three days. Blood even flowing out of them, the day he witnessed a partisan ambush and saw forty of their soldiers falling into rich puddles of scarlet. People died like flies and only flies thrived at that time. The adults seemed not to notice the blood as it grew into black shadows in the street gravel, but he saw it everywhere.

'Mama,' he would say, 'tonight I am cooking kransky klabasha the way you always cooked it. I will fry the sauerkraut in onion and garlic and capsicum and then I will put it all in the baking dish and bury within it the kranskies, and over it all I will sprinkle like heavy rain bacon pieces, and I will bake it all slowly, because slowly is the best, and then Mama, then I will eat it and taste the time before the war, I will swallow belief and hope and enjoy it for soon my plate will be empty and there will be no such things left.'

And because he was young, and because he learnt quickly to run and hide and never tell the truth or say what you meant or to trust anybody, no blood ever ran out of him. But something else was washing out of him, and he wanted it back. He wanted it back and he knew it was not possible.

He had watched his world break into pieces and he had learnt that any attempt to make it all whole again was hopeless. He had survived by camping in the fragments, eating raw turnips stolen from frozen fields of a night. He remembered how people would talk of battles being fought in places that he had never heard of before and how they would say that the war would be soon over, some convinced they would win, some that they would lose.

'No,' said Bojan Buloh. 'No reply.'

The Italian smiled and held his arms out wide as if gesturing defeat.

'Well, half a dozen stubbies then.'

'No,' said Bojan.

And after the war, they'd said, life would once more be normal. He did not know what normal was. He knew it had a taste and possibly a smell different to that of cordite and fear, but for the war to end was for his world to end. Whether that was good or not, he did not know. What people were, that he knew. People were bad, and people would still be bad whether it ended next month or next year or five years hence. What the world was, that he knew.

The world was empty of anything that might matter.

'But is that it Mama? Is it right in here?' he would say pointing to his head, and then laugh, and go back to his cooking, because the taste had to be right, even when everything else was wrong, the taste had to be right.

'What?' asked the Italian.

'You deaf?' said Bojan. 'Fucken deaf or what? *No reply.*'

'She is your daughter and she is having a baby.'

'Sure. And if she want me she know where to find me.'

'You should write something.'

'Well, write this: *I cannot help you.*'

'How can I write that to a daughter?'

'Well, don't write anything. I never write nothing to anyfuckenbody anyway.'

Chapter 35

———

1961

SO IT WAS that Bojan Buloh hammered and planed the emptiness he saw everywhere into the shape of tables and chests that he sold for a little extra money to buy a little extra drink; conjuring something out of a world that was only nothing, a small lie that some fragments might successfully be brought together and stay together, a deception both he and Sonja could share at least as long as the table or chest's making.

Bojan Buloh sawed the long autumn of Sonja's childhood into straight sad shapes that knew no irregularity or quirky angles, and in his sawing and hammering and planing and glueing knew a restraint that lent him grace; knew how much to sand a piece of wood and then no more; knew how to load a paint brush and hold his hand steady till the curl of its bristles had emptied all its wet cargo along the long run of the tabletop, knew not to be heavy with the lacquer nor to build things heavy: 'Must look light,' he would say, 'or otherwise is no good.' And in the dance of the hammer and the sweet rhythm of the saw Sonja saw that there was another man inside him, a good man, the man she loved as her father. Which was perhaps why she liked working with Bojan in the makeshift workshop he would inevitably set up wherever they lived, sometimes temporarily on a verandah, sometimes a little more permanently in a borrowed shed. For it was the one place where they seemed to find a small measure of harmony.

And Sonja knew that the table they now worked on was different from the others they built in the evenings and on weekends—the ones Bojan sold to workmates on the building site of a day and in the pub of a night. His tables were always well built and solid, but none had seen the care that he seemed to be pouring into the one he was now building. He had made ornate endings for the table-top, and was planing a taper into the legs to give the finished table a more elegant look.

Sonja left off hand-sanding a cupboard door and came over and stood next to her father. He looked at her, smiled, and held the plane out to her. She took it, and, with an expert eye, took over planing the leg. Bojan went to the door top and began sanding, which, along with the lacquering, was normally Sonja's job. She looked across at him and saw that he was lost in deep thought, noticed that he was smiling.

I make the table square and good, thought Bojan as he sanded the cupboard door. I make it out of blackwood, beautiful fiddleback blackwood, two pieces have I had the Finns at the mill cut for the tabletop, and the grain matches up and my join is so straight and true that it is almost not possible to tell it is there. Beautiful fiddleback blackwood not that shit pine that dents and is rubbish and quickly looks like rubbish, but two large pieces of beautiful fiddleback blackwood big enough to sit Jean and old Archie and Sonja and me.

Sonja watched a long shaving of blackwood slowly curl out of the hand plane to form a lustrous question mark that kept on retreating the further she pushed the plane down the leg. She glanced back at her father and momentarily wondered what he might be thinking. The shaving fluttered to the floor.

Beautiful fiddleback blackwood, thought Bojan Buloh, beautiful fiddleback blackwood big enough for a family feasting.

Chapter 36

1961

IT WAS AT THE TIME of the making of the table, or even a little before, that Bojan fell into the habit of leaving Sonja with the Heaneys each Sunday. He was vague as to where he went, though it was not for drinking as he never came home smelling of sour sweated bread, but instead, rather oddly, of apple blossom. Sonja presumed that he was playing cards, or visiting, or something like that: actually she didn't really care, as she preferred being at the Heaneys'—being a Heaney, being part of a family, for that one day of the week. And it was on one such Sunday that she saw that there was something else to Moira's life and the Heaneys besides, and Sonja had never known it till that day of the broken platter.

Outside it was raining and inside was a chaos of kids unable to play outdoors. Sonja was watching with great interest as Mrs Heaney pulled out from its waxed bag sliced bread, a food Bojan felt profaned the kitchen table. The house was as full as a flooding bucket with screams and squeals and quarrels of great intensity and at least a minute's duration, boys chasing other boys with guns, crying out *kill-kill-kill*, girls screaming at boys who ran through their makeshift tent—a blanket stretched between chairs—in which their dolls and teddy bears were having a picnic. Sonja was untroubled by the racket, because to her it was an ambience, an excitement that she thrilled to. Mrs Heaney, on the other hand, tried to ignore it. Instead, she concentrated upon toasting the bread under the griller, organising Sonja to butter it, and then place two slices on each plate, over which Mrs Heaney would ladle baked beans.

'Never seen 'em before have you, love?' Mrs Heaney gave the ladle a quick lick, then put it back into the pot to serve some more. 'Health food of a nation. Made us what we are today.' Mrs Heaney paused, and then added flatly. 'No wonder people want a change of diet.'

Then she suddenly shouted in the mock anger that exasperated, exhausted parents employ. 'Billy! I've told you once if I've told you a thousand times, you don't put vegemite on your toast when you eat baked beans.' She quickly moved over to a side bench and confiscated a knife and open vegemite jar from young Billy who had pulled his soggy toast out from under the baked beans and begun to spread it with vegemite. Then as an aside to Sonja. 'Kids, I tell you, Sonja, they're a trial.' Then with an almighty roar. 'Alright youse circus animals—tea's up.'

But the kids paid no heed.

Mrs Heaney shouted again.

'Cmon! For Chrissake get here *now*! and eat your bloody tea.' The Heaney kids continued running riot. Mrs Heaney tried invoking a distant image of threatening authority, yelling: 'Your father'll be home soon,' but it meant even less than her previous entreaties, because both she and they knew that if he was there—which he wasn't and wasn't likely to be for some weeks with the scalloping season in full flight—he would have done nothing anyway, just ignored them and had a quiet drink and smoke while listening to the wireless.

The mayhem proceeded without pause, her shouts only one more discordant element in that raucous house. Mrs Heaney cursed herself for using such a hollow, stupid threat that showed to the children only her own lack of authority. Sonja noticed that she seemed to sag, and glimpsed something of what Mrs Heaney really was: not the powerful easygoing maternal presence of whom Sonja was more than a little in awe; the vast, unshakeable centre of a world Sonja loved to orbit. For a single, extraordinary moment Sonja saw Mrs Heaney in all her frailty: a despairing woman upon whom too many people depended, her pregnancy only one more burden to be borne by someone worn out before her time, who regarded herself as unappealing and spent as the threadbare, grubby tea-towel slung over her shoulder.

For a third time Mrs Heaney shouted, but her voice no longer had force, and was simply desperate, pleading.

'Can you cut it out. Please. Just come and eat your tea.'

But they paid no heed, continuing to jump on chairs and run under the kitchen table. One boy started climbing up a cupboard.

'Giddown off there, Sean,' said Mrs Heaney, but before she had even finished speaking there was the sudden noise of something smashing, and Sonja saw lying in pieces on the floor in front of her a shattered floral serving platter, one of Mrs Heaney's few valued items, a wedding gift. As if a switch had been flicked, the children went silent and stopped racing about. Sean, the perpetrator of the terrible deed, climbed slowly down the cupboard, head hung low.

Mrs Heaney stared at the floor.

She stared for what seemed to Sonja to be a very long time, and her eyes never once moved.

Then, as surely and completely as the platter, something broke in Mrs Heaney.

With a single movement she spun around to the kitchen bench and snapped the jug cord out of its socket. Brandishing the cord as a whip, her face reddening, she roared: 'Get in the corner! All of youse! Now!'

The children eyed each other nervously, avoiding the gaze of their mother.

'Moira told me . . .' Sean began to fabricate, but his mother was in no listening mood.

'Shutup, Sean,' said Mrs Heaney. 'In that corner, I said.' Mrs Heaney was no longer shouting. Her voice had become quiet, without passion, as icy as the Frigidaire. 'Now.'

All the kids save Sonja, who remained on the other side of the room as a spectator, formed an uneasy, fearful huddle in the corner.

'I've just had it to here with youse all,' said Mrs Heaney. She was breathing hard and heavy and just wishing they could and would understand how hard it was to do what she did, to bring them into this world, to raise them on next to nothing, to do without, to work so hard that you are suddenly a fat old hag long before your time and your children forever fighting and whingeing and in trouble and your husband never ever there, and when he was, wanting her all the time and she so, so tired and then him not wanting even to know her—did they know; did they? did they? how hard, so bloody hard it all was, did they know any of it, because they would know, she would make them know how much her life hurt.

'I'm gunna give all youse such a hidin' ya wont ever forget it in all ya days.'

Mrs Heaney started to move in on her terrified children.

Though not the eldest, it was Moira who edged her way in front of the others. Her eyes met those of her mother. Moira trembled, her sing-songy voice now quavering with fear.

'Mum . . .'

But Mrs Heaney kept advancing.

'. . . Mum . . . Mum . . .' Moira swallowed.

But Mrs Heaney was coming for them.

'Please, Mum,' said Moira, her arms outstretching in a hopeless attempt to cover those who cowered behind her. 'Don't do this to us.'

Mrs Heaney stopped. She pulled her bottom lip under her top teeth and felt surprise at the way her body was seized by a violent shaking that made her feel most terribly light, as if she might suddenly rise into the air, as if she were no longer rooted to the earth, as if something she normally kept well hidden had momentarily liberated her body from its daily heaviness. She saw the rain-streaked window, how the rain seemed to be running down the glass like tears.

Sonja watched how Moira then hesitantly, slowly, so very slowly began to walk toward her mother, all the time eyeing her as one might a mad dog, and she did not stop walking all that very great distance across that small kitchen when Mrs Heaney began to softly cry, but kept walking, her hand stretching out now, and Mrs Heaney, she just stood as if frozen to the spot, as if the world was taking off around her, spinning faster and ever more crazily, her head rocking back and forth, and all the while she was sobbing. When Moira finally reached her and opened her mother's hand, Mrs Heaney offered no resistance. Her hand was hard and dry, covered in cuts and dirt, fingers big and tough and shiny, nails chewed back and filthy. Moira took the jug cord out of that extraordinary hand, felt her own soft thin fingers sliding slowly away from that venerable quarry shaped by the life stolen from it.

Moira went to walk away, but Mrs Heaney gently cupped her hand around the back of her daughter's head and drew the child into her belly.

Then, after a time, she put out her left hand in an expansive way. The other kids came over warily, slowly, but still they came. Mrs Heaney looked at Sonja and with a slight sway of her head invited her over too. In those big, flabby, welcoming arms Sonja joined the others. Mrs Heaney circled them all with her arms and they let themselves fall into her embrace for she was their Mum, their beautiful, beautiful Mum and she held them all there safe and together that day in her kitchen.

But, thought Mrs Heaney, for how long?

She had been about to hurt them, them whom she would do anything to shield from hurt, whom she would have died to protect, and it tormented her something terrible that she had been brought so low and shown to them and to herself such a bad person and how could she protect them from others if she could not even protect them from herself?

'I'm sorry,' croaked Mrs Heaney in a barely audible voice. 'So, so sorry.'

The kids said nothing. All any of them could hear was their mother's sobbing. Mrs Heaney held them all, and she felt an overwhelming pity for them and for herself, and then she felt the children against her waist as a presence as mysterious and huge as the universe itself and for a time she lost all sense of time and of herself and she felt a pity and a love as infinite as the universe for all things, both the living and the dead, that lay within it, that existed for that brief moment within her and her children.

Afterwards the rain stopped, and Sonja followed the other kids outside to play, and no-one spoke about what had happened. There was too much to it, and no-one spoke about it.

Chapter 37

1961

TWO TARTAN-PATTERNED PLATES bearing buttered toast sat upon the pink marble-laminex table that took pride of place in the strangely empty and desolate room that was Bojan and Sonja's kitchen-cum-living-room. Two tartan-patterned plates with buttered toast and baked beans now pouring over the toast, and above them, holding the tilted saucepan, Sonja standing in an apron serving the Australian meal which she was so proud to have prepared. Here was something about which she knew and he did not. Bojan sat at the table, looking at the strange meal being assembled upon his plate in awe, eyes balanced between contempt and utter bewilderment.

Bojan looked down at the table and looked back up at Sonja, and sensing her pride in her achievement turned back to his meal. From the salad bowl in the middle of the table he piled up oiled endive on his fork, then plunged the green-laden fork into the baked beans and toast and brought the whole remarkable combination up into his mouth. He chewed, and chewed some more, but no amount of mastication was going to alter the utter strangeness of what was in his mouth. He uncharacteristically cast his eyes heavenwards and asked the Mother of Jesus to give him strength, and then swallowed.

'Sonja,' he said when his gullet was thankfully free of the salad and beans, 'the . . . *the* Heaneys, you are sure they eat such things?'

'Yes,' replied Sonja seriously, almost earnestly. 'But never with vegemite.'

Bojan's eyes looked at Sonja, then at the meal, then at Sonja, then back at the meal, and he pretended to understand.

'Ah, yes,' said Bojan, 'but of course not.'

And he plied more salad and more baked beans on his fork and continued with his meal, all the while inwardly cursing the infernal, comic backwardness of Australians and all the awful things they mistook for food.

Later that evening Bojan did a strange thing, an unexpected yet welcome thing. He went to the wardrobe and reached up on his toes to the top and got down the ancient Singer sewing machine. He sat it upon the pink marble-laminex table. He unwrapped pieces of tissue paper covered in dotted lines as indecipherable to Sonja as Morse code, and pinned these papers all over Sonja, running scissors hither and thither, muttering and sometimes softly cursing to himself. Finally he unpinned the paper, and from a brown paper parcel took out a roll of shiny pink cotton, to which he then pinned the paper patterns. He became totally absorbed in cutting the shape, and seemed not to notice that it was way past the time he normally made Sonja go to bed, seemed not to notice her whatsoever, and this sight of him, so intensely focused upon a task, Sonja found mesmerising. Illuminated by the little yellow pilot light on the old sewing machine, his hands skilfully placed and pulled the pieces of pink material back and forth beneath the hopping needle. Those hands, so confident at making. She listened to the rolling sound of the old black Singer at work, speeding up and slowing down in thrumming bursts, as though it were on a journey and them all travelling with it.

Then, after a considerable time, the thrum ended and the dance of the hopping needle halted. Bojan flicked up the catch on the needle, stood up, stood Sonja in the middle of the kitchen table in her bare feet, took off the clothes she wore, and in their place let fall over her head and upraised arms a neatly made pink party dress.

Sonja twirled around.

The dress fitted well. Bojan laughed. Sonja looked at a distant image of herself in a small mirror on the far wall, ran her hands down the dress, to feel it, to smooth it, to stroke it. Something strange was going on, and she did not know what, but she was grateful for it, even if the cause remained to her unfathomable. Never before had she had her very own party dress. Never before had she seen her father behaving so strangely. He had made clothes before for her, but only the necessary things: school dresses and the like. Never anything as frivolous as a party dress. Something *very* strange was going on. First a beautiful table. Then a pointless dress. And him being so good to her, as he was now, opening out his arms, and she leaping from the table to his chest. He held her lightly and together they danced around the sewing machine to an old country song playing on the radio. Then he put her back on the kitchen table, so they could both admire his handiwork once more.

Sonja felt happy. She felt a certain grace. A lightness, an understanding that there was this fundamental goodness in life that could be danced and that one could be part of in the dancing.

And she twirled around and around and around—

Until she was so dizzy that she momentarily thought she was lace in the wind and that it was her mother twirling her so.

Chapter 38

——

1961

BEST-BRAVE-PINK-COTTON-DRESS dressed and white-cardigan clad, Sonja sat in the front seat of the FJ, long legs drawn up to her chest, scabbed knees scalloping into her chin. Bojan sat side-on in the driver's seat, one listless leg hanging out the open door, the other waiting, half drawn-up, resting on the door frame. They had arisen early, and with some haste—unusual for Bojan, who most always did things in a measured, careful fashion—he had tied the blackwood table upon the FJ's roofrack. And after having sped like lunatics down the winding, wild gravel road to the Huon, the FJ wallowing around endless corner after corner and Sonja trying not to vomit, they had suddenly halted on this hillside. Here and there an early morning mist rose and dusted the orchards that spread out below them. They were high enough to be in the sun, but in spite of its intensity the chill of the spring night had not yet gone, and the feeling was at once hot and cold.

'That's it,' said Bojan, and though he did not point, she knew it was the old cottage some distance below them, scrubby hill on its near side, apple orchard on its far side, at which her father was staring.

From the hillside the cottage, its snub-nosed verandah like an old cap pulled down over the green-painted weatherboards rippling in the low light, looked to Sonja little different from hundreds of other houses that similarly stippled the orchard valley. They were close enough to the cottage that Sonja could distinguish detail. Its orchard, the apple trees still semi-skeletal. Its garden, resplendent with rose bushes beginning to bud, a few large pine trees, the horseshoe-shaped gravel drive in front of the house. The long shadows and alternating shafts of early morning light covering a side window in tremulous stripes, moving so gracefully that she wondered if the cottage were losing its solid form and transforming into wisps and waves. Surrounding the window frame, blistered and flaking and in bad need of a fresh coat of paint like the cottage's scaly weatherboards, a large bushy climbing rose with mauve flowers also beginning to bloom. She could just make out a white lace curtain gently blowing in and out of that old window in the early morning breeze.

Lace and weathered wood. Both moving. There is something here, Sonja decided, something good. But the proximity of the combination of lace and wood also unsettled her, was too close to who she was for her to feel comfortable.

For two hours they sat there in the FJ, looking at that house in its idyllic setting, before Bojan threw his tenth cigarette that morning out of the window, hefted a healthy gob after it, looked at himself in the rear-vision mirror, tightened his tie, loosened his tie, tightened his tie, wet the tips of his fingers with his tongue and ran them through the sides of his freshly barbered hair, took a deep breath, rolled the ignition over and drove down the hill.

'You remember at the Hisketts' last year?' Bojan asked as they descended into the mist and came closer.

Sonja nodded.

'You remember that Jean we meet there?' Bojan asked as they turned off the road and headed up the cottage's driveway.

Sonja nodded once more. Sonja remembered. Jean Direen. Quiet, but strangely not out of fear. A hawkish face, accentuated by the way she pulled her long greying hair back into a ponytail, and by her winged glasses. And her unusual eyes: green and soft. Sonja never looked adults in the eye unless she had no choice, such as at school when teachers demanded it. But Sonja found she could look into Jean Direen's eyes and not feel threatened. She had seemed to Sonja old, perhaps even older than her father but with a body unexpectedly youthful. Strong, lithe, an argument against the way the face was presented, and the plain clothes in which she dressed. She was gentle, Sonja remembered. Gentle and easy.

And then Sonja knew where her father had been going to on the Sundays he had left her at the Heaneys. Even back at the Hisketts' Jean's feeling for Bojan had been evident to Sonja, and perhaps that was why Sonja had retained such a strong memory after only one chance meeting. Because Jean's interest in Sonja's father had risen like a blush from within Jean and Sonja had felt it as a glowing heat. And, at first, Sonja liked the idea of her father striking up a romantic liaison with Jean, because it was interesting, even exciting, and infinitely preferable to card nights or sitting in a pub car park waiting for him to be done inside.

And then it was night and then it was morning and then several weeks and then almost as many months had passed in a way that went on forever but seemed as short as the span of time it took for Bojan Buloh to tighten his tie, loosen his tie, and then tighten it once more. Life took on a pattern Sonja found both reassuring and increasingly delightful. Every week work and school in Hobart, her father now a different man, happy, easy with her. And every weekend they returned to the Huon, to Jean's. There Bojan would help out on the orchard, fixing machines, fences, working on the trees, spraying, pruning, picking and packing. Sonja too helped with the picking and packing of the apples, working sometimes at the side of Jean, sometimes at the side of her father. The packing shed was warm and full of light and the rattling sound of apples tumbling down toward the half-dozen packers, men and women and children, and Sonja would wrap her apples as carefully and quickly as she was able in the soft purple tissue paper until she grew tired of it, and then she would run out into the green tumble of the orchard and help pick a while and then drift back into the shed and she was never in the way and no-one was ever angry or spoke harshly to her, for in the industry of that small orchard that summer there was a harmony and she felt blessed being part of it, as if the work of the whole summer were some unspoken yet communal prayer and she one integral element of that prayer.

And each Sunday morning she would rise just before sun-up, sensing in sleep when the low light of dawn was beginning to fill the house. She would go to the kitchen, stand in her nightie between the curtain and the window and watch the rising sun turn oppressive grey clouds apricot and pink and silver, and the sky looked to her like a huge rainbow trout leaping over Jean's cottage. She would see the orchard and beyond it a hill covered in bush rising away from her vision. Even from where she stood in the kitchen the view, while not expansive, suggested a feeling of space, of openness.

Sonja would place paper and morning sticks in the small ash-rimmed hutch of the old range. She would light the paper and soon have a fine morning fire: noisy, cracking, hissing, leaping yellow flames. Lest the fire smoke out the kitchen she would close the creosote-crusted cast-iron range door. As the morning sticks spat and fizzed she would fill the large black kettle from the single brass tap, place the floral teapot so big and heavy she had trouble holding it, two cups and sugar and milk on a serving tray; get the tea canister down and fill the big teapot with tea-leaves. And waiting for the water to boil she would often think how their lives had changed since that morning they had arrived with the new blackwood table upon which the tray now sat.

They had all stood around Jean's kitchen admiring it, her and Bojan and Sonja and old Archie, who lived in the house and had, since the death of Jean's parents, helped Jean's brother Merv run the orchard while Jean worked at the local school in the office. They manoeuvred the table this way and that to see where it best fitted. Jean liked the way the table was plain but well proportioned in its design, elegant without artifice, commented on how it was so well finished off. And all that spring and that summer and that autumn Bojan and Sonja returned weekend after weekend to eat at it, to sit down to meals of strange exotic foods—some of which Bojan had never allowed into their house—such as pumpkin and parsnip and mint sauce. They ate roasts and casseroles made of lamb which Bojan had always maintained was only fit for Serbs but, rather than abusing Jean, he complimented her on how beautifully it was cooked. And they made soups using cream and milk, which astonished both Bojan and Sonja, although Jean's bread, Bojan said—and he meant it—was actually better than his own mother's; ate at least two dozen different varieties of apple puddings and drank sweet white tea out of great cavernous mugs big enough to do the washing in.

Jean carried with her the scent of apple blossom, and Sonja and her father would privately joke about this, for whatever the time of the year, her scent was as inescapable as it often was unseasonable.

But when one day Sonja discovered, at the back of the old apple packing shed, a straw-lined wooden crate that a chook had nested in full of yellow chicks, live fluffy balls, chirruping and cheeping and rolling higgledy piggledy everywhere, Jean's presence for once was not foretold by the smell of apple blossom. Thinking she was alone Sonja began to sing to the chicks.

'Spancek, zaspancek
crn mozic
hodi po noci
nima nozic'

Sonja sang softly, full of love, a song she had known for so long she could not remember learning it, a Slovenian lullaby.

'Tiho se duri
okna odpro
vleze se v zibko
zatisne oko

'Lunica ziblje:
aja, aj, aj,
spancek se smeje
aja, aj, aj.'

And only just before the sound of clapping did Sonja smell the apple blossom. Startled, she looked up to see Jean standing at the end of the shed, smiling. Sonja jumped up.

'That was beautiful, Sonja,' said Jean. 'What do the words mean in Australian?'

Sonja smiled back out of embarrassment. She moved along the side wall quickly like a spider seeking shelter, all the time facing Jean, ran out of the shed and kept running through the orchard toward the river.

What did the words mean? They were without meaning. They were nonsense words like 'Humpty Dumpty'. Yet they meant everything. She knew they meant everything. She knew they meant love, but why?

She was running hard, her breath galloping, rolling— and Sonja came to her senses and realised that it was the kettle come to the boil, bubbling furiously, splashing and sizzling water on the hot stove.

She grabbed the kettle with a bundled tea-towel, took it off the stove and slightly scalded herself in her rush. She poured the boiling water into the teapot. Then, as she had done every other Sunday morning, Sonja walked from the kitchen down the central corridor, still dark and musty with the peaceful close smell of sleep. She backed into the bedroom slowly, carefully, eyes turned downward, focusing intently upon the heavy tray to ensure that it stayed level and she did not spill anything. She placed the tea tray on a small, old table set against a wall, below a lace curtain fluttering in and out of the window.

Sonja looked up from the tray at Jean's bedroom. It was a most beautiful room, painted a faded dappled green, with high ceilings and overlooking the now blossoming apple orchard. The sun ran like a river through the window, pouring light over Jean and Bojan who lay together in a high wooden bed.

Sonja thought how tranquil and happy they looked; here, for both her and her father, was an island of peace. For a long time she had brought the tea into the bedroom, sometimes talked a little, but shy of Jean, would soon make her excuses and leave. But that morning Sonja realised that her shyness had passed and that what she wished now more than anything else in the world was simply to climb onto the island with them, to get into that high wooden bed with both Bojan and Jean and feel that river of light flow around them. She raised her eyes to Jean, and Jean pulled the covers back ready, and Sonja was almost in Jean's warm muzzy embrace when Bojan, unseen by Jean, shook his head, and shooed her away with a flick of his hand.

Two small gestures, no more, but they tore at Sonja.

Sonja halted, looked hard at her father, then dutifully climbed back down off the big bed. Jean turned and looked at Bojan who was spooned into her back. He smiled and kissed her on the nose, and Jean never saw the weight of solitude collapse Sonja's face as she walked past the lace curtain and out of the bedroom.

Chapter 39

1961

THERE WAS NO SMELL of sour sweated bread, so Sonja knew that she did not have to be fearful. Nevertheless, it was unusual to be picked up from school by Bojan, driven home, with him in a mood that she could only find infectiously silly, then at the door made to stop, close her eyes, and allow him to place his hands over her eyes.

In the blackness, total and whole, she heard Bojan's voice speak, not as it had in the FJ and had always done, in rolling Slovenian, but in stilted Australian, as though with almost every word he were starting a new sentence.

'From now on we speak English proper.'

In the blackness, complete and mysterious, her own voice, upset.

'But, Artie!—you are funny when you speak Slovene and make all your jokes.' Though Bojan generally insisted that they speak English and not Slovene, he would, when feeling easy, tease her softly and play with words in his mother tongue.

But in the black universe, his English words were adamant.

'No, Sonja, you will go nowhere if you speak Slovene, you will end up like me. From now on you speak English proper. Then maybe you have a chance.'

'English is no good for jokes.'

'English is good for money.' Still he held his large hands over her eyes. 'Now come with me.' With him behind her she shimmied in the direction he was gently nudging her. It was a curious dance, through the door and across their kitchen-cum-living room, and she was reminded how graceful he could be in his movements. Then they stopped.

He laughed, then cried gleefully, 'Open your eyes!' And with that he took his hands away.

Her vision filled with the most peculiar sight: there in front of her, in the corner of their living room, was a 24-volume set of encyclopaedias. Their brown and black spines were neatly arrayed within a brand new bookcase of the stunted variety that one received free with the set. Bojan had accorded the books and shelving a placement in their home akin to that of the grottos, scattered around the fields of Slovenia, dedicated to the Virgin Mary in the hope of divine interventions, for this was a gift of love that Bojan hoped might also prove miraculously liberating. To accentuate the prominence of the encylopaedia he had placed the stumpy bookcase on top of a pine chest he had made in which they stored clothes and linen. Sitting on the chest, at either side of the bookcase's base, was an unlit red candle in a saucer. Apart from the encyclopaedia, the rest of the bookcase was empty, for there were no other books in the house, and so on the top of the bookcase Bojan had proudly displayed their salad bowl.

Sonja stared. She felt bewildered. Bojan stood back, beaming.

'*Encylopaedia*-bloody-*Britannica*,' he said after a long silence, and his voice was full of righteous wonder and pride. He was excited, as if he had finally found the key to their mutual liberty in the shape of twenty-four uniformly bound volumes.

Sensing this weight of futile faith congealing around her, Sonja approached the books. She ran her fingers over the caterpillar tread of their dark spines massed together. Emboldened she took one volume out, feeling its weight, watching its crowded pages stumble past her fingertips as she peered inside.

'Now you learn the English good,' said Bojan with pride. 'Now you don't end up like me.'

Curious and alien as the gift was, Sonja felt a certain thrill both with it and more so by her father's obvious pleasure in giving it to her. But she also felt somewhat apprehensive. Without reading a word she wondered if she could ever understand all or any of it, for there was no story, no identifiable person to guide her through this labyrinth of words. And without a guide she knew she was lost. There was also another matter that suddenly struck her as a cause for worry.

'Artie,' she asked, 'how much did it cost?'

'Don't you worry. The salesman and I make a deal so that I don't have to pay for it now.' Bojan smiled benignly. 'Instead I pay for it over three years, so much a month.' He shrugged. 'But that's my problem.' He sank to his knees next to Sonja, looked glowingly up at the encyclopaedia set as though it were an apparition of the Virgin Mary herself, and put an arm around her waist. 'The salesman, he say no better way of learning the English than by reading the *Encyclopaedia Britannica*.' Sonja seemed unconvinced so Bojan spoke further to enthuse her. 'All you have to do,' he said, 'is read.'

For a short time, a very short time, perhaps twenty minutes in all, Sonja found the encylopaedia interesting. For a much longer time, she simply read it out of respect for her father. She began with Volume One and resolved to read the entire encyclopaedia page by page, volume by volume, however arduous a labour this might prove. Bojan felt this to be both a wise and industrious use of the books. Sonja read some hundreds of pages dutifully, before she found it impossible to stop her eyes glazing and skidding over words then sentences, then entire articles, then large sections. She realised it was possible to read such writing closely and for it to mean nothing and for it not to have enlightened her in any way whatsoever, and as she slowly came to admit this to herself, the futility of her ambition became ever more apparent.

Still, for some months they would each morning sit at the pink marble-laminex kitchen table eating breakfast. In front of each would be two bowls, one with steaming hot golden polenta, the other empty. Sonja would fill the empty bowls with the thick black turkish coffee. Then each would put their spoon in the polenta, and with it full of the bright yellow cornmeal, place it into the dark sweet coffee, and then leaning over the bowl, put the syrup-covered polenta into their mouths. Bojan would glance the *Sporting Globe*, folded into an easily handled quarter and held out at arm's length from his eyes, because that was the way some of the older blokes held their papers at smoko, because it seemed appropriate and right to do, even if he could only make sense of the occasional sentence and some of the pictures; while Sonja would have at her side a hefty volume of the *Encyclopaedia Britannica*. She would read dutifully, rather than with any enthusiasm or interest, and occasionally he would ask her where she was up to, and she would reply, 'Volume Two, page 316,' or, 'Volume Three, Cr to Da, page 1,562', and to prove her dedication and to assure him that this was not folly, ask him curious unanswerable questions, such as: 'Do you know there are over 782 types of crustaceans?'

'Bugger me,' Bojan would invariably say in his best Australian and sometimes laugh, at his own ignorance and out of his pride at her command of such facts. But he also was laughing at the inanity of wisdom, for Bojan was no fool, and he thought, rightly, that such things were generally useless to know, but he also thought, wrongly, that the

difference between failure and success in life was the pos-
session of a sum of such useless knowledge. Sonja would
smile back, and be reminded, as she always was by the
sight of her spoon of heaped golden polenta sinking into
the blackness of the coffee, of the sun setting into the
night.

Chapter 40

1962

THEY HAD PICKED APPLES, Cox's Orange Pippins they were, all that unseasonally bright and hot day and most of the previous day and all the time Sonja wondering how long it would take for her hessian bag to fill, whether it would be that many trees, or would she reach the end of her row before Bojan did on the other side and if she did, if she filled her bag before his would he always stay with her and would it always be like this or would that only happen if he filled his bag first?—and always his bag full twice over before hers and ever the question unanswered—could it be like this for ever and ever? Could it? Could it? and the question not answered and the bag never full.

Then Sonja had gone to the toilet she loved of a day and feared of a night, a wooden outdoor dunny, with a lean the equivalent of the tower of Pisa, and an interior for a child more wondrous, wallpapered from top to bottom with pictures from magazines and newspapers. Some old and yellowed, some peeling off, some new and bright.

Parts of the wall were pocked by postcards of far-off places. An old picture of tourists in a piazza in Venice; a double-decker bus in London; an aged, tinted photograph of Dubrovnik.

How Sonja loved to linger in the languorous confines of that dunny. Sunlight fell through the gaps in the door and lit up its interior—the wooden bench seat, freshly painted green, upon which sat Sonja, knickers around her ankles, the heavy wooden seat-cover painted bright red. And those pictures, those enchanting pictures!

She heard old Archie coming up the small hill to the dunny singing in his flat old voice, clattery as the apple-sorter and as assuring, his end of picking farewell to the Cox's Orange Pippins—

'The season's last pippins are gathered
And yellow leaves drift from the trees
The last case, packed, labelled and branded;
Is railed to be shipped overseas.

'We have toiled like dumb driven cattle
With a picking bag yoked to our neck;
And battled the pest and the weather
That threatens the harvest to wreck.'

Sonja sat looking at these magazine pictures that adorned the walls, pictures of remote and romantic places, her practical purpose for being on the toilet long forgotten, her mind wandering through tinted dreams of Europe over which Archie's song murmured and meandered—

> *'The plow handles I now have forsaken;*
> *I let them go without even a sigh;*
> *And to the apples that grow in the future,*
> *I say, goodbye, Mr Pippin, goodbye.'*

'Have you ever been to Dubrovnik, Archie?' asked Sonja.

Sonja gazed at the curling picture of Dubrovnik, which looked to her exactly how she envisaged a city out of tales about genies and sultans.

'Have you, Archie? To Dubrovnik, Archie?' asked Sonja.

Outside, Archie readjusted the nappy pin that held his braces to his pants, tucked a faded blue flannel shirt back in, then took one final drag of his rollie, and threw the butt away.

'No,' said Archie and he spoke as if to the sky. 'But I have been to buggery and back waiting for you to get off that bloody throne.'

By mid-afternoon the heat and work had taken their toll on Sonja, and she lay down to rest in the orchard and promptly fell asleep. She awoke all muzzy to see Jean standing on the uppermost rung of a stool picking some apples from a tree not far from where Sonja lay. Bojan stood beneath her, collecting the apples in a wooden case, and the rows of trees formed a green grotto around them. Then Jean got down and they gently embraced. They kissed.

'Sonja . . . ?' asked Jean, motioning to where Sonja appeared to be dozing in a nearby sunny patch of grass, clearly not wishing to give offence to the child.

'Don't worry,' said Bojan. 'She's asleep.'

Sonja blinked, squinted, and without moving, focused on what was taking place. She watched with unease as Bojan gently parted Jean's hair with his hands, then with equal tenderness cupped and ever so slowly rolled one of Jean's breasts. These gestures disquieted Sonja, in a way that seeing her father in bed with Jean had strangely not. In bed they had been homely, but now there was a suggestion of an intimacy beyond what she had ever known with her father and the consequences of that intimacy disturbed Sonja. But the sun was strong and the grass soft and her sleepiness coupled to her awareness that she had seen something that she ought not have, led her to again close her eyes.

And her daydeam gave way to a terrible nightmare. She was once more in the back seat of Picotti's Pontiac, cowering in the corner. Picotti sat in the front seat, head turned toward Sonja, smiling, beckoning her to come to him. She stole a glance out of the window and saw Bojan talking to Jean in the orchard. She screamed to Bojan for help but heard nothing, and nor, it became apparent to Sonja, did Bojan, who turned away from Sonja and embraced Jean. The more her terror grew, the more Sonja silently screamed, the more oblivious they seemed to become to her plight and the more passionate grew their embraces and kissing. There seemed to be no hope, no possibility of rescue, of security.

Later Sonja would recall the nightmare seamlessly merging into reality, for suddenly she was jolted awake by a bump, sitting up to find herself back in the FJ as it kicked up a large cloud of dust along a back road lined on either side by apple orchards. Bojan looked across at Sonja and smiled.

'You awake now,' he said.

Sonja was still sleepy and merely murmured in answer. Bojan drew breath. In front of him he saw a fence that was ageing and badly needed its ancient split posts replacing, a packing shed whose roofing iron was loose and would need to be refastened before winter. He saw things that needed to be done, but for various reasons had not been attended to.

'Good weekend, eh?' said Bojan. For Sonja it had been a weekend more or less like any other of that summer. She nodded vaguely. 'Sonja—what you think if Jean and I we marry? If Jean become your Mama?' He said it nonchalantly, as if it meant nothing, as if he was asking did she wish to have more or less vinegar on the oiled salad.

Sonja came to her senses. Her dream had left her feeling scared, vulnerable, and in desperate need of her father, who was now saying he might give himself to someone else. Outside the FJ she saw a world that was green, a sky that was blue, a world in which people seemed orderly, in which life was as it presumably was meant to be. She had had too much change and wanted no more. She felt the confusion of love pull at her, felt the desire to retain things as they were, struggling with her wish to change everything or forget it all, felt love's fear of another love possibly swamping hers.

'No. No, Artie, no . . . I don't want it. She's . . .' Sonja searched for a reason against the choice of Jean but found none. She had liked the arrangement they had through the summer, that had seen Jean giving, them sharing, but none of it threatening her. Sonja seized on the obvious. 'She's too old. I just want you. I don't want her. I want us.'

Bojan's smile slowly disappeared.

'Together. *Us*. In our home.'

Bojan swallowed. Neither spoke any more on that long trip home, this time longer than either could ever remember.

Chapter 41

———

1962

AFTER THAT things were different. The following Saturday they worked in the workshop, Sonja back to her role of sanding, Bojan marking up a piece of cheap Tas oak to be cut for the shelves of a small bookcase, smouldering cigarette in mouth, open bottle of beer on the workbench.

The oppressiveness of that day did not end with the drowsy mugginess unusual for autumn. Neither had spoken much, and Sonja, feeling her father's depression as a physical weight, summoned the courage to ask what had been troubling them both.

'Why aren't we going to the orchard this weekend?'

Bojan's wistful melancholia abruptly vanished. He looked more closely at the square, as though the next saw cut was far more important than anything Sonja might say.

'You said you loved Jean,' Sonja said, though she did not mean to say that or to say anything, but it just came out that way, because she did not have his look silencing her.

'Sure,' said Bojan. 'I said that maybe. Maybe not. But I have you.' And to make it not so much clear as final, he added, 'We're not going back, Sonja. Not ever. That is what you wanted, that is what you have.'

Sonja was not horrified at the time, because she did not know that he meant it. She knew he was upset, but thought it would blow over and then they would return to Jean's and everything would be as it had been. She could not know that it would take years in demonstrating the strength of his resolve to never return, to establish the cruel unfairness of what he had said.

Sonja would not give up. She introduced a subject about which he never talked and in which she was of late interested and thought he might be too.

'Is Slovenia beautiful, Artie?'

Bojan stood up straight and looked at her. Realising he was listening but wasn't angry, Sonja continued.

'And Europe? Is it like the pictures in Jean's toilet?'

Somehow this seemed to strike at the heart of his sadness.

Maybe Bojan had wanted to marry Jean, but did not have the strength alone to see it through. Maybe he had needed Sonja's enthusiasm for the idea, because he had been so frightened. And perhaps like her, he finally felt safer not risking anything. There were thoughts that terrified him every night when the idea of living once more with a woman came to his mind, and washing behind that were memories, accompanied by a notion of himself so low and so despicable that he was frightened what might happen if ever he embarked on such a forlorn project as another marriage. Because he loved Jean and Jean loved him, but he no longer believed in love. There were things, he had concluded, more powerful than love in this world.

'Is it, Artie?'

And when he replied he seemed to be talking as much about Jean, about him, them, as about Europe. He lingered over each word, unintentionally throwing an entirely different meaning on the sentence.

'It was,' he said, '. . . *bloody* —' He halted, seeming confused by the strangeness of English words. '—beautiful.'

He leant down and placed the square back on the Tas oak ready to start work again, but, struck by a memory, halted for a second time and stood back up. He looked once more at Sonja.

'I tell you the best story I know about Europe. It was before the war. The richest man in our village—a big, fat mean bastard he was, Jesus Christ you shoulda seen him!—and this bastard have most of his wealth in pigs which he keep beneath his big house.

'Well, one night, in the middle of winter, snow everywhere, the rich man's house catch fire. All the villagers help rescue the pigs from the burning house. But as quick as they pull them out of the burning house, the pigs run back into the flames.'

'Why?' asked Sonja.

'Why?' repeated Bojan. 'You ask me why? Who knows why? That's Europe. That's what I mean. Can you believe it? I can't. No-one could. It was as if the fire had cast a spell on them and they were in love with it.' He laughed, but clearly he didn't find the story funny. 'In the end the pigs were all burnt to death and the town stank of burnt pork for days.

'That's a funny thing, eh?'

But he didn't smile.

So it ended. Winter came. The white lace curtain hanging in the old wooden window frame yellowed, a cocoon from which the butterfly had long since flown. Jean stood inside, arms folded, looking out the window into the distance, as if waiting for Bojan and Sonja to return.

She stood that way for many days, some down the Huon say for some months, and a few even say for years. But to stand waiting even for an hour would have been pointless. The telltale cloud of dust signalled many a passing car, but never Bojan's FJ, crawling under its carapace of fresh furniture made in affirmation of a fragile idea that something even bigger than his love for her, or more beautiful than her love for him, might exist, and that was the idea of people finding a measure of grace living together.

It began to rain, at first a few gentle spots, and then a slow drumming on the tin roof. It grew darker. After a time Jean's staring and thinking came to an end, and her arms unfolded to pull the old window down, and then draw heavy, dark curtains across the window, behind the lace curtain, and the lace curtain no longer played in the soft morning breeze, but grew still and brittle, and gathered heavy dust. The rain continued falling upon the glass, forming rills and rivulets in the window grime.

The roses next to Jean's bedroom window wilted and died, and their petals fell to the ground there to lose what little colour and shape and scent remained, and Jean took no comfort from the knowledge that the flowers were passing slowly back into the damp earth. There was, she had long ago concluded, little comfort to be derived from anything except other people. And she was unsure if she had the strength any more to seek out such brittle solace.

Chapter 42

——

1962

THEN THE BOOK-READING fell apart, as if its spine had been silently snapped in the night as they slept, and everything was unable to be as they wished it, even to be as it was, and Bojan took back up with the bottle and Sonja hated him for it, o God, how she hated him for it, but she simply had to stay the course with him, because she was a child, because she was his daughter and he was her father but both these things stopped being things and became only words which neither trusted nor understood. He didn't know what to do with himself far less with her, and though she knew what she wanted she could find no way of getting there, so instead each afternoon after school she simply went with Bojan.

She would walk or bus or generally a bit of both to get to whatever building site Bojan was labouring on at the time, and there wait in the FJ through the hours until knockoff. In the FJ she would not read her schoolbooks, because reading was a stranger whose acquaintance she decided she was not destined to make. She would draw pictures of flowers. She would get out of the car, go for a wander, watch her father from a distance and admire him, think this was how she would always remember him, forever back bent and moving beautifully beneath loose old workclothes. She had done enough physical labour in the course of her short life not to envy him his hard yakka, as he called it after the manner of his workmates. Yet she loved seeing him so, and sometimes wanted and sometimes did work with him on the site, cleaning up, fetching material and tools, because that was how she saw what was best in her father, how she came to understand how he saw the world and those within it, through his work with others.

But when his day's work was done, instead of going home, Bojan would drive to the pub and leave Sonja to wait in the car in a small gravel car park.

'Don't worry,' he would inevitably say, 'I have only one drink.'

The sun would fall low. It would glint on windscreens, skid along the mirroring chrome of the new Zephyrs and Hillmans and Holdens, sink into the rich earthy ochre colours of the rust pocks in the older cars. The sun would sink. Bojan would remain in the pub. As darkness came upon the car park, the streetlights would come on and Sonja would still be waiting in the car.

Then when she least expected it, when she had abandonded all hope, Bojan would appear out of nowhere at the car's side window, waving something in his hand. At long last, Sonja would at first think, at long last we can go home. She would smile. Bojan would put his head in through the door and, with a crooked smile, proffer Sonja a large wrapped block of chocolate.

Sonja would ignore the chocolate and look straight up at Bojan. Look into his beer-glazed eyes. Quietly and impassively she would say: 'Artie, please can we go home.'

Bojan, invariably drunk, invariably laughed, and would say: 'It's a family bar.' Laugh some more. 'The chocolate—a family bar.' He always did that when he was drunk, explain his jokes, as if their failure related to someone else's inadequate command of language. It never seemed to occur to him that the joke might not be that funny in the first place. And it made her so angry, such jokes.

'I want to go home.'

'Where?' Bojan would ask. 'What home? You and I have no home, Sonja. Don't you understand?' He would laugh some more and then his laughter would turn to tears. The beer glaze would wash from his eyes. 'We have a wog flat, my Sonja. A wog flat. Don't you understand?'

And he would turn and head back inside the pub. Those men staggering from the pub later that night would see, as they saw so many other nights, the car with the small girl in it illuminated by a nearby street lamp. Sometimes they would see the small girl sitting in the driver's seat looking at the horizon, as if she were driving to some destination very far off and had already spent many, many hours on this journey; sometimes, if they

232

came close, they might find her fast asleep on the back seat. And sometimes, very late of a night, they might notice her at the passenger sidewindow, putting her hands to the window and screaming, a most terrible scream, long and thin and plaintive.

Inside, the pub would be loud, exclusive in its adult male camaraderie, deeply sad and selfishly desperate. From the height of a bar table, a child—if a child ever were to grace such a place, which of course, like a woman, it would not—a child would have seen only glasses being raised and lowered, puddles of beer on the tabletop, cigarettes being butted out in the ashtray, hands gesticulating. Between beer glasses that stood like prison bars the child might just have been able to look out through a window to the car in which Sonja sat screaming. But instead of screams the child would only have heard the tinkle of glasses and the laughter of merry male company. It might have heard one of Bojan's drinking companions whisper a confidence to his mate, have overheard him say: 'Get the wog to buy your drink. He's in here every night. He don't care what happens to his money. They only use it to bring mama out from Greece anyway.'

And heard his mate reply: 'Bojan you bastard are you gonna buy this next shout or what?'

And heard Bojan laugh and say: 'Yeh, bloody hell, I buy as much bloody beer you want. What the fuck else do I earn this bloody money for?'

General laughter. And from within the merry perspective of the pub, Sonja would have looked not unhappy in her car-prison, like an insect inside a bell jar seemingly content.

Even though the insect was screaming and even though each scream was taking the insect further away from the one person to whom she wished to be closer and who might make her human once more.

Chapter 43

———

1990

SO IT WAS as that magic summer of so long ago ended
in rain, and Bojan forsook Jean's love and resumed his
interrupted affair with the bottle, Sonja stopped eating
apples, only to dream all the more about them. She did eat
apples again, of course she did, but it was only many years
later, long after she had become an adult, when she lived
in Sydney and she felt sure that the sensation of torn skin
and ruptured flesh and sweet acidic juices filling her
mouth would not bring the power of the old world back
into her life. There were in Sydney neither Geeveston
Fannys nor Jonagolds nor Tassie Snows nor Cox's Orange
Pippins to be had, and the fruit stall in the crowded railway station had only the ubiquitous Golden Delicious. But
upon biting into the apple, Sonja tasted only total emptiness and loss, for the apple was mealy and tasted of pap.
And then she knew that all she had was what she carried
within her, and she had denied that for so long that it now
seemed not possible to reclaim any of it and, feeling everything had gone, she abruptly sat down in front of the fruit

stall on the pavement and burst into tears, as thousands of commuters stepped around and finally over her.

On a day off from her barmaid job Sonja borrowed Helvi's old Corolla and drove down the new highway to the Huon. It took her a few attempts and wrong turns and a flat tire before she finally found the place on the hillside where she had so many years before sat in the FJ the first time they came to visit Jean, with Bojan tightening and loosening his tie, tightening and loosening. This time it was raining and Sonja looked out of the car at where Jean's orchard had been through worn windscreen wipers grinding back and forth. Little remained; through cupolas that cleared and then dissolved back into rain-blur she saw that the orchard had become a paddock, the garden was entirely gone, and the house transformed into a dilapidated barn. The rambling rose was gone. The lace was gone.

As the heavy rain continued, she noticed a piece of derelict, rusty guttering break away from the roof of what had once been Jean's home and channel a long, heavy tongue of rainwater upon a budding red tulip, flattening it to the ground.

All that remained, she thought, was her. And him. But apart, they were nothing more than a home become a barn, an orchard ploughed under to become an empty paddock. The smell of a tree without blossom. The look of Jean's window without lace. The sound of one hand clapping.

In the years between Jean falling into Bojan's arms and Sonja falling onto that filthy Sydney pavement Sonja had never seen an orchard without feeling guilt at what she believed was her own treachery, had never heard the old names of the apples without seeing her father momentarily, gloriously happy looking up at Jean, and the happiness disappearing with the old apples and with them old Archie singing his clattery end of picking farewell to the Cox's Orange Pippins—

> *The plow handles I now have forsaken;*
> *I let them go without even a sigh;*
> *And to the apples that grow in the future,*
> *I say, goodbye, Mr. Pippin, goodbye.*

—and it had all vanished: Jean and Bojan and old Archie and Cox's Orange Pippins and the marvellous taste of it all, bitter and sweet and crunchy all together.

Chapter 44

———

1990

THAT NIGHT after she returned from visiting the Huon, Sonja was beset by an old dream:

She was once more a child waiting at the work site after school, watching her father and the men lay a slab for a house, a vast and wet ocean of grey mud. Jiri was not about when Bojan fell into the cement. It happened quickly and it took place slowly, so quick that he disappeared into the cement in a single motion, leaving only a wet gravelly wave where his body had been, so slow that she saw it, saw him twist and drop face first, saw all this without fear or panic, expectantly waiting for Bojan and his curses to resurface. But he only managed to bring his torso and head a little above the wet cement before dropping into it once more. She did not know, could not know, but somehow could see that his overalls had become ensnared in the hidden wire reinforcing, and the more he struggled, the more ravelled up in the wire his clothes became. The wave thrashed around, and Bojan arose a second time, his face and clothes and hair all shining wet and dark with the concrete, as if he were a statue, as if he were a ghost, and his arm extended out toward her and he cried out her name in a voice piteous and pleading but she did not know what to do or how to help him. She hesitated as his wet-iron fingers stretched as far as they could in the vain hope of reaching her, as if she could save him, as if she could reach him, and she did not know whether to scream or to rush into the dangerous pit of the slab to help her father. Her head shook, and at that moment Jiri rushed past her, bounded into the wet slab like a lifesaver into treacherous seas, and the liquid concrete splashed around his big body and above his gumboots. He hauled at the seal-like form of Bojan's upturned body, and pulled with such might that he ripped Bojan's overalls off the steel reo, and in the process put a nasty gash into Bojan's thigh. Bojan screamed in shock and pain and the relief of being freed. Jiri laughed, and his mighty saving hand slapped Bojan upon his wet back, lifting a fine spray of grey concrete into the budgerigar blue of the morning sky and then the concrete was falling and changing to crimson in colour and a curtain in form and a hand was tying it back and the morning light was filling the bedroom.

'How goes the pregnancy?'

Sonja looked up from her bed, saw that it was Helvi with a tray of breakfast: Finnish sweetbread and tea. Sonja gazed out the window. Her bladder felt outrageously full.

'Fine. I don't throw up any more.' Sonja turned her face and looked out the window, trying to reorient herself to the world outside that of her dreams. 'I've given up coffee. My back aches, my legs throb.' She got out of bed, anxious to be alone until the dream was properly gone and she knew for sure that it was not true that her father was drowning in a wet cement slab and she could not save him. 'And if I don't go now I'll flood the bedroom.'

Chapter 45

1990

HELVI PUSHED AND STRETCHED the dough until it was as pliable and roly as a podgy baby's bottom, stretched and pushed and rolled. 'That is the art,' Helvi would say, 'to stretch the dough when you knead, not hit it or beat it or crush the life out of it. But push and stretch, push and stretch, and the dough will grow softer, more compliant, until it is alive and ready to grow.

'That is all you have to do to make bread,' Helvi would say to Sonja on those long days they worked together around the house, 'show the yeast and the flour that together they can grow into something better.' Sonja watched that large ball of dough, round, elastic, being expertly kneaded by Helvi's knobbly old hands. 'I love that smell,' said Helvi and she almost touched the dough with her nose as she inhaled the beery fragrance. 'Like a baby's head. Warm and yeasty. You smell it?'

'To tell the truth, not that much,' said Sonja.

'Ah—pregnancy,' said Helvi. 'You look beautiful and feel woeful. Your back aches, legs throb, you throw up and can't even drink coffee. And you, Sonja, can't even smell bread.'

Sonja smiled.

Helvi kneaded the dough some more, and had just picked it up when Sonja began to talk. 'It's not exactly the pregnancy, Helvi.' Sonja halted, thought, then continued. Her voice was weary, slow with the telling. 'When I was young, Artie hit me too hard once.' Helvi let the dough drop onto the bench with a dull thud. She resumed kneading. But she was listening intently.

'And my nose wouldn't stop bleeding. At the hospital they cauterised it and stopped the bleeding. But I can't smell things now.' All the time she talked she had a gentle, ironic smile fixed to her face. 'Flowers. Or bread.'

Helvi did not know what to say. She had a sense that it was wrong to frame the story with any comment. She flashed a smile of sad solidarity. She pushed the dough along the bench to Sonja.

'Here—you knead.'

Sonja began awkwardly to work the dough.

'Your father write you yet?'

'No. And he won't. He never writes to anybody.'

'Maybe you should go and talk to him.'

'Why?' said Sonja, with little enthusiasm, but somewhere the slightest hope. 'There's no point. It's too far. And it's been too long.' Then wistfully, she opened up ever so slightly. 'It would be nice, Helvi. It really would. But nice isn't life. Is it?'

Helvi's hands wrested the dough from Sonja's and resumed kneading the dough properly.

'Stretch the dough, Sonja. Stretch. Unless you stretch it, the bread won't grow.' Helvi laughed. 'Like your father.'

She pushed the dough back to Sonja, who tried once more, this time with a little more expertise, stretching it back and forth, back and forth.

'Bojan bread,' said Sonja. Helvi dropped the dough into a bread tin, the tin into the oven. 'You'd need the rack to stretch that old bastard.'

And they both laughed. But then Sonja stopped, and looked up from the oven.

'What if I turned out to be like him? If I was like her? Sometimes I wonder Helvi, what kind of mother I will make. That I will be a bad mother. What if I was never there when the baby needed me? What if I became so angry that I hit it?'

Helvi said nothing. She wished she knew what to say, but she didn't. She could only offer Sonja her home, her bread.

'I'm scared, Helvi,' said Sonja. 'Sometimes I am so frightened that I won't be able to hold it all together. Parts of me are dead, but I don't know which parts.'

Sonja remembered how upon arriving in Sydney all those years ago she had been struck above all by the indifference of the city. In the airport she had suddenly screamed out her father's name and there was no reply, and she had laughed, out of fear and out of relief—and people studiously avoided her, rather than as before, simply not seeing her. Sane or insane, the city did not care, went to pains not to know, and within it she felt a sense of liberty, of having joined some huge fraternity of the fallen, all refusing to acknowledge the devil was on their tail. Lives lived with purpose existed only in rumours and advertisements. In the big smoke there were a billion particles of smog, caustic residue of millions of similarly incinerated lives. The city filled her with the anonymity of others and in that vast wash of a shared nothingness, where people were ordered like factory hens and worked like mules and only in their nightmares were human, Sonja finally found some relief.

She ended up taking a comfort in the climate's oppressive closeness, a flat heat that lay upon all things and all places, finding in it a form of security. She did not want the space that other people in the city craved, rather she welcomed the lack of it, the endless opportunities it gave to deny private life. She preferred to remain upon life's surface and was troubled when people who liked her tried to take her with them down into the murky depths, people who presumed that friendship ultimately entailed learning fundamental truths about another. She wished to stay skipping in the shallows, where escape was always a possibility, remaining a mystery even to herself.

But then had come that day, that day only a few months before.

Sonja had happened to be in an editing suite chasing up some receipts when they were cutting footage for a TV documentary on the dam-building mania of postwar Australia.

They were scanning an interview with an old union man called Preston, who was talking about the reffos, about the violence and drinking and suicides and murders. They tried running some of Preston's comments over some archival footage, grainy and scratched and without sound, of the building of a dam in Tasmania in the early 1950s.

And it was then that she saw that maddened animal wielding a sledge hammer.

It took Sonja some moments to recognise who it was. The old union man called Preston began telling a story so unspeakably sad about a woman he had never met, but whose path he had briefly crossed in the middle of a blizzard so many years ago. He had only glimpsed her from his motorbike, and it was night and he was moving and it was snowing, but he remembered she wore a scarlet coat and beneath it a dress edged in lace.

'We'll cut that,' said a short red-haired woman sitting next to the editor, 'pointless, unnecessary detail.'

The tape was rewound, then run once more, but Sonja was already running faster than the videotape, along the corridor, down the stairs, and into the street below, pulling large deep breaths in, as though she were a drowning woman just rescued from the sea.

Helvi did not tell Sonja to do what Sonja then did, or even suggest it. It was not inevitable, but it was born out

245

of Sonja's sense that if she didn't do something herself now, the inevitable that she had hitherto lived her life with would intercede. It may well all be written, as Jiri used to say, but perhaps Helvi was right when she would reply: 'Maybe, but it's better *you* be the writer yourself than some bastard who only ever writes bad parts for you.'

From now on, Sonja decided, she would do some of the writing herself, would at least try to fix some of the flux that beset her into a form that *she* wanted, instead of letting her life, and the lives of everybody around her, be relegated to the cutting bin of unnecessary detail.

Sonja looked out her bedroom window, looked as far as she could into the morning sky until the sun that sat like a flame in pale water hurt her eyes so much that she screwed them up and turned away, thinking once more of what she had tried to not think about for so long, wondering where her father was and what he was thinking.

Wondering also: But why doesn't he write? Why?

LIKE A BAR-ROOM BRAWLER who won't give up laying into his opponent even after the poor bastard has been reduced to a pulpy quivering mess that won't or can't get back up off the blood-puddled floor, the rain continued pummelling the tin roof of the bereft Tullah single men's quarters on that miserable winter's night. The wind, a banshee from the west, shrieked and beat the single men's quarters with erratic thumps. In Bojan's lousy room a small bar radiator sitting on the floor etched a thin red line, promising but not delivering heat.

Below his breath Bojan cursed the incessant din of the rain above. The glow from the light bulb fell directly onto a near-empty cardboard carton of Cascade bitter that sat on the middle of Bojan's bed next to him, and grotesque shadows grew out from the beer carton to the periphery of his small cell, as though the beer carton was the only real, substantial thing in the room.

Fuck it, thought Bojan Buloh. Fuck everything. Fuck this fucken place. Fuck me. He reached into the carton and pulled out another bottle. He slid the neck of the bottle into the side of his mouth, brought his back teeth down hard on the metal beer cap. It was then that he became aware of another presence in his room and heard her voice.

Saying: 'I'm pregnant.'

He did not bother looking up, but chose rather to twist his head sideways as slowly he levered the beer bottle up against his teeth, prising the cap off. The pressure released and the beer hissed. He pulled the opened beer bottle out of his mouth.

Spat the cap out onto the floor of his room.

Spat out the words: 'I know.'

'I thought maybe you didn't get my letter,' said Sonja.

In one hand Bojan had a smoke, in the other the opened bottle of beer. He was drunk, but quietly so. His voice was subdued. Outside the night was black and cold. Bojan alternately smoked his fag and swigged from the bottle, one hand rising to his mouth, one hand falling. The suck of the fag, the swish of the bottle. Movements of a few centimetres, movements of a lifetime. He wished he could dissolve in the driving rain and wash away into the rivers they would soon fuck up forever. Fuck the rivers, thought Bojan.

'No,' he said. 'I got it.'

They were both silent.

The rain battered the tired iron above their heads in heaving waves. Sonja felt the storm as an oppressive weight bearing down upon them. Bojan, to the contrary, found in the noise a cocoon into which he could retreat and feel some safety from others, a cocoon which both imprisoned him and succoured him. This thought gave him the strength to say something more.

'What could I do?'

Sonja said nothing.

Bojan breathed out, turned his bottle and fag holding hands outwards. 'I have no home,' he said. Sonja said nothing. 'No money, no possessions, only this job and this room.'

'You could have telephoned,' said Sonja.

'Why?'

And as if to emphasise how little he supposedly cared Bojan raised the bottle to his mouth and swigged. Sonja watched in sad disgust. There was something half-fascinating, half-repulsive in Bojan's proud desolation. As the lager fell down his throat his stubbly, wrinkly gullet pulsed in and out like that of a seagull. He skulled maybe half the bottle in a single go, though Sonja found it hard to tell with the amount of foam he kicked up within the bottle.

'No wonder Mama left,' said Sonja.

Bojan took the bottle a few inches away from his mouth so that it sat level with his chest, still on a steep angle ready for the next swig. He looked at Sonja, annoyed with her for bringing back the memory of Maria.

'What you know?' he said contemptuously.

Fuck Sonja.

'I know you,' said Sonja.

Fuck her.

'You know nothing,' said Bojan.

Maybe, thought Sonja. But I know who I am. Maybe it's not much. But I know. And without even thinking it first, she heard herself saying, not yelling out all of a sudden like, like him, but saying in a thin, hard whisper, 'Shutup.'

This was unexpected. For him. And for her. While his behaviour was normal, almost ritual, Sonja's was new for them both.

'Shutup,' she said a second time, almost a wishful comment, almost an aside, not meant to be noticed, but strong somehow.

And when she said it, when she said shutup that second time, his head jumped back, just a bit, but she and he knew it to be a big jump back, like she had landed an unexpected punch and he was dazed. Then he feigned that it hadn't affected him, thrust his jaw upwards, held his head high as if now on the lookout for another blow and warning her not to try—like it was one more hapless fight outside the pub at the end of the evening that she had once watched from inside the FJ.

And Sonja noticed this.

That he was shivering slightly.

That her father's face was quivering as if possessed of numerous tics, and she saw upon it things she thought only she knew, but which were appearing there now for all to see. His face that she thought had not aged was, she now realised, ageing terribly while she sat there that bleak night. An ageing infinitely worse than beer flab and baldness. An ageing, wretched and hideous and accelerated so that years made their cruel mark within seconds, and decades within a minute. As she watched, lines were appearing all over his face as if an invisible angel were scratching them there with an invisible nail.

Bojan was transforming before Sonja's eyes from a man she once knew, her father, her artie, into someone else, someone she could scarcely guess at. His hair seemed suddenly thinner, greyer. His flesh hollowed, puckered and fell. His eyes receded, lost their shine. And those lines! Those cuts and gouges! As if they might miraculously open and bleed, she feared this horribly etched face and the things that had created it, things that she had only ever half-guessed at—feared the avenging angel with its nail and its creation far more than she ever feared her poor weak father.

But she knew she had no choice but to continue. So she said: 'I am sick of you. I thought maybe you had changed—'

But before she had finished his quivering lips were opening and his body was heaving mightily and he was shouting, 'You know nothing!'

And she, without meaning it at all, suddenly yelled, 'Shutup! Shutup!' and she slapped him hard, hard across his ravaged, blotched cheek, his stubbly flesh like leathery sandpaper rasping her falling palm.

Never before had she done such a thing. Never retaliated. He looked at her in a way he had never looked at her before: with amazement.

He raised his hand to his reddening cheek and wiped it back and forth, feeling the heat. He ran his hand down onto his mouth, dragging his lips together, then turned his head away. Maybe he was thinking, or, maybe just trying to forget one more thing.

'You've grown hard,' Bojan said at last.

Sonja trembled. Then she shook her head, stared down at Bojan, and spoke now without pity or anger.

'I have had a hard fucking life.'

Bojan looked up into her eyes. Sonja stared back fiercely. Sonja continued with a slight tremor in her voice.

'And I am fucking hard.'

Slowly, forcefully, between gulps, she found in words things she had never even thought of, but which she knew were nevertheless inescapably true.

'And you better get fucking used to it.'

Somehow her comments seemed to alter the balance of forces between them. Bojan's contemptuous and derisive edge vanished. The momentum of their confrontation evaporated and they faced each other as equals, partners in a tragedy neither fully understood. And perhaps for that reason, neither knew what to say next.

Bojan's face seemed as slack and loose as the remnant beer froth that dribbled out the top of the bottle. He turned to his bedside table and pulled out the old shoebox of photographs. He searched through it until he found the one of the dead grandfather about whom Sonja had once dreamt. He put his finger on the face of the corpse, passed the card to Sonja, and asked: 'You remember?'

Thinking Bojan was seeking to take the conversation into the less troubled waters of family history, Sonja replied tersely: 'Mama's artie—my grandfather.'

'And how he die?'

'In the war he carry food to the partisans,' said Sonja, reciting a story she had heard often enough. 'The village priest tell the Domobran. The SS Prinz Eugen Division come and shoot him. This photograph—is after.'

Bojan pondered this reply, began to speak—halted— then recommenced. 'Maria . . .'

Sonja began to realise she had not known everything.

'Mama,' she said, 'Mama . . . see this?'

Bojan breathed out, looked away. He put the bottle down and lighted another cigarette. 'Of course,' he said. He looked as if he was disappointed with Sonja for not understanding something, though rather it was disappointment with himself for not having had the courage to tell the whole story. He said, 'She must watch—that is how it was.' He said, 'You understand what I say?'

Sonja nodded. She felt a little dumbstruck. She had never known that Maria had to watch her father's murder. And she began to make connections between this and elements of her past that had previously made no sense whatsoever.

Bojan looked this way and that, anywhere where there wasn't Sonja. He sucked his breath in, and then, still not looking at Sonja—looking instead at the floor between the V formed by his arms, beginning at an elbow balanced on each knee, converging together at the apex of the cigarette—he began to tell a story. He told it slowly, because it was a big story, but one that somehow could only be told in very few words. He told her this.

'Then they rape her sister, her mother.'

He stopped, gulped.

'Then they rape Maria.'

Sonja felt strangely light, as if all that kept her connected to this world had been abruptly severed. She had never heard of such a thing about her mother. She felt confused, concussed by the weight of this new knowledge. Silently she mouthed 'they rape Maria' twice, feeling the shape of each word like dry stones in her mouth, making certain that what she thought she heard was what she did hear.

'Who?' Her voice was quavering, her fear apparent in its uncertain pitch. '*Who* are you talking about?'

Feeling he had said too much, Bojan stopped, his anger momentarily spent. He looked up at Sonja.

He spoke. Quietly.

'Maria.'

Sonja was uncomprehending.

'The SS rape Mama?'

Bojan looked downwards. 'Of course,' said Bojan. 'Look at the back of the card. Look.'

Sonja turned the card over. On its cupped and acid-blotched back was written in faded blue ink the inscription 'ix *Avril* 1943'.

'She was twelve years old,' said Bojan.

'She told you?'

Bojan replied with vehemence, somewhat annoyed that his daughter seemed not to understand the full and total shame of it.

'She say *nothing*.'

Bojan continued even more adamantly, his fierceness arising from both anger at what happened and pride in Maria for never telling him.

He said: 'Never.'

And he said it proudly.

He realised he had Sonja's total attention, that this was a single moment of understanding that they had never known. He paused, and though he then continued to speak quietly, within him a rage had started to grow.

'But the whole village know.'

He pointed his right hand at Sonja and punctuated each word with a jab of his smouldering cigarette, flicking ash here and there, leaving smoke trails in the air.

'See.'

Bojan took the card and again looked at the photograph of the grandfather in the coffin. He drew his cigarette up to the head of the face of the dead man in the photograph and held it there, slowly burning a hole through the dead man's head. As he did this, seemingly absent-mindedly, he continued talking.

'That is war,' he said, as if talking about a far-off dream, the details of which it was impossible to properly convey. 'Don't let anyone ever tell you no different.'

Bojan's face rose upwards and looked toward Sonja. He held the photograph out to her as if it were incontrovertible evidence, and not knowing what else to do, she took it and stuffed it in her handbag. His eyes were close to tears, and they pleaded, begged Sonja to say she understood the horror of it all.

But Sonja was without words. Bojan opened his mouth as if to speak but no more words were to be had. He moved his lips and his tongue but still no words came.

And then, suddenly, the enormity of the tragedy, which he had carried as an inexpressible burden for so long, opened up to him and left him horrified.

'They kill her father,' he abruptly cried out. 'Then they fuck her. You understand! They fuck her!'

He spoke out of an infinite sadness, as if he were reciting a poem that went beyond human suffering.

'My Maria.'

He started to cry.

'They fuck her.'

He enclosed his head in his outstretched hands as if his mind might burst from the pain of memory.

Sonja turned and left. Bojan sobbed.

'Maria, Maria, Maria.'

Outside Sonja scurried away from the single men's quarters, through the night-time rain to her car, at first walking quickly, then breaking into a jog, then running, running as hard as she could, running to leave it all behind.

Trying to find her car keys she fumbled and dropped her handbag into a puddle. She fell to her knees in the wet gravel and hastily grabbed all that had spilt out and threw it back into the soggy handbag, overlooking in her rush the photograph of her dead grandfather. She put first one key then another into the car door before she found the right key. All she could hear was Bojan keening. She got in the car, slammed the door, started the motor and revved it as hard and as loud as she could trying to drown out Bojan, to drown it all out.

But still she could hear him continuing to keen in his hut, each word a terrible lament, caught between a long single heaving sob. The whole an agonised prayer of loss that pursued her all that long drive back to Hobart.

'Madonna, Madonna, Madonna.
'Maria, Maria, Maria.'

Sometime after the car had gone, a drunk Turkish boiler-maker-welder walking back home stopped to relieve himself. Illuminated by the mist-softened phosphorescence of a street lamp he saw in the piss-spiked puddle a curious thing: a waterlogged photograph of a dead man, with a burnt hole for a face, lying in a coffin. Priding himself as a sporting man, he attempted and then succeeded in angling his stream on the approximate spot of the burnt-out hole. To his astonishment a face formed where the hole had been and the face rose up out of the puddle and grew in size until it was equal to his own and the colour of alabaster and the face stared at him with a look of overwhelming sorrow that greatly unsettled the drunk Turkish boilermaker-welder. He staggered back into the darkness, mumbling appropriate apologies as he went, but he did not sleep well for several nights.

SHE WORE LACE; that much Sonja remembered.

How much lace?

She did not remember.

What type of lace? Fleur-de-lis or rose-patterned, coarsely knotted or finely woven?

She did not know.

The colour of calico or the colour of snow?

She could not recall. In any case, it was irrelevant. Whether it was only her collar or her cuffs, whatever its colour or shape or extent or pattern, it was beautiful and Sonja remembered it as a liberating beauty that took on different colours and shapes and extents at the different times she recalled it, and it did not worry her and why should it?—for she knew her mother was dressed the way she had dressed for the funeral of the Italian tunneller who had been crushed beneath the rock fall: knew she was dressed for some formal departure.

Mama wore lace and it was beautiful and she was leaving, Sonja knew she was going and it was not within

Sonja's power to do anything other than observe and then begin burying what she saw so deep within her that only the outlines of a lost memory would remain impressed forever upon her soul. And the only word she had for those traces of her past, the single, strange inexplicable word was lace. Sometimes she had a dream in which there was a piece of lace billowing in front of her and when she went to grab it, the lace would simply blow away. She would chase it. The chase was always different, but the end was inevitably the same: the lace disappeared in the wind.

Mama wore lace and it was beautiful and she had left, but before she left she had sung softly to Sonja, had sung a lullaby in a language soft and wondrous and as familiar as the close smell of milk of her mother that now sounded to Sonja foreign, the words of which she did not understand but the singing of which was both exotic and deeply sad. '*Spancek, zaspancek,*' Mama sang,

> '*crn mozic*
> *hodi po noci*
> *nima nozic . . .*'

The lace rode the strange words until it blew beyond the snow into the Butlers Gorge hut-home and shaped itself into Sonja's Mama, Maria Buloh, a young woman clad in a scarlet coat and battered burgundy shoes and within her slowly rocking arms materialised the three-year-old Sonja to whom Maria softly sang.

What was it that she sang?

A lullaby in her native tongue, familiar and reassuring.

> 'Lunica ziblje:
> aja, aj, aj,
> spancek se smeje
> aja, aj, aj.'

It is of course possible that the words which Maria was singing took her back to another land that she was trying to forget as hard as she was trying to remember. It is even possible that as she sat there rocking her child upon her knee, she saw her family's home almost buried in winter snow, nestling in the Julien Alps, saw the snow melt and the alps grow green and then heavy with flowers in spring. Maybe then she saw that which she wished to forget along with that which she wished to remember, and the pain of the inseparable nature of memory was too great for her. Certainly—in Sonja's memory—tears ran down Maria's face, and perhaps it was in a futile attempt to stem the tears, to end the memories that she stopped singing in Slovenian and spoke in English.

'My baby,' she said. 'My baby.'

After the lightness of her song, the English words were harsh and heavy, made Maria sound as if her tongue had been mutilated, cut out. She put Sonja down and spoke to the uncomprehending child once more in her heavy English, the words falling like rough-edged rocks from her mouth, a small avalanche dooming her daughter.

What was it that she said?

The truth, strange and elusive.

'Sonja, I must to go.'

Maria put her daughter back in bed. But when she went to leave the child was back up watching from her bedroom door. Maria opened the front door. Outside it was dark.

'Do not worry,' she said. 'Artie be home soon.'

Caught within the glow of an electric street light Maria saw snow falling. What, she wondered, lay beyond the light's illumination?

'Sonja?' asked Sonja.

'No, Sonja,' said Maria softly. 'I must go alone.'

Maria came back to Sonja's room, for a second time put the child into bed, held Sonja hard against her then abruptly let go, quickly turned and walked back to the front door, trying to soothe the child to sleep without daring to look back at her, saying, '*Aja, aja,*' to the walls, to the ceiling—then stepping outside and looking up and seeing only the night sky which was nothing and explained nothing and offered nothing and her despair was total and utter and in spite of her daughter's pleas the door was already closing and it was the same as Sonja had always dreamt: the lace had disappeared forever.

Chapter 48

1966

AND THEN a powerful arm had hold of her sleeping body and with a lazy force was shaking her awake. He did not know why he was shaking her.

He wished to say, There is this.

He wished to say, How beautiful you are in sleep.

He did not wish to say anything.

He wished her simply to know that was what he wished her to hear. He did not want her to know anything about how he felt. He wished for them both to escape and the terrible thought of him killing them both briefly crossed his mind, before he exorcised it once more, and his hold on her arm slackened momentarily as he involuntarily began to draw it up to cross himself, before he halted in disgust at having almost taken refuge in religion.

He wanted her to escape him, and he wished her to stay.

Because she understood completely, and knew nothing. He shook her some more.

In Sonja's mind the silence of snow falling, of lace disappearing gave way to the sound of cars pulling up outside, the abrupt overly loud noises of doors slamming, drunken voices speaking in a babble of European languages.

'Mama,' Sonja mumbled a memory from somewhere inside. Then whimpered, 'Mama . . . ?' She was listening for the wind, to hear it say, *Aja, aja*. But when she looked up into his glazed eyes and saw it was her father shaking her, she had to turn her head away from his thin spirit-heated words.

He said, 'Wake.' It was the middle of the night.

He said, 'Come. You get food ready.'

Aja, aja.

Out in the lounge-room, her eyes, previously opened wide in dreaming, had now to narrow to discern in the urine-yellow glow diffused by smoky haze the figures of half a dozen drunken European men, their number fewer than their great noise suggested. They sat around the laminex kitchen table, now moved to the middle of the room with a mustard-coloured cloth covering its pink marble wonder and upon it cards and bottles, some full and some empty, some large and long and bubbling loose froth, some small and full of mean spirit, and for a moment, before her eyes had properly adjusted, she was not sure which were the vessels emptying, not sure if the bottles were the men or the men the bottles.

They were drinking not to enjoy the present, but for the more urgent reason of wanting to forget the past and to deny the future. Their destination was not pleasure but oblivion, and they wished to arrive as quickly as possible.

They were drinking wine from flagons.

They were drinking moonshine from coke bottles.

They were drinking beer from long-necked bottles.

And every other drink they consecrated with a thimble glass of schnapps. To hasten the spirit's rapid journey into their guts, they threw their heads back violently, as if into their hearts a knife had been suddenly plunged, and this was the moment of horror when they realised that their wound was mortal and their poor souls were soon to take leave from their ruined bodies.

She wished to say, Artie, I must go to school in the morning.

She said, 'Artie—salami?'

The men gesticulated wildly and talked aggressively, short jabs of broken Polish, Slovenian, Deutsch and new Australian, their conversation chainsawing into the forest of her night, revving and then idling and then roaring as it cut and recut.

'Of course,' replied Bojan above their clamour. 'And kruha and the prosciutto and the capsicums I pickle and the mushrooms I pickle and the trout I smoke.'

Without knowing any of these men Sonja understood them all. Their voices no-one else could understand, their hearts no-one else could decipher, their souls no-one else could see. She understood them all, and hated them and herself all the more. She went to the kitchen. She prepared plates of salamis and cheeses and bread. She arranged the plates with great care, each salami slice neatly tucked in under the next salami slice, the whole a millipede of spiced pork and knuckle fat shuffling around the plate's rim toward its centre. She looked up at the kitchen clock which showed the time as being almost two in the morning and smiled a little at the thought of herself in a few short hours yet again sitting dazed through her school classes. Once it had made her angry. But now she had decided that it was coming to an end in the only way it could now end, with her leaving. When, or how, she did not know. All she knew was that her desire must override what she had until then believed to be her destiny.

As Sonja adroitly manoeuvred in and around the men, without enthusiasm or interest, but dutifully putting down plates of food and filling glasses, one of the men sought to paw her. She ignored him as the rest ignored her. Mostly the men were totally indifferent to her presence, as though the food and drink were magically summoned out of the ether into their presence simply by their alcoholic desire, as though she were as insubstantial to them as they had become to the world at large, a phantom existing only in her imagination.

The unadorned electric bulb above their heads burnt like the wordless things they carried in their hearts. She tried not to see them: these men who had loved other places faraway and had loved other people either long dead or as good as long dead for all the contact they would ever know again with one another, so their strong talk avoided talking about any matter of strength, any matter to deal with love, or, for that matter, hate. She tried not to hear them: their babble about lust and grog and work and other empty matters in such violent language to give each other but chiefly themselves the impression that what they were talking about mattered, that they might have some measure of power over it, that it might be life, and that they had not already died. They drank the moon down and the sun up, but in truth they belonged no more to the night than to day. They were lost in time, as they were in everything.

A few had kept the women they arrived with in the new land, but the mud of their youthful union had turned into stone of sharp and flinty angles. Others had had women they had lost; a few more found Australian women, mostly young and headstrong, who were willing to throw in their lot with those who most Australians not only thought but knew to be less than people, such women believing foolishly that love could conquer all, even such hate, and on rare occasions their folly was shown to be a great wisdom but the price was high.

Most men, however, had come to Tasmania alone, and at some point realised that they were going to live the rest of their days alone, and then depart it alone and they feared the night all the more.

And so they became men who by and large survived without women except for the occasional coupling with women who, for a night at least, saw something more in them than they saw in themselves, or with whores who saw only what the men offered which was little: money and moans issued in several strange tongues. If the whores were listening close, which they may or may not have done—if they put their cold ears near those cruel sensitive mouths—they might have discerned a terrible yearning in those sounds, but being in another language, they seemed only primeval, which they were, and without meaning, which they were not. So the men let the electric light beat upon their heads till their heads ached, and upon their bottles till their bottles were empty. Sonja tried not to know any of it, but she understood it all.

In the great forests beyond, the devils and quolls and possums and potaroos and wombats and wallabies also came to curious life in the night, and they roamed the earth for what little they could scavenge to keep themselves alive, and when they mistakenly ventured onto the new gravel roads that were everywhere invading their world, it was to be mesmerised by the sudden shock of moving electric light that rendered them no longer an element of the great forests or plains, but a poor pitiful creature alone whose fate it was to be crushed between rubber and metal. Having being shown by the electric light to have no existence or meaning or world beyond a glaring outline upon the gravel, each animal was killed easily by the men who drove drunk to and from their place of work, heading to or from the whores and grog and the card games of the bigger towns.

By day the roads were speckled red with the resultant carnage and startled hawks feasting on the carcasses would hastily rise into the air dragging rapidly unravelling viscera behind them, a shock of bloodied intestine stretching across the blue sky as if the world itself were wounded.

Jiri had told Bojan some people believed that the animals reincarnated as spirits or other animals or even as people. But when Bojan hit a fellow animal he hoped he had done it a favour and relieved it of the burden of life forever.

Chapter 49

1966

THE CARD GAME ended around 4 a.m. the same as it always ended: in acrimony. Dawn was close and another day's labour not far away and no-one seemed to have the desire, as they mostly had when the night was young, to sort the matter out with their fists. For which Sonja was thankful. The men disappeared in dribs and drabs until there was only Sonja and a very drunk Bojan cleaning up the mess in the kitchen and living room.

Sonja watched her wild and dishevelled father, wondering if she even knew who he was at such times. She wanted to see him as he was at other times. Not as he was now. Which was perhaps why she forgot herself and so foolishly said, 'I'll finish up now. You go to bed. You've had a few, you need the sleep.' She said it quietly, almost kindly. But Bojan's drink-sodden mind soaked up the soft sound of her words and heard what even Sonja was not fully conscious of: that she could not bear to see him so.

He raised his arm above his head in anger.

'I'm no bloody drunk—' he said.

'I didn't say you were drunk,' said Sonja, and then she knew she shouldn't have said even that.

'—what you fucken mean *I'm* drunk?'

'No,' said Sonja, feeling her breathing already growing short, rushed, the words escaping with too much tension, as if she did know and had known and had meant what Bojan thought she had said. 'No no, no nothing,' she found herself panting, but Bojan was not listening.

'So I enjoy myself every now and again. Am I not allowed to enjoy myself? Bet you fucken enjoy yourself when I not here. Bet you out fucken boys I fucken bet I fucken know you fucken slut I fucken do.'

Sonja felt her head sway, felt the earth rise and pitch, but somehow she knew she must keep her balance, must not fall. She cupped her hands and held them over her ears so that she might not hear but her head was alternately swelling and then collapsing into nothingness and her cupped hands were only shaping the horror, rather than preventing it.

Bojan was now yelling.

'A fucken slut fucken like your fucken mother.'

Bojan spat the last word out with vehemence. Then Sonja saw that her hands were shaping a shield and his hand was coming toward her face, the back of a large hand growing huger as it came closer.

'Fucken like your fucken mother.'

Sonja screamed, but not out of terror but from something beyond terror; she had unwittingly set him off but she had not meant it, she had not.

'No,' she screamed, terrified at what she knew would inevitably follow, 'No, no, no,' she yelled.

'I show you who's bloody drunk.'

His voice was cold and without emotion. Only his face shook.

'Watch,' he said slowly, as if trying to demonstrate to both of them that he was not drunk. 'I show you.' When he backhanded Sonja for the second time, she remained impassive and did not cry, and were it not for her flesh tearing and her blood starting to run it might have even been possible to think that his blows were without effect. Bojan's face shook more. Sonja pleaded with him now in Slovenian, chattering like a caged, maddened bird.

'*Ni, Artie, ni, ni, ni, ni* . . .'

But no language meant much to Bojan now. He hit her again and again. And when she finally fell to the floor he yelled out in great pain, as if he had been beaten and not her.

'They fuck you! They fuck you!'

She hated him. She wished she could hold him tight like Mrs Heaney's kids had held their mother, so that she might not hate him so much.

'They fuck you!' cried Bojan a final time, then staggered off to bed, tripping over a chair leg as he went.

She could not remember when it had started. To go back to before was for them both to acknowledge that now was no good, but now was all they had and could ever have. She could not remember how it had begun, these bashings. She did discern a change in her own response to the bashings—transforming from a paralysing fear to a feeling close to blessed release when his first blow fell, for the end was now close and her fear, with which she had to live for days leading up to a beating, was shed with her blood, and her blood smelt sweet to her like rain falling upon a drought-maddened earth. And then finally, there came a night when she realised she was no longer scared at all of his backhanders and his fists, because she knew there was something within her that hadn't broken, that hadn't bled and which he could never reach.

THE FOLLOWING MORNING Sonja lay motionless in
her bed, eyes open and alert in a face bruised and swollen.
From Bojan's bedroom came the sound of drunken snoring. She moved, felt pain jab and prickle her face, sat up
slowly, and eased herself out of her bed covers. She did not
dress, but in her pyjamas went straight to the laundry,
filled a bucket with hot water into which she threw some
detergent, found a rag from under the sink closet, and
then went to the wall spattered with her now dried and
darkened blood. She described an arc across the wall with
the dampened rag, then another and another, watching
pink patterns form back and forth as she cleaned the wall
and the similarly stained floor below. As she washed the
wall, watching the swirls form and disappear, holes within
holes within holes, she began to sing so that she would
not hear her father snoring.

'Oh Mr Sheen,' she sang softly, sang slowly, more
slowly than the song in the advertisement for the aerosol
cleaner, in a hesitant, stumbling way she sang, 'Oh . . . Mr

Sheen, you get everything . . . everything so sparkling *clean.'*

When she finished the wall, she would open the windows and front door, mop the floors, and wash up the mess from the card evening, then finally clean herself, trying as she did so to look at her face as little as possible. And then her father would awake and the house would glisten and the smell of sour sweated bread would be banished for another short, ever shorter time.

Chapter 51

1966

I'm getting used to it now.

His moods, his unpredictable explosions, horrible words and terrible things spewing out of his mouth. When he comes into a room, I go out, not to make a point or anything, not loud like, but quiet as a mouse, hugging the wall so that he will not notice I was ever there. I will turn side-on when he walks past me, so that there is more space for him to pass, I will say nothing when he talks, neither bad things nor good things, neither jokes nor serious things. I will. Sometimes when he's just chatting away I know he's trying to catch my eyes, to get me to look into his eyes. But I won't and I don't, because I get all dizzy looking into them, they're like deep blue lakes that I stand way, way above and I am so frightened I am going to lose my balance and fall all that long way into them and that I will drown in those dark blue lakes. I know he's trying to catch my eyes, and when he's trying I get the shivers, and then I have to try and stop the shivers because that makes him angry too: What you shivering for, he says, kind like at first, what's the matter? But then he gets angry because he knows why I am shivering and he hates why I am shivering and he yells horrible words and terrible things he says: Stop your fucken shivering, he yells, and his arm rises above his head and I go to run, but my feet are frozen, and I know the moment he sees my eyes his hand will fall. Fuck you, he says. Who do you think you are? Who? I don't know who I am. I should know and I am being punished for not knowing. Maybe that's fair. Perhaps that's right. Maybe when I know who I am, when I can look into his eyes without shivering and answer that question and not shiver, perhaps then he will not hit me no more. Without even thinking it first, I hear myself yelling out all of a sudden like, yelling I love you Artie, and I listen to my yelling and I think that is all I know and that is everything I know and I realise I am looking into those faraway lakes of his eyes, and I am losing my balance and falling. Fucken love, I hear him say, and he is crying, what's fucken love, Sonja? and his hand is falling and I am drowning and I cannot reach the air or the light or the sun above and I am drowning.

Chapter 52

1966

She give me fucken shits. She make me want to hit her, like a little fucken mouse, never answering me when I speak to her. Don't bloody listen to me unless I, well, hit her. Not hard though. Not fists, not much. Only backhands. Mostly. But she must learn though. She go like me if she don't learn. She go down. I hit her down to bring her up. Why don't she behave like a proper bloody kid? I know she hates me, when she looks me in the eye, I know she hates me. I don't care. Why should I care. I am shit. I am the wog, the fucken wog cunt. She not. She looks like them. Talks like them. That's good. Not like me. Not an old wood house that is falling to bits. Why do she hurt me? When she look me in the eye like, why she say such terrible things without words that she should never say even with words that make me feel like there is a hammer-drill boring into my head? I know she hates me. I hit her so she will say it. So she will say you are shit, say, hey you wog, so she will say I hate you, you fucken old wog cunt. I hit her so she will know how bad it is and how bad I am and so that she will say what I long to hear so that it will be over and I will be alone and away from it all at last.

I fucken hit her and nothing happens. Maybe I drink so much that I think I hit her but haven't. Maybe I am watching this movie and it's me hitting Sonja but it's not me and not Sonja just this movie on the TV. Because the more I hit and the harder I hit her face says nothing. Not her mouth, not her eyes, not nothing tells me anything. Nothing tells me it's wrong or bad. Nothing tells me it even is happening, because maybe it isn't. Maybe it's just the horrors from the drink. If it was real, she would cry or scream or say no. But I fucken hit her and nothing happens. So it cannot be happening. Sometimes the blood it spurts and sometimes I think I can hear her scream and even me scream, but from a distance like, like it is through a wall, something happening to other people faraway. Sometimes I think I see blood even on the walls—but it can't be because the next morning I get up and I wash like I always do and when I come out there is no blood on the walls they clean like they always clean cos Sonja is a good girl not a lazy girl and keeps them that way, she is good but clumsy and sometimes falls and hurts herself and bruises her face.

So I hit her, belt her real hard and with each backhander I ask the most gentle question: Sonja, say something. Please, I say with each blow, please say something.

Chapter 53

1966

I go out into the cold night. Faraway I can see the large river, shining like a silver paddock in the light of the moon.

I fetch myself down, lie on the grass and hold my face close to the wet earth, feel the long dewy grass all the more delicate with the bruises of my face. My face burns like a fire, and each long piece of grass traces out the contours of my bruises with the grace of a cooling feather. Wish I were a seed in that earth, a flower that could unravel into the light of the sun with other plants, know the rain as life and die with the other plants when the terrible coldness came upon me.

My hands run over the ground, flatten the worm casts. The wet grass feathers over my welts. When he has not hit me, I do not feel the wet grass the way I do now. Necklaces of grace. Pearls of dew spreading in a film over my face. And as I lie on the damp earth I whisper my mother's name. Her beautiful name.

Maria, I say to the earth, my Maria.

Chapter 54

———

1966

OBSERVE BOJAN BULOH this night of remorse.

Watch how through the frontierland of Australian suburbia he in his FJ searches for escape once more, how he travels past houses new and raw as a gutted roo, their bloody viscera carved out of the bush only an instant ago, along roads that merge into deep muddy drains, heading into this land of no footpaths, no concrete edging, few gardens in none of which would lovers ever find the star-shaped flower; see how he scans this wasteland of semi-finished and just finished buildings for a sign, an omen, an apparition of reality in a world he finds increasingly unanchored, as his head begins floating elsewhere. As if dismembered his foot hammering hard the clutch, the brake, the accelerator, his FJ alone along the empty and silent roads that wait with expectant desire for when the other new inhabitants of this new world can afford cars not only for each family but for every individual.

See how he is searching, searching and searching longer still, for something, he no longer knew what. He,

Bojan Buloh, who once had the charm that pulled women to him even when they were repelled by his behaviour, now knew all that charm to have fled him with his sweet complexion and thick hair. When he met people now he felt himself a fool, did not know what to say, felt naked and that such nakedness gave offence, felt that he spoke after too long a time and then awkwardly, giving them time to stare in horror at this naked shivering fool unable to find words in which to clothe his horror.

He felt an overwhelming desire to confirm that he still lived, that the unreal world that swam past the FJ was not hell and he not condemned already to plumbing the deep well of his cracked existence, that he would not forever be a spectre acting out a life in a world that only approximated a world, the cruellest of theatres in which punishment was simply being, and the desire grew hard and hot in his loins, a feeling curious and undeniable.

Bojan's journey ended in a muddy front yard that could accommodate several cars. He parked the FJ, got out, smiled slightly, for the brothel of the suburbs hardly matched his image of a whorehouse indelibly formed in Belgrade where as a JNA conscript in the company of fellow soldiers, he had first paid for sex in an establishment that looked to his eyes as if it had been decorated by and for a Turkish pasha, replete with great rugs and hanging drapes of all colours, the whole suffused with a huge mystery that came to an abrupt end when a fight erupted between a fellow Slovenian and two Macedonians.

The brothel of the suburbs was, on the other hand, as nondescript, as lacking in mystery as the world it serviced: a modest brick veneer house, it sat at the bottom of a steep drive discreetly shielded from its suburban neighbours by an overgrown hedge of Chinese fire bushes. He felt a chill, cutting wind that had journeyed thousands of miles of ocean from the vast white lands of the Antarctic to arrive at this strange terminus, pushing hard at his back as he went up the guardless concrete stairs and rang the doorbell. He heard footsteps, knew he was being appraised from the spyhole, and upon hearing the latch turn looked up to be greeted at the door by a respectable looking middle-aged woman wearing a neat shiny bone-coloured dress and horn-rimmed glasses. She reminded Bojan of a desert lizard throwing up its frill to frighten predators. As if to a tupperware party, she welcomed him.

'Brian, Brian how are you? April? April, Brian is here to see you.'

Bojan said nothing. Before crossing the threshold he passed her a five-dollar note.

'Brian—I am ever so sorry,' said the woman. 'Our rate has gone up—' She held up seven fingers—'to eight.' She abruptly flicked a thumb out to make up the new requisite number of digits. Apart from that she did not move. 'Eight dollars.' Then added: 'It must be confusing for you, this new decimal currency business.'

Bojan reached into his pocket and handed over the additional brown dollar notes. He asked himself, for no reason since there was no answer, why he bothered when the outcome was inevitable, and the inevitable was awful.

A small dark-haired woman, auger-eyed, appeared at the back of the lizard-woman, dressed in the same red dressing gown she had worn the first time he had visited, and which had led him for no reason he could think of to choose her over a more attractive, older woman.

The wind at Bojan's back tumbled around him and fell across the door, pushing the red dressing gown up against the auger-eyed woman's small stout form, outlining her as she was and not as the lowlights of the house's interior pretended she and her fellow workers might be, showing her as a woman as he was a man, frail and ordinary, as if to say: For what? For this? But Bojan had seen many different women in the brothel of the suburbs since his first time, and he had always gone with the auger-eyed woman with the red dressing gown, and Bojan wanted to say yes, yes, precisely for that, and he wanted to say no, because it never was possible and never would be. She looked as ever, except that she now wore her hair cropped in the new fashion, but Bojan did not think it became her as much as the long hair she wore the first time he had visited. But he did not say this to her, nor she anything to him. He closed the door behind him.

I SMELL HER and I smell things that cut me, thought Bojan Buloh as he tried to ride April who would not be ridden, things that make me sick, it is so strong that smell of woman like mutton that Serbs cook on a spit and I hate it, hate them the fucken Serbs, hate that smell of the church incense, hate the smell of apple blossom, strong and so close that you could become so dizzy that you might fall and never rise up.

As he attempted to do what he had come there to do, Bojan Buloh looked up at the Madonna and caught himself beginning to pray to Her. He halted, shook his head, closed his eyes and tried to remember how it was with Maria, to recall lying with her, to imagine that it was her and not someone else now beneath him. In that small, stark bedroom with a ceiling Bojan always found too low, its walls covered with a heavy wallpaper with purple felt fleur-de-lis, the only ornamentation was this—a cheap framed picture of the Madonna with a bleeding heart, hung above the head of the bed. And how I hate it and her, thought Bojan Buloh, hate that fucken picture. He looked back down at April, still with her dressing gown on. In her left hand, covering her face, she was holding a copy of the *Women's Weekly*, folded in half. He ran his fingers into her right hand, trying to make some sort of contact. Her hand snapped back, and grabbed the other side of the magazine.

Combine mayonnaise, wine and lemon juice, April read, *season with salt and pepper.*

I feel her, thought Bojan, and feel her flesh cold, clammy like a leg of prosciutto, feel myself limp, limp like a dead pig's ear, and unable to enter through her gates into her body, and I cannot fuck this cold meat.

'Jesus,' said April, 'you still not finished?' and went back to reading the recipe.

What I would do if I was a man! thought Bojan. But I am not a man and she is not Maria and her smell and her flesh and that smell, Jesus I hate that fucking smell, I push it away and moan for it to leave me and stop mocking me.

He fumbled to no avail between April's thighs. *If wine unavailable, substitute vinegar and sugar,* April read, trying to concentrate hard on each and every word as her body wobbled and shook from Bojan's exertions. *Stir in undrained spinach, blend well. Serve sauce over heated fish fingers.*

All that either could hear was the rustling of the magazine pages and Bojan's slow breathing, his diminishing grunts, then a few sobs of frustration, him weeping, then him saying, 'I am sorry. I can't, I just can't.'

Then he got up, quickly dressed himself, and was gone.

As the FJ started up and left, April talked to the lizard-woman.

'I suppose,' said April, 'you charged him your special wog rate—a third more expensive than for dinky-di Aussie boys.'

The lizard-woman said nothing. The lizard-woman was motionless. April continued. She was a little worked up. But only a little.

'You should give it to him half-price. He don't come here for sex. He comes here to cry.'

The lizard-woman had had enough. Her eyes suddenly darted away from the front door and fixed upon April and her mouth opened and her blue tongue started darting back and forth.

'Don't talk disgusting,' she said. 'This is a respectable house.'

April turned and walked off for a smoke. A cruel draught rose up from the floor. The red dressing gown felt to April colder than ice. She wished for warmth. She did not wish to return to the room of felt flowers. The doorbell rang with the promise of more custom. April wished it would not be answered. She was still. She knew she must remain still to endure, but her fingers shook.

The doorbell rang once more.

'Christ,' April murmured under her breath. She took one last long drag on her cigarette, tried to steady her hands and stop the ash snowing over the floor, wished she were smoke that might dissolve into nothingness, and called out, 'Hold on. Hold on. Christ, just wait.'

But no matter how long she waited she could not steady her hands.

'I WANT YOU TO KNOW,' said Dean Martin, 'that this is going to be a family show. The kind of a show where a man can take his wife and kids, his father and mother, and sit around in a bar and watch.' The studio audience brayed with laughter, Dino smirked, then the band struck up and Dino burst into song. A third of the way through he abruptly stopped just in case you—here he was reminding Bojan and Sonja who usually sat together each week watching this, their favourite show—you happened to be thinking that, having heard all the 'noo toons', you might not go out and buy Dino's new record. He joked with Ken Lane and the inevitable buxom blonde, whose inscribed bare belly Dino read instead of the autocue to introduce the next act. 'Just in case I'm seeing double,' said Dino, face perilously close to the blonde's breasts. Double entendres and triple martinis. Crooning and cleavages. Big names and booze. All equally transitory on the Dean Martin Show, in which Dino was both the old world's hope and its revenge upon the new. Dino don't give a fuck, Bojan would laugh, but unlike Bojan he was without menace. Her father as she wished him, without oppression, without history, without a shadow.

Sonja liked watching Dino with her father and he with her, and they sat together and laughed at Dino's stupid jokes, and envied him his flash wog ways that somehow he had fooled the world into admiring, the ways she had learnt to deny. In the radiating blue hue of the Victrola, she and Bojan shared something and she knew a feeling she would never after be able to describe. But like Dino's jokes, the feeling was growing tired, threadbare.

In the early summer of the previous year they had moved yet again into the place in which they now lived, which was no different from the other places, only a little larger. But it was still a wog flat, still did not feel like a home to Sonja, nor did she think it was ever going to feel like a home. Bojan earned more money now and they had proper mats on the floor instead of blankets, a new purple vinyl lounge upon which Sonja would watch their new black-and-white TV, but Bojan drank more and more and it did not feel like a home.

The winter came and she fancied she had let her body fall asleep with the plants, waiting for the sun to return, because she had nothing better to do than to wait, and Bojan drank more and more and it did not feel like a life to her, and she knew that at some point the waiting would come to an end and her real life begin. The spring of that year was far wetter than normal and everywhere there was the most luxuriant growth, and as Sonja herself grew the final few inches to her adult height, as her body filled out, she smelt the trees and weeds that seemed to be pushing through everything, even the fresh laid bitumen of the road outside. Then the rain abruptly ended and a summer even more remarkable than the spring began, with long harsh hot spells. The plants' growing halted, the weeds withered and the grass died. The sun seemed forever to sit high and burn hard. The land grew quiet and expectant.

As if it knew before it happened.

Tonight, as Dino continued schmoozing away, Bojan was not even there, not even sharing this moment. Sonja watched the show alone, trying to pretend her father was sitting next to her as usual, face puckering up in laughter. She adored the radio, she adored the television. To all the old movies Sonja knew the words; could walk like John Wayne and dance like Ginger Rogers and dangle a cigarette nicked from Bojan between her lips like Bette Davis. She adored that world of no shadows, frameable and predictable, a world in which she knew from the beginning what the outcome would be, in which goodness was rewarded and never punished, where life progressed ever forward and no-one ever had to look back—except for the occasional explanatory flashback—where even sadness was only the excuse for another song, and to all of them Sonja knew the words.

But with her father she seemed to know almost none. Sonja and Bojan now spoke few words with each other and thought in even less. The word 'love'—the one word describing the essential but hidden nature of Sonja's story—had been cast from their minds and their tongues so long ago that neither noticed its peculiar absence. Word, mind you, word, not the notion itself. Their language now was akin to the tools he used: for a practical purpose, they might use words that cut deep like a chisel or words that fell heavily to pound something like a mallet. So there was a certain artistry in their use, it was undeniable. But as they did not use tools for other than their selected purpose, they did not use words unless they were needed to describe, recall, or initiate an activity.

That evening when Sonja returned from her after-school wanderings in the bush that lay in the hills beyond their ribbon of a suburb, she had found her father sitting down at their laminex table pouring turkish coffee from a half-empty pot into a tiny demitasse cup. Around the cup were scattered old black-and-white photographs. It was unusual to see him so: not drinking or working or watching TV, or working *and* drinking, but sitting and thinking.

Then he had swept the photographs up and put them into an old shoebox, then gone outside and stood on the small balcony of his wog flat. He was unchanged from his day's labouring, clad only in a blue singlet and khaki work trousers. He leant against the wall, under the light bulb, smoking a cigarette. The smoke rose slowly up to the yellow light around the naked bulb. He seemed to be thinking.

And then, despite it being Thursday night, Dean Martin Show night, he had gone out for the evening. Sonja found the shoebox of old photographs where Bojan had hidden them at the bottom of his wardrobe. In the shoebox were pictures of people with skis and guns in European alpine country. There were pictures of a woman Sonja knew must be her mother. There was a picture that showed the same woman and Bojan in a posed embrace in front of snow-heavy alps, she holding a starry white flower, them both pressing their lips to either side of it. She was beautiful, Sonja thought, he handsome.

Sonja looked at the photographs and wondered. And had no answers for her many questions, insistent as they were half-formed and not understood by her. She put the shoebox back in the wardrobe. None of it made sense. The photographs looked too much like the movies, and she loved the movies precisely because they were nothing like her life.

Chapter 57

———

1966

DINO WAS NEARING THE END of his show when the front door opened and Bojan staggered in noisily. He was badly drunk. Sonja only glanced up from the TV as he passed her on the way to the bathroom.

'You want your tea, Artie? I cooked kransky klabasha.'

Bojan re-emerged from the bathroom.

'No,' he said. 'I don't want bloody anything.'

'Why do you have to drink so much?'

'Fuck you,' mumbled Bojan, then more loudly, 'Fucken young people think—' but then he lost the train of thought about whatever it was he thought young people did think, and retreated into a ranting that not even he could be bothered taking seriously.

'*Everybody loves somebody sometime,*' Dino crooned from the Victrola, wrapping the show.

'Fuck you!' Bojan mumbled. 'Fuck you—fuck you— fuck you.'

Sonja wanted Bojan, her Bojan, her Artie, not this bottle-emptying echo of someone she had once known.

'You said you wanted me to cook it for you,' she said.

'I do what I fucken want,' Bojan said. 'You do what you fucken want.'

'Even Ken,' Dino said from the Victrola, smiling to Ken as Ken kept tinkling long after Dino had lost all interest and was simply milking the song for a few more laughs, '—ain't that right, Ken?'

As he sidled past Sonja, Bojan accidentally half-fell, half-shoved her, then regained his balance, saying as he did so, 'Where's some bloody drink.' He opened the fridge and took a large bottle of beer out. 'Can't have a bloody beer in peace.'

He flicked the cap off with a knife, and, still standing, stubbly throat pulsing in and out, skulled the entire bottle in a single go. Then he sat down at the kitchen table and looked across at Sonja.

We are strangers, he thought. He watched her sitting perfectly still in the chair and saw nothing in her that he knew to be childlike. All impulse and energy seemed to have left her. He looked at the small, cramped room, redolent of poverty, in which she sat; looked outside and saw someone else's clothesline, and he knew only that tonight he would drink again to forget it all. Life is not life. Children are not children. Fathers are lost and mothers are gone and they cannot find their children, who have, in any case, already departed their bodies.

Ken laughed at Dino's wisecrack and kept playing the grand piano, while Dino schmoozed on, the TV crowd responding to both Dino's arrogant charm and the flashing applause light. 'Dum-de-dum-de dum-de-dum,' hummed Dino, adding, 'I wish I knew who sang this so they could teach me the words.' More cheers and laughter. 'Doo—da—da—doo—da—da—dum.'

'No more, Artie,' Sonja said. 'No more.'

'Fuck off,' said Bojan to the refrigerator, angling his head around just enough to look at her in such a way that it was like he saw nothing, and with a lazy casual action he lobbed the empty beer bottle at Sonja. It was not a violent throw, more an idle gesture of contempt. Perhaps it was hatred not of her but of everything that made him throw the bottle in the strange way that he did. The bottle slowly arced across the room between them, as if scything them apart. It missed Sonja by at least a foot, smashed on the wall behind her, and Bojan saw none of it, because he was already poking back inside the refrigerator for another beer.

There was something about this gesture that greatly humiliated Sonja. It was as if Bojan no longer cared enough even to be violently angry, as if beating her at least betrayed some emotion toward her beyond a relentless self-destruction. His utter indifference to what happened to the bottle after it was thrown—whether it hit Sonja or whether it missed her—hurt in a way she did not expect such a foolish thing to hurt.

After he went to bed, Sonja got up, dressed in jeans, jumper and a grey duffle coat, and went outside, with the vague intention of going for a walk. She was not running away, simply escaping for a while. She walked around the side of the house, and from a window she heard the sound of Bojan's drunken snoring. She turned around and looked at the window for a while, and her face set like a rock. She felt full of loathing for everything, most particularly herself and her life. Bojan's snoring seemed to her to grow louder and more oppressive. He snuffled and hacked and rumbled and she felt she was suffocating in the volcano-mouth of what he was and what he wasn't, that she was bound to him and the lava of his molten sleep was entombing her forever.

She raised one fist, then the other, closed her eyes, slowly shook her head, trying to push the noise away, trying to break out. But the sound of his snoring grew worse, more insistent, more complete and inescapable. If only she could free herself and feel something, anything. Suddenly, unexpectedly, she threw her fists at his bedroom window. The noise of the glass shattering shocked her far more than the sensation of her flesh tearing.

For she felt nothing.

She had grown beyond pain, and she wished to hurt and now she knew nothing hurt. No matter how much she hated herself, lost herself, allowed others to hurt her, or hurt herself, she might never burst the dam that held back her suffering.

She shook. *Nothing hurt.* She felt terrified. *Nothing hurt.* How could she know herself what had happened if she could not even feel this. Her hands were inside his bedroom, her arms outside it, her twitching wrists embedded in the broken glass of the window. Was she dead? Was this hell? Or was she alive? And could this then also be hell? Being alive but not knowing life.

She felt weak. She felt tired. Red-tipped shards of glass broke away and fell to the ground.

Sonja's eyes remained clear, and she watched, unmoved, as her hot blood ran from her wrist onto the cold damp windowsill. She felt weak. She felt tired. She felt nothing. She saw little. She rocked her wrists along the remnant broken glass, as if it were ham she were so slicing. She felt nothing. It did not matter now.

It did not matter when sometime later—a lifetime, a deathtime, an unknown time later—she heard Mrs Heaney find her on the ground and yell for help, then ask, 'Where is your father?' Mrs Heaney, who never swore, or at least not badly like a man, swore terrible things quietly as she cradled Sonja in her lap.

'That useless fucking bastard,' she said in a low slow cursing whisper, then again asked, 'Where is he?'

Sonja knew he was asleep in his bed, but where was he? Where he was, she couldn't say. She couldn't talk. She couldn't tell Mrs Heaney what made no sense: that they were both waiting for the wind to rise one more time.

An ambulance siren later awoke Bojan. Then stopped. He turned on his side and went back to sleep.

And in the silence before the gale, slowly growing in strength, came the pulsing, swirling sound of a heartbeat on a monitor, pushing hard, hard through that darkness.

Chapter 58

1990

THE DRUMMING GREW QUICKER and quicker, an ever more insistent rapidfire pattering, *woosh-wish—woosh-wish—woosh-wish*, and at first the white scratchings of shapes that appeared, merging with other shapes then disappearing in strange jerky motions on the gridlined screen seemed as difficult to place as the loud sounds emanating from the machine. Then, with an unexpected clarity, she understood the sound as that of a beating pulse amidst a washing-machine of white noise, the ultra-scanned amplification of the heart of a five-month-old foetus sailing the ocean of its mother's womb.

Her womb.

Her child.

Sonja gulped.

As the foetus continued to pound out in staticky rhythm its mesmerising heartbeat, one shape, though far from stationary, came to predominate.

A soft, podgy finger appeared in front of the screen and pointed at the white image of her child.

'The foetus seems fine. No sign of placenta praevia.'

Upon the finger a large, somewhat ugly gold ring embossed with a crescent pattern.

'Head and the body, arms, legs, fingers . . . all seems fine.'

The ring-finger disappeared.

'Haemorrhaging?' another voice asked, but Sonja could not find the strength or the energy to look up and see who it was doing the asking. It was a higher-pitched voice. Perhaps that of a younger doctor. Perhaps that of a woman doctor. Perhaps that of her mother. She did not know. She did not care.

'Not for six hours,' said the voice she presumed belonged to the ring-finger. 'It looks as though the edge of the placenta lifted and that caused the excessive bleeding.'

Her vision began to blur, and a figure she had difficulty making out—but she presumed it must be a doctor for he was mostly white and could not therefore be her mother for he was a man and he wore no lace—this figure moved toward her until he seemed to loom threateningly above, like some late-night horror movie figure. He smiled in a grotesque fashion, his voice sounding distorted, distant, as if it was calling from far, far away, from another time and place.

'Ms Buloh? Ms Buloh, you are a very lucky woman. You lost a lot of blood, but you will be okay. And so will your baby.'

Sonja started to shake as if she was about to break down sobbing, though whether it was from relief or disappointment even she was not clear. She did not cry.

You must never cry, she remembered. No matter what happens, you must never ever cry.

'Ms Buloh?'

But she was already going somewhere beyond her body, sliding out of it, for a time at once infinite and limited, feeling both intensely conscious of her surroundings—of the suffocating closeness of the hospital's air, the strange hardness of the gurney mattress, at once unforgiving and comforting, the immodesty of the hospital nightie, cleaving to her body like two loosely strung tea-towels—and at the same time increasingly liberated from these and all other things.

From this world that after a time turned blue then turned green. Then after a further time that was both long and short, that went on forever and had only just begun, the green swished open and Sonja realised she had become the curtain and that she was flying up in the air and folding around a person who had come to see her but couldn't see her because she had become the curtain, and the person who she now knew was Helvi kept on look-ing at the bed—in which lay a very ill-looking woman who she now knew was herself, but couldn't be herself because she was the curtain—and a nurse came in also through the curtain that was Sonja and together the nurse and Helvi looked at the ill woman who was also Sonja, whose face was a waxen grey-green, who looked drained of all life, whose arms hung limply down her sides.

And Helvi said, 'I was so worried, I thought she might die,' and the nurse said, 'No, not now, everything will be fine now. It was close, but it's fine now.'

Chapter 59

1990

Sonja she's mine.

No, fuck what I mean—

Sonja, she's everything and we lived, we lived worse than dogs and I would not want it for a dog and did not want it for her or for me but could not help it that it was her that I had to hit, had to hit to stop this pain, had to drink this pain, had to let her know this pain, had to let her know that I felt this pain, that it was burning me, that it was a red hot knife and it cuts me every night into less than a fucken dog and every morning I've grown back into a man and it won't stop, Madonna Santa, it starts again, that red hot knife starts to cut me back into a dog and Sonja my pain is yours and I must fight it and you must feel it.

I hurt. I hurt. I hurt.

And it never ends. And I am not a dog, am I? For if I were, someone would surely shoot me, would be at least that good, at least show that kindness to me, but you came back and you will not put me down so if I am not a dog, what am I?

Chapter 60

———

1990

WHEN SONJA finally woke to a babble of noise, she felt
weak, but her head was finally clear, and her overriding
desire was simply to recover, to get better and get out of
hospital. Helvi was still sitting at her side, though her
clothes were different, so Sonja presumed that another
day, or perhaps even some days, had passed.

The noise manifested itself as flesh in the form of a
large brown-uniformed woman slashing through the
green curtain, advancing upon Sonja bearing a tray upon
which was arrayed the collection of stainless steel that
denoted a hospital meal.

Helvi put one arm under Sonja and pulled her into
an upright position, stuffing pillows behind her back.
Both Sonja and Helvi looked on conspiratorially as the
orderly placed the meal on the bed table and then left.

Helvi took away the cover of one plastic bowl to
reveal a thin reconstituted soup, in which floated flecks of
a chewy red substance that passed for carrots. In another
was a small puddle of red jelly encircled by a collapsing

edging of package custard, and the main meal took the form of two paper-thin slices of roast lamb next to which puddled some gelatinous gravox and two small mounds, one yellow, of mashed pumpkin, the other white, of mashed potato.

'They bloody poison you,' said Helvi, horrified, quickly covering up what she regarded as a travesty of a meal.

As if out of air Helvi conjured two massive slabs of continental bread. Sonja, moving carefully, leant over and peered down. Helvi was delving into a very old blue vinyl ANA bag which had a picture of a DC-10 flaking off its side. From this venerable give-away, meant only to be discarded some decades previously, Helvi pulled an oil bottle and spattered some oil over the bread. The bottle was returned to the bag, and Helvi's hand re-emerged holding a small vegemite jar. She unscrewed the yellow cap. 'Now,' said Helvi, 'you get better.' And with that she flourished a kitchen knife, which she pushed deep into the vegemite jar. The knife came out piled high with a mass of smashed white pulp, which she thickly smeared over the bread.

'Garlic,' said Helvi. 'Good for the baby, good for the soul.' And while still waggling a finger in the air with her left hand, brought up a thermos full of real coffee from Jiri's bottomless bag. Sonja suddenly grimaced, then the grimace dissolved into a look of confusion. She ran a hand over her belly. 'Coffee is good for the—' said Helvi, mis-understanding Sonja, cupping her hands under her breasts, one hand still clutching the thermos handle '—the milk.' Helvi dropped her hands, nodding seriously.

'Helvi,' Sonja said, 'I think . . . *it* moved.'

'You must eat,' said Helvi. She picked up a slice of garlic-smeared bread and, smiling, passed it to Sonja, but Sonja was too absorbed in her own body to take any notice.

'The baby,' said Sonja in excited wonder. 'The baby just moved.' She turned and looked up at Helvi. 'I felt it kicking me, Helvi.'

'Well, of course,' said Helvi. 'Of course it moved. It'll kick the shit out of you later.' She cackled like an old witch. 'Now, while you can, eat.' And Sonja, without relish but with an undeniable purpose that seemed new to her, took the bread and bit into it. She smiled at Helvi. Then giggled a little, then laughed a lot.

'Oh Christ,' she suddenly said.

'What?' asked Helvi.

'I think, as I was laughing, I just wet myself.'

Chapter 61

1990

BOJAN BULOH might have broken out of this life in some spectacular way, as he had broken out of Slovenia so long ago, spending months secretly climbing the Julien Alps each morning to observe and learn the patterns and routines of the border guards, planning and re-planning, watching how the natural world might betray them in their escape and how it might protect them. Impatient to leave, Maria would ask when they were going. But he was waiting, waiting and waiting longer still till his brother was released from jail, till he felt ready. Working out routes, checking them each day up there in the snow country, then re-thinking, re-calculating. He carried a pair of binoculars his brother had taken off the body of a German soldier, and the binoculars still held the disconcerting warmth of human flesh when he held them close to his eyes. No matter how much it snowed and the wind blew like a thousand knives of ice, the binoculars always felt as warm as blood against his chill eyes. One day he saw through them that rarest of all flowers, the edelweiss, in its most favoured habitat, a cliff. The starry white flower of love that men risked their lives to reach to give to their women. He waited until near darkness when the patrols were changing shifts and, without a rope, climbed out along the cliff face to take it. He did not get home till after midnight to find his family greatly distressed, thinking he had been caught or shot by the guards.

The following evening he gave Maria the edelweiss. With its pointed petals it resembled a mariner's compass. She laid it on a map, and the pointed petal that showed the direction of their route she plucked off and ate in front of him. 'North-west,' she said, slowly rolling her white speckled tongue over her lips.

This curious, for Bojan strangely erotic, gesture, Maria repeated in the Austrian refugee camp two years later. Somehow she had managed to retain the dried flower. This time she laid it upon a map of the world and—in celebration at being finally accepted as emigrants—she plucked the petal that indicated their next destination. 'South-east,' she said, and Bojan looked down at the world in a single page in a schoolchild's atlas and saw that the missing petal would have just touched the northern tip of Australia. And, in turn, he repeated his response. He leant forward to kiss her while slowly running his hand up the inside of her skirted thigh, and as before she let him feel the petal disintegrating into flotsam upon her tongue. But this time she did not push his hand aside. She laughed. 'And when there are no petals,' she said, 'there is nowhere left in the world for us to go.'

So, in a strange coupling Bojan found as troubling as he did exciting, Sonja was conceived.

Bojan might have broken out of his wretched life before, but he was waiting, waiting and waiting longer still, till something—he no longer knew what—happened. Sometimes he was taken with the thought that he ought be dead, that he would be better dead, but the ache he had known those months before they had fled across the Alps was back with him, except now it was vague and without purpose. So he waited for the ache either to grow into something he could make sense of or to disappear and leave him to die.

Sitting on the side of his steel bed, looking less a man and more a bent coat hanger off which hung a faded blue singlet and khaki work trousers, Bojan swayed and thought. In one hand he held a near empty Bundaberg black rum bottle, in the other three old photographs which he grasped like a hand of playing cards. From the very slight rock of his body back and forth it was evident that he was drunk, though how much so it was difficult to know.

There was a raucous knock on the door, and a shout. 'Eh—Bojan—coming to the pub?'

'No,' said Bojan. He paused and drew breath in through his nostrils. 'No. Not tonight. Bloody hell. Piss orf. I got some thinking to do.' Something had turned within him, something had changed him and he had crossed into another land. Even to other wogs he had become a real wog: forever different, alien even to other aliens.

Bojan swayed some more, back and forth, eyes intently fixed on a nothingness in the mid-distance. He put the bottle down and picked up Sonja's letter from the small chipboard chest of drawers. He held the letter in front of him, then rubbed his fingers over it, as if it were braille, as if there was a clue hidden in it, an answer to his wretched dilemma. With one hand he held the letter up to the light, with the other hand he held the photographs similarly, and looked at one swaying handful then the other, as if comparing x-rays, as if able to discern a connection, as though through careful study one might reveal a problem in the other. Finally he placed them all in a neat pile on his lap, and went back to his brooding.

How I long for such queer things, thought Bojan, such strange little things not even big that it might seem wrong or offensive to ask for, but only to feel Maria's breath once more, listen to its song as she slept, hear her snuffling and even snoring and wheezing and sighing in God knows what dreams for who or for what I care not only that it disappeared into the wind and the wind is everywhere and I know her breath is lost within it.

He remembered how when he went to bed with her, she would lie on her side and he would lie behind her, head nuzzling into her back, smelling her and forever thankful to smell her so. Binding memory to desire, the fragrance of her once more returned to him. He remembered his loins on her rump, feeling her power and forever awed to know it, and his top arm running along and up her torso to where his hand would cup the soft

weight of her breast and he would wish to hold that
weight for her forever. He remembered how they would
make love and sometimes it would be wild and he would
excite her greatly and she him and she would groan like
an animal, and it frightened him that her body went
places his was unable to know—and he knew she liked
him far less for having made her feel so. At other times
he excited her less, took fewer liberties with his love-
making and she liked him more though her satisfaction
was greatly reduced and this paradox puzzled him, for he
felt honour bound to pleasure her, but wished her to love
him as he loved her.

There had been a time when he had promised her
foolish things that were not possible: a house made of per-
fume, clothes spun out of songs; and she had promised
him what was possible, that she would work with him and
lie with him and if necessary fight for him if only he
would be with her. And he felt the dried white eidelweiss
petals upon the tip of her tongue and his hand was part-
ing her thighs, her beautiful sweet strong thighs, and he
knew he was falling into the wind and it smelt of the sea
and felt of the sea, and the fingers of his other hand ran
through her hair and then wrapped tight around her hair
and by her hair pulled her head backwards until her
mouth and her throat and his thrusting and her heart and
his desire were all in precipitous alignment and her low
moans unimpeded rose up as if from the earth itself.

After some time there was another knock on the door. A knocking different from before, more restrained, almost polite. Bojan again looked up to the door and yelled, 'Piss orf! Jezuz Chrise . . . I already tell ya. I don't want to go to the bloody pub. I hate the fucken pub.'

There was a second polite knock on the door. Bojan reluctantly got off his bed and a little shakily walked to the door, swearing some more as he did. But when he opened the door Bojan's expression changed from annoyance to surprise. He stopped grumbling, stared at who was standing in his doorway, framed by the darkness. The two men looked at each other, Bojan in shock, Jiri looking not at Bojan's face but at his body, his dress, his stance, as if seeing Bojan for the first time.

'Bojan,' said Jiri, 'I've been telephoning the canteen for weeks. You are never here. That's what they say. You are not to be found.'

Bojan stood back from the doorway and indicated his room with an open hand, waving at it in an impatient gesture.

'You comin in or what?'

Jiri walked in. Bojan offered him the one chair in the room and the rum bottle. Jiri shook his head, declining both. His mission was serious, and his manner accordingly awkwardly formal. Bojan sat back on his bed, and waited.

'Bojan . . .' Jiri began, but then halted. Ran his big full fingers through the few long thin strands of hair that remained to him. He was glistening from the rain. Bojan did not speak. Jiri looked at him and wondered whether this was not the most foolish thing he had ever done in a life that had known its fair share of folly, driving the old Corolla near six hours in the rainy dark on the treacherous windy road from Hobart to Tullah, to tell Bojan what he had to tell him, then to turn around and drive six hours back. But there was no escaping it, for it had to be said.

'She nearly died.'

Bojan skulled from the rum bottle and the rum tasted of nothing, ran down his throat as easy as the lukewarm tea they served by the gallon in the single men's mess, and he knew he could have finished the bottle there and then, and wanted to, and start another and another and another and finish them all and hopefully himself in the process, rather than listen to what Jiri would tell him. But he took the bottle from his mouth, because he had to say something, anything.

'I know that. So?' And having unburdened himself of the necessity of reply, Bojan took another lengthy swig.

'You must stop, Bojan.'

Bojan let the rum bottle slowly fall from his lips, then quietly, slowly, as if he were talking of someone else rather than himself, spoke.

'How can it stop? You so clever you know, Jiri, you tell me—how?'

He remembered all the times he thought it would stop, how he hoped if he could turn his soul to ice nothing would penetrate, how if he anaesthetised himself enough with drink he would feel no pain when he fell over or when he got hit in the bar, and that it would then follow that this other pain, that had no physical reality, would also no longer be felt.

'It's like a knife,' said Bojan. His eyes filled with tears. 'Like a knife that won't stop turning in my guts.'

His voice trailed off. Then the rum leapt up his throat like a flame, his whole body began to tremble, quivering under the weight of the most enormous anger.

'You tell me, Jiri, please, please, I beg you, you tell me—how can it ever stop?'

Chapter 62

___

1967

THE TRUTH WAS the knife had been in there a long time, longer than Bojan cared to remember. The truth was that the knife had been slashing and shredding back and forth, and it—him, her, them—had in consequence all been falling apart for some time now, all heading toward a moment, an action that both would instinctively understand meant that it was over. It wasn't the things that were said, but the growing mountain of things that were unsaid, the way the silence between them which had once bound them together like hoops of steel had now reformed into an ever widening abyss.

Put your back into the plough, Jiri said, pull harder on the net, Jiri would tell him, do not give up. But it was beyond trying or not trying because it was beyond them, because it was not even about them, not about things they could grasp in their hands and shape like a piece of wood, but greater things which grasped them. And though neither understood this, both knew it intuitively, and both waited, as he had waited once before in a cold construction camp in the middle of nowhere, assailed by a growing feeling of horror. Maybe Jiri was right and they were wrong to abandon themselves to a larger destiny, but nothing they did seemed to add up to anything and their agony only returned each morning, stronger, worse, more unapproachable.

So on that still Saturday morning when the only sound in the world seemed to be the transistor radio in its dark leather pouch purring Patsy Cline from the top of the refrigerator, when Sonja opened the door from her bedroom and walked into the main room carrying a small suitcase, Bojan was not pretending to ignore her. He sat in what was to be their kitchen only a little longer, drinking turkish coffee from a tiny demitasse cup yet again, looking at the old photographs of his wife and, though she noticed the photographs at which he was looking, he simply did not notice her.

She watched him and thought of the times they had known together, and how there ought to have been stories about it she could one day tell her own children, but there were no such stories, no happy stories she could at that moment recall, only sad stories that did not deserve the honour of being told. And perhaps the saddest story of them all was the one from only a few days before.

Sonja had held a sixteenth birthday party for herself. Bojan was drinking too much to either oppose or support the idea. She asked for money and he threw his wallet to her and told her to take what she wanted, take it fucking all for all he cared. She wanted the party to be like the adults' parties she imagined, not like the ones she had witnessed. She baked some cakes, not kids' cakes, but two lush chocolate cakes and a cheesecake of the type Australians liked. She bought salamis and cheeses and good bread and arrayed them beautifully on the plates. She made Bojan buy her four bottles of Kaiser Stuhl Cold Duck. She bought chips and peanuts and filled little bowls with them. She invited her friends, and she invited some more she only vaguely knew, but liked.

In the hours preceding the party she changed four times, torn between the beauty of her favourite—and only—dress, or the casualness of her only jeans. Casualness won. She asked Bojan to please not drink and for once he listened and for once he did not touch a drop. They waited watching TV. Sonja smiling and laughing and even Bojan unable to resist the infectious high spirits of his daughter. They waited, and as they did so joked and played foolish games, he holding a potato chip over each eye and making a loud buzzing noise pretending to be a blowfly. This is how it ought to be, she thought but did not say. Then, more boldly: This is how it will be, and the thought grew like a confident sapling into the notion that their lives were poised on the brink of a momentous change. Perhaps, after all, something better was possible.

They waited until 6 p.m., and when no-one had arrived half an hour later she checked the invitation, but the time and the address were unmistakeable. They waited until seven and her smile disappeared and her laughter ceased. They waited until eight and then Bojan went to the fridge and opened his first bottle for the day.

Half an hour later she changed out of her jeans.

People made excuses like people do. Some were good reasons, some were not. But at school the following day she heard a girl she did not even know tell another girl in a stage whisper behind Sonja's back, 'The wog sleeps with her, the wog and her, you know what I mean,' and Sonja turned and asked what did she mean? and the girl told Sonja that she meant what everybody knew, the reason no-one had gone to Sonja's sixteenth party.

So the following day Sonja did not return to school but instead walked into town and with the money Bojan gave her for housekeeping bought a blouse that had the pattern of brambles and the colour of cream, and that was edged with lace, and she never wore it until that morning she stood there in their kitchen waiting for her father to look up at her so that she might tell him what suddenly seemed always to have been inevitable.

Chapter 63

1967

BOJAN TURNED and smiled slightly. He was calm, defeated. Knew that he could no longer pretend to hold the fragmenting pieces together. That even his anger and rage could not halt the disintegration. Beyond the bottle, nothing left to hang onto.

'I am leaving,' was all she said.

He laughed. He smiled a little more, albeit grimly. He was ready, trying to accept what fate presented him with grace. He had not known much dignity in his life, and he wanted to have it at this moment. Maybe it was pride. Maybe it was only trying to prove to himself that if she left something remained in the exploding chaos that would ensue.

'You better take this,' Bojan said. He stood up, and from a cupboard above the refrigerator he produced a box wrapped in fancy paper which he handed to Sonja. He had bought it for her birthday but had in his drunkenness forgotten all about it. Too ashamed to admit his folly and give it to Sonja late, he had saved it for this moment that he had been anticipating far longer than she had been planning it. 'Don't open it now,' he said. 'You'll need what's in there. I have no need of it. You have every need.'

He held the box out toward her. His eyes—broken dowel joints set in a splintering piece of furniture—caught Sonja's, but only briefly. She accepted the box, leant across, gave him an awkward kiss on his cheek which he showed no sign of wanting or accepting, then farewelled him in Slovene.

'Adio, Artie,' she said.

Bojan Buloh looked at her, at his beautiful child and he felt so much love for her he thought he might shrivel into nothingness, as if his love were a fire and he only the ashes of its burning. Because his love for her was something beyond him, enduring where he was transitory, solid where he was melting into air. He wished her to stay, and he wanted her to go immediately, before he came between his love and her.

He replied in Australian.

'Goodbye, Sonja,' he said.

He made no movement toward her, and she was grateful that he too wished to avoid any acknowledgement of what they felt. So they didn't touch. She turned around and had begun to walk out when Bojan Buloh suddenly cried out to her.

'Sonja!'

She stopped, swung around and saw him holding his hands out in front of him, not begging but moving crazily, as if trying to shape a mystery into something knowable.

His mouth too was moving, but no sound was forthcoming. He stood before her, a potter with no clay, a tongue with no words. Then—as if recognising their own absurdity—his arms abruptly stopped moving, fell away, and his gaze followed them, away from her to the floor. Then Bojan's mouth rediscovered speech.

'Sonja!' he cried out—the last word he was to speak to her for twenty-two years. For upon lifting his eyes upwards searching for a voice of absolution and penance, he saw nothing—nothing, save an empty doorframe.

Sonja was gone.

And with her gone, he finally found the words for what he had long wished to tell her. 'You and me,' he said in a quiet, halting voice, 'we lived, we lived worse than dogs. I am sorry. I don't expect you to come back. Believe me I never wished it, the drinking, the fighting, these wog flats, sometimes things happen in your life and, despite everything, despite your hope, you can't change them.'

And his confession complete, his eloquence abandoned him as rapidly as it had come.

Before going to the fridge for his first bottle for the day, oblivious to the early hour, he said only one thing to the breeze washing in from the world outside.

'We came to Australia,' said Bojan Buloh, 'to be free.'

Chapter 64

———

1967

BACK THEN, it was the summer of the great fire the monstrous like of which even the oldest could not remember and which the youngest, huddled like nervous whiting in the shallows of beaches along the great Derwent and Huon rivers, would never forget. Early one morning a great wind had begun to blow, and as the day continued the sun burnt hotter and the wind grew fiercer and the sky darker and a few sparks grew into a number of small fires and the small fires grew into numerous bigger bushfires and then the many bushfires joined together in invincible alliance. People stopped trying to fight what was now a single monstrous fire-storm as large as the land and the sky joined, and realised that the best they would be able to do now was simply escape the terrible conflagration that was eating the island. As Sonja observed it from their Moonah home—the fire forcing itself into the very city—watching the air turn into smoke, seeing it turn as dark as night as ash filled the sky and the heavens rained cinders, she had found herself feeling both terrified and excited.

Before the sun rolled earthwards that terrible day like a huge ball of boiling blood, over a thousand homes were to burn to the ground, countless creatures, domestic and wild, to be incinerated, and sixty-two people to perish. In the following weeks, in whichever direction Sonja looked, the view always ended in the most silent and desolate blackness. Nothing was like anything people had ever known. The town was numbed, full of refugees who had lost everything in the moving maelstrom of flame that had sucked half the island into its transforming heart. The once blue forested mountain that backdropped the town was now a black blasted rock. Where once had been vast forests, a dense and mysterious dank green world, now only the trees' skeletal essence remained, great stags arising from the scorched earth like accusing pillars of salt and beneath them soot and ash. And beneath that black earth? Beneath it, Sonja found when she had one morning walked into the hills and scratched at the ground, the first evidence of new life—embryonic green shoots of the new forest.

Because of the fire Sonja had come to think that things could change utterly. And now she wanted that change, wanted to join the refugees and leave everything she had known. She wanted to leave this land of water and become as the fire itself.

Back then, time was different and a childhood was not part of a lifetime but several lifetimes rolled into a single interminable dusty morning. Things were not as they are now, and it is a mistake to think of people then in the way you think of people now. Standing there that morning waiting at the bus stop with her skinny legs in a pair of cheap skin-tight slacks and her thin torso in the lace-edged blouse, holding in one hand a gift-wrapped box and in the other an old cardboard suitcase, Sonja wasn't like the woman she would soon become.

Something had consumed everything Sonja was. She felt what Mrs Maja Picotti had suspected in her prayers, that her soul had departed her body. Sonja could have complained most bitterly about her life, but that was not how she saw it or even how she felt it. She felt as if there was nothing encased within her but ash. And as she boarded the bus she saw that her bare arms were already covering in smuts blowing down from the desolate hills beyond, so recently burnt into nothingness in the cataclysm, and when she shook, then rubbed her arm the greasy soot only smudged into blackness.

The bus driver looked up at his rear-view mirror. Behind him the sun shone through the dirty windows of the bus and shafts of light illuminated the dust that slowly spiralled within. He saw that the bus was empty save for the thin, young girl, sitting up the back, who by trying to dress as an adult had, he thought, succeeded only in accentuating her youth.

Sonja undid the wrapping around Bojan's present. Inside she found a wooden music box of Asian origin, black lacquer coated, a cheap thing that must have cost far too much. She opened the box. It had a lid inlaid with mirrors and a base of red felt jewellery compartments. Its centrepiece was a ballerina figure that rotated around a flat round glass mirror when the clockwork mechanism was wound up.

In a side compartment were five twenty-dollar notes wrapped around an old photograph.

Sonja unravelled the notes, put them in a compartment at the bottom of the box, and gazed at the photograph. It was of Bojan and Maria at Butlers Gorge, with Maria holding a baby—Sonja—on her hip. Sonja had never seen the photograph before. In it her parents were happy. She smiled: they had been happy as she always knew they had been happy, even if it had only been for a short time, even if it had been only for a year, for a few months, a week, a day, even if it had only been for the moment that photograph was taken, they had been happy and had known happiness together. And then her smile vanished and she wanted to cry, but she didn't.

Sonja wound up the mechanism, and watched the ballerina as she pirouetted and circled around the miniature mirrored glass floor, while the clockwork mechanism played 'Lara's Theme' from *Dr Zhivago*. She watched the ballerina's figure in multiple reflections in the mirrors inlaid diagonally in the lid, as if a wondrous company of dancers had been summoned into existence solely for her.

Back then, Hobart was empty, and the emptiness was exacerbated by the vast violence of the fire that had come upon the place like the most terrible war, and a huge silence wrapped itself around everything, even around large buses lumbering through the town with only a handful of passengers all lost in their journeys, even around Sonja, heading into the heart of Hobart with the intention of leaving it forever, a music box open and playing upon her lap, watching the toy ballerina and her reflections continuing dancing around the music box's interior of red felt and mirrors, watching several lifetimes suddenly finish with all the unexpected abruptness of a car smash—and there was no sound in that silent cocoon other than that of the clockwork mechanism melancholically chiming 'Lara's Theme'.

In that magic cavern of mirrors, Sonja saw the spinning dancer dissolve into new forms: of herself at eight, twirling around in her communion dress on the Michniks' kitchen table; of herself, older, in her new homemade pink party dress circling on the kitchen table and dancing with Bojan. Then that too was lost as the clockwork mechanism ran down and all that remained was the toy ballerina ever more jerkily pirouetting. The music slowed, grew lonelier and lonelier until the last chime sounded and the tiny toy ballerina stopped altogether, though her arms remained held beautifully aloft, her face frozen into a perpetual smile, her left thigh permanently drawn up and out, her left foot forever touching her right knee with its perfectly pointed toes.

If only I could become that toy ballerina, thought Sonja, if only I could be forever frozen in a single beautiful dance, circling within a circle forever.

There is no going back, Sonja thought. Wood and lace. There is none, she thought. That was a luxury reserved for others. Wood and lace, both gone, forever. As Sonja closed the box, as the mirrors gave way to the black lacquer casing, as the ballerina was felled by the closing lid, several lifetimes and a dreadful silence came to an end. Sonja looked up and out and felt the bus's labouring diesel engine rumbling up through the shuddering seat into her body.

In the silence of Hobart then that is not like any town in the world now, the only sound was that final chimed note of that music box's song.

Outside the gentlest of breezes lifted a swirl of ash, the driver cursed the black smuts sullying his windscreen and, beside the road, feathering up through fecund soot, the smallest of yellow-green shoots began pushing toward the light.

Chapter 65

1967

BOJAN BULOH sat alone in his kitchen as he had done since the morning, brooding dark, deep thoughts. Maybe then he saw things he did not wish to see. Whether he saw monsters or pestilence or the war or only his own inability to decipher, to understand anything of all that he had seen and knew only as a malevolent mystery, it is difficult to know. Normally such feelings were transitory only, and he would drink determinedly through the day they beset him and several thereafter to ensure he was properly rid of them forever. But this feeling could not be so easily dissolved.

The kitchen was filled with the languid light of a late summer's early evening. His demitasse coffee cup was empty and he upturned it on a saucer. After letting it drain for a time he turned it right side up and peered into the resulting pattern of coffee grounds to read his own fortune.

Bojan Buloh stared at the laminex tabletop, the cup, the prophesying grounds within it, the assorted objects

that to him seemed to bear no relation to one another—
the ashtray with smoking butt, the photographs randomly
laid, his right hand. His eyes could only see an abstract
array of forms and colours. They could see no pattern, no
future foretold. They saw only a terrible chaos without
reason or consequence, an unending storm of unconnected pain. And within his head the wretched clockwork
'Lara's Theme' would not stop sounding.

Christ, I wish it wasn't this way, thought Bojan
Buloh. I wish I didn't hear that fucken clockwork song
playing over and over. And I wish it wasn't this way and I
wish it would just shutup and I wish I wasn't this way I
wish.

The extended fingers of his right hand trembled as
they rose off the laminex and were drawn over the top of
the cup to hide the awful secrets revealed by the coffee
grounds. The fingers slowly curled—as if the hand itself
were in agony—into a shaking fist in the middle of which
was clasped that small coffee cup.

With a sudden, violent movement he raised his fist—
the infernal cup within it—into the air and brought it
crashing down on the table. As his fist hit the table it
opened out like a flower briefly blossoming, fingers splaying like petals, the cup for the brief moment before
smashing the stamen. The cup shattered, pieces of broken
china flying from out beneath Bojan's now flattened
hand.

He no longer saw chaos. The storm had ended, the
song finally over.

Blood pulsed out from beneath his spread hand, and with a strange feeling approaching tranquil terror Bojan watched his blood pool around the scattered fragments of a life foretold.

And I wish, he thought, and I wish and I wish and I wish.

Chapter 66

1990

JESUS! thought Bojan Buloh.

How little he remembered of Maria, so little he kept on mistakenly thinking he was seeing her. Sometimes when visiting Hobart he would see a face in a crowd—but on closer examination discover it was not her body below; sometimes he would catch a glimpse of a body—a gesture of fingers, a swing of hips—but on chasing the small distinctive motion discover that the face joined to the hands or the hips was not hers. As if something of her continued to echo mournfully in strange and curious moments. As though her presence was too powerful to have simply disappeared so, and the world formed curious vaporous moulds of odd parts of her.

Sometimes the woman he had chased down the street would turn at his voice and when she saw his face—that was no longer a face but an unanswerable question—her expression would change from that of bewilderment to fright. And once, the woman who turned had a face that was most wickedly deformed, covered in pig-like flaps of flesh with one eye missing. She said nothing, only meeting his pitiless stare with her own, as if recognising herself in what she saw. And then she slapped him hard across his face and like all the others walked away.

Like an incarcerated lunatic the white light cast by the single electric bulb bounced around the gloss-painted walls of his room, bleaching Bojan Buloh, so that his blue-checked flannelette shirt, khaki work trousers, and thongs, his very body and face all seemed faded and drained. Sitting without movement on the side of his bed, he did not appear drunk, though he was.

He listened to the endless rain falling forever upon the tin roof, heard the dull drip from the sagging gutters building to a heaving rush then relaxing then building again, and was grateful for the way in which this rhythm of the rain blanketed out almost all other sounds from outside. He stopped staring at the black hole that was his window and returned his gaze to the two black-and-white photographs he held in his hand.

Who had she been? thought Bojan Buloh. Sometimes a foolish notion would possess him that he even recognised the outline of her lips in the greasy red lipstick smudge on a crushed cigarette filter still smouldering in a pub ashtray, but upon looking up the departing woman was never her. Nor was it the woman whose profile momentarily mocked his memory in its similarity; nor was it another, whose voice was the same, so achingly the same he thought burning oil was being poured into his ears and searing its way into his poor brain.

Very hesitantly, as if it were some tarot card predict-
ing a dreadful fate he wished not to know but was
doomed to suffer, he placed one of the two old photographs upon the fading acrylic quilt, that had once blos-
somed brightly with iridescent purple irises. The
photograph was of Maria, holding the baby Sonja at
Butlers Gorge.

Who had Maria been? Sure as he wanted to be, he
was increasingly unsure. For he thought he wished to
remember, but really he worked incessantly upon forgetting her completely, scared lest, like sanding a piece of
wood too long, he would ruin what impressions he still
had of her if he ever dared focus upon them. Without
being able to admit it he felt that somewhere within his
mind, somewhere mysterious and remote, hidden far, far
away for its own safety the whole memory still remained,
and that these traces of the past, though complete and
intact, were exceedingly fragile, and would break into a
thousand pieces of dust if he tried to extricate them.
Somewhere deep within him she remained, and it troubled him greatly, this knowledge of an irretrievable
memory that was answerable only to its own law of recall
and never to his powerful desires. Something within him
was not subservient to his powerful animal will and it
both distressed him and gave him the strength to continue
living. Who had she been?

He placed the second photograph onto his bedcover.
In it a much younger man whom he had once been held
the baby Sonja at Butlers Gorge. Bojan slid the photograph

of him holding Sonja, and the photograph of Maria holding Sonja together, until they overlapped so that they looked like a single picture. Like the photograph that was missing, the photograph he had given Sonja when she left home, of a family that had once been and no longer was— of Bojan and Maria and the baby Sonja together.

He shuffled the photographs together, stood up, and put them back into an old shoebox, upon the top of which lay Sonja's letter.

The only thing worse than working was not working, thought Bojan Buloh. If he drank enough he would feel like a man without a shadow. So he told Pavel. 'The only man without a shadow is a dead man,' replied Pavel. Which was why at that moment he wished to be back within the womb of his work, within the joinery shop, within the entombing noise of bandsaws and planing machines and drills and extractor fans, comforted by the dust and wood shavings and stench of adhesive, a place within which it was sometimes possible to dissolve into a world of making. In the joinery shop they made nothing flash, only the ordinary things, the cupboards and wardrobes and tables and drawers for the new hydro villages, for the offices of the staff, for the single men's quarters that housed more and more of their own kind, the ordinary things for the ordinary people. Sometimes when he knew exactly where he was and who he was, Bojan Buloh botched joins and made things ugly especially for them, made his hate for them into those doors that jammed and desks that rocked and drawers that were not square.

'Look at this,' Pavel said to Bojan Buloh one day, pointing at a piece of chipboard. 'All them little splinters of scrap wood—that's us.' But what was it that held us together? Bojan Buloh wondered. Made us something that might matter?

And Bojan Buloh thought about this you see, as he worked in that large, loud neonlight-lit workshop, he thought about what Pavel meant by saying they were wood, and he felt lost again, so terribly lost.

And then he started making things for everybody else who he worried might be lost like him, and he made them tables and wardrobes and cupboard doors no longer with hate but with love, a poultice for their sad wounds, good solid things that would not let them down when everything else in life had failed, and he hoped that people might feel it in the smoothness of the wood, in the careful edging of the laminex, in the sturdiness of the chipboard, in the straightness and correctness of the angles; might maybe know that he knew they had seen their children die and their mothers never return and had buried their fathers too young, had watched innocents executed as he had, watched men go mad, good men and bad men alike, watched their sisters give themselves to a soldier for a frozen turnip, seen what he had never wished to watch, a man lashed with timber put through a sawmill. Bojan Buloh did not care whether they knew or not that the chipboard was held together with his tears and the laminex with his love and every day he was smuggling out of that cavernous workshop his message to them all, just as he had once run messages hidden in hollowed-out onions for the partisans, and the message was that others knew—*others knew*—and all that they had together, the one thing they shared, that allowed them to be human, to be different from the mad drunk dogs everybody thought they were was knowing that this happened not just to him but to them all—and he told it all in the tables and wardrobes and cupboard doors he made, and he tried to tell it all with love.

Bojan Buloh picked his daughter's letter up, passed it slowly across his cheek, as if its touch might possibly offer the promise of a caress, put the letter to his nose and sniffed it, as though its scent might impart to him its hidden meaning.

Maria, thought Bojan Buloh. My Maria.

Chapter 67

1990

BOJAN'S DOOR WAS OPEN. Inside, Bojan was at work. Arrayed around his normally tidy room were tools, pieces of timber, and furniture in various stages of construction. On the card table an unopened bottle of beer. A bedroom transformed into a workshop. Bojan gave a quick final sand to a turned piece of wood. Then he fitted it into a long piece of timber containing a number of identical turned spigots, to form part of a half-finished cot.

The other single men who each weekend wandered back and forth outside, carrying washing, stopping to yarn and smoke, no longer saw the old wog drunk at the pub. On the rare occasion they glanced into his room they saw him only as he was captured in the shafts of sunlight tumbling through the small window, as a silhouette, working amidst rising spirals of dust motes, as if he were erasing himself from their world.

As he worked, as his hammer drummed and his saw zipped and his drill whined, Bojan grunted and groaned and swore and wheezed. No sound other than these, that of a man labouring. No sight other than this, that of an outline, back bent, head and arms and wood entwined and one.

Chapter 68

———

1990

BOJAN BULOH felt the mist sitting low in that treacherous marsh of a town that was Tullah, a fetid swamp in which water and men festered in a bleak valley's sag, a rotting hammock slung between high blue mountains, and was grateful to feel it, to feel the blanketing white wetness reducing his horizon only to that of his FJ, upon the roof of which he was tying furniture.

The mist dampened Bojan Buloh's clothes, made them sit heavy and wriggly upon his flesh like snakes. 'You don't know what trouble a daughter is,' he said to the Italian who was helping with the tying on of the tarp over the furniture. As Bojan Buloh stretched and tightened the ropes, the snakes writhed over him. And then he laughed. 'And I don't fucken know either. Know fucken nothing that's what I fucken know. Know there's nothing left up here,' Bojan Buloh said, tapping his head. 'It's not right, but I can't remember things. Now that's a funny thing.'

'Are you going to tighten the bolts?' asked the Italian, pointing to the antiquated rusty roof-rack.

'They fine,' said Bojan.

'Better than the car,' said the Italian, who was rightly sceptical of the FJ's capacity to make such a long trip with such a heavy load. 'You sure you don't want my Valiant?'

The Italian's concerns were not unfounded. The FJ blew so much smoke it looked like a mobile bushfire; the steering was terrible; and there were bags of cement in the boot to help minimise the body roll, one bag of which Bojan had broken into to make a concrete mix that he had then poured down the front passenger side door to end its problem of rust. The speedo hadn't worked for years; the odometer spun erratically as if it were the FJ's mind; sometimes meditative and unmoving, at other times racing quicker than an olympic clock. The grey hydro blanket kept falling off the ripped front seat it was meant to cover, exposing horsehair and rusty wire coils. The rubbers on the doors had long since perished, and had been replaced with duct tape run around the inside of all but the driver's door. This served to stem rather than end the problem of leakage, the car still dripping whenever it rained, and the interior had the humid closeness and scent of humus more often associated with a greenhouse than a car. The FJ held together with the fibreglass bog that had been roughly shoved into its many dents, the silicon poured into its ever growing rust holes, and a foolish feeling on Bojan's part that the car would get him wherever he wished to go, because his will and the FJ's had at a distant point merged. To get rid of it, as the Italian and a few other fools sometimes advocated, filled him with a dread others might know only at the prospect of amputation. Bojan shook his head.

'Why I want your bloody Valiant?'

The mist was now so heavy Bojan Buloh's face was running with water. It ran over his face, shaping his nose and cheekbones and reminding him what he was, what the awful shape of him was. A mindless moss upon the face of this earth.

'You must care for her a lot anyway,' said the Italian. His eyes seemed particularly large and dog-like that day. For the Italian did not even have an estranged daughter. He had a wife and one son who had both died immemorably in a car smash some years before. Nothing remained of his wife and son, not even the road they died upon, which long ago had a new four-lane highway built over it.

I don't know whether I care or don't care, thought Bojan Buloh. 'I'm just going to Hobart, that's all I know,' he said to the Italian. Maybe I should care, but I don't know what the word means, thought Bojan Buloh.

'I care for Fabrizio,' said the Italian. 'For Adriana.' His eyes seemed then to water, though whether it was tears or mist droplets or embarrassment at his confusion of English tenses in speaking of his long dead son and wife whose souls were lost upon a road it was no longer possible to find, it was impossible to know. For it could as well have been anger at having nothing left to cleave to, neither a life nor even a place of death.

But, thought Bojan Buloh, maybe some know at least a few things. Believe something. Care for one thing, even if it is no more.

But not me.

Not anything. Not anymore. I am only an old tree at the edge of a new hydro lake, thought Bojan Buloh, full of canker and parasitic insects, its base rotted almost out by the rising waters, its crown no longer luxuriant but only heavy.

Waiting.

But for what, he did not know.

The sun was sinking and Bojan wanted to make at least the first hour of his journey in light. He made one last check of his knots which tied the blue polytarp over its cumbersome load on the roof-rack. His thick fingers plucked the ropes' tension and momentarily held it as he drew breath.

Then let go. Then opened the car door, got in and kicked the motor over. He said nothing to the Italian, only nodded.

For now it was time to begin the journey back.

And when he reached third gear at the bottom of the hill, he looked down the road, marvelled at the speed of a car—even an ancient FJ—fleeing so easily, and wondered whether anything good could come of so much that was bad.

Chapter 69

─────

1990

BOJAN BULOH drove down the twisty road to Rosebery and then on to Queenstown and in the last of the light turned eastwards, making his way up the serpentine road that clung at dizzying heights from that sad town's bald mountains. Somewhere past the ghost town of Linda he switched on his lights, and soon after, when the rain squalls hit, his windscreen wipers. As he climbed up mountain passes and slowly came down their treacherous flanks through that vast peopleless land, an occasional bolt of lightning lit up the FJ and he would momentarily glimpse the wild country through which he was journeying.

The rain came down heavier and heavier.

If he had not been so intent upon his journey Bojan probably would have turned back long before, for the rain now fell not in drops, or even sheets but as a vertical lake and the FJ's windscreen wipers had little effect. His visibility became so bad that he ended up crawling for well over an hour in first gear, which only exacerbated the problem as the wipers, which ran off the engine, slowed down with the car.

Beyond seeing, the rain scrubbed the mountains and forests and filled the rivers. Moving things that did not want be moved but whose destiny it was to be reshaped and reformed.

Bojan's resolve finally began to falter. His spirits, fragile in any case, were further lowered by the steady dripping of water inside the FJ, leaving him damp and chilled. What he was undertaking was hard, so hard, and he did not know if he was strong enough. Doubts fell heavier than any rain. What if she did not wish to see him? What if she did but they fought once more, worse than ever, and he saying terrible things about her he never even thought? At the best what would he achieve with his ridiculous offerings which to her eyes no doubt would appear ugly?

And then a little past Tungatinah, as he was approaching Tarraleah, he found himself overwhelmed by the ineluctable desire to finally return to the one place he had vowed never to return. Why that night of all nights such a strange passion came upon the sad, soggy Bojan Buloh, remains as inexplicable now as it was improbable then. Perhaps he was unknowingly avoiding in his own mind the issue of whether he would—or would not—carry through his mission of finding Sonja. Certainly the conjunction of extraordinary events that was to follow was not foretold. There were no omens, no harbinger, nothing whatsoever that could be construed as portending what was about to take place. Even if there had been, it is doubtful if Bojan Buloh, labouring under the draw-backs of bad eyes coupled to the practical limitations of the FJ—bad lights, worse windscreen wipers and no demister—would have noticed them. But when the sign indicating the turn off from the highway to Butlers Gorge was dimly illuminated in his headlights, it was simply as if he were being washed there by the rain, and he was some distance down the rough gravel road before he even fully comprehended what he was doing.

And then, realising where he was going, still he did not consider why. He only thought that if it was to be in the darkness, in the terrible rain, so much the better. He would return but the night and the weather meant that he would not stay so long that it would trouble him.

So the poor lights of the FJ described candle-lit curves upon the sweeping gravel track that led back to where he had left so long ago.

As he approached the rise leading to the dam he became aware that far below the car, even though he could not see it, the Derwent River was in massive flood, huge rapids crashing through the rain and over the sound of his whirring, steaming engine. The gutters on the side of the road ran as rivers and the river far below ran as a huge cataract.

And then there it was in his headlights, and he was shocked by what he saw. He knew of course—how could he not know?—that dams were not meant to spill except under the most exceptional circumstances. Water was money, and water spilling was money washing away, water that could never be retrieved to make power. Dammed river systems were managed to ensure that they never flooded, that their whole cycle was one of exploited restraint, of constant, never varying flows. This dam, which he had with his sweat helped raise so many years ago, whose concrete felt entwined with his very flesh, whose form with his soul had set like rock—this dam was meant to hold everything within. But there it was, water falling with a fury, and he thought he had never seen anything so extraordinary in his life. The dam was spilling, a mountain of water avalanching down the spillway to end in a violent white maelstrom so huge houses would disappear at the point where the flume met the river bed.

Bojan Buloh got out of the FJ, stretched, shook himself, then, although he was quickly becoming drenched, undid his fly and relieved himself into the gutter that roared alongside the car. He watched his foamy urine race off to join the cataract in the blackness below.

He did not see—how even in light, far less such darkness could he?—the fissure lines, at first only a suggestion of a rupture, so thin that one might need a microscope to see them. Perhaps it was that curious thing so inadequately described as a sixth sense; an animal awareness of impending danger—

Suddenly he turned and tried to run for the car, yet try as he might he could not run, could not even move, for Bojan Buloh found that he had turned into concrete. But behind him a huge wild river was pressing and he was breaking, so slowly and inexorably breaking, and what he had held back for so many years was no longer able to be contained.

The fissures were opening into thread-thin fractures, and the penned-up water was pushing hard, infiltrating—countless tons of water pushing the dam face ever outwards. The fractures were expanding into cracks and the cracks growing ever larger and the water like some caged animal that had recognised its time now pushed the pieces, at first pebbles then boulders of concrete outwards with the force of missiles.

When the first ominous yet strangely dull thud of concrete collapsing came to Bojan's ears through the muting rain, he did not know what it was finally cracking into pieces. He did not see—how in such darkness could he?—how could he see when it was he also that there and then began to fall apart? He who had been stone and water bursting into dust and vapour. He who had been inert, without movement, was now riding the wind, was now running, and without knowing how, reforming into a different person sitting in the FJ desperately gunning the engine.

Bojan Buloh had driven only a few hundred metres when he came to a junction where a second road branched off and turned back upriver, up a steep hill toward a lookout on a ridge above the dam wall.

He knew the main road ran down the river valley for some kilometres. To follow it downriver, fleeing the collapsing dam and the avalanche of water that would follow, at least had the virtue of momentum. In a car

Bojan thought he might—if he could just go fast enough—be able to outrun the flood and leave it all behind.

But his right foot seemed to have a separate idea, as indeed did his entire body, for while he continued contemplating his chances of escaping by accelerating down the valley ahead of the damburst, his body knew that there was no time to think. His right foot leapt from accelerator pedal to brake and the FJ lurched violently, half-slewing, half-skating around 180 degrees and his body was already ready, one arm crunching the gearstick back up into second, the other riding the steering wheel's wild gyrations. The FJ lurched uphill, an old trout ungracefully leaping back toward the dam. But the second gear was inadequate to the climb and the engine suddenly cut out, and with it the car lights.

Darkness slashed Bojan Buloh's eyes, and in a lightless world all he could hear was the most terrible roaring, as if a mountain were falling. His stomach went watery, his breathing hard. He twisted the ignition key with such force he bent it in the ignition barrel. The motor kicked over slowly, without determination once, twice, then came to life with a roar as he flattened his foot to the floor. The engine screeched but beneath the car he could feel a different, much greater vibration.

For the very earth was shuddering.

The back wheels spun, then making proper contact with the gravel, the old car leapt forward howling up the rutted gravel road. Bojan Buloh was pushing the ancient machine so hard that on flying over one bump he smashed the muffler such that it fell apart upon landing, so that the shaking of the earth was accompanied by the unmuffled roar of the screaming engine and the tinny clattering of the exhaust pipe, and it was at that moment that Bojan Buloh saw in his headlights a sight so remarkable that it momentarily dissolved his terror.

At first—though only very briefly—he thought the road was heading straight into a cliff. And then he realised that the cliff was advancing on him, quicker than he was advancing toward it, and he saw that the cliff was a huge wall of water into which he was driving, and he knew the utter strangeness of that moment was as inexpressible as its horror was complete.

And Bojan Buloh, feeling that this was his fate, unavoidable and predestined, no longer wished to flee from the shadow of his fear, but rather to complete his journey into its vast mysterious heart. He hammered his old car as hard as he dared up that hill, into that cliff, that water, that darkness, his only remaining desire to arrive as quickly as possible.

And at the very moment when he thought he was about to die and felt strangely resigned to his death and felt that death was only right for someone so wretched, that the only strange thing was that such punishment was so overdue—at that very moment the huge wave did not carry him and the FJ away, but passed beneath him, and Bojan realised that he had managed to rise above the damburst's peak and was continuing to rise. He looked down then, and wondered in awe if the FJ was not actually flying, had grown wings and was rising into the nighttime sky, and he in it, an angel granted a second life.

Behind and below him sounds, strangely gentle and beautiful, of rock and valley washing away in water, of concrete tossed as light as water foam.

And then he turned the motor off. He got out of the FJ. He listened to the river running free below. And heard the wind in the forest. Saw his heart and her heart forever together, dancing in that mad storm, riding its terrible sudden squalls, sliding into its eddying swirls. It was a moment of measureless lucidity, and when it was over, Bojan Buloh sat back in the FJ and buried his face in his hands.

Chapter 70

1990

BOJAN DROVE SLOWLY down an old logging road that ran along what had until a short time before been the dammed lake and which was now nothing more than a drained muddy crater, the FJ making so much noise now that it did wake the dead and their spirits fled in front of the FJ in the shape of wallabies and wombats and quolls and possums and devils and tigers and among them were Fabrizio and Adriana and Kenny, the son of the truck driver, as well as the history professor from Krakow, and so many others that in the end it looked as if he were a drover and the mass of creatures in front of the FJ his herd.

After a time the road headed into the forest. Following the spirit animals blindly, he eventually arrived back on the main road, at which point they vanished as inexplicably as they had appeared. At the crossroads Bojan did not turn west to head back to Tullah but without hesitation swung the car east, toward Hobart, toward Sonja.

He drove slowly, carefully. His heart feeling hope and his stomach knowing fear. Driving through that long stormy night.

His foot shaking on the accelerator.

His hands shuddering on the steering wheel.

Bojan Buloh knew now that he was pushing on, pushing back. Past the forest and beyond Butlers Gorge. Dismembered objects momentarily flashed up in his headlights and flew past him. A scarlet coat. Burgundy shoes. But Bojan Buloh was pushing on, pushing back. He drove at and through all the apparitions of horrors that beset him that night. Through a snake coiling around a neck. Through white flower fragments speckling a blue tongue. For Bojan Buloh was rolling that dark night back as hard as he could, heading into the northern suburbs and into the old town.

Until he came upon a blue angel.

Chapter 71

———

1990

SONJA GAVE THE BAR a perfunctory polish with a counter towel. Through a window she watched the rain outside, falling in shudders and shakes, wild scratchings across the dull, greasy light of the streetlamps. Across the road, the neon blue angel continued to fly above the seamen's mission through the mizzly night. There was little else to do but look and dream, the pub being empty save for a table of bus drivers in a far corner, and an amphetamine-crazed crayfisherman who sat pin-eyed and face flushed red, a lobster of a man, at the far end of the bar drinking American whiskey neat and mumbling to himself. A stormy Tuesday night. Not a night for anyone to go out anywhere. She caught a deep breath, leant backwards to ease the ache in her back, and then returned to her task, standing side-on to the bar so that her swelling belly did not get in her way. She heard the door open but took no notice. Even if she had retained her sense of smell it would have done her no good, for there was no forewarning scent of sour sweated bread. She looked at the clock and calculated how many minutes left before she could give the Metro boys and the pin-eyed lobster their marching orders and close up for the evening. So it was that she turned and, until he spoke, did not recognise the rain-glistened face.

He was nervous. He smiled awkwardly. He spoke quietly.

'Hell-oh,' he said.

And then Sonja knew it was him.

An embarrassed silence ensued.

Bojan had no intention of telling Sonja about the damburst. Or how he had been standing outside in the rain for the last half an hour wondering whether or not he would come in, his clothes so saturated that their weight pulled him earthwards and held him anchored to the pavement with the force of roots, and him staring up at the neon blue angel that flew above the seamen's mission, its extended arm pointing across Morrison Street to the waterside pub in which his daughter worked.

Sonja fidgeted with the bar towel. There was no denying it, she was shocked to see him.

He thought it reckless to mention that he had asked the blue angel if this was wise, if it was even right for him, who had so little to do with her for so long, to now return to her life? The blue angel said nothing, but continued pointing to the pub, and Bojan felt even more stupid and confused for fooling himself that neon signs might be omens.

'A beer,' Sonja said finally, grabbing a glass from overhead and placing it under the beer tap. 'On the house.'

Bojan looked up at Sonja, and shook an out-stretched hand. 'No. No beer.' His face a book she could no longer read. 'Wait,' he said. Before she could reply, he had turned and walked back out the door. Sonja swallowed and shook her head and her hand fell from the spigot.

'What did the wog want?' asked a bus driver who had sidled up to order another shout.

Sonja, her gaze fixed on the door through which she thought Bojan had fled, said, 'Nothing.' She filled the glasses, took his money, then looked at the bus driver, and said, 'Nothing at all,' rang the till, held the change above his opened hand and said, 'He was my father,' and let the gold coins tumble with the weight of guilt.

He *is* my father, thought Sonja, suppose he is. I ignored him even longer than he ignored me when he brought me up. If you can call it that. But I can't balance his life with mine. Can't do to him what he did to me. Don't want to even try. Never wanted to see him again.

To see the bastard ever.

My father the bastard.

The bastard, the bastard, the bastard.

Sonja returned to cleaning the bar. The bus driver wandered back to his fellow workers with his tray of beers. The low drone of the pub resumed, only to be then interrupted by loud clunking and banging sounds. Sonja looked up to see a largish object being manoeuvred into the bar. Behind it, awkwardly hanging on, the shoving and puffing figure of Bojan Buloh.

Once through the doorway he stood in the middle of the bar-room. He and Sonja looked at each other as if across a distance, a great, seemingly impassable gulf of time and emotion and both wished it were possible to look elsewhere. Yet neither moved, for both were mesmerised by the sight of the other. As if they were seeing each other for the first time.

And both were entranced.

Bojan by the sheen and strangely tormented veneer of a pregnant woman. A stubbornness and courage he recognised. She saw him as anyone else in that pub would have seen him that night: a man who had no home other than such pubs; an ageing wog who had a face that might have seemed fine under normal circumstances, but which when cruelly glazed by the night rain seemed somehow battered by life, full of the fleshiness and the ruddiness of those who have worked too hard and drunk too much. The clothes, thought Sonja, Jesus the bloody clothes. Her father who had once been so dapper, who despised the peasant dress of the Australians, whose snappy clothes spoke of his ambition, his pride, his virility—her father now wore clothes that spoke of nowhere, nothing, nobody, cheap clothes that were neat but shiny with wear, suggesting nothing more than a desire for comfort and warmth, of protection against the cold. And something else too she saw that night that she had never before seen in her father.

That he was frightened.

The clinking, chattering sound of the bar died away. The Metro boys stopped swapping stories and began watching with interest. Even the pin-eyed lobster stopped mumbling and twitched around in their direction.

In front of the old wog they saw standing a cradle. It was made of Huon pine and was built in an ornate Mitteleuropean fashion, all fretted timber and elaborate edges. It was even fitted with new bedding, lace bumpers and all. Wood and lace, thought Sonja. She smiled a little. Bojan was unsure what her smile meant, fearful as to what it boded.

The pin-eyed lobster came over and ran a claw over the cradle. 'That's Huon pine,' he said. 'Bloody beautiful, that is.' Bojan said nothing. 'I'll give you a hundred bucks now for it,' said the lobster, claw diving into his jean pockets.

'Jiri tell me what you doing,' said Bojan. He halted, not sure whether he had already said too much, but then deciding to press on regardless. 'That you stay. So-o-o, I think.' He halted again, wiped his mouth, looked at the ground, then back up at Sonja. 'I think, I take holiday and come over see Sonja.'

'Two hundred,' said the lobster. 'The missus is expecting again and she'd love this.'

Bojan, unable to ignore the lobster any longer, said, 'It's not for sale.' He turned back and noticed that Sonja was no longer looking at him, but at the cradle, in a some-what perplexed fashion. 'Oh—that's for you,' Bojan said in an off-hand way. And then laughed. 'Well, not you—the baby, but . . . you.'

Sonja didn't speak and Bojan drew the wrong conclusion.

'It's not good I know,' he said. 'I make it in the work-shop. After hours. The shop ones very expensive. But maybe you prefer shop one?' He shrugged his shoulders, as if his offering were trivial. With a shock Sonja realised she was letting love in, and she felt sick with loathing, felt her whole body and soul rushing away from where she stood and felt fearful that the small piece of secure ground beneath her feet was disintegrating and there was nothing below her, felt a powerful sensation of falling at such a great velocity that it was also akin to a floating, a flying, but was she rising or was she falling? She grasped the beer taps to anchor herself in the dull world in which she had chosen to live. Keep love away, she warned herself, lock it out.

'No!' she suddenly yelled, 'No!' Then embarrassed by her own sudden outburst, Sonja moved out from behind the bar and came over to the cradle, flashed a smile, mur-mured, 'No,' again but in a way that she hoped managed to obscure her original meaning. She shook her head and said, in a still quieter voice, 'No, I don't prefer.'

She squatted down and examined the cradle up close as a joiner might, checking to see if it was true and square. Bojan looked at her wistfully for a time without saying anything, then announced, 'Now I go and—'

And Sonja, startled out of her own private thoughts, said what she really thought: 'No, Artie, please—please don't go . . .'

'—and come back in a moment,' said Bojan, permit-ting himself the hint of a smile.

He disappeared and came back with a newly made wooden cot. Sonja smiled a lot, though it was a smile of bemusement, for Bojan's offering, while both generous and touching, seemed woefully inadequate to all that had passed between them.

'I be back,' Bojan said, 'in a moment.'

He reappeared with a high chair, so that by now half the pub seemed full of baby furniture. Sonja stood there caught between smiling and crying, between love and contempt. These offerings—so silly, so futile—and yet they had been made in good faith.

So . . . *so* beautiful.

There was about Bojan Buloh that strange evening something that approached the most curious innocence. As if innocence, thought Sonja, were not something one had before it was lost, a natural state into which one was born before life sullied it forever, but rather something that could only be arrived at after one had journeyed through all the evil life could manifest. He was lost and condemned to loss, he was damned and lived with the damned, but somehow, somehow because of what he had lived through he had acquired an innocence.

That wet awful evening Sonja saw innocence in her father, it was as though she was seeing her father for the first time, as if for the first time their love was both naked and visible and it stood before them as a cot and a high chair and a cradle.

As she stared at that bedraggled, stubbled old man, who looked like the men she so often ordered out of the bar, she felt as if she were a rain cloud, heavy with a fluid soon to take shape and fall, yet light with being. It was a most extraordinary feeling, and it struck her that it had taken a lifetime to know it.

She wished to say: I love you.

I love you, you bastard, you bastard, you bastard.

Chapter 72

1990

MAYBE IT WAS THEN. Or maybe it was later. Maybe it was something big or maybe it was something small. Or maybe it was the sum of the little things that finally got to Sonja, that made her start to feel something was perhaps different between her and her father. The way he would run errands for her. Give small gifts unexpectedly. Be so obviously happy to be with her, and yet avoid seeing her too much, as if he was worried she might tire of his company. A profound, and to her unexpected, gentleness in his dealings with her.

And it wasn't so much that he talked differently, but that he talked at all. Admittedly about little of consequence—what was on a TV gameshow the night before, a politician's latest comment, the weather—but it was *that* he talked and the *way* he talked that mattered, the way he listened to her and seemed to want to know, to understand, rather than pretend not to hear—it was all this that made her feel what she feared above all: hope.

Maybe it was just that he was there for at least part of those final months and she knew that she was not alone, when she felt so listless, so tired, so stupidly emotional, elated one moment, depressed the next, knew she was not by herself and that in this at least she was not abandoned, that the door was not opening on a nighttime blizzard to close forever leaving her behind.

Still she felt a fool, for such feelings could only end up being broken like glass and he would break them. She knew him, she knew he would drop the prism through which the invisible light of their feelings was being so curiously and quixotically refracted into a rainbow of hopes, he would drop that precious prism and let it shatter. Yet perversely, because she did feel touched by his presence, his attentions, his desire to be different, Sonja feigned indifference when he was around, a pretence more for herself than him, wishing her heart to believe that it did not matter whether he was there or not.

But when Bojan disappeared after three weeks—evidently back to Tullah and his melancholy existence there, his holidays spent—Sonja felt it keenly. Yet she was also relieved. She had let love visit, true, and she cursed herself for it, but it had been given no chance to grow and though she knew herself to be less, she knew herself also to be safe.

Neither Helvi nor Jiri commented upon her father's leaving, and she concluded that they, like her, felt it could only be for the best. They were in any case otherwise occupied, Helvi working double shifts, Jiri seeming to have a great deal of carpentry work on the go.

The final months of the pregnancy were tedious and difficult for Sonja, and passed, for her, far too slowly. She kept on with the job at the pub, though on reduced hours. Even this exhausted her, but everything exhausted her, even resting, for she found herself unable to sleep properly, and her dreams became stranger, more elusive. Every time she seemed on the border of revelation, of understanding in her dreams, she would groan and suddenly find herself awake with a dull backache and a pressing fear that she might wet herself if she did not rush to the toilet immediately. Her hair lost its lustre, her skin grew as greasy as that of a teenager. Pains slashed up and down her legs, her belly felt so tight she thought she might just burst open like a grape pressed between two fingers, and all she could look forward to, Helvi assured her with a laugh, was the advent of piles. She felt ungainly—an oiltanker of a woman wallowing her way through town—her walk somewhere between a shuffle and a swagger as she tried to balance the growing load within.

She was still living with Helvi and Jiri, though she had been supposed to move into Ahmet's house some months before. Ahmet, however, had told Helvi that there were a few things he had to get fixed, which Sonja thought was something of an understatement.

She would waddle around the house cursing Ahmet, cursing herself, for she wanted a home, her own home, wanted it very badly, wanted to paint out a nursery for her baby and hang mobiles above Bojan's cot, make the kitchen warm, a home, that thing she had never known, a home, a home fuck it, a fucking home for me and my baby, she wanted her child to have what she had never had, and she would have it, if it took the last bit of strength in her ballooning body, she would have it. Yet every time she went to ring Ahmet to abuse him, or to ring a real estate agent about finding another place, Helvi somehow managed to dissuade her.

All this waiting, thought Sonja, it drives me crazy: waiting, waiting, and waiting longer still for Ahmet, for my baby to be born and my baby also waiting, for the time when it will drop into the wedge of my pelvis, for the moment when it must begin shoving its way out, and though I know it's not true, that he will never return, I can smell the wind rising and my only thought is strange:

Out there my father waits also.

Chapter 73

1990

WHICH IS WHY nothing could have prepared Sonja for the day Ahmet called to say that her prospective home was finally ready. The house, Sonja guessed, would be much as it had been on the day they had inspected it: filthy, rotting, damp, pungent with the scent of cat-piss. No doubt the plumbing now worked after a jerry-built fashion, and a few of the more obviously dangerous switches and power points had been replaced. Perhaps—though this was a vanity of a thought—perhaps a new stove.

A small ageing man in a budgie-blue acrylic suit waited for them at the front door of what was to be Sonja's house. Sonja had not met Ahmet. The suit hung off the old man's small frame at odd angles, as if he and the suit were not on the most familiar of terms.

'Ahmet don't normally dress so flash,' said Helvi.

There was about him something slightly dashing; though badly shaven with wayward beds of sprouting silver stubble, his long, dark face with its strong nose and dapper moustache suggested a body bigger and bolder than that which was below.

Ahmet rocked from foot to foot. He shot Sonja nervous glances. 'You are like her,' he said finally, in a strange accented voice, high and thin, like a reed pipe. 'Your mother. Your face—not the nose—but the eyes, yes, and the mouth and the hair, very much, very much like her.' He handed Sonja two keys. 'I knew your mother,' said Ahmet. 'She beautiful woman. She good woman. Butlers Gorge I knew your mother.' And then, assuming a more confident pose, he held her hands and he finally sustained a long look at her face, saying once more how Sonja was so like her mother, and that was why he had done this, because her mother was a good woman and he had not forgotten her goodness and this home was to be Sonja's for as long as she would want it. And then he abruptly turned and walked off down the street.

Sonja was struck by Ahmet's powerful memory of her mother, moved and flattered by the idea of similarity, and bemused that in light of such feeling, Ahmet thought she would view renting his hovel as some sort of gift.

But on entering the front door Sonja was shocked. She turned to Helvi, who only laughed. The hovel had gone. No trace of carpet slimy with rot, no sign of damp lathe-and-plaster about to fall remained. For the house had been transformed from Australian squalor to modern Mediterranean.

'Come,' said Helvi, and they walked into what had formerly been a cramped living room. There, one wall had disappeared, along with the union jack fireplace, which had been replaced by a wonder of abalone shell in which amethyst-silver encrusted splendour was enshrined a gas heater; doorways had been replaced with arches, peeling wallpaper with bright purple and sky-blue and aqua-green paint, mouldy carpet with terracotta tiles, broken wooden windows with aluminium powder-coated sky-blue, and the decrepit kitchen now revealed as part of a larger family room, an iridescent marvel of shining laminex and tiles.

A kaleidoscope of colour. Modern styling and an older decorative urge clashing and colluding. Sonja found herself beginning to smile. And there, sitting on a pine lounge suite, each with a can of beer in hand and a number of empty cans at their feet, she saw Jiri and Bojan beaming up at her.

'Surprise,' said Jiri, in his deep, oddly inflected voice, so that the word came out sounding like *soap-prize*. 'Surprise.' He raised his can in Sonja's direction and made an extravagant gesture to the surrounding walls. 'Is this not—' He paused, trying to remember what he was going to say next, what it was and what it was not, belched, then giggled, then said, '—a thing of wonder and beauty?' And twirled his can in delicate waves as if it were a conductor's baton. Jiri was clearly drunk. So too, Sonja could see, was the beaming figure of her father. But it was a different drunk from what she had ever seen in him, not a forgetting drunk or a wild, angry drunk, but something else. Something entirely different.

'Yes, it is,' said Sonja. 'And laminex.' She laughed. They laughed too.

'Fucken laminex alright,' said Jiri. 'It's not easy getting that good purple stuff anymore.'

Sonja almost said that it was all extraordinarily over the top. But then halted. For in that abalone-shelled and terracotta-tiled and sky-blue aluminium-framed house she for the first time recognised her world and herself, and with a shock she knew this was her home. She did not know what to say. She asked, 'But why?'

'Because,' said Jiri—the word came out sounding like *bee-curse*—then he took a swig of his beer, and before he had properly swallowed, continued, 'because Helvi she say I must.' He finished swallowing, his florid face swelling up like an iced doughnut around a belching mouth, and he resumed talking without a trace of embarrassment. 'She say—Jiri—*Jiri* you useless bastard get off your fat arse and do something useful for a change. And Bojan too, bloody hell, he say, Jiri, before my holidays finish and I go back to Tullah we must do a proper job for Sonja and her baby. So we tell Ahmet—Ahmet, we'll make your place. And Ahmet, he's no fool, he say fine, go ahead, just make it good. And so we do. And now I am so happy.'

Bojan was giggling. 'He is,' said Bojan, 'he is, he is so bloody happy.'

'Yes, I am,' said Jiri, round bollard-face glowing ruby with drink. 'In fact the beauty of this room is all the more because all of us are so happy.'

'I am not so happy, Jiri,' said Helvi, gently but firmly taking Jiri's stubby away from him.

Jiri looked up. Jiri said, 'O.'

He looked sheepish, then became inventive. 'Well, you know that is good, because if you were happy too Helvi I think there would just be too much happiness, and the whole thing would explode.' With growing authority he expanded on his newly found theme. 'You know the world can only take so much happiness. So much happiness is good, but too much is a very bad thing.'

Helvi motioned to him. 'I take little happiness home.'

After they had left, Bojan and Sonja were quiet. Sonja wandered the house, and came back to stand next to her father. Bojan looked at Sonja, then around at the redecorated room and, as if finally satisfied, nodded his head.

All that long time, all those many, many years between when Maria had walked into the wild night and when he had finally emerged back out of the wet darkness, carrying a cradle into the Blue Angel on that evening of rain, Bojan realised he had known only as a nightmarish hallucination and not as a life that could be understood.

Unable as Bojan was ever to tell of what he had glimpsed before his daughter had awoken him from his dream, it was implicit in every alteration and addition he had made to Sonja's new home. His truth had always been expressed through his body, in his work for others. And in his work for Sonja he had come to see how he was changing as rapidly as Ahmet's house.

But in his heart he suddenly felt unsure. He dropped his eyes to the floor, too embarrassed to look at her.

'I go back to Tullah tonight,' he said. 'It's finished.'

Sonja didn't speak. She, no more than he, knew what to say.

'Over,' said Bojan, trying to help them both.

With some tenderness Sonja said, 'Drive safely, Artie.'

Bojan partly raised his eyes from the floor, smiled at Sonja, swallowed, and then softly said, 'Sure. Sure I will.'

But now, as he looked upwards at the imposing form of his pregnant daughter, a looming figure of possibilities, he felt once more old, and worried. 'Sonja,' he asked meekly, '. . . is okay? You like?'

Sonja looked about, at the arches, the laminex, the tiles, the aluminium, the kitchen in which she would pre-pare food for her baby, the lounge-room floor upon which the baby would first roll and crawl and then walk, the world in which she and her child would come to dis-cover life together. Her breasts felt suddenly, strangely damp, and she knew her nipples to be leaking. Then seek-ing to explain this curious response without talking about it, to say all that she felt, Sonja finally settled on one word, a word of the old world.

'Doma,' she said.

A smile slowly came to Bojan's face. He repeated the word in a murmur. 'Doma.'

Then he smiled some more, and his movements grew more confident and as if he were a bird about to take flight he spread his arms like wings, saying, more loudly, more confidently, 'Doma,' and one unfolding wing, his left arm, accidentally brushed Sonja's protruding belly. His hand jumped back. His smile vanished. 'Sorry,' Bojan said, fearing he had offended her by touching her body. 'I am sorry.'

'It's fine,' Sonja said. 'Truly.'

They looked at one another. Then she reached out to him, and cupping her hand behind his head slowly brought it toward her, until her father's head was resting on the hard dome of her belly.

Through the gnarled flesh of his face Bojan felt the warm immensity of a world being created. His bottom lip trembled upwards. Short breaths he drew in through his nose. Words stumbled haltingly out of his mouth.

'Jesus,' he swore slowly. 'Jesus Christ.'

Chapter 74

––

1990

WHEN FOR THE LAST TIME Sonja saw herself in that dream she was again eight years old, clad in a floral nightie, huddling up inside Bojan's bluey, again in phantasmagorical flight forever in the FJ with her father. They were where she knew they always had been: fleeing through a dark, frost-rimed night along the empty road to Butlers Gorge.

At first her mother was not her mother, but rather Mrs Maritza Michnik, appearing out of nowhere, face framed by the front passenger window, contorted with hate, only inches away from Sonja. And though the car was moving, Sonja wishing it to move faster, still Mrs Maritza Michnik was standing staring in through the passenger window and there was no escape. 'You ungrateful little slut,' Mrs Maritza Michnik yelled. Her words seemed to mingle with the whine and hum of the 138 motor as Bojan pushed the car ever harder, until it was as if the FJ and Mrs Maritza Michnik were screaming in unison. 'Don't think you can ever come back,' they roared.

And then as abruptly as it had appeared Mrs Maritza Michnik's face was gone, but her voice continued, except now the words were tumbling from the mouth of Sonja's mother, Maria. 'You can never come back,' said Maria, but her tone was entirely different from Mrs Maritza Michnik's, at once wistful and sad. A lace-covered ghost, forlorn and desperate, wanting but unable to touch the flesh of her daughter, her face close to the window and her hands pressed up against the moist glass, wet fingers splaying out like a starfish falling.

'Can I come?' Sonja asked.

'No,' said Maria, and her voice, unlike her distorting face, was now her own. 'You don't want to come with me,' said Maria. Her tongue began to loll out of her mouth and her eyeballs started to distend, and with that she was sucked back into the forest that was flying away from Sonja into the clear night.

'Why she go?' a nightmarish voice asked from behind the front seat. 'You know?'

To escape that voice Sonja moved closer to her father but he did not look like her father, for in the weak yellow light of the speedo clock his face wore an eery look, shadowed and jaundiced. With a shock she realised her father was sick. Terribly sick. Look forward, look forward, she thought to herself, away from him and never back into the darkness inexorably closing in behind. She gazed up at the giant eucalypts that towered over all sides of the car. But pierced and divided by the FJ's onward journey, they too seemed to be in constant flight, and gave her no comfort.

'You know what she do?' the voice from behind her began again. 'You know?'

Sonja turned slowly, fearfully. Slouched across the back seat was Umberto Picotti, relaxed, half-smoked cigarette between his thin lips. He took the cigarette out of his mouth and gazed wistfully down at it. Then, exhaling a languid cloud of smoke, he looked up and smiled.

'Of course *you* know,' said Picotti, winking at Sonja in a familiar, knowing fashion. 'Women like her are no good, Sonja.' He waved his cigarette around playfully. 'Your mother did not love you or she would be here now. Eh?' He pointed the cigarette at her in a precise gesture, to emphasise the precise thing he now wished to say. 'If she loved you, she would be here looking after you.' Picotti paused, then shrugged his shoulders. 'This is hard for you I know, but it is better you know it all.'

Sonja searched desperately for her father, who had disappeared. The driver's seat was empty, but even driver-less the FJ continued hurtling along on its hellish journey, for it could not halt, could never stop.

'Eh! Sonja!' said Picotti. 'Come over and sit with Bertie.' He patted his knee, scattering light-grey ash upon his dark suit pants. He was still leaning back in the seat, completely at ease, leering and grinning. 'Come.'

She spun around looking for her mother, for Jean, for Mrs Heaney, for anybody who might save her, and outside the FJ she saw them all, all the people from her past, but only she could see them and none could see the others, and none was connected, and none could help either themselves or the others or her.

'Do not be frightened, my child,' Picotti said, in a voice deceptively gentle and persuasive. At first Sonja didn't move, but then, when what seemed the inevitability of her fate took hold of her, she began to climb slowly and awkwardly over the front seat into the back. She began to sob silently. She looked to her side, and was astonished to see falling out of an impenetrable darkness above the giant trees her father. He was clearly drunk, for his flight through the air was more a collapsing roll earthwards than a graceful glide. He tumbled onto the ground, ending up flat on his face. With an uneven vigour, he picked himself up, brandishing before him a large block of chocolate. He collapsed against the front passenger window, proffering the chocolate. Sonja ignored his offering.

'Artie,' said Sonja, 'I want to go home.'

Bojan laughed. 'Where? What home? You and I have no home. Don't you understand?' He continued to laugh and then his laughter turned to tears. 'We have a wog flat, my Sonja. A wog flat. Don't you understand?' He turned, and seeing Picotti in the back seat, smiled. 'Hello, Bertie. Want some chocolate?'

'Why she go?' Bojan asked, again sad, as Picotti took the entire block. 'Where my Maria go?' And with that Bojan vanished into the night. Sonja looked back at Picotti, lewdly peeling the foil off the chocolate.

'Where she go?' asked Picotti. Sonja did not move. Picotti leant back into his seat and slowly pushed some chocolate between his lips with a single finger, chewed, and then spoke again, in a nonchalant manner. 'You know?' He narrowed his eyes, leant forward, and waved the remnant chocolate at Sonja to make his final, emphatic point. 'Of course *you* know.'

Sonja sat there, terrified, straddling the front seat, one leg over each side. Her eyes were welling with tears; her head shuddering; snot falling and then receding back up her nostrils with each anguished, half-stifled sob. Picotti was laughing. Sonja looked down at the seat top to see a dark stain of urine, spreading out from her crutch and across her nightie and she was peering into the darkness, far, far into that darkness.

And then she was awake. In her bed in her new home, and the bed was wet. Between her legs a warm deluge gently spilling. With a shock, she realised that her waters had broken and her labour was just beginning.

Chapter 75

1954

IF THIS TALE could be told properly it would be filled with everything. There would be an ocean of what had been and the dreams of what would be and you could swim within the shallows of those memories and surf the waves of those dreams as they rose up before breaking into nothingness. Watch as their foamy wash swirled up schools of reffos arriving day after day pushing their scant belongings to the single men's quarters in mangy old wooden wheelbarrows, them thinking that at last their journey was ended, in this, the strangest and most unexpected of places, all those Poles and Krauts and Czechs and Lithos and Yugos and Eye-ties and other Balts and wogs, the wheels of their wheelbarrows leaving thin muddy corrugations in winter and lifting roostertails of dust in the hard ruts of summer.

If this tale could be told fully, you would be able to swim through the strangeness of the weather that could deliver four seasons in one day, snow and sun and rain and wind, and the men who took to dressing according to their moods rather than in accordance with the fickle nature of the alien weather, wearing coats when despondent and singlets when cheekily defiant. You would be able to see properly the bearded bushmen who came in to the camp selling wallaby meat and be able to taste the wondrous salamis that were then made out of that lean meat when crossed with fatty pork and blessed with garlic and pepper and paprika. All of this and more the story would be filled with. With tales that ran like rivers into the sea of that place: of the priest so different from the village priests the Europeans had known, for Father Flannery was almost always drunk and frequently swore worse than the Maltese tunnellers, confused names at christenings, borrowed wine from them for services then drank it all before he even reached the altar upon unsteady feet. The way the place was all so new and would soon seem so old, the way they worked hard to make the place nothing more than a memory for them, how they coped with the awfulness of it by dreaming that one day this would simply be something they would tell tales about in the comfort of good homes like they had seen on American movies, homes with electric kitchens and good plumbing and plush padded seats and happy families in them.

All of this and more. All of this and more and more and the sea would still not be full or the story told, but of a night the child Sonja lay in her bed staring at the sea above her, where the ceiling masonite was already buckling and bowing where moisture was seeping through the tin roof, and the ceiling swelled in waves like an ocean, like a buttongrass plain, like the pocked earth stripped of its trees, and she sometimes felt her world to have been turned upside down, that the house, far from offering protection from the natural world, only amplified and distorted it, recreating it in grotesque forms, and she would be scared that all that upside down sea and earth might crush her, and she wondered what would happen if the earth and the sea fell upon her, whether she would have the strength to find her way out to where the real world was. Then she would dream of what the real world might look like and she knew it must look like nothing she knew.

So that night long ago, as on other nights when such bad thoughts troubled her, Sonja got out of bed and went to the door of her mother and father's bedroom. There she saw her mother packing an old, small cardboard suitcase that lay open upon her bed.

Sonja watched the odd array of items her mother placed in the suitcase: a scarf from the old world and stockings from the new that she had never worn lest she tear them, a frayed child's handkerchief with a fading teddy bear pattern which Sonja was allowed on special occasions, some rope, a jumper of Bojan's, a photograph of an old man lying in a long box. She put each item in slowly, staring at them for a time, lost in strange distant thoughts which she did not share with her three-year-old daughter. As if she simply felt a need to fill the suitcase, but the contents that filled it were irrelevant but still somehow meaningful, somehow located her. When the suitcase was finally full of these strange things she placed on top of all the other items a pressed white flower, which had unusual pointed petals. She turned the flower first this way, then that, as if taking a bearing on some distant place and time. Then somewhat absentmindedly Maria Buloh put on a pair of battered burgundy-coloured shoes and a scarlet coat.

The child Sonja saw it all from the doorway of her room, quietly. She was dressed for bed where she was supposed to be asleep; wearing a floral flannelette nightie, old and pilled where it was not already showing the warp and weft of its weave, and a green woollen jumper which, despite being a little too small in the sleeves and having one frayed elbow, was nevertheless snug. In her bedsocks, one still running up her calf, the other fallen, Sonja walked across to Maria and, avoiding looking at her mother, stared into the suitcase, hoping perhaps that she might camouflage her presence by her interest in the ongoing activity of packing the suitcase. She picked up the pressed white flower.

'What's this?' Sonja asked.

'You should be asleep,' Maria scolded.

Sonja wished she could tell her mother that she was scared that her ceiling had turned into the sea and then the earth, and she was frightened that her world was being turned upside down and she worried she would disappear forever beneath it. But she had no idea of how to begin to say such an enormous thing, and instead said she was thirsty, and then asked once more what the flower was, for she did wish to know what the beautiful thing was that her mother cradled in her hands.

'The flower of love, Sonja,' Maria said, though absently. 'An edelweiss. It grows in mountains, in cliffs, high, high above the ground, and to pick it you must be very brave and climb the cliff to reach it. Young men do such things, risk their lives, to pick such a flower to show their love for their woman.'

'Flower of love,' repeated Sonja, then correcting her English to please her mother—'*The* flower of love.' Then asked: 'Did Artie pick this for you?'

Maria nodded. 'When he first know me. And I press it to keep it.'

Maria Buloh picked her daughter up. Beneath her red coat she wore a black dress with a white lace yoke, into which Sonja buried her face. She wore lace and it was beautiful and Sonja pressed her face against the lace and knew her mother was leaving and that her mother was held within the power of something beyond the child, a terrible spell she could not break. Maria Buloh took the three-year-old Sonja in her arms and began softly singing a Slovenian lullaby as she rocked her.

> '*Spancek, zaspancek,*' she sang,
> '*crn mozic*
> *hodi po noci*
> *nima nozic . . .*'

Maria felt a tear gathering in the corner of an eye and she closed the eye and rubbed it hard to brush the moisture away, all the while continuing to sing:

'Lunica ziblje:
aja, aj, aj,
spancek se smeje
aja, aj, aj.'

She looked at the child cradled within her arms.

'My baby,' said Maria Buloh. 'My baby.' She put Sonja down. This time she rubbed both her eyes and then turned away from her daughter.

'Sonja, I must to go,' said Maria Buloh. She gathered herself, turned to face Sonja, picked her up and carried her back to her bed. As she pulled the covers over her daughter she whispered reassurances. Then she returned to her room, picked up the suitcase, walked through the main room, opened the door to the darkness outside.

She heard Sonja getting out of bed and walking back out to her. But Maria did not acknowledge that her daughter was again up. She did not turn when she spoke. 'Do not worry,' Maria said to the open door. 'Artie be home soon.' In the glow of an electric light she saw falling snow scratching the blackness beyond.

'Sonja?' asked Sonja, hoping her mother might still relent.

'No, Sonja,' said Maria Buloh softly, her words already losing their way in the blackness. 'I must go alone.'

'But it's dark here,' said Sonja, 'and I'm scared of the dark.'

'I leave light on,' said Maria. Her voice momentarily choked, then she continued. 'I cannot stay. I must go.'

Then Maria turned around, fell to her knees, embraced Sonja, pulled slightly away, made a hurried sign of the cross and looked into Sonja's eyes with both fear and hope. As if the child were a priest that could grant redemption.

'Forgive me, Sonja.'

'What for?'

This was too much for Maria Buloh. She rose quickly, turned her back upon Sonja, picked up her suit-case, and left.

Outside Maria Buloh's shoe had just touched down onto the third and lowest snow-powdered step when she heard the sound of Sonja's voice from inside—'Mama . . .' but Maria abruptly cut her daughter off, quickly and firmly shutting the door. Then Maria tried to soothe her child in Slovenian—'*Aja, aja,*' before she turned and headed off down that street, leaving the imprint of her shoe on the snow-covered step. A flurry of snow, then another, and the footprint was already disappearing.

Everywhere it was silent.

Outside, the snow blew ceaseless.

Inside, the little girl tried to imagine the shoes from behind as they trudged off through snow. But the door had closed and outside a gale was rising, and it was the same as Sonja had always dreamt it, a dreadful foreboding confirmed.

The lace had gone forever.

SONJA SCREAMED.

My mother is lace. My father is wood. I am not.

Opened her eyes and looked around the dimly-lit hospital delivery room and screamed with all her guts and all her heart and all the wind in her throat. Sonja screamed and her body heaved like a huge wave and she felt it breaking her being apart, felt that she was being split into a million pieces of pain.

My mother is lace. My father is wood. I am the lace tearing in two. The wood breaking in half.

Then the wave ebbed and the agony momentarily abated and her breath she caught in short, shrill pants. 'I can't do it,' she whispered in a broken voice, and she almost cried in rage at her own weakness, at her own inability to control either her mind or her body. 'I just'— and she halted momentarily to catch breath—'just can't,' she sobbed, 'can't.'

'You must and will,' said the midwife whom Sonja knew only as Betty. 'Will and can. You have come so far and we are going to make it.' But Sonja was again too far away to hear her. The room around her was blurring.

'O my God,' Sonja cried as the next contraction came, quicker and even harder. 'O my God, my God, my God—' she whispered as if He might hear her if she showed sufficient humility, then abandoning both humility and faith she simply screamed once more.

'Let it out,' Betty urged. 'Let it out and get it out.'

Sonja no longer knew where she was or who she was or why her body and her mind seemed to be simultaneously ripping apart in agony. All she could hear was herself screaming, but even that sound was growing distant.

And then she finally knew that she had always known. It did not come back to her in a sudden moment of revelation, nor did it come to her in a rush, because it had never gone away. It had always been within her and she had let it grow slowly within her, nurturing it without ever intending to nurture it, as she had her child, letting it build from a scattering of half-formed, unconnected memories into something whole and complete unto itself.

Sonja's eyes were closed and as she journeyed into the whiteness of an indescribable pain she could see something at once so huge and so small that at first it was impossible to recognise herself as the small child clad in only a floral nightie, old green jumper and socks—one running up her calf, the other fallen—trudging through snow, on a winter's night all that dark time ago.

'Now push,' she heard Betty exhort once more, but the voice was ever more remote and only its rhythmic incantations remained with her, '*Push. Push. Push. Push.*'

Chapter 77

———

1954

HOW COLD THAT NIGHT! How white that snow! How completely the small camp of Butlers Gorge was already disappearing into that whiteness and darkness! The child Sonja stood at the top of the steps of her home, looking out at the shimmering mirage of what passed for a town, trying to catch some glimpse of her mother. It was hopeless of course, though the child did not think that or think much at all. The child simply felt this. She saw the town as fragments of black shaped between intricate, ever changing patterns of falling white snow. She saw the town as lace. And she wondered how long before this—the only world she had ever known—how long before this too was gone.

At that moment she had the most terrible premonition, that was shapeless, more a pain than an idea, and because of this strange, awful feeling she slowly, awkwardly began to half-walk, half-clamber down the steps. If her mother was lace and the town was lace and all were disappearing, who was she and would she remain or simply vanish as surely as her mother had and the town would? Could it be that she too was lace?

Sonja knew that she must find her father before he too turned into lace. And then comforted herself with the thought that he was too loud, reeked too strongly of tobacco and beer and garlic ever to be lace.

Feeling braver, she trudged through the snow, oblivious to the snowflakes covering her green jumper like desiccated coconut, the ruts in the road that still held slush beneath the fresh white layer of snow and thin ice shell, not caring as the ice water reached through her socks and seized her toes and began to clutch in cruel spasms her still warm body, but simply taking and being a straight line to that place where she knew her father to be. To say she walked is to describe inadequately what Sonja did. Some of those who saw Sonja from the canteen entrance later said that she tottered, trying to keep her balance, and the rough road with its white undulations looked a wild sea and the child a small boat being tossed upon it.

The gaggle of women who stood around the empty wooden beer barrels outside stopped chatting and giggling as Sonja approached the canteen's main entrance. Their eyes followed Sonja as she toddled up to them, and then, as if they were earth to be turned over and Sonja the plough, they parted without a word as she walked through them, opening up to let the child pass through into the men-only canteen.

The women watched as Sonja pushed open the double slat door, was momentarily illuminated by a cone of yellow light, then disappeared into the low hanging haze as the door banged shut.

Inside, a dun-coloured crowd of men sat on bench stools at crude tables, drinking, smoking, playing cards, drinking, talking, listening, drinking, thinking, drinking, not thinking, drinking, drinking. The room was strong with the close smell of smoke, of damp clothes and stale sweat and spilt beer; loud with the roar of all the languages of the Levant and elsewhere, a maelstrom of laughing and cursing and gossiping. Words took startled flight round the amber-hued room like flocks of frightened exotic birds, and a few of the words soaring above her she understood, but many of the words, and almost all of the tongues were entirely unknown to her. Some of the men looked to her loud monsters, others wispy ghosts. Sonja walked down the long rows between their huge, heavy bodies, looking up at the forest of musty backs of men still in their heavy workclothes and boots. Here and there she glimpsed their faces and they looked to her like the fallen trees and broken rocks that lay at the fringes of the settlement, but no tree or rock bore the face of her father. Suddenly, with a resounding thud, a giant slumped backwards and fell off the back of a stool onto the floor immediately in front of Sonja, blocking her path. She recoiled in fright, but upon recognising that the man was neither her father nor dead, but only a dead drunk stranger, she stepped over the fallen giant and kept on walking until finally she found who she was after and tugged at his bluey coat.

Bojan Buloh swung around, drunk.

'Madonna Santa! What the . . . Sonja, you not supposed to be here. What you want? Your mother send you? Here, sit here.' He waved to another man getting up. 'Eh—Pavel—six beer here.'

Bojan placed Sonja on his lap. He laughed. He ran his hand through her hair. She turned and buried her head in his chest. Bojan, for the benefit of his mates, pulled a comic face, pulling his lower lip up over his upper lip, simultaneously shrugging his shoulders, throwing his arms in the air and turning his extended hands outwards in a theatrical gesture. Pavel returned with the beers, and seeing Sonja on Bojan's lap, looked at him queryingly.

'Kids,' laughed Bojan, 'Bloody kids.'

Outside, the snow blew ceaseless.

How white the snow. How cold the night. How chill Sonja's small body. How dark the world outside her father's pungent, powerful arms. And how completely the small camp of Butlers Gorge seemed already disappearing into that whiteness and darkness and coldness as she turned inwards for that life before this life.

Chapter 78

———

1954

WHERE? thought Bojan Buloh. *Where?*

He glanced around the other labourers, a score or more of new Australians, standing around waiting to be taken to their work.

All avoiding his eyes.

It was Saturday, and Maria had still not returned. It was as if the other men already knew. But knew what? He had told no-one that she had left the previous night. If they did know, why would they not tell him? And what was it they knew? What? Perhaps she was hiding out with someone else's wife. Perhaps one of the drivers had taken her out this morning in a truck bound for Hobart. Perhaps—he hoped against all his despair—perhaps she would be back home when he returned from work. Then she would pretend and he would pretend as they had for so long that everything was entirely normal, whereas nothing was normal and nothing had ever been normal. But he would do whatever it took to have her back, if only she would return: he would believe whatever she told him, even if he thought she was lying, for lies were the bitter bread of banishment for them both, and with what else could they hope to sustain themselves?

But where she now? thought Bojan Buloh. *Where?*

Was she still in that room waiting for her father to perish in such wretched humiliation, for her and all her family to die their various deaths, some quickly, some as slow as a lifetime? Or had she found some way to escape that room? Perhaps she was sharing the edelweiss with another man who offered her something he did not, and this thought both enraged and comforted him, because it suggested that there might actually be some happiness beyond what they had known.

But where she? he thought. *Where?*

The men waited, stamping their feet in the snow, smoking a lot, talking a little. Not being able to tell them that she had left, how could Bojan confess to them his fear that she might never return, might have walked out of his life and their daughter's life for good? He told them nothing, of course, but instead put on a front of bravado.

Joked.

As he listened to the others laughing with him, his unease only grew and his pain was great. On the other side of the gravel road, in what passed for a park—a bare patch of gravel with a flagpole and a tatty union jack—the local scouts were meeting. The scoutmaster, an English engineer, was delivering a talk on the perils of Communism.

A small Albanian, indicating the scoutmaster with his cigarette butt, said, 'Dunno why I left. They clearly did some good if they got rid of bastards like that.' A few smiled, and with the discovery of some diversion from the cold and the boredom, the others began to concentrate on the scoutmaster's oratory in order to mock it.

They were interrupted by the arrival of their lift, an old army truck pressed into domestic service. The driver did not even bother to turn his head, but merely bellowed his destination at the windscreen—'Canal works!'—and the labourers clambered up into the uncovered tray.

Where? thought Bojan. *Where?*

A Pole with a heavy beard was first up on the truck, and as he helped haul others up, spoke to nobody in particular. 'Uncle Joe,' he said, 'you weren't so bad. You got rid of Hitler and you got rid of scouts. It's just a pity you didn't stop there before you decided to get rid of us.'

A short, blond-haired Czech banged the top of the truck's cabin, and shouted at the driver, 'Don't forget you pick us up early today so we back in time for our natu-ralisation ceremony.'

'Yeh,' said Bojan. 'We Aussies never late.'

At that they all laughed.

Where? Where? Where? And the thought jackhammered his heart and mind. He must have gulped and shaken at the same time, for the Albanian put a kindly hand on Bojan Buloh's forearm and said he must have a fever and really ought report to the sick bay. Bojan Buloh turned and stared at the Albanian and knew he was shaking and that his stubbled face was an unanswerable question.

Where? asked Bojan. *Where?*

But the Albanian did not answer him. The Albanian looked into Bojan Buloh's eyes longer than it was right to look into another man's eyes, swallowed, ran a finger over his moustache, and cast his eyes downwards.

The early morning sky spread over the central highlands. There were clouds above them, but they were high and wispy and moving slowly across the largely clear sky, boding a good, if chill day. There were drifts of snow below them, up to a metre thick from the blizzard of the night before. The truck turned off the main gravel road, onto a narrow dirt track, along which they bounced through thick, tall rainforest. The labourers rocked back and forth on the truck's tray on which some sat and some squatted, rubbing hands, stamping feet, smoking, talking only occasionally.

'They say the tallest hardwood trees in the world are not far from here,' said the bearded Pole over the truck's roar.

Bojan, attempting to regain his composure, looked up and forced out a laugh. 'Lucky for the Aussies we drown them all with the big dam.'

'What the bloody hell they want all this bloody electricity for anyway?' asked the Albanian.

Bojan waved dramatically at the bush. 'For all their bloody industry, of course, you wog fool.'

The Albanian turned and looked at the wilderness that enveloped them and laughed. The bearded Pole spoke once more.

'They think if they get the electricity then the industry will come, and then they will be like Europe, then they will have factories instead of forests, battlefields instead of potato fields, rivers that run with blood instead of water.'

He paused.

Nobody laughed.

Nobody spoke.

Some turned and looked away, into the forest. The Albanian looked down at his feet and the thudding tray of rotting wooden planks, in which gravel was jumping up and down with each jolt. The Czech hacked and spat into the passing bush. The bearded Pole let his gaze roam around their faces. The Pole was bitter. So were most of them. But they did not want to hear it. They all avoided the Pole's gaze. They were trying to leave it behind them, dissolve it in the way the truck was turning the snow in front of it into mud behind it. With chill palms Bojan kneaded his hammering forehead. The Czech wiped his mouth with the back of his hand, his stubble rasping the hand's skin, thinking, *O lungo drom, o lungo drom.*

But the bearded Pole continued. He spoke not so much to them though, as to himself, because he knew none wanted even to begin to think that they were all complicit in what they had left. 'Europe is a cancer,' said the bearded Pole finally. 'It spreads death everywhere.'

The Czech managed to roll another cigarette as the truck jolted along, letting the rhythm of his hands rolling the tobacco be dictated by the lurching and bucking of the truck. The exercise forced him to concentrate upon his hands rather than on the bearded Pole's ugly truths. The words of a song the Gypsies had sung began forming like curds in his mind. *The crack of . . .* But he pushed them away. With a wry smile to himself, proud of this small triumph over adversity, the Czech put the rollie in his mouth, lighted it between cupped hands, and then looked up into the forest.

It was at that precise moment that he saw in the trees what he had hoped he would never see again. It was, admittedly, only a glimpse, but the sight was one he had seen before in the Bohemian forests, and though he never thought about what he had seen there except in his nightmares, he knew with a terrible coldness exactly what it was.

With a single movement, sudden and urgent, he pulled the cigarette from his lips, stood up, threw the rollie away, and brought his fist down hard, once, twice, on the truck's cabin roof. The truck braked, the men rolled back and forth like an ocean wave and looked confusedly first at one another, and then, as the truck came to a halt, in the direction the Czech was pointing. The men jumped out of the truck quickly, but then, abruptly, lost all their haste. A few turned and walked back to the truck, preferring to stay and look down the snow-white road that led away from that place.

The rest, slowly, hesitantly, walked into the forest, acutely aware of their every movement, and it was as if the sound of the bush breaking beneath their feet, the sound of their shallow breathing and swallowing were the only sounds for them in the world at that moment.

In this manner they walked fifty metres or so through the snow, and then came to a halt.

Chapter 79

——

1954

SOME HAD to look away.

Some had to stare.

And those that stared forced themselves to look up from an old suitcase that lay half-buried in the snow and saw suspended in mid-air what should never be seen suspended so, saw the worn-out soles of two dangling shoes.

A woman's shoes, the holes in them stuffed with newspaper, iron-grey with iced wet.

Some had to look away.

Some had to stare.

And like unwilling birds caught in a spiralling updraught, the gaze of those who stared circled inexorably upwards: past the battered burgundy shoes to the small, delicate icicles already growing from the coat's frayed ends, and higher, higher yet, up that snow-rimed scarlet coat, and though now giddy with horror still their gaze continued to rise; from the ice-stiffened old grey hemp rope that collared her garrotted neck like a snake-coil of steel; to the white face above it, with lolling tongue and milky, dead eyes.

What were once her eyes, thought Bojan Buloh, whose soft roundness he once had delighted in feeling with his lips.

Now embedded in a stiffening corpse suspended upon a rope from a tall tree.

Below, a dozen men from faraway lands gathered, and above them hanging what was once her, the now forever still body of Maria Buloh.

Had she, for some undivinable reason, run out of petals and there been nowhere left in the world for her to go? Or had the star-flower indicated this final direction, or another she had not wished to take?

For speckling her blue tongue were strange white fragments, which might have been mistaken for snow rather than what Bojan Buloh knew them to be, the terrible flotsam of the broken flower of their love, the remnants of the petals of an edelweiss.

Chapter 80

1954

BOJAN BULOH DID NOT KNOW. Bojan Buloh did not think why. He did not cry then, nor for some time after.

He seemed strangely unmoved until later that day in the movie hall when the naturalisation ceremony took place. It was then, during a long speech by a politician, that he began to sob uncontrollably. The room swirled in front of Bojan Buloh's rheumy eyes and he felt himself being sucked out of that room into a vortex of the most terrible maelstrom from which he wondered if he could ever emerge. He held Sonja on his chest and she cradled his heaving head between her shoulder and encircling arm. He clutched onto his daughter as if she were a life-preserver ring. He sobbed and then moaned like some dreadfully wounded animal not allowed to die.

But she did not cry at all.

Some had to look away. Some had to stare. Some said it was then that her face became a mask, though how would they know such a thing, or even what they mean by such words? Some said it was a shame, of course. And so for the child Sonja there was some sympathy for a time, until the shame of it outgrew the sadness of it in other people's minds and she was simply dismissed as strange and ungrateful.

After the naturalisation ceremony, two engineers' wives came to take Sonja off to play. They were English. They believed in charity. Bojan Buloh did not let them take his daughter. It was just that he had no power to hold onto Sonja any longer when their insistent hands gently prised her from his arms with the full, unshakeable force of good Christian intentions. Bojan Buloh did not want his daughter to go, but they insisted it was for the best for the both of them. They had lots of words.

It astounded him, how many words some people might have. He said nothing. There was nothing to say. There is only this, thought Bojan. Stretched flesh and bones and shit and wood that grows in trees that stretches flesh and flesh that flattens wood to make meaningless things such as the hut in which they were gathered and this noise that meant nothing. There was birth and there was love and there was death, and there was death and there was noise, this endless noise that confused people, making them forget that there was only birth and love and that each and everything died. There is only that, thought Bojan, only that, and he suddenly realised he had lost his daughter as well as his wife and he did not know how to get either back.

Sonja did not cry as those strange hands fought to wrest her from her father. She did not speak, nor did she scream. But she resisted those good Christian intentions with all the dumb ferocity of a fish trapped in a rock pool after the tide has gone out, and with the same inevitable result. She did all she could to hang onto her father, trying to swim back into the depths of his body so as to be part of him, invisible to all but him, but now he too had become lace and the lace was shredding into pieces as she clung ever more desperately to him and then the lace pieces dissolved into air and a fish cannot survive upon lace or in air. The women were walking off with her in their grip, and she suddenly ceased struggling, for something fundamental had become lost to her and she intuitively knew that there was now nothing to fight either for or against. There was simply a world that had turned upside down into the sea and which with the silent monumental force of an ocean's undertow was sweeping her ever further away from what she wished to cleave to. One day she would escape the sea, no matter how many years, no matter how many lives after this one that had just ended, she would escape and find her father once more and he would no longer be air or lace or wood but be himself, and until that time she would wait, as still as the moon, playing dead, no-one knowing she was still alive, taking breath in gulps measured so slow.

With Sonja having ceased her thrashing about, the shorter of the two engineers' wives put the child down, took her hand and made her walk alongside, parading the small girl as a cantilever of contrition buttressing the engineers' wives' notion of themselves as caring women.

Above Sonja's head the engineers' wives talked a curious language of abbreviations and euphemisms, occasionally hacking in their throats, and twisting a censorious chin in the child's direction. Sonja knew that this meant they were talking about her mother, though the sounds ran in and out of her ears like bathwater, though the women looked as grotesque in their stilted conversation as the chooks that ran up and down the main street pecking at the frozen earth in jerky motions.

'Where's Artie?' Sonja said, more of a demand than a question, but the women either did not hear or paid no attention to what the child asked, for they continued clicking and clucking. 'Where's my Artie?' Sonja asked once more. The tall woman turned and smiled at Sonja, and her smile terrified the small child, who instinctively knew such powerful good intentions so firmly held were impossible to dispute with.

'He's fine,' said the tall woman, 'and so shall you be. And we—*we* are going to have a tea party.'

As they walked down the main street Sonja looked at the filthy slush. She wondered how the beautiful earth, from which she made cakes, and the pure white snow, with which she had the day before made snowballs with her mother, could combine to form something as unpleasant as grey slush. She kicked at it, and the slush splashed up the wool-stockinged leg of the shorter of the two engineers' wives. Sonja felt her hand suddenly crushed in the woman's grip and a voice icier than the air announcing: 'That'll be about enough of that, missy.'

'Mama!' cried Sonja. 'Mama!'

'Mama's away on holidays,' said the woman with soggy stockings. 'We don't know when she's coming back,' added the other. And even Sonja sensed the small cruelty intended.

Two women talking together, with a child at one's side, and although it was not possible to make out precisely what the women were discussing, it was clear enough to Sonja that it was her father of whom they now talked. Occasionally, she unwittingly let some phrase register in her mind, before she once more tried hard to hear nothing. Phrases such as 'perhaps there was another,' and 'nobody knows why, mind you, a few drinks and they say his temper is something terrible.'

But it meant nothing to the small girl who walked next to them, because at that moment she had decided for ever and ever and ever from that time on she was nothing, until that distant day when she would once more find her father.

They came to a staff house—a proper house, not a shack like the one in which Sonja lived—and went around to its back garden. There, on a concrete apron, an upturned gelignite box was neatly set up as a table, covered with a makeshift red chequered tablecloth, upon which was formally arrayed her toy china tea-set.

We drink tea now.

The women pulled their knitted cardigans closer to ward off the cold, their backs facing the rear of the house. Framed between their torsos a long way away was Sonja, in her party dress and pigtails, standing at the upturned crate with the tea-set upon it.

Because it is Tasmania and not Slovenia.

'I went to their house and found it for her,' said the woman who had crushed her hand, 'so she'd have something to take her mind off all that has happened.'

'To help her forget,' said the other woman.

'Yes,' said the hand crusher. 'That's right, help the poor little thing forget.' Her tone became more intimate. 'She kept the house surprisingly clean, I'll say that for her. Not what you'd expect.'

Sonja picked up the teapot, found that it did not stop to pretend-pour in one of the toy cups but continued to move till it was above the ground onto which it fell and shattered.

Because our world is upside down.

One of the engineers' wives yelled out to Sonja and she must have heard, for she looked up at the two women, looked at them and through them such that neither spoke again, not when she smashed the milk jug, nor when she smashed the first saucer nor the second or fourth or sixth cup.

Because in her eyes was a question to which the engineers' wives had no answer. Teapot and milk jug, saucer and cup upon concrete. Porcelain, pearl-smooth on the outside, sharp as glass and dry as death upon breaking. Had they broken? Had they? Teapot and milk jug smashing. Her mother singing. Her father sobbing. Saucer and cup breaking. Had they? A howling inside that would not leave.

Her mother singing. Her father sobbing.

Her father. Her mother. Her.

Had they?

But the engineers' wives would not answer her, and only pulled their cardigans in tighter, no matter how many cups and saucers Sonja Buloh smashed before the scudding sky, no matter how many shards of porcelain splintered into that poor child's soul, they could never answer her.

Chapter 81

———

1990

'SLOW IT!' shouted Betty, '*Pant, Sonja, pant, pant.*'

Sonja no longer had a will or a mind but only waves of sensation, pain, cascading down her body in waves from head to toe. From a distant oblivion of pain, she heard herself faraway lowing like a cow in agony.

There was no obstetrician in constant attendance as Sonja was a public patient, but Betty seemed to have an infinite array of positions into which she would manoeuvre Sonja between contractions, and now Betty had her sitting up and told her that she could see the head, that it was coming, coming quickly, quickly. Sonja had not called for pethidine yet, but was sucking the gas hard and panting like a lousy dog and had her eyes tightly closed and was clenching her fists so hard that they were numb from lack of blood when she felt her womb suddenly, violently jump backwards and up into herself. She was at that moment possessed of the foolish fancy that her womb was some giant rainbow trout returning home in huge skipping leaps upriver, each leap traversing yet another previously impossible fall, and each fall another person—Jean, Picotti, Mrs Maritza Michnik—*leap*—another place—Sydney, Hobart, Butlers Gorge—*leap*—another time, now all only water and stone to be traversed: until the trout had reached the third and lowest snow-powdered step at the bottom of a wooden hut—*leap*—and then there was a door, a door! and with each leap the rainbow trout became younger and smaller and lighter until it rode the very wind, until it was simply a piece of lace and it was no longer as she had always known for the door was opening and the lace was returning and shaping itself wet and slippery and bloody as it was coming toward her and out of her and she was dying and she could no longer pant or talk or even low like a cow but was screaming forever.

Chapter 82

1954

LIFE HAD REVEALED ITSELF to Bojan Buloh as the triumph of evil.

He stood in the bright light thrown by the unshaded light bulb in the corridor of their house, heard the rain that had followed the snow flogging the iron roof, felt the walls and low ceiling close in on him further like some mediaeval torture press, smelt his own fear and felt that his whole life had been a journey downwards to what he now believed to be true hell.

Out of his time. Far from his home. Forever bound to her, yet no longer a husband. Where was the sun? Where was his rightful place? Where could such a man and his child who was as surely her child now go? And the edelweiss that once gave its enigmatic directions in lands that he knew only as mysteries now gone.

He knew he simply had to live each day—as much as it was possible—without hope and without despair. This required of him that he think as little as possible, and this he largely achieved, emptying his mind not only of troublesome thoughts but of the capacity to reflect upon events. Life did manage to stick in his mind sometimes, troublesome burrs of experiences, and these could only be pulled out with a furious eruption of anger. There was, he had discovered, good and bad in everything—in life, in the very earth itself—and in everybody.

But in the end darkness prevailed.

There is only that, thought Bojan Buloh.

He put one arm out against the wall to stop it crushing him, to steady himself. What was his time? When was his home? He staggered the few short steps to Sonja's bedroom, feeling his body to have found the immobile weight of lead, as agonised and as difficult as the crawl of wounded man to safe shelter.

But when at her doorway he raised his head, Bojan Buloh saw a sight of such exquisite beauty that for a moment he thought he had truly lost his mind. For Sonja's bedroom had burst into blossom and even in the dim half-light he saw that it was full of edelweiss in full bloom, their starry white petals filling the room with a lunar luminosity. Arising out of the mass of flowers like an old stunted tree he saw an upturned wooden box down the edge of which was stencilled in red letters the word GELIGNITE. On top of the box was a frayed lace doily laid diagonally, and upon the doily sat three postcard-sized pictures. On the left was a picture of the Virgin Mary with her hands outstretched as if in compassion; in the centre a photograph of Maria's father laid out in his coffin, a man who looked tired and worn-out even in death, who looked without hope even when surrounded by flowers; and on the right was a photograph of Maria and Bojan in their best clothes, with Sonja as a baby dressed in an old-fashioned long christening gown, being held by her father. Next to the gelignite box, Sonja lay asleep in her bed, the old iron frame painted a cream colour through which suppurated numerous chancres of rust.

Bojan noticed, though strangely it did not disturb him, that the edelweiss were growing out of his daughter's nostrils and ears, and that their petals pointed in every conceivable direction. There was no proper bedspread, only an old blanket, but all was neat and clean, and the only discordant element was the child of flowers herself, who had kicked her covers away. Beneath her nightie he could see the raised impression of what he could only assume were more flowers growing out of her sex, embossing the thin cotton with striking stellar shapes, and he momentarily wondered if it was the starry night sky he was seeing, wondered if the vast southern heavens had been transformed into his small daughter or she into the heavens and he felt dizzy with the thought and the sight.

Bojan's hands gently and silently pulled the covers back over his daughter. Then, his face brushing the edelweiss petals, he kissed her on the cheek and whispered to the heavens, '*Aja, aja.*' Still asleep, the child stretched out her arms in an embrace and held her father around his neck. He felt her small body stiffen, shudder in a nighttime spasm, then relax back into sleep. Her arms went limp and fell away, and Bojan crossed them on her chest beneath the covers.

Then he went back out into the harsh white light of the corridor, and returned dragging a mattress which he laid on the floor next to Sonja's bed. He noticed, though strangely the observation did not disconcert him, that the flowers had all gone. As he made a bed up with some blankets, he thought to himself and knew it to be a curious thing to think, that the bedroom had simply returned to its winter state and that the flowers had all died and now he must sleep until spring returned. Then he lay down, with Sonja asleep in her bed on one side of him, and Maria laid out in her coffin on the other.

Bojan Buloh let his body of lead run into the mattress until all that remained was his soul and his soul was the universe and he let it fill to overflowing with the snuffling and movement of Sonja, let the sound of his three-year-old daughter sleeping fill his universe.

There is only this, thought Bojan Buloh, and only this.

Outside sleet once more began to slap the small windowpanes. But Bojan Buloh had fallen asleep and did not hear its icy scratch.

For there is this, Bojan Buloh was dreaming. *This.*

BOJAN BULOH HAD SEEN MUCH in his life before he fell asleep that night, and he was to see much thereafter. Flowers growing out of the living and the dead. A Tasmanian tiger, and what's more one that carried a vision of hell within its gob. Pigs incinerating themselves, and people behaving similarly. Great dams being built and great dams falling apart and rivers once more running free. He could, if he so desired, which he did not, and would never have even conceived of the idea—he could have written a treatise on how he had seen people die: how the disinherited did not even die easy, but as hard as they lived, slow protracted deaths at which they had to labour as hard as if they were dumb driven cattle; how both the corpses of his race, as of the Germans who once thought Bojan's race inferior, started white at the moment of death and ended up—if not buried—as black as coal, the corpse in between inflating, deflating, rotting, until it was little more than a skeleton clutched hard by a tarry skin that resembled nothing so much as a worn-out old black boot. He had seen animals of all types give birth and seen newly-born calves and piglets and foals, and had known the curiously empty, wrong feeling of killing a roo and finding a living joey in its pouch.

But Bojan Buloh had never seen a newly-born baby, not even his own daughter, Sonja, having then been forbidden by the hospital for three days after her birth to see either her or Maria.

When Bojan Buloh had woken up on this morning he had, without thinking about it, driven to a florist's. His momentary look of disappointment when the shop assistant told him she had never seen an edelweiss in any florist in all of Tasmania in all her years, gave way to an enigmatic smile when the shop assistant then showed him a bunch of white carnations as being the next best thing. They weren't, of course, but Bojan was still smiling at the absurd idea of two such different flowers being thought in any way similar when he was back in the FJ and the motor was misfiring and rattling as he was driving into the heart of town, and he was just hoping to Christ that it got him there and he praised it in Slovenian (*Dobra staryr auto*) for all its years of faithful service and beseeched it in Italian (*Per favore cara macchina*) to last the few more miles that would see their journey finally ended and ordered it in Deutsch (*Raus! Raus!*) to continue going and cursed it in Australian (*Shitfuckingbucket*) for spluttering worse than himself in the morning.

But, once the promise of a new Australia, the FJ was now, like its owner, aged and decrepit. The FJ was not the car it once had been, and, Bojan had to ruefully admit if only to himself, it had not been much of a car in the first place. So when the FJ went ominously silent as he was driving down Macquarie Street, Bojan was philosophical in his realisation that after two and a half decades the FJ's 138 motor had finally died, and he was looking forward to either buying a new car or never returning to Tullah. He rolled the car to the side of the road, did not even bother to raise the bonnet for a look, but grabbed the flowers and a plastic shopping bag from the front seat, hopped out and without even bothering to shut the car door began what, for a man of his age and proclivities, was less than easy: to run.

And in this manner, without any conscious thought, with legs feeling like lead, heart hammering, breath heaving, Bojan found himself some minutes later in the elevator of the maternity hospital, wondering if he wouldn't end up in the emergency ward for a heart attack he was feeling that awful, heading for the labour wards.

Chapter 84

1990

AS IF JUST BUTTERED, vernix covering her frog-like face, there she was: a freshly swaddled newly-born baby, strange-looking stranger to her mother. The baby gave a small cry, somewhere between a scream and a yelp, and her naked arms spasmed out and up in an L-shape, tiny fists clenched, as if she were surrendering to life. Sonja put her nose against the baby's head, and gasped. For the first time since she had been a child in Jean's kitchen Sonja recognised strong odours: of yeast, of bread—of her baby.

In the dimmed light of the labour ward Sonja held her child close, and looked at that alien animal in awe and with not a small amount of fear. Sonja heard herself gulp and moan, knew her face to be smiling, to be frowning, to be shaking. She kissed the baby on the forehead, then—so very hesitantly—she put out her tongue and lightly touched the baby on its head with her tongue tip, once, twice, and then, feeling braver, she licked the baby's neck and face, long, delicate licks, all the while drawing in deep draughts of that extraordinary scent of bread.

Betty, who had left the room some time before, returned to tell Sonja that her father was outside. Sonja did not look up from her baby. Betty was concerned about such an intrusion so soon after giving birth. 'I can tell him that you are not up to seeing him yet,' she said, 'and for him to come back tomorrow.' Sonja ran a finger over her child's small, puckered face. The baby, after her initial brays, had not cried. Instead her wide eyes roamed the dimly lit room, as if serenely appraising the curious world she had arrived in, and it seemed to Sonja that far from being wrong, it was somehow right her father would wish to see his only grandchild at such a time, and right that her daughter should meet her grandfather so soon after birth. There was a magic to the moment that Sonja did not understand, but which she vaguely apprehended, and she knew it had a power that would only be manifest for a short period. In that year after the revolutions, she was now circling time. And though it seemed dreams were being born within dreams, it was not so. It was only a mother and her child waiting.

She told Betty to ask him in.

Bojan entered apprehensively, frowning, one hand held behind him, the other carrying a plastic shopping bag, eyes scooting back and forth, as if appraising the room ready for a quick exit. He looked at her and he looked at the baby and his nervous frown gave way to a nervous smile. From behind his back he produced a large bouquet of white carnations, which he placed at the foot of her bed.

'So you haven't gone back to Tullah yet, Dad?' Sonja smiled.

'No,' said Bojan. He paused, but then felt what was for him the unusual need to explain himself more fully. 'I'm not going back. Told them they could shove it. Jiri thinks he can line me up a job. I don't need much. Anything is okay by me. Maybe I even look after the baby when you work, things like that, I dunno. But I am not going back, not now.' He looked down on his newly-born granddaughter, and moved closer. 'Not ever. Not to that.'

He went to put the plastic carry bag on the floor, then halted. 'Ah—now,' he said. 'Helvi give this to me.' He reached into the bag. 'She tell me how much you want to repair it.'

And proffered in his hand was the bramble-patterned teapot Sonja had smashed so long ago. Finally together in one piece, once more complete. She saw that his work was, as ever, true and careful, the few fractures that remained apparent only as hairlines.

He leant down, handed the repaired teapot over to Sonja, and she, as if in exchange, passed her daughter to him. Bojan held the baby not awkwardly, but in a relaxed manner, cradled in his right arm, cooing and cackling as he stroked her chin with the knuckle of his index finger. 'Anyway, now it's fixed,' continued Bojan, playfully pressing the baby's nose as if it were a button. He laughed at his own convoluted speech. 'Not like my English.'

As Sonja turned the teapot around and up and down admiring its reconstruction, Betty, not knowing what else to say to the strange man of heavy odours and curious accent, asked, 'How would describe your feelings about your new granddaughter, Mr Bellow?'

'Oh,' said Bojan looking up from the baby, his head rolling in an uncharacteristically loose way, like a treetop feathered by a fresh wind. 'Oh, I, eh, I think there are some things that matter more than words.' He pressed the baby's nose in again and laughed, and said: 'She's beautiful, eh?'

He smiled once more and now there was no trace of nervousness. Sonja felt that perhaps it might just be, after all, possible. Maybe one afternoon when the baby was crawling around the kitchen floor, pulling lids and pots from cupboards, maybe they would sit and talk long, long into the night, about her, about him, about the baby—and about all the things she had long thought she would stand over his grave regretting she had never told him, asked him, reproached him for and laughed with him about. They would talk for so long that the sun would fall and night would come and they would put the baby to bed and keep talking through her night feeds into the next morning about them and her and what had happened and what might be. They would talk only about what they could hold onto, and they would not use words they could hide behind, but use words like timber to build a table they could sit around.

A beautiful table, big enough for a family feasting.

And after Bojan left, a small miracle took place. For the first and not the last time in this new lifetime, Sonja cried and her tears fell like summer rain upon her baby's head.

Chapter 85

SOMETIMES A VAST LONGING would come back over her.

And when it did she would not fight it, but sought to celebrate it, would gather some things together in a carton and put the baby in the car and they would drive back. They would drive up that long empty road to that empty place where once stood a construction camp called Butlers Gorge and where there was now nothing, nothing but strange bird cries and wind and cold.

Though she did ask twice, Bojan never came with her. He still drank, but infrequently, and Jiri was only rung four times in the following two years by frustrated barmen asking him to pick up a hopeless drunk who had given them this number. He still drank, but with the exception of these occasional bust-outs, the quantities were small and his behaviour—apart from becoming sometimes tedious with his repetition of stories— unobjectionable and even quite likeable. It was impossible, of course, to know how long it would last, but both

Bojan and Sonja wisely treated it at best as a day-to-day proposition, and each showed genuine delight when the other honoured the day by calling around or ringing.

Sonja and Jiri secured Bojan a housing department semi-detached unit with which he seemed genuinely happy and where he grew vegetables that he gave away, and strawberries which he kept for only his granddaughter to eat, along with yoghurt he would make by letting milk sour on top of his hot water boiler. He fought with the housing department over his garden, not because of his vegetables or strawberries, but because of the FJ, which he parked there permanently and used both as a children's playground and the site of some of his garden, making beds out of the engine bay and boot and headlight cavities. After Ahmet intervened on his behalf Bojan won, and the flowering FJ full of kids became something of a local landmark. Occasionally he would grow tired of the racket and yell at the kids to bugger off, but sometimes, late in the afternoon, he would open a stubby and sit at a short distance from the FJ having a quiet drink and smoke, as kids darted like gannets and pilchards around him. He would look out over his garden and see it all again, a gale which he cursed and which had cursed them all, which transformed time into a dam and the dam into dust and dust into earth and the earth into a garden in which he found himself sitting staring at a rusted-out car, seeing it all again, though this time there was mixed with his desolation a certain wonder.

Chapter 86

———

UPON ARRIVING at the old construction camp site, Sonja would get out of the car and draw herself erect and look around at the tall manferns dripping rain upon the ageing stumps of huge eucalypts felled so long ago to clear the site. She would do as she did every visit: look up and see the new trees that had grown since that time. Then, with her baby in one arm, and the carton under the other, she would walk into the desolate, harsh noises of Tasmanian rainforest, toward the scrawk of black cockatoos and the cries of the currawongs, into the slow *thrush-thrush* of the wind up high in the forest canopy, and sometimes she thought she heard sounds most peculiar: of her mother singing—

> *'Spancek, zaspancek*
> *crn mozic*
> *hodi po noci*
> *nima nozic'*

And Sonja, baby cradled in her arms, would sing softly back, full of love, a song she had known for so long she could not remember learning it, a Slovenian lullaby.

'*Lunica ziblje:*
aja, aj, aj,
spancek se smeje
aja, aj, aj.

'*Tiho se duri*
okna odpro
vleze se v zibko
zatisne oko

'*Lunica ziblje:*
aja, aj, aj,
spancek se smeje
aja, aj, aj.'

She would spend some time making sure her bearings were exactly right, then, when finally satisfied, push four sticks into the wet, soft warm earth. Out of the carton she would take a large reel of red ribbon and with it she would mark out the boundaries of what had been their home all that long time ago. Each stick a corner and around each stick the red ribbon wrapped and strung to the next corner. Out of the carton she would take a blanket that she would spread in the middle of that nowhere defined by the ruffling ribbon and place her child upon it.

Sometimes Sonja would close her eyes and imagine what a strange sight it must make from a distance: the green blur of the forest and in front the thin blood trickle of the red ribbon where once had been Maria and her hoping for what they would never know and now were her and her daughter searching for what they never had, holes within holes within holes, and she would feel dizzy seeing it all so clearly. Sometimes she would daydream that she opened her eyes and the whole plain was filled with red-ribboned rectangles, as far as the eye could see, and in each rectangle sat a parent with a child, saying, 'This was my home,' as she would always say to her uncomprehending child. 'Once.'

Red-ribboned rectangles receding into infinity.

Then Sonja would take out some lunch things and they would eat, she feeding the baby first then herself. Finally out of the carton she would carefully lift an old and battered music box, which she would wind up, and set upon the ground.

Then she would lie down on her side upon the blanket, hold the baby to her belly and slowly raise the lid of the music box that sat only inches away from her nose. The clockwork mechanism version of 'Lara's Theme' would start up. The ballet dancer would begin her endless twirling, circles within circles within the music box's valley of mirrors, and within each mirror were the trees of the forest in which Sonja's mother had hanged herself, those vast, huge bluegums that swayed back and forth in the wind.

They would watch, as they watched mesmerised every visit, how the music box's frame of black lacquered wood wrapped around the mirrored forest, and how in front of that vast wilderness the toy ballerina would twist and turn until 'Lara's Theme' slowed down and then stopped altogether. Then Sonja would shut the box and the mirrored forest disappear. The baby would cry out in disappointment.

Sonja would turn on to her stomach on the wet ground. Faraway she could see the forest, wet from the last shower of rain, glistening like an animal in the shafts of sunlight that punctured the ink-blue clouds above. The child's crying would ebb, then stop altogether. The child, sitting on the blanket, would look unknowingly, wide-eyed at her, and all that would remain would be the sounds of the wind in the huge eucalypts.

Sonja would hold her face close to the damp ground, close to the acrid, fecund peat that overlaid the hard clay, the sour gravel, and feel the long dewy grass with her chin, run her lips along the earth. Her body burning like fire. Her hands running over the ground. Her face being feathered by the wet grass. Bowing buttongrass threading water droplets. Pearls of dew spreading across her cheeks. Necklaces of grace. And as she lay so on the ground she would hold her child close and whisper her daughter's name. Her beautiful name.

'Maria,' she would say to the earth, 'my Maria.'

And Sonja would put her finger in her baby's pudgy fist and draw the fist to her trembling lips, for how would she ever tell her daughter of what only those who lived it can ever know?

For it was all long, long ago in a world that has since perished into peat, in a forgotten winter on an island of which few have ever heard. In that time before snow, completely and irrevocably, covers footprints. As black clouds shroud the star and moonlit heavens, as an unshadowable darkness comes upon the whispering land.

At that precise moment, around which time was to cusp.